Talia
Enjoy the exciting conclusion
K. M. Doherty

# Thomas Holland

## and Pandora's Portal

Book Three

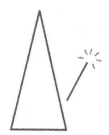

by

# K. M. Doherty

Wizard's Mark Press
Dover New Hampshire

Wizard's Mark Press

ISBN-13   978-0-9915720-7-6
LCCN: 2020910611

First Edition: Oct 2020

The Thomas Holland Series
Book 3

Visit the website: www.ThomasHollandBooks.com
Signup for the author's newsletter:
https://thomashollandbooks.com/newsletter.html
Visit us on Facebook: www.Facebook.com/KMDoherty.author
Tweet with the author on Twitter: @authorKMDoherty

Printed in the USA

Cover art by: Daniel Johnson of Squared Motion
www.squaredmotion.com

Map Graphic by: K. M. Doherty

# Acknowledgements

I'd like to thank everyone who helped make this book possible. First, a big thanks to all the kids who entered my 'creature naming contest'! Their creativity and thoughtfulness were outstanding! And the winners were: Benjamin Blackstone for the name "Kiki" which Goban named one head of his two headed pet raptor. And Nathan Nardini for the second head's name "Squinkles" though Goban calls him, "Mr. Squinkles." And also, to Laura Bourdeau for coming up with two winning names: "Frost" Kiran's dragon hatchling, and also for the name "Bubbles" which Mab, the whacked fairy queen, named her ferocious pet zhanderbeast. Also, thanks to Laura Shanks for coming up with the idea of naming both heads of Goban's pet, brilliant idea! And to all my 'beta readers' who gave me critical feedback which greatly improved the novel: George J. Callis, Geof Tamulonis, Stephen Paul Tamulonis, and Rebecca Shea. I'd also like to thank a young fan who came up to me at an event and said, "You should have goblins in your next book!" So, I added goblins! Thanks to my cover artist Daniel Johnson for another stunning work of art! He's a true master! And to my proofreader Dianne Donovan for her detailed and thorough work. A special thanks to my grandson Thomas, who informed me of the 'secret scene' that every bestselling novel must have. And thanks to Mackenzie Lipe for her suggestions for getting the teen girl tensions right between Avani and Zoe. Plus, a huge thanks goes to Travis Marshall for his thoughtful insights into characters and scenes throughout the book, but especially on helping me decide which of two possible endings to use. What's more, his ideas for heightening the ending's suspense, action, and surprise twist made the ending fantastic (in my humble opinion.) Thanks, Trav! And lastly, to my wife Lin for putting up with all this 'being a writer' nonsense.

# Recap

Hi, I'm Tom. Are you a science geek like me? You don't believe in magic and then one day, you go through a portal at your mom's lab and end up in Elfhaven, a place where magic is everywhere! I know, right? Happens every day. Well, at least it happened to me. Worse, blood thirsty trolls immediately captured me. If it wasn't for Max, that's my giant slobbering Saint Bernard, I might've died! Max ran off and found some elf kids who rescued me. Then we had to save the world. But I'm getting ahead of myself.

Me and my new friends had some great adventures. Oh. I guess I should introduce you to some of them. My two best friends are Avani and Goban. Avani's a magically gifted elven girl. She's bright and self-confident. Avani's also the chosen one by the magic crystals. The crystals magnify her magic. And she's also the last Keeper of the Light, an ancient society that protected the Citadel. Then there's Goban. He's a dwarf. He's a prince, but he'd rather work on building inventions with his uncle than have anything to do with royal stuff. There are other friends. Prince Devraj is a bully, but he's OK once you get to know him. And Kiran, Avani's younger brother.

If you haven't read our adventures, or it's been a while, I'll bring you up to speed. In 'Thomas Holland and the Prophecy of Elfhaven' we figured out a way to break into the Citadel, meet the Guardian who told us that not all we thought was magic, was really magic. Like the barrier, for instance. It's actually some sorta force field and its power was running out. The whole of our first adventure was finding my robot Chloe, who'd been captured by trolls. We had to sneak into the heart of the troll encampment, late at night, free Chloe and get her back to the Citadel before the barrier failed completely. Turns out, the evil wizard Naagesh, was helping the trolls. We barely managed to jump-start the barrier, using Chloe's battery, before the troll army destroyed Elfhaven. Later, we found out a wizard named Larraj helped us out along the way.

In 'Thomas Holland in the Realm of the Ogres' we had to find the crashed spaceship that was supposed to deliver the replacement power source to the Citadel. On our way, we took a shortcut through the Demon Forest and the Cave of Dreams. Just outside the destroyed Library of Nalanda, we got caught in a freak snowstorm and nearly died. Somehow Max found some fairies who rescued us, though Mab, the fairy queen, turned out to be a bit whacked. Anyway, we traipsed up an active volcano and found the ship. Everything was going great until Malak and Chatur, a couple of screwup elf kids, blew up the ship and got my friends captured by ogres. Max and I, along with one of the ogres, fell in a crevasse and went on the wildest water-slide ride you can imagine… only ice instead of water and with giant ravenous ice worms and an angry ogre who kept trying to kill us. Max and I survived the ride, the ogre not so much. But then we had to rescue our friends from the ogres, take back the power supply Naagesh had stolen from us, and with the help of a dragon, get back to Elfhaven before the war with the ogres began. After saving Elfhaven for a second time, Max and I, oh—and mom, forgot to mention mom. She came through the portal after us. The Guardian opened a portal for us, and we went back home to Earth.

This adventure, the third book in the trilogy, starts a year later. Hope you enjoy it!

# Prologue

A tall hooded figure stepped from the atrium into a small room and glanced up at the stone slab ceiling high above. A dry, tart mustiness filled the air.

Opening his hand, the room lit with a dull red glow.

A short, hunched, and badly gnarled beast shuffled up beside him. "There it is, Master," rasped the servant, pointing a long, crooked finger.

The tall one lowered his gaze. In the center of the room a book floated above a pedestal, rotating slowly, bathed in a soft golden magical light. Leather-bound, the ancient text had a large silver seal embossed on its aged and deeply cracked surface.

Striding to the platform, he reached for the book.

As his skeletal fingers crossed the pedestal's threshold, orange magic lashed out, attacking his hand. Flicking his wrist casually, there was a flash, and the magic dispersed in a flurry of tangerine sparks.

Plucking the book from the air, he gave it to his servant, then waved his hand over the pedestal. An exact replica of the book he'd just stolen suddenly appeared, floating as before. A sickly thin smile spread across his face.

"We have it, Master," hissed the servant, scratching its left horn. "We must leave!"

"Just one final task," said the Master. Spreading his arms wide, he opened his hands, palms upward. Emerald lightning arced around his fingers and launched up. Crackling, the magic playfully scampered across the ceiling, seeping into cracks between the massive stone slabs. Once concealed in its hiding place, the magic's green glow faded.

Gazing admiringly at his forgery a moment longer, he smiled and said,

"The trap's baited and set." The wizard's cape flew as he spun and strode from the room, his hideous servant scampering along after.

# Avani

Beads of sweat formed on her brow. She knew this was going to hurt, and hurt a lot. Her hand trembled as she reached out.

Avani hesitated. *It's been nearly a yara. Why did it take the king and the wizard so long to act?*

She absently flicked a lock of her long, golden hair behind her tall, pointed elven ear. *I know you're here. Show yourself.*

Extending her fingers yet farther, Avani half-turned, anticipating the pain.

The magic didn't attack.

Rubbing her stiff neck, Avani glanced around the plateau where only a yara ago, she, Tom and Goban had stood. Just ahead lay the boulder-strewn rubble-field they'd seen back then.

Beyond the debris, a sheer cliff towered above, its peak engulfed by roiling clouds. At the base of the cliff, an ancient, arched, stone entryway stood mostly hidden, blocked by boulders.

Taking a deep breath, Avani stepped forward and reached out again. As her hand approached the spot where the magic had struck, the hairs on the back of her head began to tingle.

*This is the spot. I know it is.* Avani closed her eyes and thrust her fingers through the exact spot.

Nothing happened.

One eye popped open. *Huh?* She extended her arm. *Still no response.*

*I'm certain it was here.* Avani glanced over her shoulder. The cowl of Larraj's dark cloak lay back, exposing the wizard's beard and his long gray hair. Larraj stood engaged in conversation with Prince Devraj, a young, tall, regally dressed elf, and Sanuu, one of the head palace guards. Several elven soldiers stood nearby, listening intently to the conversation.

Avani heard fragments of their conversation.

"It will take several solar cycles just to find and catalog them all," complained the prince.

Sanuu said, "And more days to crate them up."

"And haul them all the way down the treacherous mountain pass back to Elfhaven," agreed Devraj.

Avani turned back. Inhaling deeply, she took three bold steps forward, waving her hands in front of her as she went. Still nothing.

Half-turning, she called, "Something's wrong."

Larraj glanced in her direction. Twirling the tip of his white beard absently, the wizard gave a guard a last instruction then walked over. Prince Devraj and Sanuu trailed behind.

"What's wrong?" asked the wizard.

"It shoulda been here," said Avani.

The corner of Larraj's lip curled up playfully. "Could you be a little more specific?"

"A yara ago, Tom, Goban and I were here. Goban reached out, and the magic attacked him." She smiled at the thought of Tom.

"Why are you smiling?" asked the prince.

Her smile evaporated. "Nothing."

Devraj stared at her. Avani looked away.

"So?" Larraj prodded. "What's this about Goban being struck?"

"So, Goban stood back there." Avani pointed at a spot five paces behind. "But now I'm standing here." She glanced down at her feet. "Beyond the point where the magic attacked him."

Larraj frowned. He scanned the ruins and raised his staff. A golden owl, perched atop the staff, rotated its head to face the rubble, ruffled its metallic feathers and blinked.

The staff began to glow. Arcing, popping strands of magical lightning flicked out, touching stones, boulders, and finally the cliff-face itself. Avani squinted, but kept her gaze fixed on the scene ahead. The light slowly faded.

"You're correct. The protection magic that's guarded this entrance for the last hundred yaras is no longer present."

"No longer present?" Avani said. "You mean—someone destroyed it?" She paused. "Was it me? Last yara, I created a hole in the magic and let our gremlin friend in. Did I destroy it?"

"Perhaps…" The wizard cautiously approached the stone archway. Two boulders blocked the entrance.

Larraj waved his hand. Twin magical, glowing ropes launched from his palm and wrapped around the massive stones. With a flick of his wrists, the ropes snapped taught and the boulders launched skyward. The ground shook when they crashed down across the plateau.

The ropes dissolved in a shower of golden sparks. The entrance now stood clear.

Larraj asked Sanuu to post guards at the entryway, and not to allow anyone in until he returned. "No matter what you hear—under no circumstances are you to enter."

"Why?" Devraj gestured to the elven guards scattered across the plateau. "We have soldiers to protect us."

"Soldiers would be useless against—"

"Against what?"

"I'm coming with you," Avani interrupted.

Larraj faced her. "No. Something's amiss. I sense…" He studied the entranceway intently. "If you destroyed the magic, there's little danger. If it wasn't you…"

Avani leaned forward defiantly. "How will I ever learn if you won't let me test my training?"

Larraj scanned her face thoughtfully, then asked the prince, "And I suppose you want to come as well?"

Devraj nodded.

"Your father would be displeased, should I bring home his only son and heir to the throne, dead."

"As you wish," Larraj told Avani. "But if a giant three-headed fire sloth leaps from the shadows, use the duratus statim spell to freeze it in mid-leap."

"You know I don't know that spell. You haven't taught it to me yet."

"Then I suggest you run."

Avani glanced at the prince.

Larraj whirled, his long cape billowing. "I was joking about the fire sloth." He strode through the threshold and entered the legendary Library of Nalanda. From inside the mountain came his hollow, echoing voice adding, "It'll likely be something far worse."

# The Library of Nalanda

Walking down a cold, dark hallway, the faint hiss of their boot-heels on the dust-covered stone floor announced their presence. Row upon row of bookshelves towered over them like shadowy monsters poised to strike.

"We should have brought the guards," huffed the prince.

"As I explained," began Larraj. "Soldiers would be no use against—"

"I know," said Devraj. "Soldiers are useless against... What? You would not say."

When the wizard didn't respond, Devraj continued, "In any case, we need the guards to complete our mission."

"There'll be time to locate what we came here for," said Larraj, "but circumstances have changed."

"What has changed? We are here, in the Library, are we not? We should acquire what we came for and leave!"

"Once we know it's safe."

The prince slammed his fist against a bookshelf. The sound echoed hollowly through the vast dark room. Larraj glanced at him but said nothing.

Larraj led the procession, his staff glowing, dimly illuminating a narrow swath ahead.

Avani shivered, not from the cold but from the noises: the chittering, scrapping sounds of small animals, and the deeper grunts and hisses of larger... things. Worse, far worse, were the occasional distant moans and cries, their echoes lasting several sectars before finally dying away.

Avani shivered again. Raising her hands, palms upward, she mumbled an incantation. A globe of light flickered, then went out. She glanced at Larraj. If he noticed her failure, he didn't show it.

Concentrating harder, she tried again. This time two glowing orbs appeared, floating above her hands. Avani sighed and tossed them into the chill air. They drifted up, up, allowing her to see a short distance down the dark aisles.

Avani hurried up beside Larraj. "There are chandeliers. Why not light them?"

"Your magic failed again, didn't it?" said the wizard. "Conjuring your light orbs."

Avani fidgeted. She glanced over her shoulder. Devraj had fallen behind. "Second time worked!"

The wizard didn't respond.

Avani pulled one of her magic crystals from her satchel. "What's going on?" she asked, "Why are the crystals failing me?"

"It's not the crystal's fault." Larraj drummed his fingers lightly on his staff. "It's you. You're holding back. You seem torn. Distracted of late."

Avani rolled the crystal in her palm. She used to hear voices when she touched them. Hundreds of soft melodic voices, singing to her. They were always too faint. She could never make out what they were saying. Anyway, the voices stopped recently, about the time her magic started failing.

She sighed.

Larraj glanced sidelong at her. "Becoming a wizard requires total commitment. Can you do that? Are you sure you want to?"

"More than anything! You know I do."

Larraj studied her closely. "As I recall, the last time your magic failed you were attempting a simple incantation to invoke the aid of a watcher nymph. Instead, you conjured up an acid spitting nimbus toad, a particularly nasty one at that." He glanced sidelong at her. "Destroyed half my lab before I could stop it."

Avani squirmed again. "That was different. You distracted me—on purpose!"

Larraj's voice assumed the now familiar tone of her mentor. "There are always distractions. At times, a wizard must even deal with multiple threats at once. A master wizard lives in the here and now, no matter how many distractions surround her. If you lose focus, or worse yet—panic, your magic will fail you. A distracted wizard might mean the difference between life and death, not only for herself, but for those she's charged to protect."

"Yes, but—"

"What's more," Larraj continued, "when a novice's magic fails it often damages their self-confidence, making it more likely to fail when they need it most."

Larraj walked on in silence, letting his words sink in.

Avani gazed at the dimly pulsing crystal still clutched in her hand. She changed the subject. "I thought the magic crystals would only respond to one person."

"That's right. One person, born of this world and chosen by the magic crystals themselves. Actually, it's the spirits who choose."

"Who?"

"The crystals are just a manifestation in our world of spirits, composed of pure white magic."

"The voices…"

"Voices?" said Larraj.

"Nothing. Pure white magic? But that means—"

"The crystals are all powerful. They can do anything. Not just create, move or destroy matter. They can even alter time!"

"Can you teach me?"

"No! No one should ever alter the past. The consequences are infinite and unfathomable and far too dangerous." He stared at her. "Understand?"

She nodded. "So how come Tom could touch them?" she repeated. "And the crystals responded, even stronger than to me."

Larraj drew in a deep breath. "Tom's a special case. Tom is not of this world. Strangest of all, Tom possesses heightened magical powers, perhaps even stronger than my own. But he hasn't been trained how to safely wield them. So he's afraid, and rightly so."

"Could he use the crystals by himself, without me?"

"I don't know. The crystals seemed to accept him. Not sure why. But if he tried, I fear he'd badly hurt himself or worse." Larraj hurried ahead. "In any case, we'll never know. Tom's on another world."

"Come! We must hurry."

As they walked through the dimness, Avani again stared at the dark chandeliers, high above. "We'd move quicker with more light."

"True, but it would also alert others to our presence."

"Others? You mean—if it wasn't me who destroyed the protection magic, whoever did might still be here?"

"Perhaps."

"Besides, with more light, if someone's here, it'd be harder for them to sneak up on us, right?

"With the security magic gone, I sense other things now inhabit these halls."

She glanced down a dark aisle between shelves. "The things making those creepy noises?"

"Those aren't the things you should be worried about."

"I wanna see the whole library," she insisted. "Please?"

Larraj's lip curled up into a slight grin. "Very well." Raising his staff, he chanted an incantation. Hundreds of chandeliers sprang to life, one after another, filling the cavernous room, ahead and to each side, with light. "The things now know we're here. Keep sharp."

"Wow!" Avani gazed wide-eyed down long aisles of towering bookshelves. "This is more books than I've ever seen!"

The wizard smiled. "This is nothing."

The area ahead grew brighter and the moans and whispers louder. A moment later, the three stopped at a large circular balcony overlooking a vast chamber.

"This is the hall of white magic," said the Wizard.

Leaning over the polished wooden railing, Avani gasped delightedly at the sight. Books backed out from bookshelves on one side, floated across the vast open space and re-stacked themselves upon shelves on the far side. Even more striking, here and there, whole bookshelves moved. One shelf slid out and hovered above the gulf while another shelf slid sideways behind. Then the first shifted over and glided back into place.

One of the books floating past stopped and hovered in front of Avani. It was titled Fun Spells: Amaze your Friends, Befuddle your Enemies! Another book glided over and nudged the first book aside. The second book's title read Potions to Ward off Evil Spirits. Avani gave Larraj an inquisitive look.

"The books are trying to get your attention. Each wants you to choose it, over the others."

Avani grinned delightedly. A third book swept down in front of the other two. The 100 Most Critical Incantations You Must Learn! Avani plucked it from the air. A spark of magic flared across its well-worn surface. She glanced at Larraj, then opened it. Flicking through the pages, she stopped, read a few lines, then flicked some more. She began to close the book, when suddenly, the pages started turning themselves, then abruptly stopped. Avani bent closer, studying the unfamiliar incantation, straining to decipher the ancient script.

Hmmm, a protection spell. She read on. *This incantation is used to avert physical danger. Example: in case of fire, flood, explosion, or natural disasters such as avoiding being crushed by an avalanche. Note however, the spell has proved ineffective against being devoured by ravenous beasts. Avani flipped the page. The spell works by enclosing the wizard in a protective bubble of magic, keeping him or her safe from the impending danger. WARNING: this incantation must only be used to protect one individual. Wizards tried using the spell to protect more than one person, but sadly, each of those attempts failed...*

The incantation followed. Avani's lips moved silently, memorizing the ancient verse several times.

Larraj had been watching her patiently. The prince, less so.

"We waste time," rasped the prince. "Why are we not doing what we came here to do?"

Larraj scanned the prince's face. "Which is?"

"To secure the most valuable books!" shouted Devraj.

The wizard waited until the echoes of the prince's voice faded. "And which books might those be?"

"Royal documents, of course! History of the realm, proclamation and treaties, my royal linage."

"Books on magic!" piped up Avani.

Larraj paused. "I'm on a—*secret* mission."

"A what?" snapped the prince. "On who's authority?"

The wizard's brow rose slightly. "Your father and I discussed it. We both agreed."

Devraj and Avani just stared at him.

"It's a similar mission, actually. But I came here for just one specific book. One that is far more valuable than those you mentioned. If it should fall into the wrong hands..."

Devraj continued to stare. "What book could possibly be—"

"I'll explain later. Suffice it to say, our priorities have changed."

"Our priorities!" snapped the prince. "Or yours?"

"My priority *is* our priority."

"My father would not have kept secrets from me!"

Larraj waved his hand. A mist-shrouded image of King Dakshi materialized before them. Larraj twisted his wrist, and the image grew clear.

"If the rumors be true," began the king, "you must secure the book before it falls into the wrong hands. Oh. And keep this a secret."

"From your own guards?" came Larraj's voice.

"For now."

"From your son?"

There was a slight pause.

"Yes," replied King Dakshi. "Especially from Devraj."

Larraj waved his hand, and the image dissolved.

The prince's jaw tightened.

"I'm sorry," began Larraj. "I'm sure your father would have told you in time—"

"Silence!" cried Devraj.

The wizard glanced from Avani to Devraj. "Someone broke into the library. We have to assume the worst. We must secure the book at all costs. Nothing else matters."

"The book?" said Avani.

"You'll understand when you see it."


They made their way down two flights of stairs to the ground floor. Larraj extinguished the candelabras and turned left.

Avani and Devraj crept down a narrow hallway a few paces behind the wizard. Here the faint glow from Larraj's staff was their only light.

Avani shivered, feeling the cold stone walls pressing in upon her. At least the creepy moans and voices sounded farther away.

She glanced at Devraj. "I don't need your protection," she whispered. "If that's why you came along."

"You are not the only one who is curious what secrets lie in the great library." The prince took her hand. "Besides, as my betrothed, I feel I should take an interest in your—hobbies."

Avani dropped his hand and spun to face him. "Is that what you think? Magic's just a hobby?"

Devraj shrugged. Avani stormed off.

The prince sighed and hurried to catch up. Avani slowed but didn't look at him.

"I am sorry," he said. "I am not good at making little talk."

"Look." He grasped her hand again. She stopped.

"I know we have not always been the best of friends," he said.

"You can say that again."

"I know we have not always—"

She slapped her palm over his mouth. The prince kissed it.

Avani stepped back in shock. She studied his face intently, then abruptly strode away. As she walked, Avani gazed down at her palm, still moist from Devraj's kiss.

"Could you two love cherubs speed it up?" came the wizard's distant voice.

Avani's face flushed scarlet as a newborn lapter chick.

Did the dwarves built the Library?" Avani asked once they'd caught up with Larraj.

"Designed by elves, though," insisted the prince.

"It was designed by and for all races."

"All races?" Devraj said skeptically. "Surely not trolls and ogres?"

"All races," repeated Larraj. "Even giants and goblins, when they existed."

Devraj chuckled, "How could giants possibly—"

Avani froze. "Wait! None of those are magical beings. Why was the library open to them?"

"The great library contains much more than just books on magic." Larraj turned down a narrow hallway, the smell of leather, dust, and mildew hung heavy in the stale air.

They continued in silence for a time, until the hallway ended at a blank stone wall.

"Are you lost?" Devraj asked the wizard.

Larraj rapped his knuckles against the wall. *Tap, tap, tap*. A brief pause. *Tap*. A longer pause. *Tap, tap*.

The transparent head of an elderly ghost jutted out from the wall. "Who's there?" The specter squinted. "Not another wizard, is it? This neighborhood is going to the werehounds!"

"Another wizard?" said Larraj. "It's been a hundred yara since wizards last trod these halls."

The ghost looked shocked. "A hundred yara? My how time flits away. Seems but a few solar cycles." The spirit looked around and frowned. "'Cept fer all the dust." The specter stared at them expectantly. "Password?"

"The ghost of idiots past," snapped Devraj.

"A bit long fer a password," replied the spirit. "Better ta toss in a few numbers n' squiggly accent marks." The ghost said knowingly. "Makes it harder ta guess."

"Wizard protocol level 5!" said Larraj.

The ghost's hollow eyes grew wide. "Level 5 is it? Haven't had a level 5 in…" The spirit addressed the prince. "See! Letters, numbers, marks. Always a wise choice." The ghost winked, then exploded in a flurry of whizzing orange sparks.

Larraj pressed his broad hand against the wall. The area surrounding his hand glowed and a section of the wall swiveled inward with a groan. He motioned to the prince. "After you."

They entered a large circular atrium. Three doorways, equally spaced about the chamber, led into three separate rooms. Larraj hurried to the far door. Raising his staff, the room grew slowly brighter. Larraj sighed, his shoulders relaxing slightly.

"What is it?" asked Avani.

"See that book hovering above the pedestal in the center of the room?"

She peered around him into the room. "Yeah. So?"

"That's the book I was most worried about. But it's safe."

"Good," said Devraj, trying to push past him. "Let us take it and be gone."

Larraj blocked the prince's way with his staff. "I thought you were interested in the royal documents?" said the wizard.

Devraj glared at him. "What? Where?"

Larraj pointed over his shoulder. The room across the way lit up. "History of the realm, royal documents, etc."

The prince hurried across the atrium and disappeared into the royal records room.

Avani stared at the book floating above the pedestal. "What's so special about that book?"

"This is the Keeper's room. Only Keepers of the Light are allowed in there. Not even I am allowed in."

She craned her neck through the doorway, gazing at the small room crammed with books. "All these books? What do they contain?"

"They contain your birthright." Larraj began. "The Keepers' beliefs, rituals, and responsibilities." He paused. "The books contained within that room reveal secrets known only to its members."

"To my father?"

"Yes."

"Go on," she said in a hushed tone.

"Beyond the Keeper's secrets, it also contains information about the Citadel itself: history of the alien race who built it: their culture, their society, their technology, and why they chose Elfhaven as one of the places to build a Citadel."

"One of the places? There are more?"

He gently grasped her arm. "Are you all right? You look pale."

Avani inhaled slowly. "So what's that book?" She pointed at the text floating above the pedestal. "Why's it so special?"

Larraj studied her again. "The most important book in the Library, and the reason for this mission. The Manual."

"Manual?"

"The users' guide," he explained.

She frowned.

"For the Citadel itself," he added. "Someone has to maintain it. Keep the Citadel running. Program it up to do all the things the Keepers desire it to do."

"You mean—the Keepers controlled the Citadel? But I thought the Guardian—"

"The Guardian is just the interface. The Keepers control the Citadel." He paused. "You control the Citadel." Larraj waited for his words to sink in. "Or you will, once you've read that book."

"Me?" Her face grew pale. "So, if I control the Citadel, that means I control the barrier."

He nodded. "You choose who the barrier lets in, and who it keeps out. Trolls, ogres—even wizards."

She blinked. "What about portals? Do I choose what worlds to open portals to?"

"All but one. Pandora's Portal must never be opened again."

"Pandora's Portal?"

"A discussion for another time."

"But—"

"Go on," he gestured into the Keeper's hall. "It's yours to explore." Larraj walked off.

Avani hesitated. "Where are you going?"

"The third chamber."

"What's in it?"

"Dark magic."

Avani stared into the Keeper's hall. She bit her lip. "Can I come?"

## Missing Books

As they walked toward the arched entrance, the wizard warned, "Careful! Only master wizards were allowed to view these dangerous texts," adding, "Be on guard that the dark magic doesn't burrow into some dark recess within you."

She laughed. "You're pulling my arm, right?" He didn't respond. "Are you saying these books are alive—and—evil?"

She followed him in. "That's odd."

"Hmmmm?" replied Larraj.

"All those creepy sounds. They've stopped."

The wizard paused, listening. It was true. All sounds: the distant moans, skittering noises, and ghostly whispers had all ceased. Raising his staff, it flared to life, bathing the room in its brilliant radiance. As the powerful white magic brushed past, the leather-bound books on dark magic steamed.

A few shelves stood empty. Texts lay strewn haphazardly across the floor.

"Something's wrong." Waving his staff slowly side-to-side, the staff began to hum. A ghostly image materialized before them, an image of recent times past, an image of books arranged neatly on shelves, brimming with books. Larraj lowered his staff. The image faded. "Someone's stolen books on dark magic."

Avani's eyes sprang open. "The hall of the Keepers!" She sprinted past Larraj.

"Avani no!" cried Larraj. "Stop!"

# Responsibility bears a heavy load

Avani burst into the Keeper's room. Her room. Striding forward, she mumbled the incantation for her light globes. Nothing happened. Swallowing hard, she concentrated and tried again. This time a handful of floating, glowing orbs sprang forth, illuminating the shelves, the walls, and the stone ceiling high above.

In the center of the chamber stood a tall stone pedestal, the one she'd glimpsed earlier from the anti-room. As she approached, beams of golden light spotlighted the pedestal, casting a warm glow on the single book floating above it.

The book had the raised seal of the Keepers of the Light boldly embossed in silver on its cover. The title read, 'Manual de Citadel' with the subtitle 'May the power inside be used for good.'

Larraj appeared at the doorway. "Avani no! It could be a trap!"

"Don't worry!" she shouted gleefully. "It's still here. It's safe." Her hand trembled as she reached for the Manual.

"Don't!" he screamed.

Avani's fingers passed right through the book. Her eyes widened. She jerked back her hand. Too late...

An ominous roar sounded. The room shook. Cracks formed in the ceiling, raining dust. The cracks widened, and beams of emerald light burst forth.

Avani's gaze dropped to the Manual. It had disappeared.

"Avani run!" cried Larraj from the atrium.

A deafening explosion rocked the chamber.

Avani glanced up as enormous stone slabs came crashing down.

# Kiran

Kiran, Avani's younger brother, rotated, making a complete circle. The banners flying atop the turrets of Elfhaven castle snapped in the crisp afternoon breeze.

Halting when he faced north, Kiran stared at the jagged glacier-capped peaks to the east, that seemed to float magically above the clouds in the distance.

Inhaling deeply, Kiran cupped his hands round his mouth and gave off a strange deep bugling call.

Kiran's arms flopped to his sides, disappointedly. *Where is he? He said he'd visit when the sun passed its highest point on the midsummer solstice. That was days ago. He's never been late before.*

Behind him, a faint rustling slowly changed into a leathery flapping noise. Kiran spun round. There was nothing there. But a moment later, guards standing atop the castle's parapet shouted, pointing skyward.

Kiran raised his hand above his forehead and squinted. A thunderous scream ripped the air as a massive dark shape rocketed past, barely clearing the castle wall. Guards yelled, dropping face down onto the narrow walkway.

The monster pulled in its long leathery wings and dove. Villagers screamed and ran for cover. Just before it slammed to the field, it flared its huge wings and extended sharp talons straight for Kiran. More townsfolk leapt out of the winged demon's way.

The monster's talons touched down, ripping deep rents in the long outer field, rocking violently forward, jerking to an abrupt stop beside Kiran. The dragon lowered his head, his wings creaking like an old shoe as he folded them to his sides.

"Do ya always hafta scare everyone like that?" asked Kiran.

Ninosh swiveled his long serpentine neck to regard those behind, just now getting shakily to their feet and dusting themselves off, many glaring at the dragon and Kiran 'the dragon whisperer.'

"Making an entrance is good for dragon lore."

Kiran had gotten used to hearing the dragon's voice inside his head. It no longer seemed strange.

Ninosh turned back and flared his nostrils. A warm, humid blast of ash and steam enveloped the young elven lad.

Kiran coughed. *Did Ninosh just grin?* Kiran shook his head, stepped forward and rested his delicate hand on the dragon's rough, armored hide.

The dragon widened his nostrils once more. This time, thankfully, only a warm moist breeze with the faint odor of charcoal washed over Kiran.

"I waited all last week," said Kiran. "And every day since. Why didn't you come?"

"I was otherwise occupied."

Kiran stared at the dragon.

"I fear this may be the last time we see each other."

"What?" Kiran's eyes watered. "No! Why?"

"Rumors are spreading."

"Rumors?"

Ninosh raised his head and gazed beyond the outer shield wall. "Foul rumors. Further unrest amongst the trolls and ogres. Rumors of Queen Mab preparing her sprites should the rumors prove true."

"What rumors?"

"From all five realms, rumors are spreading of dark magic rising from the underworld and flexing its dark talons."

Kiran frowned, skeptically.

Ninosh regarded the boy.

"That ol' end of an age stuff, right?" Kiran picked up a stick and poked it idly into the soil. "That's all the adults ever talk about."

Ninosh continued to study the boy. "The Prophecy predicts Drekton will rise again and the Age of Light will fall into darkness."

"Drekton?"

"Do they not teach history any more boy?" The dragon snorted, smoke curling from its flared nostrils. "Drekton is the King of the demons. When the forces of light, dragons, fairies, and other magical folk, overthrew Drekton and his demon army, the world entered the Age of Light. Before they could destroy the demons, however, Drekton escaped with most of his followers, into a dark realm where beings of light could not follow."

"And the Prophecy says?" Kiran prompted him.

"That Drekton waits for the right moment to reemerge and reclaim the world, plunging it into the Age of Darkness."

Again, Kiran looked skeptical. "So why now? What's different?"

"The Prophecy states that the light will dim into darkness when three things come to pass. First: the elves will lose their magic."

"Some of us can still do magic," argued Kiran.

"How many? Fifty? A hundred?"

Kiran counted on his fingers. "Five. Not counting Larraj and Naagesh."

Again Ninosh snorted. "Not that many yaras past, every elf knew and used magic!"

"So, that's one," Kiran reminded him.

"Two: giants go extinct. Fairies will leave, wizards and dragons will soon follow. Those are the last protectors of white magic. With us gone…"

Kiran continued to probe with the stick. "You think too much."

"I'm a dragon. Thinking is our nature." Ninosh paused. "Dragons live a thousand yaras. I've had plenty of practice."

"It's not true!" Kiran stabbed the stick down so hard it snapped. "It can't be—can it?"

Ninosh scanned Elfhaven's vast outer field all the way from the castle to the outer shield wall. "There are no more giants. The fairies hide in a land beyond time, a fantasy realm of their own making. And there are but two wizards left."

Kiran dropped the stick. "Not the end of dragons, though. Not dragons?"

"There are only five of us left." Ninosh inhaled deeply. "And we are all male."

"No more baby dragons?" Kiran's face paled. "You said the Prophecy says three things must come to pass." Again, Kiran folded down his fingers. "Elves lose their magic. White magical beings go away. What's the third thing?"

"The final event, the one that heralds the beginning of the end."

"Yes?"

"The return of goblins."

"Goblins? They're real?"

The dragon nodded solemnly.

Kiran shivered. "Well." He swallowed with a dry mouth. "At least that hasn't happened yet."

"At least there's that," agreed Ninosh.

Kiran's eyes moistened. He turned away to hide his tears, while gazing at the jagged peaks on the horizon.

Ninosh studied the boy carefully, then followed his gaze northward.

"Come." Ninosh hunkered down. "There's yet time in this age for one last ride."

Smiling, Kiran wiped away the tear, clamored eagerly up the dragon's scale-clad leg, clinging tightly to his neck. Kiran felt the dragon's ribcage bulge beneath him as Ninosh stretched his powerful wings.


# An uninvited guest

Nanni, Kiran and Avani's grandmother, stepped from the kitchen into their cozy living room, the kitchen door swinging back and forth behind her. Reflected crimson flames from the crackling hearth danced across Nanni's eyes. Candles, scattered about the room, added their rich warm glow.

Holding a steaming tray of fresh-baked tarts in her hands, Nanni smiled at her husband Nadda. "Sorry they took so long ta bake, honey!" She held them out. "Better get one before Kiran gets home." She gave Nadda a knowing look.

At that moment, the flames in the hearth flickered, and the door bulged inward, as if made of rubber, with the faint outline of gnarled claw-tipped hands pressing against it.

Nanni glanced at her husband, a horrified look on her aged, elven face. "Nadda?"

Suddenly, the front door exploded in green flames. Through the smoldering remains, a tall hooded figure glided over the rubble and stopped.

Nanni gasped and dropped the plate. It shattered, sending tarts and shards of pottery skittering across the rough wooden floor.

Nadda stepped in front of her. "I demand you leave our home at once! Else I'll summon the palace guards!"

"You demand?" The intruder sounded amused. Pulling off his long, black leather gloves, he strode forward, stopping directly in front of Nadda. "Where's the key?"

"Key?" replied Nadda.

The figure stomped his foot, causing knick-knacks on the shelves to rattle.

Raising his arm, jade-colored sparks danced playfully around his clenched fist. "Avani's key! Where is it?"

The couple remained silent.

The hooded figure snapped his fingers and a ball of emerald flames burst from his upraised palm. He tossed the ball at the over-stuffed sofa in the corner. There was a silent explosion of light. From the center of the light stepped a gnarled, hunched being with wide-set beady eyes and a wicked grin.

Scampering around the room, sniffing as it went, the thing stopped in front of the fireplace. Its grin widened, exposing jagged teeth.

The beast pointed a long spindly finger at the silver cube resting atop the mantle.

"No!" cried Nanni, lunging forward. Nadda stopped her.

The creature leapt up, grabbed the cube, raced back and presented it to its master.

Snatching the cube, the figure held it up to the light. Three raised buttons, all in a row and each of a different color, adorned one side of the cube. Directly below the buttons, three knobs, also of different colors, pointed off at various angles. The buttons glowed, each pulsing with a soft warm light: one red, one green, and one blue.

The hooded figure swept his hand over the cube while mumbling an incantation. All three knobs began to spin. A soft *click* and a button pressed in, locking in place. The knobs continued to spin.

His attention still focused on the cube, the figure flicked his wrist and suddenly Nadda and Nanni's hands were tied. He flicked again. Gags now covered their mouths. "Put them in there." He gestured toward the kitchen.

"Can I kill em?" rasped his servant.

"Once I'm certain I have the key."

A second *click*. A second button depressed.

With surprising strength, the beast dragged both grandparents, kicking and struggling, through the swinging door into the kitchen.

The levers stopped their mad race, all pointing straight up. The third button depressed inward. One final *click* and the cube sprang open, spewing forth a chill mist. Reaching inside, the figure pulled out a black, star-shaped object. Holding it up, flickering flames, cast from the hearth, reflected off the object's polished surface.

# Prince Devraj

"What happened?" cried Devraj, sprinting into the atrium, dust and rocks still clattering to the floor. The entrance to the hall of the Keepers lay blocked by stones.

Barely above a whisper, Larraj answered, "Naagesh." He stared blankly ahead, dust slowly settling at their feet.

"Naagesh? What are you talking about?"

Larraj didn't respond.

"Where's Avani?" Devraj grabbed the wizard by his shoulders and spun him around.

Magic flashed. Devraj blasted back, struck the far wall and slid to the floor.

"How dare you strike me!" shouted the prince.

The room darkened. Larraj seemed to swell, his presence filling the room, golden lightning crackling around him. Larraj's voice boomed. "Never—touch—a wizard in anger!"

Devraj got shakily to his feet, glaring at the wizard cautiously. "Where is Avani?" he repeated, softer this time.

Larraj relaxed, and the room returned to normal. He gazed past the rubble into the Keeper's hall. "I tried to warn her, but—"

"NO!" screamed the prince.

# The evil wizard

The kitchen's swinging door burst open and in strode the cloaked figure holding the key triumphantly in hand.

"Master, can I kill em now?" asked the goblin.

"Yes. You may."

Nanni and Nadda tried to scream, but the figure raised a finger and the two only managed a faint gasp.

Grinning, the beast raised its spindly arms and extended its claws.

Nanni and Nadda struggled against their bonds.

From outside came a loud *whoosh* and a flapping noise. There was a deep *thud*. Pots and pans, hanging above the stove, clinked together.

The wizard raised his hand. "Wait!" His gaze flicked to the curtained window.

The beast hobbled over, rose on its claw-tipped toes, and peered outside. It snapped the curtains shut. "Master. There's a dragon! Just outside the window!"

* * *

Ninosh had spotted the curling smoke immediately. He landed in the street, near the charred remains of Kiran's grandparent's front door.

Ninosh raised his head, flared his nostrils, and sniffed the warm afternoon air. "Something amiss." Ninosh swiveled his long, serpentine neck, positioning his massive head near the kitchen window. The blinds snapped shut. Ninosh reared back and blinked.

Kiran vaulted off Ninosh's neck, slid down the dragon's muscular shoulder, leapt to the ground, sprinted up the steps, and raced through the smoking doorway.

"Careful boy!" Ninosh warned. "I sense dark magic! And something more—a foul stench I've not smelt in…"

"Nadda? Nanni?" yelled Kiran, bolting into their living room and stopped. Fragments of pottery and fragrant squamberry tarts lay scattered across the floor.

"Nadda?" Frowning, Kiran picked up a tart, sniffed it, brushed bits of pottery off the still warm morsel and then popped the whole thing in his mouth.

"Whaas up? Whheerree are youssszz guysszz?"

A muffled moan came from the kitchen.

Swallowing hard, an avalanche of crumbs cascaded to the floor as he ran over, slammed aside the kitchen door and froze. Curling wisps of smoke rose from the charred edges of a large, newly formed hole in the kitchen's back wall.

Kiran's gaze dropped. His eyes popped.

# Devraj

*This cannot have happened!* Devraj tried to lift yet another heavy stone, but it slipped from his sweaty palms. Grabbing it again, he tossed it aside. *Avani cannot be dead!*

Beside him, wizard magic arced out, attached itself to a massive block and hurled it away.

Devraj wiped sweat from his forehead. *I was distracted. I failed to protect Avani, like I failed to protect my mother.* "Wait! There!" A glint of light leaked out from between two slabs.

"Stand back!" Larraj aimed his staff at the rubble. Devraj turned his head as rocks exploded from the area.

Avani sat calmly on the floor, mumbling an incantation, surrounded by a sparkling bubble of protective magic.

She stopped chanting and the bubble burst, bathing them all in a gentle shower of golden sparks.

"Naagesh stole the Manual!" she said. "We have to get back to Elfhaven!"

# Naagesh

"You must be The Guardian," said the intruder.

Bright 3-D displays hovered in mid-air. Sirens blared. Scarlet warning symbols flashed.

The Guardian of the Citadel, having chosen the holographic image of an elven warrior dressed in full battle armor, advanced to within a foot of the intruder and stopped.

"How dare you disturb the sanctity of the Citadel!" The image flickered, accompanied by a faint crackling sound. The Guardian's image stabilized. "In the thousand yaras since this shrine was built, no one has ever broken into the Citadel. How did you manage it?"

A ripple, like that of a pebble tossed idly into a lake, formed in The Guardian's image as the intruder poked a long skeletal finger right through him.

The hint of a sickly grin appeared in the shadows beneath the intruder's dark cowl. The figure lifted a small black object from inside his cape and set it on the console.

"How did you get that?"

"I *persuaded* the Keeper of the Light's grandparents to *lend* me her key."

"Avani's grandparents would never do that! Certainly not to the likes of you—Naagesh."

"Ahh," The evil wizard tossed back his hood. "And I was *so* looking forward to surprising you. How did you know it was me?"

"I scanned you the instant you entered the central chamber. You *and* your companion."

Naagesh snapped his fingers, and a hideous, stooped, and gnarled beast grinned up at the Guardian.

"My database contains thousands of renderings of goblins. 3-D holographic images, primitive digital photographs, pictographs, even a few fanciful sketches. Curious, though. Not a single one depicts a *horned* goblin."

The goblin raised a long, thin, claw-tipped finger and tapped its left horn. *Thunk*. "Grew these myself."

Naagesh glared at the beast. It withdrew into the shadows.

"Back to the topic at hand," resumed the Guardian. "The key would allow entrance, but how did you get past the Citadel's defenses?"

The wizard cleared his throat. From his mouth came Avani's clear, crisp voice, "Avani Dutta. Keeper of the Light."

The Guardian stared at the wizard. "What do you want? Why are you here?"

Ignoring him, Naagesh strode to the main control panel. Strange glowing crystals jutted out from the panel at odd angles. Streams of numbers and alien symbols hung in the air above the instruments.

"I assume you are here for a reason," pressed the Guardian.

By way of answer, Naagesh leaned over the console and pressed a series of glowing symbols, then grabbed hold of a crystal lever.

"What are you doing?" demanded the Guardian. "I, and I alone, control the Citadel."

"Yes," Naagesh said absently. "About that..." From inside his cloak, the wizard pulled out a large leather text. "I've been doing a bit of light reading, of late." Naagesh released his grip, and the Citadel's Manual *thumped* down heavily on the console.

The Guardian stared at the book, static rippling through his image. "What good does that do you? You're no engineer. It takes more than mumbled spells, and bubbling potions, to control a technological marvel as advanced as the Citadel." Again, the Guardian glanced at the Manual.

"Perhaps." Naagesh thrust the crystal lever forward. A panel opened on the console's surface, and a small hexagonal block rose from below. Diamond shaped keys, with glowing hieroglyphs, covered the block's face.

The wizard's eyes widened in mock surprise. "What have we here?" He pursed his lips. "Could it be what the book termed—the Manual Override Interface? Did I get the term correct?" He touched three lit symbols in rapid succession. A low hum dropped in pitch.

"Oh no. What have I done?" Naagesh said. "The barrier's down. Elfhaven is no longer protected." He shook his head. "And without even a single *mumbled spell.*"

Naagesh pressed a symbol and a 3-D holographic map of the known universes appeared. He tapped another symbol and the map twisted, distorting oddly as it expanded. A bright red sphere pulsed to the wizard's right.

Naagesh extended his arm. The space around his finger wavered as it passed through the image. The map zoomed outward, then abruptly stopped.

A dark planet slowly rotated at the center of the display. Sparkling crimson rivers of lava crisscrossed the planet's black surface, while jagged tendrils of orange and violet lightning arced around the planet's poles.

"Pandora's Portal?" cried The Guardian. "You're mad! If that portal were to open—"

"It would release the creatures. I know."

"Those creatures nearly destroyed this world, once before!"

"I know that too."

"Opening a portal is a complex task. A task only I can perform." The Guardian's voice steeled. "And I will not do it!"

"Oh? I seem to recall—" Naagesh glanced at the book. "—there's a device which can accomplish the task. Without the *need* of your help."

The Guardian's image blinked. "The remotes were all lost Long ago."

"Oh. What a shame." Naagesh casually took hold of a lever while watching the Guardian's reaction.

The Guardian's image remained motionless.

Smiling thinly, Naagesh slammed the lever forward. Up from the panel rose a small black object, similar in size to the Citadel key, but oblong instead of star-shaped. There were two shallow indentations on the object's surface, each with a glowing symbol. Naagesh grasped the device.

"NO! cried The Guardian. "I will not allow it!" Across the console's surface, small hatches sprang open. From within, a horde of tiny silver-gray robots, nano-droids, swarmed up and across the counter, sprang from the console and like fire locusts, swarmed across the startled wizard's body, forming a ridged gray covering. As the last one skittered into place over the wizard's nose, the room fell silent.

Naagesh stood frozen, entombed in gray.

A crack formed. One of Naagesh's fingers twitched. Blazing emerald magic blasted the nano-droids against the chamber's walls where they clattered to the floor, motionless.

All but one.

The Guardian glanced at Naagesh's left knee-length, black leather boot. A single droid wriggled up from inside his boot, paused, then disappeared back inside. The Guardian's eyes popped back up.

"Have you forgotten who I am? The power I possess in a single finger!" Naagesh glanced at his boot, scowled, and shook his leg.

"I was not trying to hurt you," the Guardian assured him. "Merely distract you."

"What?"

The Guardian cried, "Emergency destruct protocol 517—"

With lightning speed, Naagesh's hand flew across the console. The Guardian's image froze, his mouth open, his holographic eyes blank, unblinking.

"Enough!" Naagesh stabbed his finger onto a glowing red button. The Guardian's image flattened to a line, then to a single bright dot, then vanished with a faint *pop*.

Stepping from the shadows, his goblin servant pointed at the device still clutched in the wizard's hands. "Is that it, Master?"

"Yes." Naagesh rolled the object over in his palm, thoughtfully. "My revenge, and my father's." His grip tightened on the device.

He pointed the remote at the image of the dark planet and pressed the glowing red symbol. A flat mechanical female voice spoke, "Voice recognition must be completed before remote can be synchronized. Please state your name and title."

"Naagesh. Wizard. Master class."

"Voice recognition recorded and accepted. Synchronization for remote portal access may now begin."

Again, he aimed the device at the planet.

"Syncing remote to planet's coordinates." A series of beeps, chirps, and clicks ensued. "Synchronization complete. Do you wish to set a failsafe timer?"

Naagesh paused. "Yes."

"State the date, time, and place to open portal, should you choose not to open it before then."

Naagesh grinned. "I know the perfect time and place."

"Master!" cried the goblin. "The plan was to open the portal now!"

"Plans change," replied the wizard.

"But—"

"Silence!" shouted Naagesh.

"Time and place?" queried the remote.

Naagesh gave the device the details.

"WARNING: once failsafe timer is activated, it can only be disabled by you. Confirm timer activation?"

Naagesh gazed thoughtfully at the dark planet slowly revolving before him.

"Confirm timer activation," the voice repeated.

The evil wizard's teeth gleamed dully in the Citadel's cool blue light when he spoke, "Confirmed."

# Kiran

Kiran rushed over, removed his grandparent's gags, and untied their hands. "What happened? Who did this?"

"He stole her key!" gasped Nadda, helping his wife to her feet. "Are you all right, sweet gum?" Nanni nodded, shivering.

Kiran glanced from one to the other. "Avani's key? To the Citadel? But that was locked in Father's cube."

"Tell me everything that happened," ordered Kiran.

They quickly recounted all that had happened from the moment the front door first exploded until the tall one blasted the hole in the kitchen's back wall and escaped.

"What did they look like?"

"The tall one wore a long, hooded cloak," Nadda began. "Couldn't see his face. But his voice sent shivers down my spine."

Nanni shuddered. "I never heard such an evil voice."

Nadda squeezed her hand.

"And the short one?" Kiran said. "You said it entered through a ball of green fire."

"Yes. Over there." She pointed. "Where I tried to hide that rip in the sofa by covering it with that pillow, the one with the colorful gremlin embroidered on it." She shook her head. "Shoulda repaired that darn tear ages ago."

Nadda continued, "From the fire burst a hideous being."

"Short, hunched way over," said Nanni. "With long twisted teeth and a wicked grin."

Nadda agreed, "Sickly greenish-brown skin, its hands and feet all gnarled and twisted."

"Oh, and it had two short stubby horns on its head and there twas something odd about its eyes. Fer a moment, red flames flickered deep within its beady eyes."

"Its eyes?" said Nadda.

Nanni nodded. "They flickered. Just for an instant. Like they was on fire. Didn't you see?"

"Don't remember no flaming eyes."

"No?" Nanni laid her wrinkled hand on top of his. "Musta imagined it."

Nadda glanced at the glowing embers, softly crackling in the hearth. "Probably just the fire reflecting off its eyes."

She grinned sheepishly at her husband. "Course it was. It all happened so fast, ya know."

He patted her arm affectionately.

Nanni smiled at Kiran, her lips curling back over her gums.

Kiran drew back. "Nanni? What happened to your teeth?"

Nanni stopped smiling and covered her mouth.

Nadda bent over, picked up a set of wooden dentures from the floor and handed them to her. Opening wide, she popped them into her mouth, ground her teeth back and forth and smiled. "Better?"

"Much!"

"Anyway," said Nanni. "Guess that's bout it."

"'Cept fer the smell," Nadda reminded her.

"Gracious yes. The smell! Rotten river eels with a pinch of ogre droppings."

Nadda leaned close. "More'n a pinch, I'd say, sweet gums."

"Musta been Naagesh," said Kiran.

"Naagesh!" gasped Nanni.

"The evil wizard?" Nadda replied.

Kiran nodded. "Not sure what his servant was."

"It was a goblin," said Nadda.

"That was a goblin?" Nanni covered her mouth with her wrinkled hand. "Thought they was all dead."

Nadda's voice quavered, "No one's seen goblins in a hundred yara. Not since the War of the Wizards."

"The Prophecy..." muttered Nanni.

"What happened next?" urged Kiran.

Nadda said, "The tall one—ah, Naagesh—"

"Told the—goblin—" Nanni continued.

"To kill us," finished Nadda.

Kiran's jaw dropped. "How d'you escape?"

"We heard a loud flapping," Nanni said.

"Just outside the window," added Nadda.

"Ninosh!" Kiran leapt up and threw back the curtains. A gigantic eye filled the window.

Nadda and Nanni gasped.

"It's OK," Kiran assured them. "This is Ninosh, my dragon friend I told ya about."

Wide eyed, arms wrapped tightly round each other, the couple stared at the monstrous eye gazing in at them.

Ninosh blinked.

Bolting from the room, the swinging door smacked loudly against a kitchen cabinet. "Don't worry," he called from the other room. "I'll get help!"

# Open channel D

Devraj, Sanuu, and Larraj stood on the plateau near the entrance to the Library of Nalanda, discussing what to do next. Avani watched from a few paces away. The sun had sunken low, painting the horizon with the first golden brush strokes of sunset. A chill breeze had begun to blow.

"The books on dark magic make sense," reasoned Sanuu. "But, why steal the Manual of the Citadel? What could Naagesh possibly want with that?"

Avani glanced at the prince. He glared at Larraj with disdain. She walked up, glanced from Devraj to the Wizard, then said, "Naagesh can't enter the Citadel without my key," she reasoned, "and that's safely locked in Father's cube, at Nadda and Nanni's house."

Larraj just stared at her.

"No!" she screamed.

The wizard glanced first at Sanuu and then back at Devraj.

Sanuu spoke first, "If Naagesh somehow broke into the Citadel, armed with the knowledge from this book, could he shut down the barrier?"

Avani shuddered, "Ah—I'm not sure."

Devraj said, "That would give Naagesh's forces a distinct advantage," adding, "should they attack Elfhaven." Everyone stared at the wizard.

"I have an uneasy feeling there's more to it." Larraj studied the grave faces surrounding him. "In any case, Avani's right, we must return to Elfhaven immediately."

"What of the books?" asked Avani. "Especially the books on magic. Our mission was to bring them to Elfhaven." She glanced sheepishly at Larraj. "Originally."

"Sanuu," began Devraj. "I shall take half the men to Elfhaven and warn Father. The other half can remain here with you and complete our mission."

"What about the dwarves?" Sanuu said. "They're in danger too. We should send word to King Abban."

The prince paused. "I agree. The books have waited a hundred yara. They can wait a bit longer. Sanuu, take the rest of the men to Deltar and warn King Abban and the dwarf High Council."

Sanuu addressed his men, "Gather your things."

"Wait!" said Larraj. Everyone stopped. "We can't afford the delay. There may be another way."

"Do you have one of Thomas Holland's magical talking boxes?" Sanuu asked.

"No. Tom took them with him back to Earth."

"Are your magical powers so great then," began Sanuu, "that you can commune with the dwarf king over such vast distances?"

"No. Not by myself. For that, I'd need the help of other wizards."

"Other wizards?" said the prince. "There are but two wizards yet alive. You and Naagesh. And I think it highly unlikely Naagesh will aid us."

Larraj strode off into the center of the plateau's petrified forest and faced them.

"Technically, Devraj is correct. By most definitions, only two wizards yet tread the paths of this world."

The others glanced at each other.

"These petrified trees were once wizards. It's true, they're not alive in this plane of existence, yet there is another realm. A realm where they yet live. It's called—The Void. A yara ago, when I was here searching for the artifact, the source of the Citadel's power, these same wizards aided me. Perhaps they will again." With that, he tapped his staff on a tree trunk—and vanished...


# Avani's promise

Avani strolled through the petrified forest. Nearing the cliff, the chill wind whipped her clothing about her. Avani shivered, drawing her cloak in tight.

Larraj had been gone a long time. The sun had since set, plunging their surroundings into darkness. The only sounds were the wind rustling through distant trees, the buzz of night-flying insects and the flapping wings of their predators.

To the west, beyond the 'U' shaped, glacier-carved valley below, Avani could see the faint outline of jagged peaks. On the far side of those peaks, she knew, lay the dwarf city of Deltar, perched on the slopes of MT Drakus. That's where her friend Goban lived.

She glanced over her shoulder. On the far side of the petrified forest, flames from their campfire highlighted Devraj, nervously pacing, impatient for Larraj's return. His soldiers, however, sat comfortably by the fire, their faces flickering with a faint orange glow. A soldier stirred the coals, sending red embers spiraling upward.

Avani followed the ember's path. In the sky above, The Ring of Turin, Tom had called it an—asteroid belt, sparkled like diamonds in the dark night sky.

She smiled at the thought of Tom. *A yara ago to the day, the three of us: Tom, Goban, and I stood on this very spot.*

Avani recognized a constellation she knew by name, *the Gremlin!* Her smile widened. *And there's Blattor—the Toad King. Oh—and the Archer.* Her smile abruptly faded. The archer brought a bitter-sweet memory. The archer reminded her of her father, killed these many yara ago during a troll uprising.

"*If anything should happen to me.*" *Her father laid his broad hand on her shoulder.*

"*It won't!*" *Avani assured him.*

*He smiled.* "*No. But if it should—I want you to promise me you'll always protect Kiran.*"

*Avani nodded.*

"*And your grandparents, too. Promise?*"

"*I promise.*"

A tear trickled down her cheek. She wiped it away.

With each passing day Avani feared she would forget what her father looked like, so she continually forced herself to remember: his dimpled cheek. His long-pointed ears. That rebellious sprig of hair that would never lie flat. The twinkle in his eye when he pulled a jest on her or Kiran. She sniffled.

Her father had been the head of the Keepers of the Light. A secret sect that had maintained and protected the Citadel for the last thousand yara, ever since the star beings built it. When her father died, along with all the other Keepers, killed in the same troll uprising, that responsibility had passed to her. *I'm now the Keeper. The last Keeper. The only Keeper.*

Still gazing at the sky, she said, "Father. I wanna be a wizard, more than anything! I want to go away and study with Larraj. Learn everything he knows, but—how can I? Being his apprentice takes all my time." She hesitated. "How can I protect Kiran *and* study magic?"

Avani took a deep breath and knelt. "Father. I swear on my life, I'll protect Kiran and Nadda and Nanni too. Even if I have to give up my dream."

She turned from the cliff to the petrified forest. "Where is that wizard?" she screamed. "I have to get back to Elfhaven. My family's in danger!"

Uncontrolled sobs washed over her.

# The Void

Larraj hovered in a non-place filled with rolling mist, vague shapes and distant voices. The air felt cool and moist, though it had an odd sour tang to it. Strangely, Larraj wasn't sure how long he'd been in this realm: sectars, oorts, a yara?

Occasionally, he glimpsed something solid, something familiar and yet not. To his left a thinner patch of mist revealed a small lake with deep blue water sitting amidst a forest of rich olive-green, large-frond ferns. At the far side of the lake a waterfall cascaded noisily—only—the water flowed from the lake up the waterfall, instead of the other way round. In fact, all across the lake's surface, water droplets lifted, *bloop*, rising, rising, creating a gentle rain shower from below.

Larraj reached out and touched a raindrop. The water spread across his finger. It felt normal: cool and wet. But then the drop wound round his finger, reformed at the top and rose jiggling from his finger, continuing its

38

upward journey. The swirling mists engulfed him once more, and he lost sight of the lake, and everything else.

Sometime later, he heard muted hollow voices in the distance, up and to his right. Though he wasn't sure there was such a thing as up or down, left or right, in this realm.

Focusing his attention on the voices, he somehow began drifting in that direction. At least, he thought he was moving since the mists swirled past him faster and the voices grew louder.

Larraj squinted. His staff began to glow. Within moments, vague outlines of twelve hooded figures appeared, gliding toward him. As the figures drifted close, they formed a circle around him. Like Larraj, each held a staff in their right hands. Beyond them lay only more swirling mist, interspersed with pockets of darkness. The Void.

Larraj tossed back his hood. The twelve did the same.

One of them floated forward. "I am the wizard Dandrol." His voice sounded odd, as if coming from a deep well.

"Master Dandrol," Larraj bowed low, his own voice sounding muted and distant. "I know you. We met last yara. But even before that, when I was a young student at Dragon Hollow wizard school, your name was oft spoken in hushed reverence. Our textbooks deemed you one of the greatest wizards of our time, of all time."

"I remember your visit. Larraj, was it?" asked Dandrol.

Larraj nodded.

"Why have you returned to us, Larraj? Have you finally come to free us, then? Bring us back to the world of flesh and blood, of good works and valiant deeds?"

"Alas, I wish I could. But I do not possess the tools required."

A murmur passed through the twelve. Someone said, "Dark magic put us here."

"Aye," agreed another.

"Needs be dark magic to free us," added a third. More murmurs of agreement.

"Sadly," began Larraj. "I do not possess knowledge of dark magic."

"No matter." Dandrol glanced at his fellow wizards and placed his hand on Larraj's shoulder. "Then what need have you of us, today?"

"I need your help again. I need to enact the Colloquium Vocationem. As you know, the technique requires the services of at least six wizards to open a multi-channel vortex."

"You wish to converse with several others, in different locations, at the same time?"

"Yes, myself, and my companions outside the Library of Nalanda. We wish to speak with King Dakshi, the current king of Elfhaven, and also, to King Abban of the dwarf nation."

"Why come to us? Why not ask the Wizards Council?"

"This will come as a bit of a shock," began Larraj. "But the Wizards Council was disbanded a hundred yara ago. Shortly after the unfortunate incident that left you all trapped here." Indignant shouts and cries spread throughout the circle.

Dandrol raised his hand. The voices fell silent. "Disbanded. What folly is this?"

"Not just disbanded, I'm afraid. The council was destroyed. As a result, there are but two wizards left alive. Myself—" Larraj fixed his gaze on Dandrol. "—and Naagesh."

More indignant murmurs.

"Quiet!" shouted Dandrol. Once the voices fell silent, Dandrol continued, "Naagesh? Lord Vandon's son?"

"Yes."

Dandrol scowled. "A bad sort, the father. That incident with the demon and his daughter…" Dandrol squared his shoulders. "Yet if memory serves, I'd heard young Naagesh showed great promise."

"He was one of the brightest students at Dragon Hollow school," agreed Larraj. "At any of the schools!"

"Yet?" Dandrol tipped his head expectantly.

"Yet, eventually he, like his father, turned evil." Larraj paused. "The event that trapped you all here, was but a precursor of the unrest that followed, eventually culminating in the War of the Wizards. It was Naagesh and his followers who started the War, which nearly wiped out all our kind." Larraj fixed his gaze on Dandrol.

Dandrol tapped his fingers absently on his staff.

"What's more." Larraj sighed. "I just learned that Naagesh stole the Citadel's Manual from the Library of Nalanda, as well as books on dark magic. We have to act quickly else…"

Dandrol scanned the faces of his companions. One by one, they nodded. He faced Larraj. "We are at your service."

Dandrol extended his arm toward Larraj, then pulled back his sleeve, exposing the mark of the wizard, a simple triangle with a diagonal line with radiating squiggly lines at its tip, representing an old-school wizard's hat and magic wand. Above the mark, a wide brass wristlet embossed with silver studs surrounding a mesh of fine golden threads wrapped around Dandrol's arm. Beneath the threads, swirling clouds of multi-colored energy obscured what lay within. "This may be of use to you."

Larraj's brow rose. "A vortex bracelet?"

"You recognize it."

Larraj leaned closer. "Vortex bracelets were used to contain ancient and powerful beings. What's in this one?"

"A seeker."

Larraj jerked upright. "I thought them lost?"

"True, the seekers were all lost hundreds of yaras ago."

"Then how—"

"While the dwarves were building Castle Dunferlan—"

"That was nearly three hundred yaras ago."

"Precisely," confirmed Dandrol. "During the excavation, the dwarves happened upon a hidden cave. In that cave they found a treasure trove of ancient magical artifacts. Not known for their magical abilities, the dwarves presented the items to the Wizard's Council."

"Including this vortex wristlet," Larraj guessed.

Dandrol smiled. "Two bracelets, in point of fact. Each containing a seeker."

Larraj stared in awe at the seething cloud hovering just above Dandrol's wrist. "Amazing. I was head of the Wizard's Council for a time. I never knew."

"It was a closely guarded secret," Dandrol confided. "The council wisely split them up. I, as the head of the council in my day, took this one."

"And the other?"

"We thought it best if no one knew who possessed the other seeker, not even me." Dandrol thrust his arm toward Larraj.

Larraj paused, then drew back his sleeve. Waving his hand over the bracelet, Dandrol muttered an incantation. A soft glow spread across the wristband. On the underside of the artifact, golden bands released, wriggling tentacles dangled below like a giant, golden, multi-legged centipede. The artifact floated up from Dandrol's arm and over to Larraj's and settled down, its squirming legs slithering around Larraj's arm. Dandrol finished the incantation, and the golden legs froze solid.

Larraj rotated his wrist, opening and closing his fist, then pulled down his sleeve and bowed, accepting the rare artifact with humility.

"The seeker will aid you in finding Naagesh," said Dandrol. "But back to the original purpose of your visit. The Colloquium Vocationem, eh?"

Larraj nodded.

"The Colloquium Vocationem: opening a voice channel—allowing people to converse across vast distances requires great skill, great concentration, and great power. Simultaneously opening a channel to two other locations, even more so."

Larraj studied the wizards' faces. "You do remember the technique? Do you yet possess the ability?"

Dandrol hmmphed. "We do indeed. But you underestimate us—" He glanced knowingly at his fellow wizards. "We can do you one better."

# Goban

Goban clomped down a narrow ledge on the outskirts of the dwarf city of Deltar. He smiled, feeling the warm summer breeze blowing through his coarse, dark-brown hair. The dwarves built the city on Mount Drakus, an active volcano which provided both security and easy access to heat to power the dwarf forges. Deltar was the last city of the once great dwarf nation.

As he trudged along, jets of steam rumbled and hissed from vents on the volcano's steep slope. Some vents were natural, Goban knew. Others, however, were dwarf-made. Those had the dual purpose of supplying fresh air to the forges and underground workshops housed deep inside the volcano itself, while at the same time clearing smoke and steam from those same chambers.

Goban glanced over his shoulder. A vent to his left erupted, sending a plume of foul-smelling steam high into the air.

The dwarf lad wrinkled his face, his bushy eyebrows welding together into a deep 'V.' *Stinks of rotten zapter eggs.* Goban snorted. *Think I'd be useta the stench by now.*

A shrill cry caused Goban to gaze skyward. His face blossomed into a huge grin. "Kiki! And Mr. Squinkles!"

A fearsome two-headed raptor landed heavily on the dwarf's outstretched arm. The bird's heads resembled snapping turtles, with orange and blue feather rings around each neck. Likewise, ample feathers surrounded her two legs. Bare three-toed feet protruded from the leg feathers. Each toe ended in long, sharp talons. Oddly, her body lay covered in a shaggy, blue fur.

The strange *bird* tightened her grip, easily piercing Goban's leather smock. A trickle of blood dripped out from under his sleeve. Goban didn't seem to notice.

His pet fluffed its orange and blue feathers on her twin necks. Bending its left head downward, it cooed softly as Goban scratched the back of Kikiboo's neck. Though Goban knew better than to call her that. Preferring to be called Kiki, she strongly objected each time Goban slipped and called her Kikiboo.

The second head, Mr. Squinkles, butted the first head aside. Goban switched to stroking it. Kiki hissed at Mr. Squinkles.

"There, there," soothed Goban. "Plenty a pets ta go round."

Goban spotted a small scroll tied to the bird's foot with fire snake gut twine. Goban gently untied the tiny missive, unrolled it and read aloud, "The Mastersmith wants ta see me." Goban glanced knowingly at his pet. "Needs my expert advice, no doubt."

Kikiboo screeched.

Goban scowled. "What would *you* know?"

Both heads lowered and thrust themselves firmly against Goban's shoulder, resuming their nuzzling in earnest.

"All right, already. Hold yer zhanderbeasts!" Goban scratched the back of his pet's necks, alternating between necks every sectar or two, and continued on his way.

Nearing the entrance to one of the volcano's many hollow lava tubes, Goban threw up his arm, saying, "Enough pets fer one day."

Squawking their displeasure, his pet launched skyward. Circling above, the pair let loose a barrage of irate, scolding cries until Goban disappeared inside the steam-filled tunnel.

This particular tunnel formed the entrance to the Mastersmith's vast network of workshops.

Goban's heavy leather boots, laced up almost to his knees, echoed in the cavern. The sound was soon drowned out by a deep volcanic rumbling, the continuous clanking of tools and the gruff arguments of dwarf smiths. The noises became louder the deeper he strode down the dark stone passageway.

He felt the heat even before the tunnel veered left. Navigating the corner, he saw the distant, wavering, red glow reflecting off the tunnel walls. That way led to one of the inspection windows overlooking the molten lava lake at the volcano's heart.

Luckily, before it got too hot, Goban took a right turn and sauntered into the Mastersmith's workshop.

A handful of oil lamps, suspended from the ceiling via heavy iron chains, dimly lit the large space with their flickering yellow glow. Ventilation shafts provided fresh oxygen, even so, the lamps gave off a tangy tar smell that stung Goban's eyes.

An aged, grizzled dwarf, sporting a large gray beard and an even larger belly, leaned over a wooden bench. Wrinkled, badly stained parchment pages littered the bench. Apparently lost in thought, the dwarf studied the pages intently.

Holding a large magnifying glass made of brass, wood, and glass, he gazed through the device at a drawing, covered with hand-scrawled notes highlighting important details. The dwarf's bushy, deeply furrowed brow showed him totally absorbed in his work.

"Master Zanda," said Goban heartily. "How goes the battle?"

Setting down the device, the Mastersmith stood upright, his frown morphing into a smile at the sight of his favorite nephew.

"Prince Goban," said the smith, tipping his balding head ever-so-slightly.

Goban fidgeted. "Cut that out. Ya know I hate being called—*prince*."

"You'll someday be king, will ye not?"

Goban frowned.

"Which makes ya a prince. Like it or not."

"And speaking of such, shouldn't ye be studying statecraft: observing yer father negotiating with the dwarf High Council?"

"You sent fer me," Goban reminded him.

Zanda laughed. "Ye showed up so fast, you was already on yer way here, weren't ya?"

Goban's scowl deepened. "I hate that stuff! It's a heap a lapter droppings:

buttering up those pompous arses on the council."

"Those *arses,* as you call em, control the whole of the dwarf nation. *'Control the council, you control the kingdom'* your father always sez." Zanda aimed a pair of calipers at his nephew. "Your father is a master of control. You would do well to learn from the best."

Goban sighed. "It's boring. I just wanna build things like you do." He sighed. "Besides, I hate being called prince."

"I know's ya hate it." Zanda slapped Goban's back heartily. "I just loves ta see ya squirm."

Goban grinned. "So, how're my projects going?" He motioned to the tools and materials stacked atop stout wooden benches and scattered across the wide stone floor. Several smiths quarreled over a triangular piece of wood easily as tall as the dwarves themselves. Nearby, a well-tanned animal hide lay draped over a large bench, cascading down the sides and across the floor. Some smiths used wooden handled knives to cut the hide, while others sewed the pieces together using bone needles and animal gut thread.

This time the Mastersmith snorted. "*Your* projects, are they?"

"Ah—our projects."

Zanda studied his nephew's face. "*Our* projects?"

"They're my plans!"

"Which the Earthling Thomas Holland gave you."

"Tom and I discussed them. I suggested improvements." Goban stared off across the hall.

The Mastersmith regarded his nephew critically. Goban continued to stare.

"Thinking of Thomas again?"

Goban blinked. "No!"

Zanda stared at him.

Goban shrugged. "Well, maybe."

"Miss em?"

"We had adventures."

"And?"

"He got us into no end of trouble!"

"And?"

"We talked science, he shared inventions, told tales of another world."

"And?"

Goban sighed. "And—I miss him."

The Mastersmith nodded, knowingly.

"Back to these *secret* projects," said Goban. "My father put me in charge of overseeing the projects."

"Tryin' ta pull rank on me now, are ye? Now who's being a pompous *arse?*"

Goban's eyes narrowed.

"Aye, the king did indeed ask ya to oversee the projects," agreed his uncle. "Under my expert guidance, a course." Zanda extended his hand. "Agreed?"

Goban shook hands with his uncle heartily.

The Mastersmith chuckled and placed a broad, heavily calloused hand on Goban's shoulder. Glancing around, Zanda's gaze froze on a long brass tube lying on his cluttered workbench.

"Tom's telescope design!" said Goban.

Zanda picked it up and handed it to his nephew. Goban peered through the device's larger end. Goban scratched his head in confusion. "Makes things look far away."

The Mastersmith's stubby finger traced a circle in the air.

Goban flipped it over and tried again. "I can see Kael!" Goban lowered the telescope. "Hey Kael! You should trim yer nose hairs." Off to Goban's right, a dwarf looked up from his sewing and glared at Goban.

The Mastersmith chuckled, "Think you'll find you was commenting on Caitlin, not Kael's nose grooming habits. And she don't look too *pleased* with yer suggestion." Zanda took back the telescope.

"Ok, mister *project overseer*, I'll show ya the progress we've made on yer *other* project, but first—" The smith leaned over the pile of wrinkled parchment documents scattered before him and squinted. "This note here—" His plump stubbly finger stabbed down onto the plans. "—has me baffled. It's labeled *CG* and they're several bold red arrows pointing at it."

"Stands for Center of Gravity." Goban puffed his chest, proud to know something the Mastersmith didn't. "Tom told me it's critical to the design. Get it right, all's well. Get it wrong…"

The Mastersmith once more furrowed his brow in concentration.

Goban explained, "If the CG is too far forward—" Goban held his palm out flat, parallel to the tabletop. His palm tipped forward and dove. "RRRrrrrrr boom!" His hand crashed to the table and his fingers flew apart in a dramatic mock explosion.

"Get the CG too far back and—" Goban repeated his hand demonstration only this time, his palm tipped back, hesitated; hovering motionless for an instant, then tipped forward, dove and crashed to the desk, again accompanied by ample sound effects and finger graphics.

The Mastersmith pursed his lips thoughtfully. "I get yer point."

"What about the *other* project?"

"This way." Zanda led Goban from the room, down a long corridor. Dancing shadows cast by lanterns above followed them until they entered another large, well-lit chamber. Massive rough-cut wooden beams littered the floor.

Goban's belly rumbled. "That reminds me. Supposed ta meet dad at the palace fer dinner."

"You'll wanna see this first," his uncle assured him. "Twon't take long."

At end of the cavern, a rope net hung from the high ceiling above all the way to the floor. A hastily painted, crude red circle adorned the net's center. Below that, another net stretched taut, suspended at waist height and parallel to the ground. Two dwarves groaned as they lifted a large wooden wheel onto an equally large wooden axle.

"Why the nets?" asked Goban.

"You'll see."

Across the room, a lone dwarf sat atop a bowl-shaped platform attached at the end of a long shaft. Checklist in hand, the worker seemed to be inspecting something. Below, another pair of workers cranked a handle. The effort wound a rope tightly around a wooden drum. There was a loud clacking noise. The rope creaked. The platform lowered.

The workers stopped cranking. One of them drummed his fingers lightly on a lever while glancing at the Mastersmith with a mischievous grin.

"*Observe!*" Zanda whispered to Goban while nodding to the worker. The dwarf leaned back, straining to pull the lever. It didn't budge. His partner joined in. It still didn't budge. The first dwarf picked up a large iron sledgehammer, drew back and swung. When the hammer collided with the mechanism, a loud *thump* echoed throughout the cavern.

The dwarf sitting in the bowl above, leaned over the edge. "Hey! Yer not tryin' ta—"

The mechanism groaned. There came a loud *whoosh*. A look of shock and sheer terror crossed the dwarf's face as he soared through the air across the chamber.

The dwarf stuck the upper net just outside the red circle, missing the target by a dwarf beards' length. Disappointed groans came from dwarves who'd lost their bets.

Now falling, arms and legs flailing, the unwitting daredevil landed in the lower net. The net creaked, its heavy burden dropping almost to the floor. The dwarf bobbed up and down for several sectars before finally coming to rest.

The room erupted with raucous laughter. Dwarves ran over to help their co-worker from the net. The dwarf in the net, however, was not laughing. In fact, he was yelling a stream of unmentionable dwarvish curses!

Still watching the thrashing figure, Goban said, "I see Tom's other design is coming along nicely."

"Mostly there," agreed the Mastersmith. "Just one or two tiny insects yet to be extracted." Zanda paused. "At least we've gotten the net tension correct. Poor Bodhi's backside may never be the same after our earlier attempts."

Goban's laughter echoed throughout the stone hall for several long sectars.

Though, if he or the Mastersmith knew the fate of their world depended on the success of Goban's 'projects' they might not have been laughing.


# A delicate matter


"Have the scouts reported back yet?" asked King Dakshi, ruler of Elfhaven, the largest elf kingdom on this world.

"Two are back, my lord," said Tappus. "We are awaiting the third." Of all his men, Tappus and Sanuu, his two head palace guards, were the king's most trusted advisors.

King Dakshi's face looked grim. "What of the other two scouts, then? What news bring they?"

"Grave news, I'm afraid, sire. A massive troll army, led by Phawta, left the Tontiel Mountains, heading through Tontiel Pass."

"Heading here?"

"It's not clear. They're traveling south, following the trail that parallels the Tontiel river."

"Hmmm." The king drummed his fingers on the desk. "And the ogres?"

"They're still hold up in the ogre city of Ogmoonder, but the scouts said the ogres are stockpiling weapons, and food and supplies."

The king's frown deepened. "Trolls and ogres are sworn enemies. Were, anyway. 'Til Naagesh bent them to his evil plans."

"Sire?"

King Dakshi drummed his fingers two more times, then abruptly stopped. "What is the dark wizard up to now?"

"My lord?"

King Dakshi glanced up at his lieutenant, and then changed the subject,

"I sent for Larraj's warrior friend, Zhang Wu. Why has he not yet arrived?"

Tappus grinned. "Sire, the quirky monk is probably busy sharpening his swords and polishing his magic infused throwing stars."

King Dakshi didn't respond. Tappus coughed awkwardly, all traces of the grin now wiped from his face. "Zhang Wu is on his way, my lord."

The king still didn't respond. In fact, he just peered off into space.

"My lord, are you all right? Is something wrong?"

King Dakshi blinked. "No, no. I was—somewhere else—somewhere far away."

Tappus tipped his head. "May I be of service? Is there something you wish to discuss?" He paused. "While we wait for the monk, I mean."

The king rubbed his tired eyes and then scanned his lieutenant's face. "It is—a delicate matter."

"Have I ever failed you? You know you can count on my discretion, my lord."

King Dakshi clamped his hand down firmly on Tappus's shoulder. "I know I can." The king strolled around the great hall, his hands clasped behind his back. "I have been—troubled for nearly a yara."

Tappus hurried to his liege's side. "What troubles you, sire? Is it the news of the renewed ogre unrest? Or the raids on the supply caravans from the lake elves?"

"No, I am afraid it is something far more serious."

"What then?" Tappus's voice trembled. "I promise you I will do all in my power to right the wrong, to destroy your enemy."

King Dakshi half-sighed, half-chuckled. "Nothing that dire is required, I assure you."

Tappus waited for the king to go on.

"As I said, my thoughts have been preoccupied, of late. They keep returning to a certain person, to her face, to the last words she spoke to me."

Tappus's jaw dropped. "She? A female then." The king nodded.

Tappus spoke delicately, "Is she—er, rather—are you two?"

51

The king returned his stare. "Yes. I am in love."

Tappus's face blossomed into a huge grin. "That's wonderful, sire! Have you set a date for your joining ceremony?" Now Tappus paced the room. "Is it Lepara? She's bright, very perceptive. Or Terisa? She's witty, good in battle, and quite attractive. She would make the perfect queen."

King Dakshi stared at him gravely.

Tappus's smile faded. "I'm sorry if I offended you, my lord." Tappus bowed. "I spoke out of turn. It was just that—that I'm happy for you. Please disregard my remarks. I was just—"

"You have not offended me. And you are correct. Lepara is intelligent. Terisa is witty. They are both strong-willed. Either would make a fine queen. Still—" The king hesitated, glanced at his feet, then up at Tappus. "—the woman that haunts my thoughts, my dreams, is neither of them. In point of fact, she is not even elvish."

Tappus paused. "Um—a dwarf?" He cleared his throat, then rushed on, "That *is* unusual, to say the least, but there are historical precedents, rare occasions when—" He again paced the room, faster this time. "It would definitely solidify the bonds between our two nations, our two kingdoms." Tappus brightened. "And King Abban *is* your best friend, after all. I assume he will be your best elf, er—dwarf."

"She is not dwarvish either."

Tappus froze, all color drained from his face. "Not elvish. *And* not dwarvish. Surely not a troll?"

"Of course not a troll!" boomed the king. Tappus wisely remained silent.

King Dakshi sighed. "The female who occupies my every waking thought is—Juanita, Thomas Holland's mother, the boy from the Prophecy."

"A human?" Tappus blinked.

At that moment, the massive doors that spanned the entrance to the great hall groaned and swung inward. A palace guard entered, followed by Zhang Wu. The guard snapped to attention.

"The monk Zhang Wu, as requested sire," boomed the guard.

Zhang Wu's yellow eyes glowed brightly, and his spiky orange hair set him apart. Most people seemed nervous in the King's presence, yet the monk appeared totally at ease. Zhang gazed calmly at the king and did not bow.

King Dakshi gestured to the guard, who bowed and withdrew. Facing Tappus, he said, "We shall continue our discussion at a later time."

## Kiran

Kiran bolted down the front steps, two at a time and ran past the startled dragon, saying, "Bye Ninosh! Gotta go."

The dragon blinked.

Racing down the street, Kiran took a shortcut down a back alley, onto the main street, past the cobbler's shop, a dry-goods store and two ale houses.

Anxious shouts from townsfolk caused him to glance up. Ninosh flapped by, heading north. Kiran waved.

Rounding the last corner of the town proper, he dashed beneath the teeth-like wooden spikes of Elfhaven Castle's portcullis, across the courtyard and up the castle's broad steps through the massive iron clad doors that led to the inner chambers.

Skidding through a hard left, barely managing to keep from slamming into the wall, Kiran picked up speed, the soft *slap*, *slap* of his leather moccasins echoing down the long hallway.

At the far end, two soldiers stood guard. Twenty paces beyond them, the door to the great hall, where the king oft held council, stood half-open.

"Stop!" yelled a guard. Kiran didn't even slow down. The guards clanged their steel tipped pikes together, forming a large 'X', blocking the way.

"No time to talk." Kiran dove beneath their spears, sliding on his stomach, skidding halfway across the polished marble floor where he leapt to his feet and sprinted on.

"Wait!" yelled a guard. Spinning round, he tripped on his partner's spear and fell. The other hopped awkwardly over his fallen comrade and gave chase.

## Council assembled

"Zhang." King Dakshi beamed. "Thank you for answering my summons so promptly."

Calmly folding his arms in front of his floor-length leather duster, Zhang stared at the king but remained silent.

The king's gaze dropped to the pearl handle of one of the monk's legendary twin swords. Noticing, Zhang adjusted his cape, covering it from view.

The monk's eyes flicked coolly from the king, to Tappus and back.

King Dakshi addressed Zhang, "The reason I requested your presence, was to—"

Suddenly, a young boy burst into the room, chased by first one, then a second palace guard. The guard reached for the kid, but the boy squirmed from his grasp and ran on. Screeching to a halt a few paces from the king, Kiran gave a quick bow. "Someone stole her key!"

The guards rushed up and grabbed Kiran by his arms, "Sorry for the intrusion, my lord. We'll remove this—impertinent lad immediately." The guards backed toward the doorway, dragging a struggling Kiran with them.

"He tied up Nadda and Nanni!" Kiran jerked, but the guards held firm. "He stole Avani's key!" The guards started through the doorway. Using both hands, Kiran grabbed tightly to the doorframe. The guards tugged his legs. Kiran's body swiveled upright, suspended horizontally above the floor, his fingers white from the strain.

"Release him!" cried King Dakshi. "Let the boy speak."

Kiran crashed to the floor, sprang up, dusted himself off, all the while glaring at the guards.

"Go on," urged the king, "only—slower this time."

"He used magic. Tied up my grandparents. Stole her key. Hurry! He might still be there."

"At Nadda and Nanni's cottage?"

"No! At the Citadel!"

King Dakshi glanced inquisitively at Tappus.

Kiran screamed in frustration, "Naagesh stole Avani's key to the Citadel!"

"Take a dozen men," the king ordered Tappus. "Go to the Citadel. But do not go in. The Citadel is well defended. Wait outside. When Naagesh comes out, capture him and bring him here for questioning."

Tappus ordered the guards to follow him and hurried from the hall. The guards bowed to the king, glared at Kiran, and took off after Tappus.

"Thank you, Kiran," acknowledged the king. "You may go." Kiran scooted out.

Once he'd gone, King Dakshi returned his attention to Zhang Wu. He cleared his throat. "What I was about to ask you, before Kiran's interruption and his disturbing news, was—"

A blinding flash lit the great hall, forcing those present to shield their eyes.

As the light faded, a surprised looking King Abban and his son Goban, stood before them. King Abban was King Dakshi's oldest and closest friend. The dwarf king wore a ruby red bib with golden trim, tucked haphazardly into his matching crimson tunic.

In one hand, his majesty held a massive steaming bird's leg with a single, large bite taken out of it. The succulent drumstick oozed with a dark, fragrant sauce, smelling of cinnamon, sage, and squamberry spices.

The portly dwarf wiped his mouth with the back of his stout, hairy hand, swallowed loudly, then burped.

Another flash followed and now four more individuals stood beside the dwarves: an equally startled Avani, Prince Devraj, Sanuu, and the only one who didn't look surprised, the wizard Larraj.

Larraj stepped forward. "Sorry for the intrusion, my lords." He bowed to the kings. "But a troubling matter has come to my attention, so I took the liberty of assembling this council."

# Council divided

"What's going on down there?" asked Kiran.

"Shush!" Avani hissed, glaring at her brother. "Listen."

Having been politely asked to leave the hall, Goban, Avani and Kiran raced around behind the castle and used the secret passageways within the castle walls. The entrance to which Kiran and Avani had stumbled upon when they were young.

The trio now lay side-by-side on their bellies, under the balcony railing, peering down into the great hall, listening intently to the heated debate below.

"You should've been here!" whispered Kiran. "Naagesh almost killed Nadda and Nanni!"

Avani winced.

"He'd a killed me too if Ninosh hadn't scared em off."

Avani shuddered. "You know where I was, and why."

He glared at his sister. "Shoulda been here."

Avani turned away. "Shush. Just listen."

One of the king's military advisor's leapt to his feet and slammed his hand to the table, glaring at the wizard. "Shoulda killed Naagesh while ya had the chance!"

"And the trolls and the ogres," yelled another. The room erupted as more angry voices joined the chorus.

Zhang Wu sat between Larraj and the enraged advisor. A magic-infused throwing star suddenly appeared in the monk's hand. He flicked it spinning high into the air. The star crackled with barely contained power. All eyes followed the spinning disk. All except Zhang's. His eyes bored deep into those of the elf who'd threatened his friend.

Time slowed.

At the top of its arc, the spinning star seemed to hover for an instant before falling back down—straight for the advisor's outstretched hand.

Beads of sweat formed on the advisor's forehead, but to his credit, he held his hand firm.

Zhang eyes locked onto the advisor's, yet the instant before the whizzing star plunged into the table between the advisor's outstretched fingers, Zhang's arm shot out and he caught the star between his thumb and forefinger, its glowing spikes a hair's width above the table.

Time sped back up.

"You missed," said the advisor. "It would've struck the table, not my hand."

"Did I?" the monk's voice remaining calm and clear.

The advisor glanced down. Zhang's other hand held a dagger poised to pierce the elf's heart.

"Besides, if the star had struck the table," Wu continued in a relaxed tone. "This table, and all those sitting at it, would no longer exist." In a blur, the weapons disappeared inside the monk's coat.

The advisor sat back down uneasily.

"Stay calm, everyone." King Dakshi looked from the advisor to Zhang. Finally, he said, "I sent guards to the Citadel. If Naagesh is there, we shall have him shortly."

"He's not there," said Larraj.

"How do you know?" demanded Prince Devraj.

King Dakshi touched his son's arm lightly.

Devraj jerked away. "What?"

"I called for calm," his father reminded him.

He glared at his father. "I am the successor to the throne. I have the right to ask questions!"

"Lower your voice—*Prince*—Devraj. In case you have forgotten, as long as I am alive, I am still king *and* your father." He paused briefly. "If you wish to be king, act like a king."

"You never give me the chance! When will I learn to lead? When I am standing over your dead body?"

Several people gasped. The room fell silent enough to hear a quill drop.

"You are not yet ready to lead," said the king in a quiet yet commanding tone. "As evidenced by this childish outburst."

When Devraj didn't speak, his father continued, "If you want to lead, you must stop bullying others in your mis-guided attempt to prove yourself. A wise king leads by example. His people follow him because of his actions, not his words. Because his actions are noble. Because his actions stand for something larger than himself. And because of that, his subjects are proud to die for him, if need be." The king stared at his son. "Which king will you be, Devraj?"

Devraj leapt up, barely contained rage seething within. "I'm not a child to be lectured to, Father!"

"Enough!" King Dakshi stood. "We shall discuss this matter at a later date, in private!"

The prince glared at his father, then stormed from the room, slamming the great hall's door behind him.

"Devraj! Come back here!"

King Dakshi stared at the doorway, his jaw taught. He shared a look with King Abban, then briefly with General Kanak.

"Sorry for the interruption." The king sat and in a calm voice addressed Larraj, "Go on."

"Before transporting us all here, the wizards from the Void gave me this." Larraj rolled up his sleeve, revealing the wristlet.

A hush fell over the room. Everyone gazed in awe at the shinning, golden wristlet. Roiling clouds of light from within the bracelet's raised sphere painted the startled faces around the table with eerie waves of tangerine-colored light.

"Is that—" began King Dakshi.

"A vortex containment bracelet," Larraj confirmed.

"Containing?"

"A seeker."

A loud creak came from above. Everyone looked up. The balcony appeared empty. Tappus signaled the guards. They drew their swords and raced for the stairway.

"Stop!" ordered Larraj. The guards froze, glancing from the wizard to King Dakshi, then Tappus.

"Relax," assured the wizard. "Nothing to worry about."

King Dakshi studied the wizard's face, then told his guards, "As you were."

"A seeker you say?" blurted King Abban, "But I thought the seekers all lost?"

Everyone leaned forward, their full attention once again focused on the rare magical artifact wrapped around the wizard's arm.

Larraj glanced up. Three small heads slowly appeared beneath the balcony's lower railing. Larraj winked. The heads dropped out of sight.

"As did I," Larraj said, agreeing with the dwarf. "Apparently two seekers were recovered. By a relative of yours, no less. Unfortunately, no one knows the whereabouts of the second."

Raising his wrist, Larraj muttered an incantation. The eye of the vortex opened, releasing a swirling cloud of neon blue smoke that coalesced into a gently undulating sphere hovering just above the bracelet. Shocked murmurs rippled through the hall.

"Show us the wizard, Naagesh," commanded Larraj.

The swirling smoke roiled faster, then the clouds dispersed, revealing a dim image of a forest.

"Closer," Larraj commanded. The scene zoomed down beneath the treetops. Dark outlines appeared, hurrying down a forest path.

"Again. And seen from ahead."

The view jiggled around as if viewed through the eyes of a wildly banking bird, shifting to fly backwards in front of the procession. The view stabilized.

A tall figure, wearing a long dark cloak, its hood thrown back, strode briskly along leading the pack. A single troll and ogre walked a step behind and to either side of the wizard.

"Naagesh," cried a guard, leaping up and drawing his sword. King Dakshi placed his hand lightly on the soldier's arm. The guard sheathed his weapon and sat back down.

Larraj gazed thoughtfully at his childhood friend, now enemy, Naagesh. "Show us his underlings. The small ones behind." The image whizzed past the troll and ogre, focusing on a hobbling group of twisted beasts.

"Goblins!" spat someone.

"Least a dozen of em," agreed someone else.

One of the goblins stopped.

"No one's seen goblins in—"

The goblin looked up.

"Goblins are of no concern," responded Zhang. "Where is Naagesh now?"

The goblin tipped its horned head to one side and pointed a long, spindly finger toward them.

"Higher," Larraj said. "Show us the wizard's location."

The image zoomed upward. The goblin, along with the rest of the evil wizard's group shrank, disappearing beneath the trees and still the scene kept rising until it finally slowed, then stopped to hover far above the dense forest canopy.

"Pan left," commanded Larraj. The scene slowly rotated left. From this height they could see gentle, tree-covered rolling hills and behind, jagged peaks.

"The Icebain Mountains," shouted someone. The view continued to turn.

"That smoke in the distance." King Abban pointed. "That's Mt Drakus, at Deltar."

As the rotation continued, banners appeared, flapping atop tall castle turrets.

"And there is Elfhaven castle," said King Dakshi. "Where we are now holding council."

Larraj spoke, "Show us the direction that Naagesh is heading." The view whizzed around and froze. A deep fissure in the earth lay directly ahead. Sheer cliffs to their side of the fissure plunged deep into the ground.

"That canyon," remarked King Abban. "That's the Pillars of the Giants."

"And there," said Tappus. "To the left, beyond the Pillars, that mist is from the upper falls at the spot where the Icebain and Tontiel Rivers meet."

"Where's the demented wizard headed?" said King Abban.

Larraj stood and flicked his wrist, and the vision dissolved in a cloud of blue smoke. "He intends for us to follow him."

"How can you know that?" Sanuu said.

"I know Naagesh well. Better than anyone alive."

An awkward silence ensued. Finally, King Abban spoke up, "Why would Naagesh want us to follow him? An ambush?"

"With only a troll, an ogre, and a dozen goblins?" said someone.

"If he intends to set a trap," began King Dakshi. "Where might that be?"

"Inside the Pillars?" suggested Sanuu.

Tappus shook his head. "Too confined. Perhaps the ferry crossing?"

"Neither," said Larraj. "Knowing Naagesh, he'd choose a spot where elven soldiers would be at a disadvantage."

General Kanak began indignantly, "There's nowhere on this world where elves—"

Larraj cut him short, "Naagesh would lay his trap in the lands *beyond* the Icebain River."

"Beyond?" laughed someone. "Beyond the river there's only the Plains of Illusion!"

"And the Deathly Bog," shouted another.

The dwarf King broke in, "Few unfortunate souls who tried—ever returned from those accursed lands." Shouts of agreement.

An advisor said, "Naagesh would have to be insane to go there." The room fell silent.

Larraj was first to speak, "Nevertheless, that's what he intends."

"Then we best stop him before he crosses the river," said King Dakshi.

"If possible," agreed Larraj. "But the Bog and the Plains are the least of our worries. He has knowledge of the Citadel, from the Manual. We know not what he intends to do with it, but the possibilities are frightening. What's more, if Naagesh masters the knowledge contained within the books on dark magic, no one—*including myself*—can stop him." He stood. "Zhang and I will capture Naagesh and bring him here."

"I shall accompany you," said King Dakshi. He motioned to his guards. "Along with a hundred of Elfhaven's finest."

"As will I." King Abban tapped his axe handle. "Won't be left out of a good fight."

King Dakshi smiled, slapping his hand onto his friend's broad shoulder. "I was counting on it."

"But what of the royal joining ceremony?" said an advisor. "That's in three solar cycles."

King Dakshi paused.

"We will have the crazed wizard in our dungeon by tomorrow evening," said Sanuu.

The door burst open, and in rushed a guard. "My lord!" He dropped to one knee.

"Rise!" The king boomed. "What is so urgent that you deem it necessary to interrupt this high council?"

"Sire, the barrier is down. Elfhaven is unprotected!"

# Avani, Goban, and Kiran

It was nearly dark by the time Avani, Goban and Kiran hurried out from the secret entrance at the back of the castle. Avani and Kiran pulled back on the unicorn's leg and the ivy-covered wall groaned back into place.

Avani's hands trembled from the weight of what they'd heard.

"The barrier's down!" said Kiran.

"If the barrier's down—" Goban stared at Avani. "—that means—"

"Naagesh." She nodded. "Naagesh's been inside the Citadel. Come on!"

When they entered the main street, they heard shouts.

"What's going on?" asked Goban.

Avani led them around the corner. Halfway down the castle wall, flames leapt up from torches on either side of the castle's main gate. The voices seemed to come from there.

She raised her hand, stopping just outside the Castle's open gate. The three peered through the gate into the inner courtyard.

The king's troops rushed about, hurriedly making preparations for their journey.

"Wow!" whispered Kiran, "That was quick."

Avani glanced up. Tall black clouds approached from the north, accompanied by distant thunder, promising a gloomy sendoff.

Well-oiled leather saddles slapped down onto horses' backs. Swords and supplies *clanked* as they were hastily lashed onto the horse's rumps.

Powerful hooves pawed the ground, steam erupting from the massive beast's flared nostrils. Eager to be off, the horses' eyes gleamed with excitement.

Avani whispered, "There's Devraj."

Goban squinted. "Where?"

She pointed. "Over by the steps. With Sanuu and General Kanak. The prince is arguing with Sanuu."

A bolt of lightning lit up the courtyard.

"Doesn't look too happy," Kiran muttered.

Thunder echoed off the castle walls. It began to drizzle.

Avani flipped up the hood of her long cape. "Come on. We gotta get to the Citadel."


## The Guardian


A crack of lightning lit up the Citadel's covered entryway, exposing two elven soldiers standing guard. A moment later, thunder replaced the light.

Half a block away, Goban and Avani huddled underneath a shop awning, their clothing drenched. "Why's the door open?" said Goban.

Avani watched the guards. "It shouldn't be."

"Where's Kiran?" asked Goban.

Avani glanced around. "He was right behind us, wasn't he?"

They gazed out into the softly drizzling rain. Within moments, they heard splashing feet.

Kiran ran up and stopped. He was completely dry.

The other two looked him over, suspiciously.

Kiran grinned and pointed up. A transparent half-bubble floated above him.

"Where did you learn that spell?" said Avani.

Kiran muttered something, and the bubble burst, spewing a cool, fine mist.

"Larraj taught me. What?" Kiran gave his sister a shocked look. "He didn't teach it to you? His apprentice?" Kiran shook his head sadly. Then pulled out a bright orange fruit with spikey spines protruding from its fuzzy surface, and bit into it. More spray flew, this time of fragrant juice.

"Guess yer not teacher's pet anymore." Kiran took another bite. "Larraj must like me better. Hey! Maybe I'll be the first wizard in our family stead a you!" He chewed smugly.

At the Citadel, another guard rushed up and spoke to his comrades. A moment later, the three raced off toward the castle.

"Why're they leaving?" asked Kiran.

"They know Naagesh already left," explained Goban.

Avani flipped up her hood, sprinted to the Citadel, and ducked inside. The others joined her.

"Least we're outta the rain." Goban tried shaking water from his cloak, to little effect.

"Doesn't seem right." Kiran motioned to the open doorway. "The Guardian never leaves it open."

"Good thing he did," replied Goban. "'Cause we don't got a key."

"Something's not right," agreed Avani. "Come on." She hurried down the hallway.


"Guardian?" Avani flicked rain from her cloak and tossed back her hood. "Guardian. You there?"

Goban rubbed his chin, his bushy brow forming a deep 'V'. "It's not like the guy not to answer. Usually, he won't shut up."

Avani nodded absently. "Guardian? It's me, Avani, Keeper of the Light."

Crystals on the main control panel pulsed with energy. Holographic displays showed rows of rapidly scrolling numbers projected before them in midair. One of the displays flashed red.

"Maybe he's away," suggested Kiran, ambling over to the console.

Avani ignored him.

"Does he sleep?" asked Goban.

"Tom called the Guardian a—" Avani squinted, searching for his exact words. "an artificial intelligence *bot* with a quirky human interface program."

"Good memory!" Goban scratched his cheek. "Didn't understand it then, either."

Avani shrugged. "Pretty sure it means the Guardian doesn't sleep."

"Hey look!" cried Kiran. "It's your key. And some old book."

Avani walked over, slipped the key in her pocket and lifted the well-worn book. "The Manual."

"That proves it," said Goban.

Avani nodded. "Naagesh's been here."

A glowing see-through hand suddenly appeared, hovering above the console. The hand's index finger pointed down at a red button. The hand bobbed up and down as if to get their attention.

Kiran reached for the button.

"Wait!" cried Avani. "It might be a trap."

Kiran hesitated, grinned, and pressed the button.

The three leapt back as a tiny image popped to life before them. There was a crackling noise. The image disappeared. Another crackle. It reappeared.

"Help!" said the image. "Is someone there?"

The three glanced at each other, then at the Guardian.

"Um, it's us," began Avani. "Avani, Goban and Kiran. Can't you see us? Are you blind?"

"The image flickered and turned toward her voice."

"Blind? Yes, that is an apt description. I have lost control of most of my sensors."

"Lost control?" she said, tipping her head sideways. "How can *you* lose control of your sensors?"

"What's a sensor?" said Kiran.

Avani ignored him.

The image dimmed. "More precisely, control was *stolen* from me."

"Naagesh," they replied in unison.

"You know?"

"Some of it," Avani dropped the Manual onto the console. "We know Naagesh stole this book and the key to the Citadel."

The Guardian looked grave.

"What do you know?" added Goban.

The Guardian's transparent shoulders slumped. "It is a long story. Suffice to say, Naagesh now controls the Citadel. He tried to destroy me, but before he could manage it, I copied myself into a small, hidden partition of memory. In short, I let him think he'd destroyed me."

"What? How?" said Avani.

"Well, it is quite technical, but stems from the fact that I am brilliant, and Naagesh is but a mere wizard. First off, I surrounded him with my nano-droids. Then, while he was distracted, I—"

"No. I mean, how would Naagesh know how to do all that?"

"Oh." The Guardian sounded disappointed. "You said it yourself. He possessed the Manual."

Avani stared at the book.

"So what do we do?" asked Kiran.

"We must stop the mad wizard."

Goban stepped forward. "Everything's under control."

"What do you mean?"

Goban smiled. "My father, King Abban, is leading an expedition. He, King Dakshi, Larraj, Zhang, and a company of elven soldiers just left to capture Naagesh."

"Oh, no..."

"Why?" said Avani. "What's wrong?"

The Guardians gave them a bleak look. "They do not stand a chance."

Goban huffed, "My father's unbeatable with an axe. Plus, he's got a wizard, a Cimoan monk, plus a company of Elfhaven's finest soldiers. Not enough to defeat one crazed wizard?"

"Yeah," agreed Kiran. "Larraj is more powerful than Naagesh."

"Shush!" Avani scolded. "Guardian. What do you know that we don't?"

"Naagesh set in motion the unthinkable. Unless we thwart his evil plan, all intelligent life on this planet will die."

"What? What did he do?"

"I'll explain later. Right now, we need help if we're to prevent this disaster."

"Larraj already left," Avani reminded him.

"Not a wizard." The Guardian shook his holographic head. "We need someone who understands technology. Someone who's good at problem solving and can think on their feet. We need someone from another world."

"Yer builders," suggested Goban. "The beings who built the Citadel."

The Guardian nodded. "I admit they were my first choice."

"So call em."

"I tried. They did not respond. I tried all the usual sub-space frequencies as well as the worm-hole priority one channel. Nothing."

"If not your builders?" said Avani. "Then who?"

## Tom

Tom's drone, the one he'd gotten for his fourteenth birthday, rested on his dresser atop his favorite Chicago Cubs hoodie. He tapped his wristwatch screen. The drone's rotors spun up. He tapped the screen again. Its engines whined, and the drone lifted off. Tom tapped the screen a third time and the drone's motors spun down. Drifting sideways, the drone crash landed in a pile of dirty laundry.

Tom lifted his hoodie.

"Ya coulda just picked up the drone and moved it," said James, his next-door neighbor and best friend.

Ignoring him, Top rubbed the pullover's soft, well-worn cloth between his fingers. At the base of the hood, a long rip and its hasty repair shone clearly.

Tom shuddered, remembering the terrifying incident as if there now.

He and Avani stood in the Elfhaven Library. Avani was looking for a book on maps so she could trace the king's route to the Realm of the Ogres in search of the artifact. As usual, books glided by magically on their way to or from the few library visitors. The library itself felt cold that day—colder than usual. Avani hurried down a narrow aisle between two towering bookshelves. Suddenly, he was there...

*I started down the aisle...*

*I heard voices. Deep, sinister voices coming from the next aisle. One mentioned 'the artifact.' I stopped and listened...*

*"Did they leave?" said a voice.*

*"Yes."*

*"When?"*

*"This afternoon."*

*Two voices were speaking, but I could barely hear em. I moved closer.*

*"Has He been notified?"*

*"Yes."*

*"Then the trap is set."*

*Avani was way down the aisle studying a book.*

*"We're to meet Him tonight," the voice continued.*

*"Where?"*

*"The old granary."*

*"When?"*

*"Half past midnight."*

*I waved at Avani. Tried to get her attention.*

*"Did you hear something?" hissed a gravelly voice.*

*"No."*

*Suddenly books flew from the shelf all around me. A hand thrust through the shelf wearing a skull ring with glowing red eyes. The hand flailed about, grabbed my hoodie and yanked me hard against the bookshelf. I tried to scream, but I couldn't speak; I heard my hoodie rip...*

"Earth to Tom," came James' distant voice. "Earth to Tom!"

James stood beside Tom in Tom's bedroom, '*Inventor Central*,' as Tom liked to call it.

James wrapped his knuckles upside Tom's head, adding a wailing siren sound effect for good measure, then gently pulled Tom's hand away from Tom's own throat.

Tom gasped. Blinked. Then slowly focused on James.

He blinked again. "What?"

"You went all *Zombie City* on me."

"Walking Dead, or Sean of the Dead?"

James wrinkled his forehead, considering. "Walking Dead."

"Darn. Sean of the Dead's my favorite."

"Bro, you were way gone this time!" James looked concerned. "Seriously, where were you?"

Tom stared at his hoodie, still clutched in his hands. "Just remembering. Remembering how this tear got there."

Tom ran his finger over the rough, uneven stitching. "We were on a steep mountain trail on our way to the Realm of the Ogres. A freak blizzard came up. There was tons a snow, we were freezing. Couldn't find shelter. Had to camp on the cold, stone steps at the edge of a cliff." He brushed his fingers across the stitching once more. "I had nothing else to do, so I stitched it up." Tom's eyes glassed over.

*"Malak was the first to pass out from the cold. I knew I'd totally lost it, when I saw Max charging to the rescue, leading a flock of glowing fairies, their wings—*

"Snap out of it!" James shouted. "You're doing it again!"

Tom blinked. "Sorry."

James shook his head. "Elfhaven. I knew it!" He nodded. "You miss it, huh?"

Tom shrugged.

"Ya haven't been the same since you got back. You hardly speak anymore."

Tom picked at a hole in his faded jeans.

"See what I mean?"

"It seems so long ago," Tom said. "Sometimes I'm not sure it really happened."

"What?"

"Maybe it was just a dream."

"Then who tore yer hoodie, huh? It happened, dude!"

"I know." Tom glanced down at his feet.

James watched his friend critically. "What is it? There's something else, isn't there?"

Tom sighed. "Kids at school said you were only my friend cause you live next door."

"That's not true."

Tom raised his gaze and stared at him. James glanced away, then back. "The kids at school suck." He paused, then put his arm around Tom's shoulder and squeezed. "I'm your friend OK? And I'm not jealous of yer Elfhaven friends. I get it. Ya can't just go visit em whenever ya feel like."

Tom studied the lime-green laces on his well-worn converse sneakers. *They were brand new when I first went to Elfhaven. They've walked miles on another world. In another universe.*

Tom bent over and re-tied his laces. "It's just that—no offense, but— It's kinda boring round here. I miss all the excitement, the adventure."

"Yeah. Plus, your friends needed you. Listened to you. Followed yer plans. You were a hero. You were *their* hero."

Tom's eyes got misty. James tightened his grip on Tom's shoulder.

The pair stared down in silence at the contraption below them. Per tradition, James was always present for the *'maiden voyage'* of Tom's many *'projects.'* This was one of those times.

"What's left to do?" James asked.

"Just this." Tom bent over and picked up a flat, two-inch square chip, an Integrated Circuit, and held it up for James to inspect.

"Is that her CPU?"

"Wow," said Tom. "I'm impressed!"

"Been hanging round you too long." James leaned forward and studied the chip. "What's that thingy sittin' on top? Kinda creepy. Like an alien bug er somethin'."

Tom gazed thoughtfully at the bizarre thing piggybacking on top of the CPU. Gray-green and lumpy, it had tons of spindly, insect-like *legs* that wrapped around the CPU, each leg grasping tightly to a single pin of the CPU.

*It does look like an alien bug.* Tom shivered at the thought, then chided himself for shivering.

"What's so funny?"

"Nothing. The Guardian gave it to Avani to give to me. The Guardian said to set it on top of Chloe's CPU. When I moved it close, the thing practically jumped out of my hands. It lit up and its legs wriggled around and attached themselves to the CPU pins, one at a time, as if tasting them." Tom shivered again.

James leaned back. "Tasting them?"

Tom chuckled. "Meant *testing* them." Tom held it up so James could get a better look.

James reached out and touched it, then jerked his hand back. "That thing moved!"

Tom dropped the chip. *Clank.* It bounced off the contraption below, spun through the air and landed upside down in his thick shag-carpet, its pins pointing upward like a dead bug.

James chuckled.

Tom glared at him. "Very funny." He bent down and snatched up the CPU, flipped it right-side-up and tapped its bulbous top. Nothing happened.

"Did move though," James insisted.

Ignoring him, Tom gazed down proudly at the shiny aluminum frame of the project he'd been working on these last many months. He bent over and flipped open the hatch, carefully lined up the CPU's pins and pressed the chip firmly into its socket. "Voilà!"

Tom flipped the hatch closed. "Screwdriver."

"Where is it?"

"Under those books."

James picked up the first book. "Medieval weaponry." He tossed it aside and grabbed the next. "Hang Glider Design." Tossed that aside. "Quantum Physics for Dummies." He laughed. "A bizarre mix."

James handed Tom the screwdriver. Tom secured the hatch.

Flipping open his toolbox, Tom tossed in the screwdriver and something caught his eye. Kelly-green light shone from beneath a haphazardly stacked pile of tools. Tools clinked as he rummaged through the box. Another flash of green. From the bottom of his toolbox, Tom pulled out a long dagger with a large gem affixed to its gnarled bone handle.

Tom lifted the knife. Its sparkling gemstone sent beams of green light dancing across the walls and ceiling.

"What's that?" asked James.

Tom stared at the blade.

"Oh no," said James, "Yer getting that faraway look again." James raising his fist over Tom's head. "Earth to—"

Tom brushed away James' hand. "Just a dagger from Elfhaven." Tom rolled the knife over in his palm. The blade was hand chipped from some hard, black stone. Shiny, like obsidian, but stronger and not brittle. Jutting out from either end of the handle were large, darkly stained animal teeth. *A zhanderbeast?* The handle itself was dark with age and oil from many hands; alien hands, large hands, *very* large hands.

So big, in fact, Tom's fingers couldn't wrap around it. *Like a tennis racket for a giant.*

"A monk named Zhang gave it to me. Said I'd earned a real knife."

Tom stuffed the dagger under his belt and pulled his hoodie over it. The pair returned their gaze to the contraption beneath them.

"Well," said James. "Go on. I know you wanna say it."

Tom grinned. "Let's fire this baby up!" He reached for the switch.

James grabbed his arm. "Wait!"

"Why?"

"What modifications did you make to her?" said James, sounding nervous.

"Obviously, the oversized balloon tires, more powerful motors, high speed transmission…"

"Ah—what about accessories? Cup holder?"

Tom laughed. "No cup holders, but she's got a camera, ultra-High Def of course, high-powered radio, infra-red sensors for night vision, electronic compass, GPS module, voice I/O—"

"Chloe can talk?"

"Just a few words. But she can understand a bunch more commands."

"Weapons?"

Tom paused. "She—can—electrify her frame."

"Huh?"

"She can shock someone who grabs her." Tom explained.

James inched away.

"Oh! And it's not really a weapon but—I gave her a laser."

"What?" James took another step back. "Are you crazy?"

"It's just a quarter watt, not enough to hurt ya. Unless—you shine it on yourself fer too long." Tom scratched his chin. "Or look directly into the beam. Which would blind you, of course."

"Of course." James took a third step back. "Any other *upgrades* I should know about?"

"There's lots," said Tom, once more reaching for the on switch. "Tell ya later."

"Tom?" came Juanita's voice, Tom's mom, from the other room. "You need to get cleaned up for dinner, honey."

"But Mom! James 'n I we're bout to test Chloe Mark II."

"You've been working on her for the last six months. She can wait a few more minutes."

"Ahh mom!"

"Come on. You've gotta hurry. Your girlfriend Zoe's coming over for dinner, remember? After dinner we're going to see the new Spiderman movie. Spiderman 25: Laser web of Death. It's a comedy."

"She's not my girlfriend, mom."

James wrapped his arm around Tom's shoulders. "Bummer dude."

Tom nodded.

"A movie?" James began. "Tonight? Thought your mom taught martial arts on Tuesdays?"

"Nah! She teaches Wu Shu on Thursdays."

"Say James?" Juanita called. "Would you like to stay for dinner? I'm sure Zoe wouldn't mind."

"No thanks!" James shot Tom a horrified look. "I—ah—mom's expecting me home."

"OK. Tell her hi."

James let out a long, slow sigh.

The two gazed wistfully down at Chloe.

"We can 'fire her up' tomorrow," James said.

"Tom?"

"Coming Mom."


# Knock, knock


Avani, Goban, and Prince Devraj huddled close together, leaning over the Citadel's main console. Light from the grainy, static-filled image hovering above the console lit their faces with a dim flickering light.

"I have not finished setting up the connection," explained the Guardian.

"Inter-universal communications protocols are complex. The process must be handled with the utmost sensitivity."

The prince yawned.

"Where's Kiran?" asked Goban. "Thought you sent him home fer something?"

"He's taking too long. Besides," Avani winked. "He hates it when he's left out of an adventure."

"So—" began Goban. "You're leaving him outta this." Goban shook his head. "He ain't gonna be happy."

"Exactly!" Avani grinned. "I'm his sister."

"Why are we here?" Devraj complained. "We can handle this ourselves! We do not need help. Especially from the likes of—"

"Connection established!" said the Guardian. "Activating remote power-up sequence now."

\* \* \*

Chloe's LEDs lit up red. A string of characters raced across her LCD display as her automated diagnostics ran. The phrase 'Diagnostics PASSED' appeared on screen and her LEDs switched from red to green. An opening appeared on Chloe's raised platform, and a long arm with a camera attached swiveled up and out and snapped into place.

Chloe began to rotate.

\* \* \*

Avani gasped as a grainy image of a strange alien room materialized before them. The image sharpened and panned left.

Huge piles of clothing, strange tools and alien artifacts first came into view. Next, a large flat cabinet stood against one wall, with a rickety shelf mounted above it, sagging from the weight of rows of books haphazardly arranged on top. On the next wall hung a strange poster depicting figures in heroic stances with futuristic mechanical walking and flying machines off in the distance.

Avani wrinkled her face in disgust. "Are those piles of dirty clothing?"

Devraj frowned. "And what is that smell?"

"This is not *smell-a-vision*," stated the Guardian. "Visual and audio only. Smell requires a full portal event."

Goban glanced at the others, then sniffed his armpit.

"Tom. This is the Guardian. We need your help." No response. "Tom? Are you there?"

## Trouble

Juanita hurried into the living room, drying her hands on a dish towel. She looked down the hall toward Tom's bedroom. "Did you hear something?"

Tom sat at one end of their overstuffed leather couch. "I didn't hear anything."

"Me neither, Ms Holland," agreed Zoe, sitting beside Tom.

Juanita finished wiping her hands and again glanced down the hall. "Strange. I could've sworn…" She dashed back into the kitchen.

The theme from Beauty and the Beast started playing. Zoe pulled out her phone. Her thumbs flew as she responded to a text. Without looking up from her phone she asked, "How many *likes* did you get this week?"

"I'm not into social media."

"What?" She shot Tom a horrified look. Raising her phone, she smiled an impossibly wide smile and took a selfie. "I got seventeen hundred likes!" She resumed typing.

Tom tried to look impressed, with little success.

Zoe sat her phone down and flashed her bright blue eyes at him.

Beads of sweat formed on Tom's forehead.

Zoe pressed tight against him.

Tom's eyes widened.

Juanita burst in holding a steaming plate of fresh-baked crab cakes and plopped them down on the end table beside Tom's cell phone. "It's awfully quiet in here. Would you two like to watch a vid?"

"No," said Zoe. "Yes!" shouted Tom.

Juanita snap turned and disappeared into the kitchen. "Play 'Lord of the Rings,'" came her muted voice. The wall across from the couch lit up and the theme from the classic trilogy began to play.

Zoe leaned across Tom and picked up a crab cake, but instead of drawing back, she left her arm draped across Tom's chest and smiled once more.

*I'm in trouble,* thought Tom.

\* \* \*

"Tom's in trouble!" said Avani.

"What makes you think that?"

"He didn't answer the Guardian."

"Maybe there's a problem," suggested Goban. "With Chloe. Maybe Tom couldn't hear us."

"The robot's systems are all operable," the Guardian affirmed. "I quadruple checked."

"We are wasting time!" grumbled Devraj "Tom is probably not even there."

"Chloe. Navigate over to the door," ordered the Guardian. "And increase your audio sensitivity gain to level seven."

\* \* \*

*Uh oh.* Tom's palms started sweat. *Whaddo I do now?*

"You're so brave," said Zoe. "Tell me again how you saved Elfhaven by riding that dragon." Zoe set down the crab cake, her face only inches from

Tom's, and began playfully curling a lock of Tom's hair between her fingers.

Tom stared at her moist lips, slathered in shinning fuchsia lipstick. Managing a nervous smile, he leaned back. "Um—a—I wasn't that brave. Kept my eyes shut, mostly, when I rode the dragon."

"Don't be modest."

Tom glanced anxiously at the kitchen door. "Mom?" He gave Zoe another half-smile. "Dinner 'bout ready?"

Zoe leaned in close. She closed her eyes. Her lips parted.

Tom couldn't lean back any farther. He snatched up a crab cake and held it in front of his mouth like a shield.

Zoe's eyes popped open. "Haven't you ever kissed a girl before?"

"No—Yes! Ah—Avani," he stammered. "I kissed Avani—well, she kissed me actually."

"You kissed Avani?" Zoe gasped. "You kissed an elf? Gross!"

"I didn't enjoy it!" He stumbled on awkwardly, "Well—maybe just a tad."

"Why that little elvish tramp!" Gazing again at Tom, Zoe's look softened. "Bet elven girls can't kiss as good as Earth girls." Zoe grabbed Tom by his hoodie, closed her eyes and slapped a full-fledged lip-lock on him.

Juanita rushed in from the kitchen. Letting go of Tom, Zoe snatched up a crab cake and smiled at Juanita. "These crab cakes are delicious, Ms. Holland."

Tom sighed and took a bite of his own cake.

"Zoe, please call me Juanita. You're practically part of the family now."

Tom coughed, sending bits of crab cake flying.

"Dinner's almost ready." Juanita pivoted on her heel and disappeared back into the kitchen.

"Mom?" called Tom. "Mom?" There was no reply, other than a soft humming coming from the other room.

Tom turned back. Zoe stared at him.

Suddenly, Juanita screamed.

\* \* \*

"What was that?" cried Avani, still listening intently to sounds from another world.

"Couldn't hear what they were saying," Goban began, "What with all the strange music and such. But someone definitely screamed."

"I heard Tom's voice," said Avani. "I'm sure of it." She glanced at the prince. "Told you Tom was in trouble."

"Quiet!" scolded the Guardian. "Chloe. Increase audio gain to level nine."

# A disturbance in the force

Tom leapt up. "What's wrong mom?"

"We're out of milk."

Tom sighed and plopped back down on the couch. His eyes lit up. "I could run to Bucky's and get a quart. It's only a few blocks away."

Juanita stuck her head through the doorway. "Oh, I don't know honey." Suddenly, the theme from Guardians of the Galaxy Six began playing, then a snobby British butler voice announced, "Incoming call, Mistress."

Juanita stepped into the living room. Tapped her silver bracelet's tiny screen. "Who from?"

"One of your scientists at your lab. Mistress Sashi, to be specific."

"I'll take it." From Juanita's bracelet came an East India woman's excited voice. "—energy spike and then—" Juanita flicked her across the bracelet's screen and Sashi's face replaced the Lord of the Rings movie and her voice now came from their home's sound system.

"—the event. I checked the logs and—" Sashi waved her hands excitedly as she spoke.

"Juanita here. Say again?"

"Oh. Sorry. The readings are off the charts! I tried running it through the—"

"What? Slow down. Start over."

Sashi paused, then began again, "There's been another event."

"What? Did you check the instrument's calibration?"

"Yes. First thing, then I checked—"

"You're saying the detection grid's energy spiked." Juanita froze. "Is it still happening?"

"Yes!"

Juanita paced the room. "All right. Run diagnostics on the sensor array, verify they're functioning properly. Then run the energy/particle analysis program Cheng wrote on the data. Verify it agrees with your initial findings. If so, inform the team. Have em meet us at the lab. I'll be there in—" she glanced at her wrist. "—ten minutes."

She tapped her bracelet, and the movie resumed.

"Tom, something's come up. Gotta go to the lab. You two can serve yourself, can't you?" She darted back into the kitchen.

"What's going on, mom? Is it Elfhaven?"

"Not sure yet, honey," she called from the other room. "The energy signatures are off, too weak for a full-fledged portal event. It'll take some time to make sense of it all."

"Can I come?" Tom asked hopefully. He looked at Zoe. She frowned.

Juanita poked her head round the door. "No dear, you've got company. Besides, I think you can safely leave it to us scientists." Her head disappeared.

"Ya sure you couldn't use my help?" he called.

"You know you're right. There is something you can do."

Tom's eyes brightened.

"You can run and get that quart of milk."

Tom sighed, stood up, grabbed his cellphone, and started for the coat rack. Zoe beat him to it. As he reached for his faded Levi jacket, Zoe stepped in front of him.

"Need my jacket."

"You don't need it. It's not supposed to rain." Slipping into her puffy, stylish, raspberry colored vest, Zoe gave Tom a pouty frown. "You weren't gonna leave me behind, were you?"

Tom's shoulders sank, though he managed a weak smile. "Come on."

* * *

"Something's going on," Avani said. "Couldn't hear every word, but something's definitely wrong."

Goban nodded. "Tom's mom rushed off. Some sorta emergency."

Even Devraj sounded concerned, "She sent Tom to get help, to fetch a warrior named 'milk'."

## Serious trouble!

*Great.* Tom said sarcastically. *It's pouring.* It hadn't been raining when he and Zoe entered Bucky's convenience store five minutes ago.

Tom flipped up the hood of his hoodie. "Thought you said it wasn't supposed ta rain?"

Zoe shrugged.

Cradling the paper bag with the carton of milk under his arm, Tom held the store's door for Zoe. "Run!"

Grabbing his hand, the pair dashed out into the pitch-black torrential downpour. At the first crosswalk, Zoe leapt off the curb, landed in a deep puddle and drenched Tom's leg.

"Thanks."

She giggled. "Come on. Last one home is a zeeb! Zoe glanced over her shoulder. Her mouth fell open, a look of horror on her wet face. Tom spun around. There was nothing there. Zoe took off running.

"Hey, that's not fair!" Tom sprinted after her. As he picked up speed, a hint of a grin spread across his face. "I'm gaining on you."

She looked back, gave a high, tittering laugh and ran faster.

Rounding a corner, Zoe bolted down a dimly lit side street.

"You're going the wrong way!" shouted Tom.

"It's a shortcut!" She glanced over her shoulder again. "What? Is the famous Tom Holland scared?"

Focusing straight ahead, Tom leaned forward and gave it everything he had. The distance between them narrowed.

Though near home, this was a section of town he seldom ventured into, certainly not at night. Once lined with small shops, the area had since fallen into disrepair. Now only crumbling, abandoned storefronts remained. Most of the streetlights had long burned out. The lone working lamp flickered, arced faintly, then went dark.

*Well, this is creepy.* "Hey, slow down!" he shouted. "The streetlight died. One of us'll get hurt!"

"You're jus' tryin' to trick me. Slow me down, so you can catch up." The slap, slap, slap of her sneakers on the wet sidewalk continued. If anything, Zoe was running faster. Tom glanced around uneasily and tried to keep up.

Here, shards of glass from a broken bottle littered the sidewalk. Trying to find a safe path through the obstacle course, Tom lowered his gaze, staring just ahead of his feet. As he did, he noticed a dim red glow at his waist.

Slowing, Tom raised his sweatshirt. The gemstone on his dagger shone bright red. *What the?* Tom jerked his hoodie back down.

Someone stepped from the shadows. Zoe slammed smack into him. He grabbed her arms, pinning her tightly to him. The streetlamp flickered back on.

Tom stopped, wiped rain from his eyes and squinted in the dim light.

"Josh?" Tom took a step forward. "Josh Mallory, from school? You're a long way from home."

"Let go you jerk!" cried Zoe.

Josh grinned and tightened his grip.

"Ouch!" Zoe glared up into his smirking face. "I said let go, you bully!"

"Let her go," said Tom. When Josh made no move to release her, Tom pulled out his cell phone and started dialing. Grabbing the phone, Josh dropped it to the pavement and stomped. *Crunch.* Cracking sounds, a faint *pop.* The phone's display went dark.

Josh kicked the broken device away. "Who ya gonna call? Yer Mom?" He spat. "Surprised she let lil' Tommy out all alone. Where is she?"

"The lab. Some sorta anomaly with the detection grid."

Josh sneered. "There ya go again. Using dose big fancy-shmancy words a yers. Think you're better'n us, don't cha'?"

"What did you say?" said Tom.

"You heard me."

"No. It's just that—that's exactly what you said in the cave of dreams."

"The cave of what?"

Zoe wrenched free, hurried to Tom and put her arm around him, then glared at Josh.

Tom wrinkled his wet forehead. "Only—this is all wrong. You were in the cave of dreams and when I turned around your buddy Tyler was standing there." Tom whirled, taking Zoe around with him. Tyler's face, above his ample girth, grinned down at the pair.

"How's the school nerd?" Tyler punched Tom, then shoved him hard. Tom fell backwards onto the sidewalk, taking Zoe with him and sending the grocery bag sprawling. Milk, mixed with rainwater, flowed over the sidewalk and into the gutter. Zoe scrambled to her feet.

Laying on his back, rain pelting his face, Tom touched his lip. Blood trickled down his fingers, quickly washing away.

Josh ambled over and kicked Tom in the side. Tom winced.

"Come on." Zoe jerked frantically on Tom's arm. "Get up!"

Josh kicked Tom a second time.

Tyler grabbed Zoe. She fought to break free. "Tom. Help!"

Tom struggled to rise. Josh shoved him back down with his foot, leaned in close and smiled. Tom blinked away rain and an unwanted tear.

The streetlight arced, popped, went out.

Suddenly, all down the block, one by one, the other streetlights flared bright and then exploded, glass shards flying.

The street faded into total blackness.

An instant later, there came a brilliant flash and a blast of wind that whipped their rain-soaked clothing. As quick as it began, the wind died, replaced by an odd green glow. The jade-colored light reflected off the wet pavement, the lampposts. Even the bullies' faces took on a sickly green tinge.

"You look like ogres," said Tom.

"What?" cried Josh and Tyler.

Zoe jerked Tom to his feet.

Tom faced their attackers. "You gonna punch me now? That's what you did next in the cave."

The bullies glanced at one another, then at Tom.

Tyler clenched his fist. "My pleasure." He grinned wide, green light reflecting off multi-colored braces.

Tom stared in amazement. "And then I said. Nice braces."

"That's it!" Tyler wound up preparing to strike. Tom closed his eyes and turned his head.

"I wouldn't do that if I were you," came a voice from behind.

Tyler and Josh spun around. Tom opened one eye.

Three dark silhouettes stood outlined by a jade halo. One had long golden hair. One was short and stout. The last, tall and thin.

Equal in height to the tallest of the newcomers, and much more muscularly built, Josh and Tyler grinned. "Let's see whacha got."

The short, stout one swung a battle axe off his shoulder, its handle smacking loudly into his open palm.

The tall figure drew a long sword.

A golden glow leapt from a satchel hanging from the long-haired one's waist. The light brightened and raced across her hands.

A streetlamp flickered back to life.

Tom's jaw dropped. "Avani? Goban? Devraj? How?"

No longer smiling, Josh and Tyler glanced at each other.

Tom's friends stepped forward. The bullies stepped back.

Before Josh and Tyler could decide what to do, Avani muttered an incantation. Bands of magical energy engulfed the bullies. The pair glowed. Then shrank. Then changed. Until there, standing before Tom and his friends, stood two of those spiky blue-haired rat-from-hades creatures that had tormented Tom in the Elfhaven dungeon. The rats blinked, their whiskers twitching as they gazed up at them.

"What did you do to them?" shouted Zoe.

Tom stared down in shock at his shrunken classmates.

Avani looked Zoe up-and-down, then turned to Tom. "Thought you said magic doesn't work on your world?"

"Guess I was wrong."

Goban leaned over the creatures and said, "Boo!"

Everyone watched the two blue, wiggling rat bottoms scurry off into the wet, dreary darkness.

"The spell'll wear off," said Avani.

"Too bad," replied Tom.


# A reluctant hero


"Mom's gonna be pissed about the milk," said Tom, staring at Avani. "Maybe I should go back and get some more."

"Milk's not a warrior?" Devraj asked.

Tom's eyes still glued on Avani, he said, "Milk comes from a cow. You drink it."

"If it's food," remarked Goban. "We should get more."

"You can stop staring," Avani said. "I missed you too."

Blushing, Tom shifted his attention to his left shoe.

Glaring at the pair, Devraj slammed his sword into its sheath.

Avani's grin widened until she noticed the Earth girl studying her from the shadows. Avani stepped up to Zoe. "Hello. My name's Avani." She stuck out her hand. "What's yours?" Zoe didn't move.

"That is your Earth custom, right?" Avani glanced at Tom. "To shake hands—when greeting someone new?"

Zoe asked, "Are these your friends from—"

"Yes. From Elfhaven." Avani smiled. "I'm Avani."

"Avani?" Zoe glanced at Tom. "The elf chick you kissed?"

Avani's jaw dropped. She glanced from Tom to Devraj. Devraj glared at them both.

"Yes—ah—no!" Tom stuttered. "Wasn't like that."

"The portal!" urged Goban. "Come on. We gotta hurry."

Tom grabbed the dwarf by his arm. "Goban it's really you." Tom hugged him.

Goban patted Tom awkwardly on the back. "Course it's me. Who else'd I be?" Goban gently eased Tom to arm's length. "But we gotta get you to Elfhaven, fast."

"What? You came to Earth—to get me?"

Finally Devraj spoke, "Of course we did! Did you think we came all this way—just to save you from those two delinquents?"

"Well—yes, actually. Kinda sweet, really."

Devraj snorted.

Zoe stepped forward. "We were managing just fine by ourselves." Everyone faced her.

Zoe locked eyes with Avani. "I had those two bullies under control."

"They knocked you down," Avani reminded her. "If we hadn't come along when we did..."

Zoe gritted her teeth and leaned forward. Avani stood her ground. Neither moved. Neither breathed. Rain dripped from their bedraggled hair as they each sized the other up.

"Come on!" huffed Devraj. "We have no time for female turf defending."

Goban glanced at Tom. The two wisely remained silent.

Tom stepped between the two girls and faced Avani. "So—if you didn't come here to save me from the bullies, then—what's up?"

"We do have to hurry." Avani grabbed Tom's hand. "The Guardian can't keep the portal open long. We can't risk Naagesh finding out."

"Naagesh?" Tom scanned their faces. "What do ya mean? The Guardian controls the Citadel, not the wizard."

The others just stared at him.

"Oh, no…"

Goban grasp Tom's arm. "Come on. The portal."

"Goban's right." Still holding Tom's other arm, Avani said, "We've got to get you back." As the two pulled Tom along he noticed, for the first time, a familiar rectangular shape. At the far end of the block, a portal loomed wide, its lime-green outline seething with energy, its surface undulating like waves on a lake, crackling where the rain tentatively explored the unnatural rift between universes.

Tom dug in his heals and stopped. "No! Gotta leave mom a note first! Tell her where I've gone."

"No time!" Devraj nodded. Avani and Goban again, dragged Tom toward the portal.

Tom struggled. "No, wait!"

They'd almost reached the portal, but a loud *crack* and a flash of light brought them up short. The portal had closed. A single green dot wavered in front of them, then winked out.

Tom jerked his arms free and strode off. "Doesn't matter now," he called back. "Guess yer stuck on Earth."

# Juanita

Juanita strode briskly into the lab. Facing the coat rack, she hurriedly slipped out of her long coat and shook it off.

"What have you learned?" she called over her shoulder to her team of scientists. Before she could place it on the rack, her brother took the jacket from her. "Thanks," she said.

"My pleasure." Carlos brushed off her coat and hung it up. "Where's Tom?"

"With Zoe. I sent them to Bucky's to get milk." Juanita faced her teammates. She froze. Everyone just stood there smiling at her.

"What's going on?" she said. "Why the stupid grins?"

"Have you written your acceptance speech yet?" asked Cheng.

"Acceptance speech?" Juanita tipped her head in confusion. "I'm here because of an anomaly with the detection grid." She studied their still smiling faces. "Acceptance speech for what?"

"The Nobel prize in physics, of course," Leroy began. "For proving that parallel universes do in fact exist."

"While at the same time," added Cheng excitedly, "disproving *supersymmetry* in favor of the less popular *multiverse* theory."

Sashi brushed lint from her orange sari draped casually across her torso. "Let alone the fact that you actually visited a planet in another universe."

Leroy leaned toward Sashi. "And survived."

"Aren't you getting a little ahead of yourselves?" asked Juanita. "The nominations haven't been published yet. Besides, there are lots of worthy scientists we're competing against for this year's prize. Hopefully, we'll be one of them."

The others just continued to smile.

"What?"

Carlos stepped forward and produced a letter from behind his back. "It's from the Nobel committee. It's addressed to you."

She gasped. Her hands shook as she accepted the envelope. "This doesn't mean—they may just be telling me we didn't make the cut."

"Don't keep us in suspense," Carlos urged. "Open it!"

Glancing at them one more time, Juanita tore open the letter, slid the contents from its envelope and scanned the page intently. Neatly folding the letter, she slid it back into the envelope and set it on the counter.

"It appears," she began. "I've been nominated! I'm in the running for the Nobel Prize!"

Everyone cheered, rushed forward and hugged her.

Carlos beamed. "You did it sis. You won!"

Tears gushed down her cheeks. With some difficulty, Juanita pulled herself away, wiped her eyes, then beamed a gigantic smile. Glasses materialized. A champagne bottle *popped*. The glasses filled to overflowing.

Sashi handed her a tissue. Juanita wiped her eyes. "I—ah, we—haven't won yet. We've only been nominated."

"It's a sure thing." Carlos thrust a glass into Juanita's trembling hand. "A toast!" he shouted.

Juanita dabbed her eyes again and smiled. "You all know this was a team effort, right? If I win, I'll make sure the world knows that."

"When will they announce the winner?" someone asked.

"A month from today you'll take the prize!" Carlos raised his glass in a toast. "To a brilliant scientist and the best sister a guy could ever have! In this universe, at least." Some cheered, others groaned. They all raised their glasses and sipped.

Juanita shuddered, turned away and wiped the remaining tears from her eyes. Carlos touched her arm lightly. She relaxed, then faced them.

"Ok. So back to business," Juanita began. "What do we know so far about the energy spike? Or was that just a ruse to get me into the office on our day off?"

"We get days off?" said someone. Everyone chuckled.

Amidst good-natured grumbles, the scientists returned to their workstations.

"Energy spike was real," Sashi assured Juanita.

"And actually," Leroy interjected, "we've learned quite a bit."

Juanita took a sip, then set her glass on the counter. "Go on."

"We've confirmed my initial hypothesis," Sashi continued. "The energy spike wasn't enough to open a portal."

"At least," Cheng qualified, "not like the previous portals."

"What do you mean?" asked Juanita. "Not like the previous portals?"

"We analyzed the energy signature. It wasn't as strong as previous events, but there's something more."

"More?"

"There appeared to be some sort of transmission accompanying the event."

"Transmission?" Juanita said excitedly. "Can you play it back?"

"We haven't been able to decode the signal yet," said Cheng. "It's not using any protocol we've seen."

"Sounds like static," Sashi added, "but if you listen closely using noise suppression software, there's a pattern."

Juanita blinked. "Theories?"

"Our best guess is that—a nano-portal opened," began her brother. "One just big enough to transmit a message."

"A message from whom?" Juanita shook her head. "To whom? Have you localized it?"

"Too short," said Carlos. "The transmission ended before we could pinpoint its target."

"Approximation?"

"Chicago."

Juanita asked, "Our lab?"

"Chicago was the best we could do. If the signal had lasted longer…"

Juanita ambled toward the detection grid, scanning the mass of wires, cables, and instruments bolted to it. "This is great news!" She turned back.

"Timely too. If we can analyze the data quickly enough, we may be able to submit an addendum to the Nobel Prize committee. Couldn't hurt!"

An alarm started blaring. Everyone rushed to their consoles.

"I don't believe it!" cried Leroy.

"Another event!" Sashi confirmed. "And this time the energy signature is far stronger."

"Its origin is Elfhaven," said Carlos.

"Excellent! Start recording data! With this added event, surely the committee will…" Juanita stared at the blank detection grid.

"The detection grid should be lit up like a Hanukkah menorah." Juanita frowned. "Why isn't it?" She slapped her forehead. "It's not directed here. Where else would the Guardian?" She spun around. "Hurry! Use Fermilab's satellites."

"How many?"

"All of em. And patch into the International Space Station's sensors, too. See if you can zero in on the portal's exact location."

Cheng argued, "We'll need authorization to access the ISS sensors—"

"No time!" Juanita shouted. "Hack into their systems if you have to!"

Cheng raised his brow, then turned back to his console.

"Triangulating," replied Sashi. Three massive flat-screen displays lit up, showing rotating views of the Earth. A grid of bright red dots overlaid the Earth. Icons representing individual satellites appeared with more being added each second.

"The northern hemisphere sats are online!" shouted someone.

"Southern hemisphere as well!"

"ISS sensors linked up." Cheng said. "They're not gonna be happy when they realize we hacked their *impenetrable* security system."

Ignoring the comment, Juanita scanned the displays. As each satellite came online, red lines shot out from their icons, scanning the globe. The area in red shrank to the northern hemisphere, then to the US, then to the Midwest. Finally, focusing to a single dot.

"Enlarge," shouted Juanita. The display zoomed in.

"It appears," began Sashi, "there's an open portal in southwestern Chicago."

"Another nano-portal?"

"No!" cried Leroy. "It's a fully formed portal! And nearby."

"Enlarge," Juanita repeated. The image expanded again. She brushed her finger in the air. The imaged shifted left, then stopped.

"It's in our neighborhood." Carlos stared at his sister. "Near Bucky's convenience store."

"Great!" she began excitedly. "We can take the van, it's got remote sensing equipment. Assuming we—"

"Where did you say Tom was?" Carlos asked.

"I told you. I sent him and Zoe to get some milk at Buc—" Juanita froze. "Tom!"

Carlos snatched up his key FOB from the counter, and the two bolted from the building.


# Tourists!


They must have been quite a sight; the bizarre, inter-species group, heading toward Tom's house. Zoe just kept staring at the kids from another world, especially Avani. Tom's Elfhaven friends, however, their emergency apparently forgotten, gazed in awe at all the bizarre alien sights and sounds.

Goban and Avani asked tons of questions: Tom tried his best to explain electric lights, see-through glass windows, and videos they saw playing through windows.

A nearly silent car whizzed by, throwing sheets of water up from its tires. This shifted Tom's lecture to self-driving vehicles, both hydrogen and electric.

"Just thirty years ago, cars were powered by burning fossil fuels, gasoline, primarily. The resulting carbon waste nearly destroyed the planet."

"Destroyed an entire world?" said Goban.

Tom nodded. "Warmed the planet beyond its ability to cool itself. If it hadn't been for the scientists and engineers who developed the bio-mass carbon reclamation technology…"

Tom stepped aside, allowing an elderly couple huddled beneath a small umbrella to pass by. They smiled at him. At that same moment, a loud *clang* of a metal trash can toppling over, followed immediately by that of a screeching cat caused Devraj to leap sideways and draw his broadsword. The couple rocked back, staring in shock at the long-eared, oddly dressed boy holding a sword.

Tom pressed down lightly on the prince's wrist, "Put that away. It was just a cat."

"Sorry," Tom apologized. "He's not from around here."

\* \* \*

"Tom?" Avani whispered.

"Yes?"

"Why d'you let those two push you around like that?"

"The bullies?"

Avani nodded.

He glanced back. "They're bullies. They're bigger than me."

Avani stared at him.

"Bullies've always beaten me up," he stammered. "I'm a wimp! What could I do?"

"You were afraid? Of them?"

"Course!" he blurted. "They're bullies! They're big and strong. I'm small and weak."

"But you've stood up to trolls and ogres—"

"Yes, but—"

"And to Naagesh."

"That was diff—"

94

"You rode a dragon."

"With my eyes shut!"

The two walked in silence until they neared his home.

"That's our house. The blue one at the end of the block." Tom sprinted up the steps. "Coulda used my phone to unlock the door, but the bullies destroyed it." He typed in the entry code and the door swung open.

## Home sweet home

Tom led them through the living room. "The kitchen's through there. My bedroom's at the far end. Halfway down the hall there's a bathroom on the left." He paused. "Ah—you flip the lever to flush." Again, he started and again stopped when he noticed Goban watching the video playing on the wall.

"Wow!" said Goban. "Is this some sorta historical record?"

Tom chucked. "Nah. It's a 3-D Vid. An old movie classic called Lord of the Rings."

"You never told me you have dwarves on your world!" Goban pointed to a shorter character with a long full beard and mustache. "Who's that?"

"The character's name is Gimli. He's my favorite. Grumpy, but in a tight spot, he has yer back."

"Course he does! He's a dwarf!" Goban scratched his chin, thoughtfully. "Got a funny accent though."

"A Scottish brogue." Tom pursed his lips. "For some reason, the dwarves in the vid speak with Scottish accent."

Goban lowered his voice and attempted to match Gimli's brogue, "Here's one dwarf she won't ensnare so easily," he began, repeating Gimli's last phrase. "I've the eyes of a hawk and the ears of a fox."

"Freeze," called Tom. The scene froze, an arrow aimed directly in Gimli's face. Tom chuckled. Goban glared at him.

95

Tom shrugged. "Supposed to be funny."

Tom's face lit up. He turned to Avani. "Hey! You like magic. You'll love this flick." He faced the screen. "Play Harry Potter and the Goblet of Fire." The wall went dark. Tinkly, suspenseful music began to play.

"We have no time for nonsense," declared the prince.

"Video off," Tom said. The wall went blank. Tom stared at Devraj. "I missed you too."

Tom marched down the hall and waited at his door. The prince followed him. As Devraj passed Zoe, she winked at him. He glanced back. She blew Devraj a kiss.

"This is my room." Tom twisted the doorknob. The door didn't budge.

Goban tapped his shoulder. "Lemme try." Tom stepped aside. Goban pushed. The door gave a little. Goban put his shoulder into it. The door groaned, swinging grudgingly inward.

Tom stuck his head through the doorway. "It's Chloe. She's blocking the door." Tom slipped inside and stared at his robot. "How'd she get over here?"

Goban pushed past him. "We'll explain later."

"You'll explain?"

The two girls entered next. Tom shook off his wet hoodie, then grabbed a tee shirt from a pile and used it to dab off his sweatshirt.

Tom's bed started sliding across the floor. Max popped his head out from under the bedframe, a dirty sock hanging limply from his ear.

"Max," Tom scolded his large, furry saint Bernard. "I told ya. You're too big to fit under there anymore." Max struggled to crawl out from under, then looked up at them all with his large brown eyes. Shaking his head vigorously, the sock, along with ample dog slobber, went flying.

Zoe stood in her drenched vest. She cleared her throat. Tom glanced her way. Zoe shivered.

Tom grabbed a sweater and handed it to her.

"Thanks." She smiled, and handed him her dripping vest. Tom tossed it in the corner.

Avani studied Zoe. Noticing her, Zoe brushed the soft fabric of Tom's sweater and smiled at Avani.

Facing Tom, Avani asked, "Is this your sleeping chamber?" She scanned the room, taking in the books on his rickety shelf, the parts strewn haphazardly across his dresser, and the mounds of clothing piled on the floor.

"Looks even worse than before," said Avani.

"Before?" Tom said.

Devraj wrinkled his lip in disgust. "Did one of your science experiments go horribly wrong—and explode?"

Goban began rummaging through Tom's toolbox, tossing tools left and right. *Clink, clank.* He picked up a tiny rectangular box with red and black wires dangling from it.

"Hey!" shouted Tom. "Careful with that. It's a multimeter meter."

"Hmmmppphhh." Goban studied the rectangular device intently, then tossed it over his shoulder. Tom winced.

Avani picked up a pair of boxer shorts from a pile, flipped them over and studied them. "You wear these strange garments?"

Tom snatched them from her, scooped up the entire stack of underwear, crammed them in a drawer and slammed it shut.

"Why's your face red?" Avani asked.

Zoe snorted. Avani watched her. Zoe scooted over, leaned against Tom and shot Avani a fake smile. Tom glanced from Zoe to Avani.

Goban walked from the toolbox over to Tom's robot and, with some effort, tugged her back to the center of the room. "Yer mechanical pet looks different than last time."

"Yeah," said Tom, glad for the distraction. "Chloe mark II. I've given her a few—upgrades."

"You're not the only one," said Avani. She gave Goban a knowing look.

"What?" Tom asked, sounding confused.

Goban reached out. "Is this her on switch?"

"Don't!" Tom grabbed Goban's arm. "I haven't tested her yet."

"It's OK. We have." Goban brushed Tom's arm aside and flipped the switch. Chloe's diagnostics started running.

"You have?"

The message '*Diagnostics complete*' flashed across her display.

"What did you mean by—"

Chloe swiveled her platform and faced Tom. "There you are, big boy!" came a sweet, feminine voice from the robot.

"What?" Tom blinked in shock. "I only programmed Chloe to have a few words."

The robot spun around and expertly navigated the slalom course of clothing piles, finally stopping at Tom's full-length mirror.

"I like what you've done with my frame. All shiny and such. More sensors, too. And you gave me a high-res camera!" She pivoted to one side, then the other. "Do you think these oversized tires make my chassis look big?"

Tom blinked in shock. Suddenly, a hologram of a tiny figure, clad in ancient Japanese Samurai garb appeared hovering above Chloe and the Guardian's voice filled the room, "I see you found Tom. Good. This little excursion cost us precious time.

"The king's party now has a six oort head start on you. Hurry, you must warn the king of Naagesh's plans, before they catch up with the wizard."

"The portal closed," the prince reminded him. "You stranded us on this accursed planet."

"I closed the portal intentionally. If I left it open too long, Naagesh might have sensed it."

Tom stomped his foot. "Stop talking like I'm not here!" He folded his arms. "I'm not going anywhere till someone explains what's going on."

Everyone stared at him. Tom stared back.

"What would you like to know?" asked the Guardian.

"First off, how can you talk to us through Chloe? No. That's second. First is, how does Chloe know all those words? And what's happened to her voice?"

"That's three things," the Guardian pointed out. "The answer to all three questions is—I gave Chloe an upgrade."

"You gave Chloe an upgrade?" Tom sounded aghast. "I upgraded her. Wait. How did you upgrade her?"

"Remember that bio-electronic device I gave you to attach to her CPU?"

Tom's eyes widened.

"She's an AI being now. Not fully sentient, as I am, but good enough to fool most. Do you like the personality I chose for her?"

"No! I don't," Tom shouted. "She's too—ah—"

"Sweet?" said Avani.

"Girly?" suggested Goban.

Zoe grinned. "Sexy!"

Tom blushed. "All of those!"

"Fine," replied the Guardian. "I'll adjust her personality index. Tone her down a bit."

"I kinda liked her," said Goban.

"Regardless," continued the Guardian, "we can't afford any more time with trivial questions." The Guardian's image rotated to face Tom's closet. From the closet came the sound of high energy cracking. The closet door swung open and a blinding olive-green light poured forth.

"Go!" shouted the prince.

Tom crossed his arms defiantly. "Like I said, I'm not going anywhere till you tell me—"

Devraj grabbed Tom's arm.

"OK—OK!" Tom jerked free. "Lemme leave mom a note, at least." Tom walked to his dresser, glaring at the prince the whole way. "You remember those two bullies you saved me from back there?"

The prince stared at him.

"Sometimes you remind me of em," Tom said. "Jus sayin'."

Devraj glanced from Goban to Avani. They looked away. He shifted his gaze to Zoe.

Zoe scratched her cheek, considering. "Now that I think about it—you do look like a furry blue rat bottom."

Someone snorted. Devraj scanned the room, searching for the culprit.

Meanwhile, Tom found a pad of paper hidden underneath an old copy of Robotics Monthly magazine, then pulled a mechanical pencil from under a smelly, half-eaten tuna sandwich.

Carefully lifting the sandwich, as if it were a live grenade, Tom took aim at the garbage pail in the corner.

"Ah hmmm," said Goban, eying the sandwich. Tom handed it to Goban. He gobbled it down in two bites. Tom began scribbling.

"How old was that food?" asked Devraj.

"Yesterday's lunch." Tom licked the pencil's eraser, then erased vigorously. "Or else last week."

Goban burped.

Tom dropped the pencil, started to lay the note on his dresser, hesitated, then laid the note on his pillow.

"I'm going with you," insisted Zoe.

"You? In Elfhaven?" Avani looked Zoe up and down. "You wouldn't last ten myntars."

"Then I won't be in your hair for long, will I?"

Avani frowned. "In my hair?"

"How long's a myntar?" said Zoe.

"You shall stay here," Devraj commanded. "On your own world."

"You can't boss me around!" Zoe stared at Tom, her eyes pleading.

"Zoe," Tom began. "Ah—I kinda agree with Devraj. It's too dangerous."

Zoe folded her arms.

Tom shrugged. "Fine. Just stay out of trouble, OK?"

An enormous grin blossomed across Zoe's face. Avani's face, however, darkened.

"Come on." Tom turned toward the closet and spotted Max pawing at a leather strap protruding from behind the door. Tom bent down and hefted his old adventurers' belt.

"Haven't used this thing since I got back from Elfhaven." He turned it over. "Restocked it, though. When I first got home. Added some new stuff. Didn't expect to ever use it again."

"New stuff?" said Goban.

Tom pursed his lips, thinking. "Glow tubes, compass, sewing kit. Some other junk." He took off the belt he'd been wearing. As he did so, the dagger bounced off the carpet. He picked it up, set it on his dresser and cinched up his adventurers' belt.

"Come on, Max. Time to save the world!" Max shook himself, slobber flying.

Chloe spun around, her new high-powered motors whining, and bolted past Tom. The others leapt aside as she sped through the portal and disappeared. Max barked, bounding after her.

Tom blinked. "OK then. Why doesn't Chloe just come along?" He scanned his room one last time. His gaze froze on the dagger. On his way to his closet, Tom snatched up the dagger, stuffed it in his belt, stepped into the closet and disappeared. Goban and Devraj followed him.

And now there were two. Avani studied Zoe.

"What?" said Zoe.

"Ah, I didn't want to embarrass you in front of Tom but—"

"What?" Zoe repeated.

"It's just that—"

"Ask already!"

"Your eyes." Avani pointed. "They're circled in blue. Plus, your cheeks are too red and your lips are an odd color. Are you sick?"

"No!" snapped Zoe. "It's called makeup! Makes you prettier. You should try it sometime. Heaven knows you could use it."

Avani continued to stare. "The question I really wanted to ask is—"

"Yes?"

"Are you—ah, you and Tom, I mean?" Avani hesitated. "Are you—"

"Are we what? Boyfriend and girlfriend?" A smile spread across Zoe's face. "Of course we are! You jealous? You got a crush on Tom? Well, that's just too bad."

Zoe pretended to inspect her long, silver-star embossed nails. "Tom's a good kisser." Zoe gave Avani a sad smile. "He told me I'm a better kisser than you."

"Tom said that?" Avani looked shocked. "Doesn't matter." Her look softened. "You needn't worry. Prince Devraj and I will wed in three solar cycles."

"Oh?" Now Zoe sounded shocked. "Kinda young, aren't you? To get married?"

Avani smiled. "Evidently, elven girls mature faster than Earth girls."

Zoe's clenched her jaw. "Engaged or not, you've got a crush on Tom, don't you?" When Avani didn't respond, Zoe grinned. "You do! I can tell. Well, that's too bad. You snooze, you lose. Tom doesn't care about you anymore. He chose me!"

Avani blinked, then gestured toward the portal. "After you then."

Zoe stormed off for the closet. As she passed Avani, Zoe *accidentally* thrust her hip to the side, knocking Avani face down into a pile of dirty laundry. Zoe stopped. "Oops! Us Earth girls are such klutzes."

Leaping to her feet, Avani peeled a sweaty undershirt from her face and threw it to the floor.

Fluttering her long lashes at Avani, Zoe pivoted smartly on her heel and took another step toward the portal.

Swirling yellow magic burst from Avani's satchel. "Oops! I'm such a— what was your term you used? A klutz?" Avani strode past Zoe and stopped at the entrance to Tom's closet.

Zoe tried to follow but couldn't move. She glanced down. "What the?" Tom's shag carpet had mysteriously grown over Zoe's shoes! Still growing, the seemingly possessed carpet wrapped itself playfully around Zoe's ankles and began moving up her calves.

Zoe screamed, desperately trying to pull loose.

"Don't worry," Avani assured her. "It'll let go—in time." Avani tipped her head uncertainly. "At least—it would in Elfhaven."

Avani stepped into the portal and disappeared.


# Juanita and Carlos


"We should have taken the van," complained Juanita, "instead of your Jeep. The van's equipped with data recording gear."

"I'm more concerned about Tom than about capturing data," Carlos chastised her playfully. "Aren't you?"

"Tom can take care of himself," Juanita argued somewhat guiltily. "I'll try redialing." She tapped her bracelet. Tom's ringtone sounded. "Pickup!" Juanita glanced at her brother. "Tom's not answering."

Carlos patted her arm. "He probably just left his phone home, *again*." There was a brief pause. "You know—you really should be more careful what you say in Tom's presence."

"What do you mean?"

"He overheard us talking yesterday."

"Talking?"

"About the Nobel Prize."

She brushed a lock of hair from her eyes. "So?"

"So you said, *winning the Nobel Prize was all that matters*."

"That's true."

"Where does that leave Tom?"

She blinked. "Tom knows he matters more to me than the prize."

"Does he?"

Juanita stared out the window. "Can you go any faster?"

Carlos shot her a sidelong glance. "So we arrive before the portal closes?"

"Yes. No!" She fidgeted. "So we can make sure Tom's OK."

Carlos studied her closely. Leaning forward, he tapped a red square on his hydrogen-powered Jeep's large, curving display. From below the console, a small steering wheel rose up and out and peddles extended beneath his feet.

"*Switching from self-driving mode to Manual,*" came a flat automated voice. "*Please confirm.*"

Carlos took the wheel. "Confirmed." Slapping his foot down hard on the accelerator, the car picked up speed. He glanced at this sister, still staring out the window.

"Why do you think the Guardian would open a portal here, now?" he asked. The engine's soft whine rose in pitch.

"I don't know. Something's going on."

"Trouble?"

She bit her lip.

"Maybe King Dakshi just misses you? Wants to ask you out on a date?"

She whipped around to face him. "The king's not—we're not—" Carlos grinned.

"Oh, be serious." She smoothed a nonexistent wrinkle from her freshly ironed jeans. "Tom might be in danger."

Carlos nodded knowingly.

Folding her arms, she glared at him.

Her phone rang. Juanita sat up and tapped her bracelet. "Hello?" She whispered to Carlos, "It's Sashi."

"On speaker," he said.

"Carlos is with me," Juanita flicked across her bracelet toward the car's dashboard. "Go ahead."

Sashi's face appeared on the car's screen and her voice blared from the speakers, "Bad news. The portal closed."

"Oh, no." Juanita's shoulders sank.

"But there's more," continued Sashi. "A second portal opened."

Juanita leaned forward. "Have you pinpointed its location?"

"Yes. We've got its exact lat-long coordinates."

"Where is it?" she asked excitedly.

"It's—it's in your house. The room in the northeast corner, to be precise."

Slamming the front door, the two rushed into Tom's room and stopped, an olive glow still radiating from the closet.

"Help!" screamed Zoe. "Get me outta here!" She pointed at her feet.

Juanita and Carlos' looked down. Zoe wore furry, knee-high-socks *over* her shoes. Odd though, the socks appeared to be made of the same material as the carpet. In fact, they were woven into the carpet itself.

"If I ever get my hands on that blond-haired elven witch! I'll—I'll. I'll rip off her long pointy ears and—and feed em to my pug Snuffles!"

Juanita tried unsuccessfully to keep from grinning. "Scissors."

Carlos, fighting a grin of his own, hurried from the room.

"We'll be right back." Juanita rushed out.

"I'll just wait right here then!"

Carlos burst into the room brandishing scissors. Juanita dashed in wearing jeans, hiking boots and a warm goose-down parka. She held an LED flashlight loosely in her hand. Green light and sharp arcing, popping noises still emanated from Tom's closet.

Carlos hurried to Zoe. Juanita headed for the portal.

"Wait!" cried Carlos. "I'm coming with you."

"After you've freed Zoe. And make sure she doesn't follow you."

"Promise you'll stay here?" said Carlos.

Zoe folded her arms and frowned.

The room rocked violently. The portal flickered.

"Gotta run!" Juanita dove through the portal a second before it slammed shut.

# Reunion

Avani stepped from the portal. Strange alien objects littered the ground: a baseball bat, a skateboard with a missing wheel, some Halloween candy wrappers. Max sniffed the wrappers, then licked them.

"Where's Zoe?" Tom asked.

Avani shrugged. "She just stood there, rooted to the spot. Must've gotten scared."

Goban snorted.

Tom's eyes narrowed. He studied their faces suspiciously. "Well, guess it's for the best. If Zoe'd been eaten by a zhanderbeast, mom woulda grounded me for a year."

Avani glanced at Goban.

Goban shook his head sadly. "Missed yer chance."

Tom's frown deepened.

"Again, we waste precious time," snapped Devraj. "We could have caught up with my father by now, instead of chasing half-way around the solar system searching for you."

"Universe, not solar system," Tom corrected. "*Universes*—plural, actually."

Devraj glared at him.

"You don't wanna warn yer father." Tom leaned forward. "You wanna prove to him you're capable. You wanna capture Naagesh yourself, right?" Tom started walking. Avani hurried after.

The prince watched them go.

"Didn't work last time," Tom called over his shoulder. "Probably won't work this time, either."

"Where are we going?" Tom asked Avani.

"To the Citadel. The Guardian needs to speak with you." On the way there, Avani told Tom all about her adventure at the Library of Nalanda, including Naagesh's trap and her narrow escape.

"Lucky you found that spell!"

Avani nodded. "Wouldn't a survived otherwise."

"Must've been scary," Tom said. "All alone, buried under tons of rubble. Too bad I wasn't there to keep you company." Adding hastily, "And Goban a course!"

"The spell can only protect one person."

Tom shuddered. "Then—I'm glad I wasn't there!"

Avani squeezed his hand. Tom glanced over his shoulder.

"Don't worry," she assured him. "Devraj is arguing with Goban. They're way behind."

As they neared Bandipur park, loud construction noise: sawing and hammering filled the air. A crew of elves were building a wide platform, while others assembled rows of wooden benches.

"What's going on?" asked Tom. "Some sorta celebration?"

This time Avani glanced back. "It's for our bonding ceremony. Devraj and mine." She picked at her tunic, nervously. "We're engaged, remember?"

Tom stopped and stared at her.

Avani blushed, looked away.

"I remember," Tom said. "To unite the royal house with the Keepers of the Light. But I thought that wasn't gonna happen till you came of—" he stammered. "I mean—when you turn—"

"My fifteenth awakening day is in three solar cycles. That's when Devraj and I—" An awkward pause. "You know."

"Become chained together fer life!" said Goban.

Avani whipped around. Goban and Devraj stood right behind them. Avani blushed again and ran the rest of the way. She opened the Citadel door. The others followed her in, calling their names as usual, then walked down the long descending hallway toward the central chamber.

"Is this the forbidden portal you told me about last year?" Tom asked the Guardian.

"Yes."

"Pandora's Portal?" Tom said. "Where hordes of life-force sucking creatures live?"

"The very same."

"I don't get it." Tom said. "Yer the Guardian. If Naagesh programed a portal to open, just delete the program."

"The wizard didn't program a portal to open, per say. Naagesh stole a remote."

"What are you saying?"

"The remote acts totally independent of the Citadel. Yes, it uses the Citadel's circuitry to actually open the portal, but it activates it remotely, at a time and place of the user's choice."

"Ok." Tom glanced at the others. "So, we need to destroy the remote."

"Not that simple. The unit is nearly indestructible. But even in the unlikely event that it was destroyed, Naagesh set a fail-safe timer. If the wizard doesn't open the portal himself, when the timer goes off, the portal will open automatically."

"Destroying the remote won't stop the timer?"

"Unfortunately, no. The timer is running here."

"So turn it off!"

"I can't. That circuitry is completely isolated. Not even I can access it."

"So—what do we do?"

Devraj sighed. "Why do you think we wasted all this time bringing you here? For you to think of a plan."

Tom paced the chamber. He stopped. "If we could get the remote from Naagesh. Could we use it to stop the portal from opening?"

"In theory," said the Guardian. "If we could access the device, we could deactivate the timer, but—"

"But?"

"The remote's keyed to Naagesh's voice. He alone can disable it."

"We could capture Naagesh," mused Goban. "Force him to stop it."

"He would never do that," said Devraj.

Tom glanced around the control chamber. "Do you keep audio logs?"

"Yes. I am recording this conversation."

"You log *every* conversation?"

"Of course! I have recorded, cataloged, and archived every conversation I have ever—" The Guardian's visage froze. "Oh. Accessing the relevant file now. One moment."

Almost instantly, the evil wizard's voice rang out, "Naagesh. Wizard. Master class." Goban grabbed his axe, Devraj his sword. Everyone spun around, searching for the wizard. Everyone except Tom.

"Bring me the remote before the timer goes off," said the Guardian, "or the world ends."

"How long do we have?" Tom glanced at his watch.

"I only know he set the timer. I don't know when or where Naagesh set it to go off."

# The Librarian

Kiran sat waiting for them just outside the Citadel. He didn't look happy. They all agreed to meet at Avani and Kiran's grandparent's house in one oort, to come up with a plan. Devraj sprinted off to the castle. While the rest headed for the Elfhaven library to do research.

"Hi Kiran!" said Tom.

"Hi Tom." Kiran shot Avani an angry glare. "You were supposed to take me with you to Earth."

Max ran over and licked Kiran's hand, then raised his paw. Unable to maintain his dower face any longer, Kiran smiled, knelt, and scratched Max behind the ears.

But on the way to the library, Kiran said nothing more. Not while they walked. Not as they shuffled up the library's long, wide steps, not even when he and Goban held open the library's massive red door and waited for the others to pass through. In fact, he didn't let out a peep until they finally reached the librarian's desk.

Kiran shot Avani an angry glare. "Shoulda waited for me." Library patrons shushed him.

Everyone talked at once, hurriedly telling the spirit what they knew, including the fact that Naagesh possessed the remote, and that the device was likely their only hope of thwarting the evil wizard's plan.

Once they'd explained everything to the ghost of the Elfhaven library, who called himself The Librarian, Tom said, "We need a history lesson."

The spirit leaned across his imposing, stout, wooden desk and glared down his long, hooked, transparent nose at them.

Ignoring Kiran's outburst, Tom asked the ghost, "Tell us what happened."

"Tell you *what* happened—*when?*" droned the apparition.

"You know! The first time."

The ghost adopted a disinterested look. "First time?"

Tom just stared at him.

The spirit shrugged. "Very well. I shall start at the beginning." The ghost flicked his wrist and a book magically appeared on his desk and opened. "As you know, there are four ages, including the one we now live in."

"We live," Kiran pointed out. "You're dead."

The spirit glared at him.

"I thought there were three ages?" said Avani.

"No. There are four."

"Are you counting the one that follows our current age or—"

The ghost's angry visage loomed across his desk again. "Who's giving this lecture?"

"Sorry," Avani whispered. "I'll be quiet."

Still glaring, the spirit crossed his arms and withdrew.

"Silent as a castle rat," she said, nodding solemnly. Kiran chuckled.

The ghost's eyes narrowed. "The first of the *four* ages was characterized by a time of powerful swirling magics, both dark and light. Magics without form or purpose. At some point, the dark—"

"Sorry to interrupt," said Tom. "But all we *really* want to know is what happened a thousand years ago. When the wizards and star beings worked together to send the creatures back to their home planet. We're not interested in hearing about the three, or perhaps four, ages past." Tom glanced at the others, "Well? Are we?"

"I'm kind of interested," said Avani. "Me too!" added Kiran.

Tom looked at Goban. He yawned.

The ghost drummed his fingers silently on his desk. Tom zipped his mouth shut and stepped back.

The spirit resumed in his flat, droning lecturer's voice, "Powerful swirling magics, both dark and light. At some point, the dark won out, forcing the light to retreat. Scholars named the period: '*The Age of Darkness*'."


Tom nudged Goban. They walked off. In the background, the ghost droned on, "It was the age of evil, filled with churning poisonous gasses, fire, and chaos. Out of this roiling dark soup, many hideous beings arose...."

"Boring," said Goban.

Tom nodded. "It's frustrating. That ghost never gives us a straight answer. He just goes on and on and—"

"I can hear you!" snapped the Librarian.

Hurrying away, Tom gazed up at the statues of monsters and beasts staring down at them from dark recesses in the library walls.

Even at this distance, the librarian's voice somehow managed to reach their ears. "...and the fairies, with the dragons help, locked the demons in a dark realm."

Tom could just make out Avani's reply, "But there are still demons in

Demon Forest."

"A few minor demons, imps and the like, managed to hide in this world," The ghost conceded. "But, having little power, they weren't considered a threat."

"There's no way for the demons to break free?" she asked.

"Not by themselves," the librarian's voice paused. "For a time, wizards routinely summoned the odd demon to do their bidding, but the Wizards Council soon outlawed the dangerous practice."

Tom turned left down a narrow aisle, Goban scrambling to keep up. Thankfully, the librarian's lecture faded the farther down the aisle they went.

"Hey!" said Tom. "This is it!"

"This is what?" asked Goban.

"The place where I overheard Naagesh's thugs." Tom absently touched his sweatshirt collar. "The two who nearly strangled me."

Tom stopped and shoved books aside. Behind the books, another large dust-covered tome lay on its side. Tom slid it out, handed the book to Goban and peered through the opening.

"They stood through there, on the other side, talking about their *'plans.'*"

Dust flew as Goban opened the book.

Tom wheezed, "What's the title?"

Goban scanned the cover. "It's written in Elvish, but—in an ancient script." His lips moved as he sounded out the words. He shrugged. "Somethin' bout a lost world."

"Cool! Sounds like an adventure novel."

Goban opened the heavy book and rifled through it. Stopping at random, he ran his stubby finger across the dry, parchment. Suddenly, the page sparkled.

"Did you see that?" said Goban.

Tom leaned close. Another faint sparkle flickered across the page. As it did, the writing went slightly out of focus then cleared.

Tom took the book from Goban. There was a brilliant flash and tangerine colored sparks whizzed away. Tom dropped the book. As it fell, a torn scrap of parchment drifted from the book to the floor.

The two stared at each other. Goban nudged the book with his foot. Nothing happened. He picked up the book and opened it.

"Whoa!" Goban thrust the book toward Tom.

Tom leaned away. "What is it?"

"Take a look." Goban shoved it closer.

Tom cautiously peered inside. It hadn't been there before, but now there was a large, round hole, the size of Tom's fist, in the center of the book.

Goban reached in and felt around. "Nothin'."

"Someone went to a lot of trouble," said Tom, "cutting through hundreds of pages, one-by-one."

"Musta taken oorts," agreed Goban.

"And they used magic to conceal the hole."

"Which worked when I held the book," Goban pointed out. "We couldn't see the secret hiding spot. But when you touched it…"

They both stared at Tom's hands as if they might explode!

Goban slid the book carefully back onto the shelf and quickly stepped back. "Let's go. Maybe the ghost's run out a words."

Tom looked skeptical. Goban started off. "Wait!" said Tom. He bent down and picked up the torn page, slid the book back off the shelf and stuffed the page inside the book. He started to replace it on the shelf but hesitated. "Let's ask the ghost what this book is and why it has a secret hiding place."

Goban shrugged.


Avani kept listening. Though, as usual, the Librarian's meandering train-of-thought had shifted the topic from the history of the ages to obscure details governing the similarities and differences between white and dark magic. Specifically, as related to *books*, of course.

"Magic books, be they white or dark—" the ghost droned on, "—are infused with magic. What's more, the books seem to exhibit a force on the reader—a persistent tug, if you will, trying to gain influence on—"

"Wait!" Avani blurted. "Larraj mentioned that in the Library of Nalanda. But he wouldn't explain. Are you saying books on dark magic are alive—and—evil?"

The ghost's voice seemed to perk up at the question, "Anything that contains magic could be considered alive. But the books on dark magic aren't evil, per se. In the hands of good, they can be used for good."

Avani listened intently.

"But the temptation is always there—" warned the spirit. "Beckoning, charming the user, making them feel powerful, convincing the foolish wizard that he or she is stronger and smarter than all the rest. Stroking the wizard's inflated ego. Assuring them that they alone possess the necessary skill to control the evil and use dark to expand the light. '*The ends justify the means*' whispers an oily, slithering voice; all the while leading them deeper down a dark path which few mortals ever escape from."

Avani swallowed. "No one's ever used dark magic without it destroying them?"

The ghost shrugged. "There are legends. Master wizards, of great integrity, who used it sparingly. I personally have heard of only two living individuals who reportedly used dark magic and survived." The spirit stared at her pointedly. "But those two only used it once."

Beads of sweat formed on Avani's brow. *He means Tom and me. That time we summoned the demon army to stop Naagesh at the ruins of castle Dunferlan.* She glanced back over her shoulder. Tom was out of sight. "How did you—"

"I overheard Larraj telling the tale to the king." The ghost almost grinned. Almost.

Avani swallowed again.

Just then Tom and Goban walked up.

"Hey," said Tom. "We found a book." He started to raise the text. "It

114

has a secret com—"

"A book? In a library?" the ghost sounded shocked. "What are the odds?"

"Avani. What's wrong?" Tom grabbed her by the arm. "You look like you've seen a ghost?"

"Ha. Ha," said the spirit. Tom ignored him.

She picked at her tunic. "Ah—the Librarian reminded me of that time in the ruins of castle Dunferlan, when we—ah-I'll tell you later."

Tom watched her strangely.

"May I continue?" huffed the Librarian.

Before Tom could answer, the ghost rambled on, "When someone uses dark magic, too much, or too often, their body will start to dissolve into churning black smoke!"

Avani eyes widened.

"Starting from the fingertips—" The ghost leaned forward. "—and working its way up."

Tom chuckled. He glanced at Avani. She wasn't laughing and her face was white. Tom addressed the librarian, "So—that's it?" Tom raised his brow inquisitively. "Ya done?"

"I am finished."

"A cheery tale!" said Kiran. "Even worse than Ninosh's."

Tom sighed. "Now, can you tell us what we *really* came here to learn?"

The ghost yawned. "Remind me."

"A thousand years ago, when Pandora's Portal first opened, how did they beat the creatures?"

"And how might that information help you?" asked the spirit. "I thought your mission was to prevent the portal from opening in the first place?"

"It is," Tom agreed, "but I thought knowing how to defeat the creatures might help." He glanced at his friends. "Just in case."

Avani's color had improved. She nodded.

"I don't recall the specifics," The spirit replied dryly, "But I believe it involved thousands of wizards, hundreds of star beings and a dozen

Keepers of the Light! None of which you currently possess."

"I'm a Keeper," Avani said meekly.

"That's not much help," Tom told the Librarian. "Can't you remember any details?"

"Sorry. That's all I remember! Perhaps the historical reference books from the Library of Nalanda might help." He shifted his scornful gaze to Avani. "Books that should've been here by now!"

Avani fidgeted. "We had more important things on our minds."

"More important than saving books?"

"Naagesh set a trap!" she argued. "I—I almost died!"

The ghost leaned forward and tapped his finger noiselessly on his desk. "Nothing is more important than the knowledge contained in those books! In fact, if you'd secured them before Naagesh got there, none of this would have happened!

"As it is, Naagesh used the Manual to do the unthinkable. If the portal opens, and the creatures are released…" The ghost floated forward, suddenly seeming much larger. "What's more, Naagesh now possesses knowledge of dark magic. If he masters that, not even Larraj can stop him."

The spirit pulled back, gazing out through hollow eyes. His voice sounding strange, distant, "The Prophecy unfolds… The Age of Darkness is nearly upon us."

Max whined and scratched Kiran's leg.

Kiran bent over and petted him. "There's gotta be something we can do?"

"Can't you at least try?" Tom agreed. "Try an find out how the wizard's and star beings defeated the creatures last time?"

The ghost appraised the desperate faces before him. Finally, he raised a spectral hand. Throughout the library, books floated off shelves and drifted their way. Once they arrived, the books stacked themselves neatly on the librarian's desk.

"I shall do some light research." The spirit patted the stack of books. "Check back with me in half an oort." He paused. "But it hardly matters.

If what you told me is correct, the fate of this world depends on you retrieving the device you spoke of, from Naagesh, and getting it to the Guardian *before* the portal opens!"

The ghost floated forward once more. "So, I suggest you get on with it."


# Juanita

*Where am I?* Juanita stood in a field, wild grasses waving gently in a cool evening breeze. A couple hundred yards away stood a medieval style shield wall with a forest beyond, and in the distance, the last rays of sunlight were quickly receding behind jagged mountain peaks.

Juanita took a step, *crunch*. She looked down. The contents of Tom's closet littered the ground at her feet.

*Must be the right place. Wonder how long Tom's been here? With the time-dilation, while traveling through the portal, he's probably been here for hours.*

She scanned the area. Far off to her right, torches flickered atop the parapet of a familiar sight, Elfhaven castle.

A crackling boom behind her caused her to spin around. Green sparks flew off in all directions, the only evidence that a portal had ever existed. *Guess Carlos didn't make it.*

Minutes later, Juanita sprinted up the castle's broad steps and turned left. As she neared the massive door to the great hall, a palace guard stepped in front of her.

"I must speak with King Dakshi. It's urgent."

"I'm sorry, lady Juanita, but the king is away."

"Away? Where?"

"I'm not at liberty to say."

"Then who *is* at liberty?"

The guard nodded to his partner, who spun on his heel and strode briskly away. A moment later he returned. "Follow me."

"I'm sorry for your inconvenience, my lady," Tappus said with a grin. "I'm surprised to see you."

"I'm surprised to be here. Why are you smiling?"

His grin evaporated. "No reason. It's just that—I know his lordship will be happy to see you, is all." The grin crept back. "But I'm afraid there's been a slight—disturbance. King Dakshi is off dealing with it." The grin widened.

Juanita studied him suspiciously. "A disturbance?"

"Um—yes. Naagesh stole books."

"Stealing books seems a bit lame for an evil wizard, doesn't it? Not really worth chasing after."

"They were texts on the forbidden practice of dark magic," he said defensively. "Plus he shut down the barrier."

"Now that sounds more like Naagesh." She glanced around the hall. "Although I had hoped to see King Dakshi, I'm actually here to find my son, Tom. Have you seen him?"

"Thomas is here?" Tappus blinked in surprise. "I have not seen him. Still, knowing your son, I'd check the Citadel and the library first."

## Malak and Chatur

An oort after Tom and crew left, Chatur and Malak sprinted up the steps, entered the library and walked up to the Librarian's desk.

"Where's master Tom and the others?" asked the ghost. "They were supposed to return half an oort ago! I found the information they asked for."

"Tom's here?" Malak blurted. "Information?" said Chatur.

"Yes. Critical information."

Chatur glanced at Malak. "Oh yeah. Ah—"

"Tom sent us here to get it from you," said Malak, glancing guiltily at Chatur.

"That's right," Chatur said. "The information about—ah—what was it again?"

"About how the wizards and star beings defeated the creatures!" snapped the ghost. Grumbling and angry shushing sounded throughout the library.

Chatur frowned. "Why would they wanna know—"

Malak elbowed his friend in the ribs.

"Yeah," said Malak. "That's what they said you'd tell us." Malak leaned on the desk. "Whadja find out?"

The ghost glared at Malak's arm. Malak removed his arm and stood up. He and Chatur stared up expectantly at the spirit.

The Librarian shook his head. "I suppose you're all I've got. Listen carefully, it is of the utmost importance that you remember my words exactly..."

Moments later, the pair burst from the library.

"We're on a mission!" shouted Chatur. The pair bolted down the Library steps, taking them two at a time.

"I know. I was there!" said Malak.

"When?"

"Just now!"

"Where?" Chatur scrunched up his face. "In the library?"

"Yes, you dolt! When the ghost told us that thing."

"Oh right," Chatur said. "We gotta find Tom and the others." Chatur continued down the steps, Malak in hot pursuit.

Chatur screeched to a halt. "Where ya think they are?"

Malak scratched his head. "The ghost said they went ta meet Devraj."

"The castle! When we finds em, I gets to tell em." Chatur turned to go. Malak grabbed Chatur's arm and spun him back around.

"No," said Malak. "The ghost told me."

Chatur glared at him.

Malak snorted. "They'd never listen to ya, anyway. Not after the way ya screwed things up last time."

"I screwed things up? You was the one what blew up the star craft!"

"Did not."

"Did too!" Chatur locked his arm round Malak's neck and threw him to the cobblestone street. Malak grabbed Chatur's thumb and jerked back hard.

"Ouch!" yelled Chatur.

"Boys," came a female voice.

Without releasing their grips, the two stared up at the tall figure standing over them. It was a clear night, with light from the Ring of Turin casting its soft glow around them. Even so, it was difficult to see who spoke.

"Have you seen my son, Tom?"

"Oh, hello Tom's mom," gasped Malak, Chatur's arm still tight around his throat.

"My name's Juanita."

"Juanita," said Malak. He glared at Chatur. "Leggo a my throat!"

"Leggo a my thumb!"

"Could you two stop fighting long enough to answer my question?"

Releasing each other, the two jumped up and dusted themselves off.

"Have you seen Tom? It's important."

"No," said Chatur.

"She asked me!" shouted Malak.

"Did not!" Chatur faced Juanita. "Besides, 'twas a general question, right? 'Tweren't specifically aimed at my lame brained friend here."

Malak's nostrils flared.

Juanita tried a third time, "Do you know where he is?"

"The ghost said they left." Malak motioned to the library.

"Where do you think they might've gone?" quickly adding, "I believe it's Chatur's turn."

Chatur grinned. "They left Elfhaven to go warn the king."

"What?"

"Yeah," added Malak. "Somethin' 'bout Naagesh, a portal, creatures." He shrugged. "Usual stuff."

Chatur nodded solemnly.

Juanita ran off toward the castle.

"She's sure in a hurry," remarked Malak.

"Not much fer conversation," agreed Chatur. "Why d'ya tell her they left ta warn the king? We don't know that."

Still watching Juanita's retreating form, Malak said, "Once they learned Naagesh's plans, whaddya think they'd do?"

"Go warn the king!"

Malak whacked the back of his friend's head. "Exactly!" He sighed. "Wish we was goin' with em."

"Be fun to see the creatures," agreed Malak. "From a distance, a course!"

Chatur glanced wistfully at his friend. "So?"

Both faces split into huge grins.

"So, we better hurry if we're gonna catch em."

# A good plan

Once they left the library, they split up. Avani and Kiran headed home to make ready for their meeting. Tom and Goban went to meet Devraj at the castle and gather supplies.

While there, Goban borrowed a small fur covered knapsack and stuffed provisions in it, including food, a coil of rope, some more food, a knife, and yet more food, etc. Tom handed Goban the book from the library he was still carrying and Goban stuffed it in his backpack, as well.

Shortly afterwards, everyone met as planned at Avani and Kiran's grandparent's house.

"Would you like a tart, Tom?" Nadda held a tray of steaming morsels. They gave off a tangy, slightly '*soured*' fragrance that smelled suspiciously like the slithertoad pastries which nearly made Tom barf last time he tried one.

"Nah, I'm good."

Looking disappointed, Nadda moved on to Goban, who's eyes lit up. When Nadda finished offering them around, Goban having taken a second tart, '*for later,*' pulled off his knapsack and reached inside, searching for something to wrap the tart in.

Nadda addressed his wife, "Come honey. Let's leave the children to discuss their plans to *save the world*, shall we?"

She frowned. "Can't we stay? I'm sure they won't mind us old folk listening in on their plans." Nanni shot the kids a hopeful smile. They just stared at her.

Nadda gently tugged her arm. Nanni's shoulders slumped a tad, but she followed him.

"Hey!" Goban pulled an ancient, leather-bound book from his knapsack. "Look what we found." As he did, the torn piece of paper fluttered to the floor.

"What is it?" asked Avani.

"The book from the Library!" said Tom. "I almost forgot."

Goban handed Avani the book, then picked up the scrap of page and stuffed it back in his knapsack.

Avani ran her fingers across the ancient book's cover, then opened it.

"There's a secret hiding place inside," Goban pointed out.

"I see," she said, thumbing through it.

Halfway to the kitchen, Nanni stopped and turned back. "What do you have there?"

Avani closed the book and read the cover. "It's titled '*The Lost Realm*'. It was written by someone named—" She squinted. "—Kila Brasscouldron."

Nanni glanced at her husband. "Isn't that the explorer who—"

Nadda chuckled. "Claimed he'd found a lost world." He nudged her gently toward the kitchen.

"The gentleman chronicled his subterranean adventures." Nanni gestured to the book. "That must be it."

Kiran scrunched up his face. "Subterny?"

"Subterranean," Nadda corrected. "Means underground, dear."

Avani held the book out to her. Nanni's eyes lit up. She hurried over and reverently took the text from her granddaughter and began thumbing through it.

"The explorer kept babbling on about hovering stones and ruins of some lost civilization," Nanni said.

Nadda chuckled again. "Buried in a tropical paradise beneath the Plains of Illusion, no less." Nadda stretched out his arm, beckoning for his wife's hand.

"May we stop this useless babble about fairy tales and move on?" snapped Devraj. "Time is not our ally!"

Everyone stared at him.

"What?" he said.

Nadda cleared his throat. "Sorry to have delayed you, your highness." He bowed, then made eye contact with his wife. Nanni started to hand Avani the book. "Keep it," Avani said. Nanni smiled, and the two elderly elves sauntered off into the kitchen.

Avani waited till the kitchen door stopped swinging. "Devraj! That was rude!"

He glanced around. Everyone kept staring at him.

"We have to come up with a plan," he insisted.

Avani continued to glare.

Devraj shifted in his seat. "I shall take our fastest steed. Hopefully, I can overtake Father before he reaches the ferry landing."

"No need for that," said Tom.

The prince faced him. "What do you propose?"

"Like Kiran said. Just tell Sanuu to go warn the king."

123

"Sanuu left with my father."

"So—Tappus then."

"Tappus is no longer here either."

"What? Your dad took them both? Who's manning the fort?" Tom paused. "Did he leave you in charge?"

Devraj's jaw tightened.

"After meeting with the Guardian," The prince continued gruffly, "I did just that. I went to the castle to speak with Tappus, but he had already left in search of Father."

"But—" Tom sounded confused. "Tappus didn't know about the portal—or the remote. Why would he go?"

"It seems Chatur and Malak told your mother we had already left to warn the king."

"Chatur and Malak?" Tom frowned. "Why would they—*wait*—what did you say?"

"Chatur and Malak told your mother that—"

"Mom's here?" Tom leapt up. "The portal! It must've still been open… Oh no! We've gotta stop her. She doesn't know about the creatures!"

Devraj stood. "For once we are in agreement. We must warn Father."

"And my dad." Goban choked down the rest of his third pastry.

"Hey, what about yer wedding?" asked Tom.

Devraj glanced at Avani. "That is not for three solar cycles. We will catch Father by nightfall and be back here by midday tomorrow." He headed for the door. "Meet me at the stables in ten myntars."

Kiran leaped up. "I'm going."

"You're staying," Avani ordered.

On his way to the door, Tom winked at Kiran, then to Avani said, "Not gonna happen."

"Might as well let yer brother come," agreed Goban. "Better'n havin' him sneak along after, like usual."

# Horses?

Tom and his friends stood just inside the royal stables. Fragrant odors of fresh-baked bread and sharp cheese wafted from the knapsack on Goban's back. The handle of the dwarf's beloved axe, Aileen, poked up above one shoulder. Avani's satchel bulged with a fresh crop of magic crystals. The hilt of Devraj's gold and jewel-encrusted sword protruded from its scabbard, hanging loosely at his side.

Tom smiled, feeling the warm firmness of his adventurers' belt. The prince headed toward the stalls. Tom's smile dropped. "Horses? No way."

"Why else would we meet at the stables?" Devraj stopped at the first stall. "Besides, catching up with Tappus and your mother was your idea," The prince reminded him. "They left on horseback. We would never catch them on foot."

Devraj worked the stall's lock: a complex series of iron rods, gears, and levers. After unlocking the first, he moved on, unlocking five stalls.

Avani helped the prince strap bridles to the horse's heads, inserting the iron bits into their mouths, then led the horses from their stalls, handing a set of reins to Goban and Tom. Kiran grabbed the last horse's reins, but Avani didn't let go. Kiran shot his sister a fake smile. She released his reins.

Devraj jerked upward, tightening the girth strap and securing the saddle onto his horse. The others did likewise.

Tom didn't look well.

Goban leaned in close and whispered, "Never ridden afore?" The dwarf motioned toward the massive beast towering above Tom. Steam jetted from the horse's nostrils. It pawed the ground and snorted. Bending its long neck toward Tom, the beast's moist warm breath blew in Tom's face.

Tom stepped back, his voice cracking, "I'm from Chicago. Closest thing to a horse I've ever ridden was a mechanical bull at a western restaurant. It was my birthday. The waitress made me sit on it. I threw up before the bull even moved!"

Goban slapped Tom hard on his back. Tom coughed.

"Don't worry," the dwarf assured him. "It's easy. Just watch me. Do what I do." Goban's face brightened. "Gotta be easier 'n riding a dragon, right?"

Tom gazed up into the animal's four large dark eyes, two on either side of its massive head. The horse's mane flew as it shook its head, then swiveled its ears forward to regard Tom. Impatient to be off, the horse flared its four nostrils, lowered its head and butted Tom.

Tom nearly puked.


# A bad plan

Chatur and Malak sprinted down the street. As they rounded the last corner, the castle came into view, two blocks ahead.

Five figures rode through the castle gate and guided their horses toward the north exit of the shield wall. Behind them, a large furry animal loped along beside a whining metal contraption.

"They haven't left yet," said Chatur.

Malak jumped and waved his arms. "Hey guys, wait up! Take us with ya!"

"Yeah!" shouted Chatur. "We gots important information!"

The group passed through the north gate without looking back.

"They didn't hear us," said Chatur.

"Too far away."

"Whadda we do now?" Chatur asked.

"They gots horses. We needs horses." Malak ran off, Chatur at his heels. Once through the castle gate, the pair headed for the stables.

On their way there, a palace guard burst from the castle and ran down the steps in hot pursuit of a small, dark critter.

The animal zigged and zagged across the courtyard.

Malak yanked open the stable door. "Quick. Afore the guard sees us." He stepped in.

"I ain't goin' in there. It's dark!" Malak's arm reached through the doorway and yanked Chatur inside. Shouts and running footsteps grew louder.

"The guard's coming," whispered Chatur.

They heard a rustle of tiny feet. "Something just brushed my leg!" Malak whapped the back of Chatur's head. "Ya didn't close the door!"

"Ya didn't tell me to."

"I shouldn't hafta tell ya everything."

"Shush!" whispered Chatur. "The guard!"

"I knows yous in there," came a firm voice from just outside. "Come out ya little vermin."

"Does he mean us?"

"No, you idiot," Malak hissed, "He means the gremlin. Quick. Hide."

"Hide? Where?"

Malak didn't answer.

Chatur flopped onto his belly. The damp, dirt floor lay littered with manure covered straw. Chatur wrinkled his nose and crawled under a gate into a stall and over to the back wall.

Chatur wasn't the only occupant of the stall, however. A tall, muscular horse swiveled its broad neck to regard Chatur. The steed snorted.

Chatur smiled. "Hi!" The horse shook its head and turned away.

"Malak?" whispered Chatur. "Malak, you there?" The stable's back door squeaked open. "Malak, don't leave me!"

The back door creaked closed as the front door burst open. Heavy boots scrapped across the floor, moving closer.

"Stop hiding! You don'ts wanna make me mad."

The gremlin scampered into the same stall as Chatur. The two stared at each other in shock. The wily critter winked at Chatur, lay down and madly tossed straw all over itself. Chatur took the hint and did the same.

"I'll go easy on ye," assured the guard. "If'n ya turns yerself in." *Clink. Clank.* The guard fumbled with a stall's lock down the row. "Might even release ya in the forest, stead a makin' gremlin jerky." The guard chuckled. "I do so love gremlin jerky."

Two stalls over, a gate creaked open, and a horse whinnied. *Twang, twang, twang,* came the sound of a pitchfork being thrust into a pile of straw. The gate slammed and was re-locked. The next stall's gate opened. More *twangs*. The gate slammed shut.

Chatur and the gremlin stared at each other through the straw.

"Hope ya kin use some ventilation," said the guard. "This fork's gonna leave a nasty mark."

The lock on their stall started rattling. The guard pushed on the gate, but it didn't budge. "Dang it all!" The guard fiddled with the lock again. This time it released, *click.* Straw flew as the gremlin scampered into the next stall. Chatur's gate swung open. The guard raised his pitchfork.

"If you're looking for the gremlin," came Malak's voice from out front. The guard turned.

"Just saw one run from the stables and into the castle. Probly headed fer the king's chambers. Ya kin catch it if yer quick."

The pitchfork clattered to the ground. The guard locked the gate and ran from the stable. The sound of running boots slapping against cobblestones grew faint.

A door creaked. "Chatur?" whispered Malak. "Come on! We gotsta get horses before the guard comes back."

Chatur poked his head out from under the stall along with a fury face from the stall beside him.

Malak snorted. "There really was a gremlin? Thought I made that part up."

Chatur crawled out, stood and dusted straw from his tunic. "Whaddya think the guard was chasin?"

"You don't smell so good." Malak wrinkled up his nose.

Chatur glared at him. "It's not jus any gremlin though. It's the same one what helped unlock Avani's cube."

"Hodja know?"

"That white patch on its head."

Malak stared at the critter. "Anyway, we gotta go." He grabbed a gate and yanked. "It's locked." He tried another. His shoulders slumped.

"The guard re-locked em," said Chatur.

"Without horses, we'll never catch em."

"We hafta," Chatur said. "We're on a mission, remember?"

Malak sighed. "A critical mission."

"Our friends need us."

"We've gotta tell em what the Librarian told us."

"Else they don't stand a chance."

"Besides, it's our duty as friends." Malak reasoned.

"It's in the friend handbook," agreed Chatur.

"If we hurry, we can catch em before they reach the Pillars."

"And save the day!"

"Probably receive medals." The two grinned, nodding like bobble-heads.

Together they grabbed a gate and yanked. Their grins faded. The gates were still locked.

"We still need horses." Malak looked wistfully at the complicated locking mechanism. "If only we was smart enough to pick the locks."

Chatur slapped his forehead. "Hey, didn't Avani say they saved the gremlin from the palace guards?"

"Yeah. So?"

"Member why the guards was chasing it?"

"A course. It picked the locks and let the king's horses loose."

Their gaze dropped.

The gremlin grinned.

# Naagesh

Naagesh stepped from the ferry onto the wide sandy beach and faced Bellchar the troll and Dumerre the ogre. "Pull the raft onto the bank," the wizard ordered and strode off.

Bellchar grabbed hold of the ferry's rope and then looked at Dumerre.

"What?" said the ogre.

"Wizard say—pull boat up."

Dumerre pretended to study the cuticles of his fat, stubby fingers. "So?"

"So help me!"

"Trolls stronger 'n ogres." Dumerre grinned. "Maybe da goblins'll help ya."

Bellchar glanced at the scrawny beasts milling about. Bellchar snarled at Dumerre and yanked the rope. The ferry didn't budge. Tugging harder, sand hissed beneath the ferry's log hull as it grudgingly slid up the bank.

Across the beach at the edge of a sparse, stunted tree forest, Naagesh studied the signpost's three gray, cracked and weathered signs. The one on the left pointed up the rocky river trail. The other two marked desolate paths, both heavily overgrown with vines and brush.

Naagesh aimed his finger at the right-hand sign. Magic lanced out, and the sign started glowing. The cracks repaired themselves and the words; long decayed and nearly unreadable, became clear.

Waving his hand at the trail on the right, the vines, brush and grass burst into flames. Just as quickly, the fire snuffed out, leaving only a dusting of gray ash and the smell of burnt tar.

Thudding, plodding footsteps brought the wizard around.

"Bellchar. Dumerre," shouted Naagesh.

"We did as you said," Dumerre responded. "Boat safe now." He grinned at Bellchar.

"Why you do dat?" Bellchar gestured at the sign and the trail. "Make it easy for dem ta follow."

"Exactly," Naagesh confirmed. "Wouldn't want Larraj and King Dakshi to get lost. The Plains of Illusion might kill them!"

Dumerre glanced at Bellchar uncertainly.

"Don't tax your feeble brains," Naagesh began. "I've a mission for you two. I want you to hide over there." He pointed to the woods beyond the beach and mumbled an incantation. The trees sparkled for an instant. "I cast a cloaking spell. As long as you hide there, no one can see or hear you no matter what you say or do, but *only* if you stay there. Understand?"

Bellchar nodded.

"Good. King Dakshi should arrive at dusk, cross the river via the ferry and make camp here for the night. In the morning, he'll follow the path on the right. Let them pass, and all his elven soldiers.

"Oh. And one more thing. Phawta and the troll army will be here by midday, long after the king's party has left. Have him wait here for me. If—by some slim chance King Dakshi manages to escape my trap, he'll show up here. If so, have Phawta capture and hold him till I return. But under no circumstances is the king to be killed. Got that?"

"If king follow," said Dumerre. "You need our help to fight soldiers."

Bellchar glanced at the hissing, squabbling goblins. "Goblins no use 'gainst soldiers."

"I have a *surprise* for Larraj and the king. Something far more dangerous than goblins, I assure you."


## King Dakshi

"The rain has stopped," King Dakshi began, "Once we cross the river we shall make camp for the night."

"Your plan is sound," said King Abban. "There's yet enough light and it'll give us a head start, come morning."

"The ferry's on the other bank." Sanuu signaled, and soldiers grabbed the rope and began pulling the raft across.

King Dakshi gazed at the far shore. "Naagesh already crossed."

"The wizard's footprints end here," agreed the dwarf.

"He's not even trying to hide his tracks," Sanuu said. "He's only got one troll, one ogre and half a dozen goblins."

"Confirming Larraj's seeker's image." King Dakshi faced the wizard.

Larraj answered their implied question, "Naagesh wants us to follow him."

"Is he insane?" Sanuu began. "He must've known we'd bring soldiers."

"He doesn't know we've a seeker," King Abban reasoned. "Thus he doesn't realize we know the strength of his forces."

"Perhaps he believes his new dark magical powers are enough to protect him," Sanuu suggested.

"Perhaps," said Larraj.

Soldiers groaned, dragging the heavy ferry up the bank.

"The river's nearly at flood stage," Sanuu pointed out. "Flowing this fast, the water's turbulent. With this many troops, horses and supplies, it'll take three trips."

"Then you'd best get on with it."

Sanuu bowed to King Dakshi and signaled his soldiers.

The kings dismounted.

As they waited, King Dakshi studied the ferry. The raft consisted of a wide platform of moss-covered logs lashed together with ropes. A stout rope, as thick as an elf's forearm, crossed the wide expanse of the river. Tied firmly to trees on both shores, the rope passed through circular metal guides mounted atop metal poles secured at each end of the raft. Two smaller ropes led from the raft, one to each shore. These ropes allowed someone to retrieve the ferry when it rested on the opposite shore.

The king had ordered the ferry built many yara ago. The job had been no small effort, due to the swiftness and breadth of the river at this point on its lengthy journey from its glacier fed headwaters high in the Icebain and Tontiel Mountains.

Dakshi's gaze shifted upriver. Not far upstream, two mighty rivers merged, doubling the river's size and flow, making it even more treacherous.

Facing downriver, the king scanned the river's path as it flowed past the Deathly Bog to the south, meandered through the marshy swamp lands to the west and eventually emptied into Lake Elsar. Today, however, the lake lay hidden, blanketed by fog.

King Abban joined his longtime friend, gazing at the distant fog. "The mist hides the beauty of the lake and the isle of the lake elves. How's King Bharat doing? Feisty as ever?"

"I have not seen my cousin in nearly a yara. But I hear it has been a banner year for the lake elves, their boats overflowing with fish on their return."

"And ale casks drained, I'll wager," reasoned Abban.

King Dakshi chuckled. "Just so."

Behind them, horses whinnied. The pair glanced back.

Two guards strained, pulling the main rope, while two others stabbed long poles into the river bottom and pushed. The ferry sluggishly glided out into the raging current, horses pawing and snorting their displeasure.

* * *

"Look," spat Dumerre. "Da elven king."

"Wizard say he'd come," said Bellchar. The pair crouched in the trees where the wizard cast his spell of concealment.

When the first group of elven soldiers arrived, they fanned out and searched the area, making sure it was safe for the king.

A guard headed straight for their hiding place. When the elf came within five paces, Dumerre drew his rusty, bone-handled dagger. Bellchar grabbed his arm. Dumerre glared at him. Bellchar shook his head no. Dumerre stomped on the troll's foot. Bellchar cried out. The two spun to face the elf. But the guard just walked away.

"Wizard say dey no kin hear or see us," said Dumerre.

"Good." Bellchar punched him.

* * *

The two kings crossed on the second trip. They stood beside each other, gazing at the frigid waters rushing past.

"May I speak in confidence, old friend?" asked Dakshi.

King Abban's face broke into a familiar broad smile. "Of course. When have we not spoken such? We're close as brothers. Closer'n most, in fact."

Dakshi glanced at his soldiers standing behind them, then motioned to his friend. The two walked to a spot where no one else stood.

King Abban rubbed his thick beard and glanced back. "Must a sensitive matter be, if ye can't speak freely amongst yer own guards."

King Dakshi sighed.

"What is it, my friend? What troubles you this fine eve? Not that crazed wizard Naagesh, surely?" King Abban drummed his stout fingers on his axe handle. "That upstart's of no concern. We've dealt with the likes of him before."

Dakshi grinned. "We have at that, my friend. We have at that."

"If not the wizard, then what?"

"It's my son. You heard him in council. Devraj is eager to take the reins from my dead hands."

The dwarf king snorted. "I've the opposite problem. My son Goban wants nothing to do with matters of State. All he wants ta do, is spend time with his uncle Zanda, the Mastersmith, working on whimsical gadgets."

"Plans the Earth boy Thomas Holland gave him?"

"Aye—" Abban nodded. "—the boy from the Prophecy. Remarkable lad."

"He is at that." Dakshi paused. "But surely Goban does more than that?"

The dwarf king grinned. "He does. The lad knows how to enjoy a good party."

King Dakshi matched his grin. "Then he takes after his father, after all." Dakshi slapped the dwarf's shoulder.

King Abban chuckled. "But what of your son, Devraj?" Abban's look hardened and his tone grew sober, "Surely you don't believe he'd try 'n kill his own father, to seize the throne?"

"Of course not."

"What then?"

Dakshi sighed. "He is far too headstrong. He loses his temper at the slightest challenge to his authority."

"Even from you?"

"Especially from me."

The dwarf king pursed his lips. "We've had this conversation before, remember? A yara ago. Give the lad time."

Dakshi gazed at the turbulent waters. "Much liquid has flowed down the stream, since then."

"And ale down our gullets," King Abban winked.

King Dakshi smiled sadly. "I fear there may not be time to give Devraj, my friend. I am old. And Devraj is no longer a boy."

"Don't be absurd, you're but a pup! Barely cresting a hundred. You've at least fifty good yaras left in dem bones."

Dakshi snorted. "Hope you are right." He paused, his voice becoming deathly serious, "If Devraj were to become king now…"

The pair watched the sandy beach grow nearer in silence.


## Way behind


Tom's knuckles turned white from gripping the reins so tightly, and they'd only just passed the shield wall. Ahead, Goban rode beside Devraj and Avani. The dwarf glanced back at Tom and grinned.

Tom swiveled slowly and gazed back. Kiran seemed comfortable enough riding. Max shuffled along beside Kiran. Chloe chugged along behind, her motors whirring softly.

Tom swiveled back. "Something feels wrong."

"You have a death grip on the reins," Devraj shouted back. "Loosen up. The horse senses your fear."

"I am afraid of the horse," said Tom. "But it's not that."

Avani's saddle creaked as she twisted to look back. "It's the barrier. It's missing."

This was the spot, just beyond the shield wall, where they normally felt the comforting tingle of blue lightning. Yet today, the barrier's protective field was eerily absent...

The barrier protected Elfhaven from anything dangerous: trolls, ogres, zhanderbeasts, mist wraiths, and all manner of frightening creatures. Or it had—until Naagesh switched it off.

Tom gritted his teeth. Adding to the tension, the forest seemed unusually silent. The only sounds being their voices and the hollow plopping of the horse's hooves on the muddy trail.

Goban slowed, waiting for Tom to catch up. Goban lowered his voice, "How ya doin?"

Sweat dripped from Tom's face. "Been better." He sat bolt upright, ridged. Each step the horse took nearly launched him from the saddle.

"Devraj's right, yer too stiff. Relax. Ya wanna stay upright but give yer back a slight arch. Curved, like that *spring* gadget ya told me about. Watch me."

Tom twisted ever-so-slightly. Goban relaxed, exaggerating the shock-absorber effect of his lower back. Goban's head barely bobbed as his horse clopped along.

Tom tried to relax.

"Better!" said Goban. "Now release yer death-grip on the reins."

Tom's hands slowly uncoiled. His fingers tingled from the blood flowing back into them.

Devraj called from up ahead. "If we are to catch them, we must pick up speed." He gestured to Chloe and Max. "Can your pets keep up?"

"Think so. Not sure I can."

The prince dug in his heels and his horse galloped off.

Panic filled Tom's eyes.

"No worries," Goban assured him. "We'll start with a trot. Like this." Goban nudged the horse's flank with his heels and his horse began to trot, bouncing him up a bit with each step. He twisted around. "Try it!"

With trembling hands, Tom flicked the reins. Nothing happened.

"No. Not the reins," Goban instructed. "Squeeze yer legs."

Tom squeezed. His horse started prancing instead of trotting. This nearly sent Tom bouncing off the horse's rump.

"Squeeze harder," urged Goban. "Dig yer heels in."

Tom drew in another breath and dug in his heels. The horse lowered its head slightly and took off in a smooth gait, quickly passing Goban.

Goban's eyes lit up. Goban caught up with Tom. "You got er! Jus relax a tad. That's it! Yer a natural."

Tom gave Goban an uneasy smile, then glanced over his shoulder. Max bounded along beside Kiran, slobber flying from his open mouth. The whine from Chloe's motors increased, but she too had no trouble keeping up.

Tom turned back. The others were nowhere in sight.

"Next lesson," said Goban. "I'll teach ya how ta gallop."

Tom looked like he might explode.

# The king's party

"I feel ill at ease," began King Dakshi. "I have felt so, ever since we crossed the river. Like we are being watched."

"I sense it too," Larraj agreed.

The pair stood across the beach at the ferry crossing, studying the three trailhead signs. Two were cracked, weathered and hard to read. One sign pointed east up the boulder-strewn riverbank trail. The second led into Southern Plains of Illusion. The third, easier to read sign, marked the western trail leading into the Deathly Bog.

Hissing footsteps, skidding through sand, caused them to turn.

"Lieutenant Sanuu," said the king.

"My Lord. The troops are nearly ready."

King Dakshi watched as soldiers broke camp, scurrying about dowsing the morning cooking fires and lashing gear to horses. "Very well."

"Are we ready to depart, sire?"

King Dakshi glanced at the signpost, then asked Larraj, "Are you certain Naagesh took the right-hand trail?"

Larraj studied the sandy ground. "The footprints lead into the Bog."

Dakshi commented, "Again, Naagesh did not even try to hide their passing."

Larraj gazed thoughtfully ahead. "As I predicted. He wants us to follow him."

"Naagesh plans an ambush?"

"I sense it's more complicated than that." Larraj drew back his sleeve and uttered the seeker's invocation. "Show us Naagesh." The image of the evil wizard appeared, hovering in the air above Larraj's arm. Naagesh walked along a narrow marshy path, a half dozen goblins scrambling behind.

"There are his goblins," stated the king. "But where are the troll and ogre?"

"Pull up," commanded Larraj. The view rose above, showing a sparse forest of scraggly, nearly dead trees covered with long strands of thick gray moss. A thin ribbon trail wound back from the wizard's current position, making several twists, loops and switchbacks, until the tiny trail merged with a wider trail. As the image continued to zoom out, they saw it eventually end at the ferry landing where a group of figures stood gazing down the Bog trail."

Sanuu waved. His image in the seeker's view waved back. Larraj blinked, and the image withdrew.

"Naagesh no longer has the troll and ogre with him," remarked King Dakshi. "That should make it easier to capture him."

"Yes," Larraj agreed. "And we have confirmed the path Naagesh took."

"The Bog it is," said the king.

## Juanita and Tappus

Tappus stopped his horse at the junction of another trail. A steep, rocky path led into the mountains to their left. The main trail continued on. "Why are we stopping?" asked Juanita.

Tappus motioned ahead. Fifty feet away stood a massive rift in the ground. Juanita stood in her stirrups. Cliffs on either side of the canyon dropped away, disappearing into shadow below. The canyon stretched at least a mile ahead and was half that in width. She sat back down. "What is it?"

"The Pillars of the Giants." Tappus dismounted, tossed the reins over his horse's head and caught them. "The Icebain river carved this canyon half a million yaras ago. Since then, the river changed course, leaving a dry canyon." Tappus led his horse onward. "We must walk through. It's rocky and uneven. Too dark to ride."

Juanita dismounted. "Why's it called The Pillars of the Giants?"

He smiled. "You'll see. When we reach the other side, we'll mount up again. From there, it's but a short ride to the ferry crossing. Hopefully, the king will have camped there for the night."

Tappus scanned the sky. The western horizon began to lighten. "It'll be daylight soon. We must hurry."

Juanita started walking, but a flash of light to her left brought her up short. She squinted. Snapping, thrashing sounds came from the same direction. "What's that?"

Tappus glanced over his shoulder. "Come. We'll be safe inside the Pillars."

"Safe from what?"

* * *

The first rays of the morning sunlight shone through Tontiel Pass, a narrow gap between the Icebain and Tontiel mountain ranges to the east, casting long eerie shadows through the forest. With the increased light, Tom could just make out the outlines of three riders sitting atop their horses, waiting for him and Goban.

As they approached, Tom meekly tugged on his horse's reins. Nothing happened. He stared at Goban in panic.

"Like this." Goban leaned back and pulled firmly on his reins. His horse clomped to a stop.

Tom pulled a tad harder. His horse slowed but kept galloping. Jerking back on the reins, the horse skidded to a stop, nearly throwing Tom over its head.

The horse twisted its neck and looked at Tom as if to say, "Is this your first time riding a horse?"

"Well. Yes, actually," Tom said. "It is."

The horse snorted indignantly.

Goban asked, "Why'd we stop?"

"We're at the Pillars of the Giants." Avani gestured to a rift ahead. To their left, a steep trail led up to a ridge overlooking the canyon.

Prince Devraj dismounted. "It is dark and rocky inside. We must lead the horses through the canyon." The others climbed off their horses.

There was a flash off to their left. Another flash, this time accompanied by thrashing sounds and snapping branches followed by a loud hissing.

"Quick!" shouted Goban. "Into the Pillars!"

"What is it?" cried Tom.

The thrashing grew louder.

"Too late," whispered Devraj. "Hide in the woods! Now!"

Everyone led their horses into the dense forest and stopped. Two more flashes and all noise suddenly stopped. Tom held his breath, though he wasn't sure why.

"I think it's gone," said Kiran.

Tom whispered, "What's gone?"

"Shush!" hissed Avani. "Listen." She pushed aside a branch and peered into a small clearing. Tom and Goban leaned over her shoulder. Light flared, and an enormous spider suddenly materialized in the clearing. Another flash and a second spider appeared. Lowering its bulbous body slightly, the first hissed at the newcomer.

Nearly ten feet tall, the arachnids were black and hairless. Long spindly legs sporting hooked horns jutted out above each leg joint. Rows of curved pincers, surrounding their mouths, clacked, snapping at each other.

"You got giant spiders here?" whispered Tom. *Flash, flash*. The second spider disappeared, then reappeared, closer to its rival, hissing loudly, answering the other's challenge.

"Giant—magical spiders," corrected Avani.

Tom's voice cracked, "You got giant magical spiders here?"

"They're only giant during mating season," Goban explained.

"What?" Tom wrinkled his forehead in disgust. "Those monsters mate?"

Goban leaned close. "How'd ya think little monsters were made?" Kiran chuckled.

"Hush you three," Avani scolded, but her tone quickly changed to one of fascination, "It's an amazing courtship ritual, actually."

"What?" said Tom. "No! Those two are gonna—"

Her attention still fixed on the spiders, Avani nodded.

"Are they dangerous?"

"Not while they're distracted with mating," she explained. "Unless of

141

course, you get in their way."

"And after they're done—mating?"

"Then they're dangerous."

"And hungry." Kiran made a chomping noise.

"Shush!" hissed Avani.

One spider scrapped its forelegs in the dirt several times. The two behemoths circled each other, tall, thin legs jerking up and stabbing down, sending clods of soil flying.

One of them reared up on its back four legs, hissed and pounced. *Flash*, the second spider disappeared, and the first came crashing down, pincers snapping—on nothing. The spider screamed in frustration.

*Flash*. The forest fell silent.

The silence lingered. "I think they have gone," said Devraj, heading back for the trail.

"Wait," whispered Goban. "I hear something."

The prince froze.

"Doesn't sound like spiders," said Avani.

Devraj glanced at Goban. "Horses?"

Goban listened intently. "Two riders. Approaching fast."

"From the north," agreed Avani.

"Elfhaven's in that direction. If they're from Elfhaven—" Tom started back. "—then they must be good guys."

Another flash.

Goban grabbed Tom's arm. A faint rustling came from directly behind them. They slowly turned. A twig snapped. There came a second flash. Meanwhile, the sound of slapping hooves grew louder.

Devraj pushed aside a branch and peered through the trees.

Two large, multi-faceted eyes stared back at him. The spider opened its mucus-covered pincers.

The prince released the branch, slapping the spider in the face. Devraj drew his sword.

The horses thundered past. The spider hissed. Tree limbs snapped. The ground shuddered.

Tom stepped back and bumped into his horse. The horse whinnied. Tom winced. Devraj glared at him.

The thrashing sounds faded away. "It's OK," whispered Goban. "The spiders're following the riders."

"I think it was Malak and Chatur," Kiran said.

"Oh no!" cried Tom. "We gotta warn em!" He started forward again. Goban grabbed his arm.

"Chatur! Malak!" shouted Avani. "Look—" Devraj slapped his hand across her mouth. She struggled to break free.

They heard a high-pitched screech. Then silence.

Devraj removed his hand. "The spiders got them."

Avani stared at him in horror.

He met her gaze coolly. "It was them or us."

\* \* \*

Chatur and Malak stopped just short of the trail that wound down into the Pillars.

"What's that sound?" Chatur twisted in his saddle. Behind them, branches snapped. Something big stormed through the forest, heading straight for them. There was a flash, a series of hisses, a blood-curdling scream. Then silence.

"What was that?" Chatur repeated.

Malak shrugged, then got off his horse. "Probably, just the wind." Tugging on the reins, he began leading his horse down the steep, narrow trail into the canyon.

"The wind?" Chatur snorted. "That's ridiculous!"

"Yer right," admitted Malak. "Probably just a giant spider come ta eat ya."

"I ain't no fool," said Chatur. "Yer jus tryin' ta scare me."

# Juanita

Unbeknownst to either, Juanita and Tappus exited the canyon on the south side as Chatur and Malak entered from the north.

Gurgling sounds of rushing water signaled the Icebain River flowed nearby.

In the deep canyon, it was still dark, but outside, the sun's rays had already scaled the craggy peaks of the Tontiel Mountains, lighting the treetops overhead.

"Odd looking rock formations back there," said Juanita.

"The Pillars?"

Juanita nodded. "Similar to Bryce Canyon back on Earth. Only—"

Tappus smiled. "Only what?"

"Why are you smiling? You know something of the geology of those formations?"

Tappus lip curled up playfully.

"Tell me."

"Wanna hear your theory first."

"Well." she pursed her lips. "Obviously, the river's erosion process formed the canyon, as you alluded to earlier."

"Go on."

"There must have been an intrusion of some harder mineral which flowed into cracks in the softer stone when they were forming. The harder mineral resisted erosion better than the surrounding, softer material; leaving the pillars. I suppose elf or dwarf artists must've carved them into statues, correct?"

Tappus grinned. "Not even close."

Ten minutes later, they rode from the dank, dark forest into a wide clearing. Juanita felt the warmth from the sun-warmed rocks and the sun's rays itself. She unzipped her parka.

They drew their horses to a stop and dismounted. At their feet, water lapped against the western shore of the Icebain river.

"I had hoped we'd have caught up with the king here," said Tappus. Across the river, the beach stood deserted. "I would've expected the king to make camp here or on the southern shore."

"How do we get across?" she asked.

Tappus grabbed a rope and started pulling. "Help me retrieve the ferry."


## Pillars of the Giants


Devraj was right. Tom hadn't seen or heard any more giant spiders since they'd entered the Pillars. That was almost an hour ago. They were at the canyon's widest point, about halfway through.

Still on foot and leading their horses, Kiran, Max and Chloe led the way. Goban, Avani, and Tom were next, with Devraj taking rearguard. The sun had risen high enough to allow narrow beams of light to penetrate the canyon, illuminating the nearest statues with perhaps a hundred more, mostly in shadow, scattered to either side.

Tom stopped in his tracks at the sight of the enormous statues. Though weather-beaten and chipped in places, a forest of redwood sized, carved stone statues towered above them. They looked similar to trolls except with flatter noses and faces with a square jaw and a single gigantic eye in the center of their forehead. But these beasts were far taller than trolls. Stouter too, and with bigger muscles.

Tom shuddered. He felt like they were watching him.

Impulsively, Tom stuck out his arm and slid his hand across the cool stone of a statue's muscular ankle. "Who carved these?" he asked Goban. "The sculptor must've been a master! A da Vinci or Michael Angelo." Tom stopped. "There's gotta be a least fifty of em. And each one's different. Amazing!"

"Eighty-two," replied Goban.

"Keep moving," hissed Devraj.

Still holding the reins, Tom resumed walking, and his horse resumed following. Tom hurried up beside Goban and Avani. "The expressions on their faces," he began, "even the fingers and toes look so real!"

Avani giggled.

"Weren't made by sculptors," said Goban.

"Not in the usual sense," Avani qualified.

Tom gave them a puzzled look.

She explained, "Long ago giants walked this world. Hundreds of them."

"Thousands." Goban kicked a statue hard. It rang like a gong. "Thousands of the monsters!"

Tom shared a look with Avani.

Avani cleared her throat. "Giants lived peacefully for thousands of yara till the wizard Vasuman, who had a grudge against the dwarves, convinced the giants that the dwarves were their enemies."

"The giants coulda said no," argued Goban.

"Vasuman probably used the spell of obedience on em," she said. Goban looked away.

"Sounds like a familiar story—," Tom began, "—problems with evil wizards, I mean."

Ignoring his comment, Goban continued, "Vasuman attacked. The dwarves were winning, a course, till Vasuman summoned the giants. The dwarves, led by King Zabund, my great-great-grandfather, sent an ambassador to plead with the Wizards' Council for help. But the wizards on the council were old and useless—"

"Actually," Avani broke in. "It's true the Wizards Council had become ineffective, but there hadn't been a war for hundreds of yaras, so the council was filled with—"

"Bureaucratic twits!" snapped Goban.

Tom changed the subject, "Where was the dwarf nation living back then, Castle Dunferlan?"

"Nah. Castle Dunferlan fell long before that. In those days, King Zabund ruled the dwarf nation from Mongavlin Castle, not far from here.

"Without help from the Wizards Council, Mongavlin quickly fell to Vasuman and the giants. Grandfather had no choice but to flee. He moved the dwarves here inside the canyon, thinking its narrow entrances would make it easy to defend and nearly impossible for the Giants to reach em. Purchasing time till the Wizards Council finally got off their tails and acted!"

Avani started to speak. Goban hurried on, "King Zabund, assumed his people safe, but Vasuman created magical ropes and the giants climbed down the cliffs and attacked. Vasuman sealed both exits with magic. The dwarves were trapped.

"Grandfather drew his battle axe and led the charge!"

"Which was suicide," said Devraj, speaking for the first time. "He should have waited for reinforcements."

The two glared at each other.

"He died in the battle, did he not?" Devraj insisted. "If King Zabund had not been so bog-beast headed, he might have—"

Avani cleared her throat. "All of a sudden, wizards from the council, destroyed Vasuman's magic seal and entered the canyon behind the giants, followed by a legion of elven soldiers.

Goban finished, "Startled, before the giants could attack, the wizards cast a spell, turning the giants to stone." Goban continued to glare at Devraj.

"Wow!" Tom stepped between the two. "That's quite a story. Do giants, live ones I mean, still exist?"

"No." Avani shook her head sadly. "These were the last."

"And the world's better off for it!" huffed Goban.

Again, Tom and Avani stared at the dwarf.

A while later, as they neared the canyon's south exit, Tom touched Avani's arm lightly and met her eyes. They slowed down.

"What?"

Twenty paces away, Goban and Devraj led their horses toward the canyon exit.

"What?" she repeated.

"What's up with Goban and giants?" Tom asked. "He never gets mad."

"Wasn't like him," she agreed, barely above a whisper. "Blames the giants for his grandfather's death."

"And the Wizards' Council," Tom added.

"And maybe the Dwarf High Council!"

"Could be why he doesn't wanna be king," suggested Tom. "If the high-mucky-mucks had acted sooner—"

Avani glanced at Goban's back, disappearing through the exit. "His grandfather might still be alive."


## Paths crossing... Almost


Juanita stepped off the ferry onto the south shore and breathed a sigh of relief. "That was a tough crossing."

Tappus led the horses ashore. "This time of yara the river's at peak flow. Takes at least three to safely navigate the current."

Tappus tied up the horses by the trail markers, while Juanita studied footprints. "These tracks are fresh," she began. "Elves and horses. They lead down the right-hand trail."

Tappus knelt beside the ashen remains of a campfire, rolling a lump of charcoal between his fingers. "Still warm. Must've just missed em."

\* \* \*

"Kin we kill em?" whispered Dumerre, peering through the trees of their magically protected hiding place. Fifty paces away, an elven guard and a human stared at the campfire's ashes.

Bellchar considered. "Wizard say 'let elven soldiers pass.' He an elven soldier."

"Da human den?"

"She wid him," Bellchar reasoned. "No kill her eder."

Dumerre groaned.

After the two mounted their horses and galloped off down the Bog trail, Bellchar said, "I gotta pee. You stand guard."

"Go far away," Dumerre ordered. "Troll pee smell bad."

Bellchar stomped up the boulder-strewn river trail.

\* \* \*

Malak and Chatur popped from the trees and sprinted to the riverbank.

"Did ya see that?" said Malak.

"What?"

"Thought I saw a troll."

Chatur spun around. "Where?"

"Not here, dufus, across the river!"

Chatur squinted. "Don't see no troll." He frowned.

"But the ferry's on the other side."

"Course it is stupid," Malak began. "Tom and the others are ahead of us, remember? They'd a already crossed."

"So. If they was nice, they'd a left the raft here fer us."

Malak shook his head. "There's so much wrong with that statement, I ain't even gonna try n' explain."

Rope in hand, Chatur leaned back, struggling to pull the ferry across the raging river.

"Pull harder," Malak urged, while idly rolling a long pole between his hands.

"Could use some help," rasped Chatur, sweat dripping off his forehead.

"I am helping. See?" Malak poked the pole lazily in the river bottom.

"Pole harder!" shouted Chatur.

After a few myntars and a few more heated words, the pair finally reached the far bank. Chatur groaned, trying to drag the raft up onto the shore, but he wasn't strong enough. All the while, Malak stood ten paces away, tossing stones into the river.

"Ha!" cried Malak. "Did ya see that splash? Was taller'n you! Can you beat that?"

"I'll tell you what I'm gonna beat." Chatur dropped the rope and clenched his fist. The raft started drifting away.

"What's that?" whispered Malak.

Chatur didn't flinch. "You're jus tryin' ta trick me."

"Am not."

"Are too!"

"Listen." Malak batted the fist away.

"I don't hear—"

"Shush!" Malak matched Chatur, glare for glare.

Thudding footsteps sounded, coming from upriver.

"Quick," whispered Malak. "Hide!" They dove behind a pile of driftwood off to their left.

The heavy footfalls neared. The thudding stopped.

"Hey," shouted a deep raspy voice. "Dumerre. Any sign a Phawta while I gone?"

Chatur's head rose slightly above the pile, then dropped. "It's a troll," he whispered.

"Shush!" scolded Malak, craning his neck to see through the pile of sticks.

"Dumerre! Get out here," shouted the troll.

At the far side of the clearing, trees shimmered and out stepped an ogre.

"Yikes!" Malak and Chatur crawled sideways, trying to keep the pile between them and the troll and ogre. Again, they peered through the sticks.

"Any sign of Phawta?" said the troll.

"Nah. Da troll army still not here. Nor Naagesh."

"Hey!" said the Ogre. "Da ferry's floatin' away! You must not a pulled it up good."

"I pulled it plenty." The troll stomped to the riverbank, grabbed the ferry's rope and pulled it ashore. He frowned. "Someone crossed river. Didn't ya see dem?"

"I was sleepin."

"Sleepin'? You was sposta keep watch!"

"Was tired." Dumerre yawned. "Needed rest. But if someone cross. Der be tracks, right?"

A pause.

"Two sets," said the troll. "Elves. Tiny, even fer elves. Must be runts a da litter."

"Where dey lead?"

Thudding footsteps.

Malak and Chatur's eyes popped.

# Tom

Tom led his horse through the narrow winding exit from the Pillars and had to shield his eyes from the unaccustomed morning light. His friends had already mounted. Tom gripped his reins tightly in his left hand, raised his left leg and placed his foot into the stirrup.

Tom grabbed the saddle's pommel with his left hand, careful not to let go of the reins. "How far to the river?"

"Ten myntars," Devraj said. "If we ride fast." He dug in his heels, and his horse galloped off. The others followed.

"OK then," said Tom to nobody. He grunted, straining to pull himself up onto the saddle. He didn't make it. His horse swiveled its neck and stared at him with big dark eyes.

"I know," Tom agreed. "Ya don't hafta say it. I'm a wimp." The horse snorted. Pawed the ground.

Gritting his teeth, Tom pulled and jumped at the same time. The effort rewarded him by getting halfway up. Gripping the pommel in hand, he strained, finally managing to crawl up onto the saddle on his belly. From there he wriggled around and sat up.

By now, everyone was long gone.

"Don't wait for me!" Tom called. "I'll catch up!" Squeezing his legs against the animal's thigh, the horse slowly ambled after the others.

Behind, unseen and unheard by Tom, there came a hissing, clacking noise. A group of trees rustled, then a tall, dark, spindly leg thrust out, immediately followed by seven more.

The giant spider watched as the lone rider rode out of sight. Opening its mouth, slimy strands of saliva dripped, smoke rising from the spot where a glob landed.

The spider clacked its pincers and vanished.

\* \* \*

Devraj jerked back on his reins, and his horse skidded to a stop. Leaping off, he strode to the riverbank. Moments later, the others arrived, Tom last in line.

"The ferry's on the other side," said Tom. He started walking toward the tow rope. Devraj caught his arm.

"Stop!" whispered Devraj. "A troll and ogre are guarding it." He led his horse behind a group of trees. "Quickly. Before they spot us."

Once hidden, Kiran climbed a tree and stared across the river. "Hey look!" he said. "It's Malak and Chatur, hiding behind that pile!"

Avani peered around the tree and gasped, "Oh no! The troll and ogre are heading right for them."

"Guess the spiders did not eat them after all," Devraj remarked. "A pity."

## Malak and Chatur

Two enormous hands grabbed Chatur and Malak by their collars and yanked them up, their legs dangling beneath them.

Dumerre studied the two scrawny elves in Bellchar's hands. "More elven soldiers?"

"Too small fer soldiers."

"Spies?" suggested Dumerre.

Bellchar grunted his agreement. "Spies."

Malak and Chatur stared at each other in horror.

"Wizard say no kill soldiers," began Dumerre slowly. "Say nuttin' bout spies," he reasoned. "So—we kin kill em, right?"

Bellchar scratched his chin, then nodded.

"No!" cried Malak. "Ahhh—we're not spies!"

"Do we look like spies?" added Chatur. Their faces blossomed into well practiced innocent looks.

The troll and ogre didn't speak.

"We're not smart enough to be spies," said Chatur.

Malak shot his friend a 'speak for yourself' sorta look but replied, "And we didn't hear nuttin' neither."

"Yeah," agreed Chatur. "We didn't hear you're waiting fer the troll army and Naagesh."

Malak elbowed Chatur.

Chatur rubbed his ribs. "That hurt!"

"What we do?" asked Bellchar.

"Dey say dey no spies," grunted Dumerre.

"And hear nuttin'," Bellchar added.

Dumerre paused. "Could let em go, I spose?"

The two stared at each other, then grinned. "Nah!"

"Drown em?" suggested Bellchar.

Dumerre rubbed his fat belly. "Kinda hungry."

Bellchar gazed skeptically at the elves. "Not much meat."

"Still," Dumerre said hopefully.

\* \* \*

"We've gotta do something!" said Avani, gazing across the river. "Malak and Chatur are in trouble."

"They're idiots," said Devraj.

Goban glanced at Tom. "He's gotta point."

Avani leapt up. "We can't just let them die!"

Tom pulled his flare gun from his adventurers' belt, loaded a flare and ran to the river's edge. Holding it up, he scrunched his face, half-turned away and squeezed the trigger.

\* \* \*

"What dat?" said Dumerre. Bellchar glanced skyward. A brilliant red dot hovered high above the river.

"Tom's sky beacon!" cried Malak.

"They've brought the army!" cheered Chatur.

"To save us!" Malak gave their captors a concerned look. "Better run."

"Yeah. Save yourselves," urged Chatur.

Bellchar glanced around.

"See no army. Only boy."

"There!" Malak motioned across the river.

Malak and Chatur's legs flailed as the troll spun around.

The ogre squinted. "Dey right. Army coming."

Bellchar grinned. "Yeah. Da *troll* army."

* * *

Devraj rushed over and dragged Tom back out of sight. "What did you do that for?"

"Malak and Chatur are in trouble. Maybe someone'll see the flare."

"Who will see your sky beacon?"

Max growled.

Kiran knelt beside him. "What is it, boy?" Max whined, gazing upstream.

"I hear something," said Avani.

"I smell something," said Goban.

# Phawta

Laying side-by-side underneath a tree, Tom strained to see out from under the lowest branches. Thudding footsteps. The thudding stopped.

"It's Phawta," whispered Goban.

Tom pulled back a branch for a better look.

"Guess I was wrong," Devraj admitted. "Someone did spot your sky beacon."

"A scouting party?" said Goban.

Devraj nodded. "In advance of the troll army."

Phawta gazed upward into the late afternoon sky, watching the bright red dot hovering above. He sniffed the air suspiciously.

Kiran sneezed. Tom released the branch.

Phawta turned and walked straight for them.

Tom's eyes widened. Devraj grabbed his sword's hilt.

Phawta stopped at the tree, his huge dark toes only inches from Tom's face.

"Look!" shouted a troll scout. "It Bellchar."

Phawta turned back.

"Across river," continued the troll. "He's wid dat idiot ogre."

"Dey capture elves," said another.

Phawta trudged to the riverbank. "Bellchar, you fool! Get over here. An bring da prisoners widcha!"

# The king's party

The buzzing of marsh insects filled the damp, stale air of the Bog. The trail narrowed, and the king's party was forced to slow.

Bubbles rose to the swamp's putrid surface and burst, leaving a dark, oily film and the foul smell of rotten zapter eggs.

Their boots slurped with each step. Mist swirled around them, giving the illusion of ghostly creatures and haunted faces which appeared and just as quickly melted back into the fog.

Crossing a narrow patch of mud-choked marsh grass, a packhorse lost its footing and fell sideways into the swamp. The Bog's surface boiled. There was a gurgling, hissing noise.

Then all sounds stopped, and the surface became still.

King Dakshi raised his hand, signaling a halt. "The ground's too soft. We must go on foot from here." Everyone dismounted.

"Sanuu?" called King Dakshi.

His lieutenant stepped forward. "Yes, sire?"

"Have one of your men stay behind with the horses and wait for us."

Sanuu gave the order. A guard stepped up and took the King's reins and led his horse away.

Soon, the path split into three trails. King Dakshi scanned the soggy, narrow strips. "This foul swamp swallowed the wizard's tracks. They could have taken any of these paths." He addressed Larraj, "It will be dusk soon. We do not have time nor soldiers enough to split up. I would prefer to confront Naagesh while there is yet daylight. Can we use your seeker?"

"No need." Larraj waved his staff slowly over the trails. Glowing footprints appeared on the rightmost path. "This way."

Half an oort later, the path they'd been following, all but stopped, leaving only moss-covered stones and a few tufts of marsh grass, poking above the swamp's rank, scummy surface.

"Naagesh plays games with us," said King Abban.

Larraj pulled his cloak tight and gazed out at the swirling mists and the moss-covered stones, slick with dew. "Think it best I lead from here."

King Dakshi nodded.

Their progress slowed. Twice they had to backtrack when the trail they'd been following suddenly ended. Each time, Larraj used magic to reveal their mistake.

"Can't ye just keep yer magic going?" asked King Abban. "So we don't miss a turn?"

"If I use that much magic, Naagesh will sense it."

"The crazed wizard knows we're comin'."

"Yes. But he doesn't know when."

Shortly after, Larraj stopped.

"What is it?" asked Zhang.

"The path ahead seems different somehow." Larraj bent down, studying the trail. "Darker. Soggier. It may not be solid." He tested the way forward with this staff. One step. Two. His staff sunk down into the muck. He tugged on the staff, but it jerked down violently. Losing his grip, the staff disappeared beneath the surface. "NO!"

Thrusting his arms outward, he shouted an incantation, "Ostende te!"

In the depths below, a faint golden glow appeared, moving off to his left.

"Protegam te!" thundered Larraj. The spot blazed brightly.

From the depths came a muffled, gurgling cry, and a wake sped away at high speed, disappearing into the mist.

Larraj held his arm over the water. "Reversus est ad me!" His staff launched from the Bog into his outstretched hand, its brilliance lighting the surroundings like midday. The swamp's surface burst into orange flame, followed by a blast of gale-force wind. Larraj's robes and hair flapped wildly. The king's men shielded their eyes, struggling to keep from falling.

The wind faded. The flames snuffed out.

"So much for our element of surprise," remarked King Dakshi.

## Naagesh

Damp gray-green stringers of moss hung from stunted trees that lined the small clearing. A host of goblins milled about, grumbling and snapping at one another.

Waves lapped against their floating island, causing it to wobble.

Naagesh pushed aside a strand of hanging moss and stared at the flames across the Bog.

Their bobbing island caused a goblin to bump into another, knocking the other face-down in the muck. The goblin leapt to his feet, extended its claws, and took a swipe at the first. Other goblins noticed and began cheering them on. Dodging the blow, the first goblin raised its claws and hissed. A commotion behind them caused the two to freeze.

The goblin spectators stopped cheering and opened a path for the horned one.

As the horned goblin passed through their midst, it glanced at the two fighters. They withdrew into the shadows.

The horned one continued across the clearing, stopping beside his master.

The two stood in silence, gazing through the fog, the light from the explosion slowly fading.

"Your guests have arrived, Master."

\* \* \*

For a time, Juanita and Tappus rode without speaking. Soon the path narrowed, forcing them to ride single file. Juanita kept ducking to avoid the thick strands of moss.

Finally she asked, "How much farther? I thought we'd of caught up by now."

"We lost time at the ferry crossing." Tappus leaned forward in his stirrups and patted his steed's neck. "The horses needed the rest, anyway. But at this rate we'll catch em within the oort. Two at the most. Unless—"

"Unless?"

"Unless they've already reached the Deathly Bog."

"This isn't the Bog?"

"This?" Tappus shook his head sadly. "This is paradise compared to the Bog."

There was a sudden flash of light followed by a resounding *BOOM*. The ground shook. Strands of moss flew back horizontally, as a fierce wind whistled through the trees. A tree shattered beside them, crashing to the ground. Their horses reared up on their hind legs and whinnied.

They fought to control their frightened steeds, but the horses kept bucking. Juanita leapt from her horse an instant before Tappus was thrown from his, landing hard on his shoulder. Juanita did an Aikido roll and was back on her feet. Before she could grab the reins, both horses galloped off. Within seconds, the torrent subsided.

"What was that?" cried Juanita.

"Don't worry," said Tappus, clutching his shoulder. "I'm fine."

Juanita knelt beside him. "Sorry. I'm a scientist. Not always the most observant when it comes to people issues." She bent down and touched his shoulder.

"Aaaah!"

She winced.

"I see what you mean." He gritted his teeth and gripped his arm tightly to his side.

Juanita opened Tappus's tunic, exposing his muscular chest, and studied his shoulder. "Does this hurt?" She poked him.

He screamed again.

"Your Humerus bone protrudes too far forward. You appear to have a simple Anterior Dislocation."

"A what?"

"You dislocated your shoulder."

## Chatur and Malak

Still suspended in midair in Bellchar's grasp, Chatur glanced nervously at Malak.

Dumerre drew his dagger and stepped forward.

Malak glanced at Bellchar, his eyes pleading. "Aaaa—your commander said to bring us to him, remember?"

"Yeah," added Chatur. "He said." Chatur cleared his throat, trying to imitate Phawta's deep rumbling growl, "Bellchar you idiot! Get over here. An bring da prisoners wid ya—*alive!*"

Bellchar frowned. "Phawta no say *alive*."

"Did so," said Chatur. Malak nodded agreement.

Bellchar glanced at his partner.

Dumerre shrugged. "Wasn't listenin'."

Bellchar glared at the ogre, then thrust out his arms, Chatur and Malak dangling in his grasp. "Here, hold deez."

Dumerre slipped his dagger into his belt and took the squirming pair.

The troll stomped to the ferry and snatched up a spool of rope. Cutting two short lengths of rope, he trudged back to the others. "Alive? You sure?"

Malak nodded. "I distinctly remember him saying *alive*."

"My friend may be stupid," began Chatur, "but he has an excellent memory."

Malak jabbed Chatur in the ribs. Chatur wheezed.

"And I'm also clumsy," added Malak.

Bellchar signaled Dumerre. The ogre let go. Chatur and Malak dropped to the ground in a heap. "Ouch," moaned Malak.

Bellchar tied their hands behind their backs, drew his dagger, and gestured to the ferry.

Chatur and Malak stumbled onto the raft. Bellchar stepped aboard. The ferry wobbled unsteadily with his weight.

Bellchar called to Dumerre, "What you wait fer?"

"No like water," explained the ogre. Bending over, Dumerre snatched up a crab-like creature from the sand and popped it into his mouth. *Crunch*. The ogre gave a satisfied grin, then burped. "I wait here."

"Take two to run Ferry!" insisted Bellchar.

Widening his grin, Dumerre plopped down, leaned back against a log and crossed his fat arms behind his fat head.

Bellchar bared his teeth, snatched up a pole and shoved off. Releasing the pole, it clattered to the deck. He grabbed the rope and strained to pull. The raft grudgingly began to move.

Nearing the halfway point, the ferry entered the deep channel where the current was strongest. Waves washed across the deck. The ferry tipped, righted itself, tipped again. Bellchar slipped on the slick moss-covered logs, but managed to catch himself, barely avoiding falling overboard.

Chatur met Malak's gaze. Malak winked.

"Looks like you could use some help," Malak remarked casually.

"Yeah," Chatur agreed. "That ogre forced ya to struggle, all by yourself."

"Not too nice a him," agreed Malak.

Bellchar spat. "Hate ogres." Glancing over his shoulder, he jerked the rope angrily. "Dey lazy." Bellchar widened his stance, but the effort tipped the boat, nearly sending him overboard for the second time.

"Takes at least two ta run the ferry," Chatur began. "Better with three."

Malak explained, "Two to pull the rope."

"And one to pole," said Chatur.

Bellchar snorted. Another wave washed across his feet. He curled his wet, stony toes, uncomfortably.

"Hey!" said Chatur. "I got an idea! We could help ya!"

Malak sat up tall. "I could help pull."

"While I poled," said Chatur. The pair stared up expectantly at the troll. Another wave crashed over the bow, rocking the boat.

"It ain't like we could escape." Malak motioned to the raging waters.

"We can't swim," Chatur assured him. "You can tie us up again, after we're through the worst current, before we reach the shore."

The troll gazed across the river. Another wave crashed down.

Bellchar grunted. Whipping out his dagger, he leaned forward and bared his teeth at Chatur, his grimy blade poised at the young elf's throat.

Chatur didn't move.

In one swift movement, Bellchar flipped Chatur over and sliced his bonds. Then did likewise with Malak.

Chatur leapt up, seized the rope, leaned back and pulled. Malak snatched up a pole and pushed.

Bellchar snorted. Grabbed hold of the rope in front of Chatur and helped pull. The ferry stopped bobbing and picked up speed.

\* \* \*

"We've gotta do something," whispered Tom. "The ferry's almost here."

Goban slid his battle axe silently off his shoulder.

"Wait!" whispered Kiran, pointing at the raft.

* * *

Malak's eyes met Chatur's. Chatur nodded. Malak jerked the pole from the river, thrust it between Bellchar's legs and twisted.

Bellchar swayed.

Chatur snatched Bellchar's dagger from his belt and elbowed the troll hard in the knee. "Oops."

Bellchar's arms flailed. He fell. An enormous splash drenched Malak. The trolls on shore howled with laughter at the sight of Bellchar thrashing about in the madly churning river.

Malak untied the retrieval lines while Chatur hacked through the ferry's main rope with Bellchar's knife.

*Twang*. A strand broke.

Malak tossed the lines overboard and faced Chatur, still frantically sawing away at the main rope. "Faster!" Malak urged.

Chatur bared his teeth, sweat and spray dripping off his cheeks.

"Help!" yelled Bellchar, his arms flapping wildly. "Can't swim!" His head dipped below the water.

Phawta cried, "Get dem!" Adding with disgust, "'N save Bellchar."

All but Phawta waded into the swirling waters. Two trolls grabbed Bellchar, jerked him up and dragged him ashore. The rest sloshed past, heading for the raft. Growing deeper and swifter, waves broke over the trolls' heads as they neared the ferry.

"Any day now," said Malak.

Chatur continued hacking. "Not helping!" More strands snapped. "How bout ya take it from here?"

"Nah!" Malak said. "Yer doin' fine."

A troll's hand slapped down onto the bow. Malak rushed over and stomped on his fingers. The troll yelped and let go.

"Hurry you idiot!" Malak yelled.

Chatur stuck out his tongue.

*Twang, twang.* Just two strands to go. The rope groaned. The ferry creaked.

Chatur's hand trembled from the strain. "This dagger's so dull, it couldn't even slice a squamberry pie!"

Malak cupped his hands and yelled, "Chatur says the knife's dull. Got any sharper ones?" Malak ducked as daggers whizzed by.

"See?" Malak elbowed Chatur. "And you said trolls aren't helpful."

"Shut up!"

Malak's previous comment seemed to infuriate the trolls. Four of the beasts grabbed hold and pulled. The ferry creaked, twisted in the current, and began moving toward shore.

"Nearly there," called Chatur. There was a loud *snap*. "Yes!" Chatur raised the dagger triumphantly. The rope whizzed through the ferry's iron guides and dropped into the water with a satisfying *plunk*. But the ferry didn't drift downstream as hoped. They were still heading for shore, pulled by angry trolls.

"No!" yelled Malak. "Help me!"

By now, six trolls tugged on the raft.

Chatur stepped beside Malak and the two stomped like possessed cloggers on the trolls' fingers. Two of the beasts cried out and let go. Another. The ferry groaned, straining against the current's pull. The remaining trolls bared their teeth and pulled harder.

Malak grabbed a pole and slapped it down hard onto the remaining hands. *Whap!* Two more let go. Only one remained. Malak thrust the pole into the river bottom and leaned back. The pole flexed, creaked, bending in a wide arc. The ferry stopped moving. Malak strained. Chatur grabbed hold and helped. Flexing farther, the pole made an ominous cracking noise. For a moment, nothing happened, then the last troll fell, sending a massive wave gushing across the bow.

The raft drifted free.

Malak and Chatur hollered triumphantly, waving at the trolls as they floated away.

Malak and Chatur dove to the deck and covered their heads. A barrage of spears splashed around them. The ferry rocked, accompanied by *thumps* and *twangs* as deadly missiles lodged themselves deep into the deck.

After a few sectars, there were no more thumps or twangs and the splashing of near misses stopped altogether.

Chatur opened one eye. The eye regarded a spear-tip buried in the log beside his face. Chatur stood up. "Why'd they stop?" he asked. "Why aren't they chasin' us?"

"They're just dumb trolls," said Malak. "Proly realized they'd been outsmarted by us two geniuses." They grinned.

Chatur's grin morphed into a puzzled look. "So—why're they waving goodbye?"

Waves started lapping across their feet.

Malak shrugged. "Say, what's that sound?"

"Sound?"

Rapids formed. They picked up speed.

Panicked looks replaced their grins. Grabbing hold of spears embedded in the deck, they held on tight. A massive wave crashed over the raft.

Malak wiped his drenched face. "What's that roaring sound?"

The two stared at each other, then faced downstream.

Their screams filled the valley as the river dropped away and the ferry launched out over the waterfall into open air.

* * *

"Go!" shouted Phawta, pointing upstream, back the way they'd come. His scouts glanced dumbly at one another.

"Ferry gone," bellowed Phawta. "Ya wanna swim? We hafta go round."

Phawta turned to leave and spotted Bellchar lying on his back in the mud.

"You idiot! I told you. Bring prisoners ta me. Was dat so hard?" Phawta glared down in disgust. "'Stead, you let em go!"

"I no let dem go. Dey escape."

"You untied dem!"

Bellchar looked away. "Needed help."

"Oh, did poor Bellchar need help? Current too strong? Water too cold on yer wittle toes?"

Bellchar turned to the others for support. All but two walked off up the trail, shaking their heads.

"I your commander," spat Phawta. "I make da rules. When you da commander, den you make da rules. Understand?"

The two remaining scouts boomed with deep troll laughter.

Phawta raised upright and thudded off.

"Wait!" cried Bellchar. "Elven king follow evil wizard into Bog. Naagesh say fer you ta wait fer him across river."

Without a backward glance Phawta called, "'N thanks ta you we hafta take da long way round."

As the two followed their commander, one kicked Bellchar, rolling him over face down. The next stomped across Bellchar's back, planting his face firmly in the mud.

\* \* \*

"Chatur!" screamed Malak, clinging to a log that had only moments ago been part of the ferry. "Chatur, where are you?" Rapids raged around him. The log rose over a submerged boulder, then fell, splashing down on the other side, drenching him. Malak lost his grip. When he bobbed up, the log had drifted ahead.

"Aaaah!" Though flapping his arms and kicking wildly produced an impressive amount of splashing, the effort didn't actually accomplish much. The log seemed no closer.

*Guess I shouldn't a skipped class the day they taught swimming.* He kicked harder, causing gushing geysers. The gap narrowed. Ten arm's length, five, two.

He made it! But when he tried to grab hold, the wet, slimy, moss-covered log slipped from his grasp. It was too slick. He tried again. Same thing.

A frayed rope brushed the back of his arm. He splashed about, desperately searching for it. The thing brushed his arm again. Grabbing hold, he yanked it up above the water. Only—it wasn't the rope. A thrashing thousand-tooth river eel wriggled wildly in his hand. Malak tossed it away.

Thrusting his hand underwater, he groped around till he felt something. Grabbing hold, he lifted the object tentatively above water. This time, he held a rope. What's more, it was attached to the log!

Gulping in a quick breath, and with some difficulty, he pulled himself halfway up, his legs still immersed in the chilly waters. Lying there, breathing hard, he raised his head and look around.

"Chatur!" *Was that a moan?*

"Chatur! Where are you? Raise your hand!" Malak scanned the white-capped rapids. He spotted something. A stick, perhaps an arm, behind him, halfway to the far shore. Just then a gigantic wave broke over him, drenching him yet again. Malak spit out a mouthful of putrid river water. Combing his limp, water-soaked hair from his face, he looked once more. Nothing.

"Chatur! I lost you. Raise your hand again!"

There it was! Downstream from where he'd last seen it, a dark and stick-thin object rose above the river's roiling surface. It was a long way off. "Chatur. Is that you?" Nothing.

Keeping his eyes fixed on the spot, he felt the solid, reassuring security of the log beneath him. *Really wish I hadn't skipped school that day!* Inhaling deeply, he slid back into the water, kicked off from the log and flapped and kicked like mad.

Another wave crashed over him, pushing him down. He bumped into a large submerged rock on his left, which spun him into a whirlpool that pulled him down to the bottom.

A pair of large eyes opened beneath him, staring up at him. Another popped open beside the first. Then three more. Malak kicked violently, trying to reach the surface. A wavering light shone from above, but it seemed impossibly distant. His lungs burned. He kicked and kicked. Finally, his head burst the surface. Gasping for breath, he coughed. Coughed again.

"Chatur?" Still nothing.

Malak spotted something floating nearby and swam madly for it. It was Chatur! Chatur lay face down, bobbing gently.

"Chatur!" screamed Malak, grabbing his friend by the hair he jerked his head above water. Chatur's eyes were closed. Malak slapped him. Nothing. Malak slapped him harder. Chatur's eyes popped open. Chatur spat out a mouthful of water, then barfed.

Malak scrunched up his face. "Whadja you do that fer?" Malak dunked his head beneath the water. When he popped up, Chatur pointed. A few brown morsels still clung stubbornly to Malak's hair.

"Gross." Malak dunked once again.

The pair flew over a submerged log, dunking them, then popped up like corks.

Chatur spit out a mouthful of slimy, water. "Hey, jus' remembered!"

"Remembered what?"

"What the ghost said."

"The Librarian?"

"Yeah! The creatures' weakness. I remember!"

"Now?" said Malak. "You remembered it now?"

Another set of rapids lay just ahead.

"Wanna know what he said?" asked Chatur.

"No! Look out!"

While they bobbled through the rapids, a small chunk of the raft drifted by.

# So much for plan A

Bellchar moaned and held his head. Flexing his powerful biceps, he raised himself, mud dripping off his rock-hard body in thick brown globs.

"Outsmarted by Malak and Chatur," said a voice from above. "That is a new low, even for a troll."

Bellchar rolled onto his side, wiped his face and squinted upward. Two figures stood over him. A young elf in royal garb held a sword, and a dwarf lad an axe.

"What do we do now?" asked Avani.

Devraj stared down at the troll.

"Thanks to Malak and Chatur," Goban reasoned, "we can't cross the river."

The prince's gaze rose. The far shore stood deserted. There was no sign of the ogre. "We do not know where my father is, let alone Naagesh."

Chloe rolled over and stopped beside Tom. A small panel opened on her side and out came a mechanical arm with a miniature hand attached. The hand reached out and tugged Tom's pant leg.

"We know they crossed the river," said Tom.

"Obviously," Devraj began, "but where did they go from there?"

"Since we can't get across," Goban gestured to the far bank. "We can't follow their tracks."

Chloe tugged Tom's pant leg a second time.

"Not now, Chloe."

"What about the bridge upstream?" suggested Kiran.

"Too far," said Devraj.

"Besides," added Goban. "The entire troll army's ahead of us."

Chloe let go of Tom and withdrew her arm. Another panel opened. Light spewed forth and the Guardian's visage appeared.

"I've been tracking Naagesh's progress," came The Guardian's voice.

Tom jumped. "What?" He stared at the Guardian's image. "How can you track Naagesh?"

"One of my *nano-droids* stowed away in the wizard's boot."

"So where's the evil wizard, now?" asked Kiran.

A transparent, 3-D floating map replaced the Guardian's image. The map showed the river, the ferry crossing and trails on both sides. At the lower right a skull and crossed bones covered an area marked 'The Deathly Bog.' A red dot flashed on an island in the heart of The Bog. A blue dot also hovered at the ferry crossing.

"What's the red dot?" asked Goban.

"Naagesh," said the Guardian. "Or—more accurately—my *nano-droid*."

"And the blue dot is *us*, I'm guessing," said Tom.

"Correct. Due to my upgrades, I can track Chloe."

"Finding Naagesh is not our goal," argued Devraj. "Our goal is to find Father *before* he catches up to Naagesh."

"How long has Naagesh," began Tom. "Ahhh, has your *nano-droid* been at that location?"

"5.67492 oorts."

"That's a long time."

"Maybe he's waiting for something?" suggested Avani.

"My father," said Devraj.

"We know the king is following Naagesh," she reasoned. "We also know that Larraj has a seeker. So, they'll know where Naagesh is too." She tipped her head toward the red flashing dot. "So King Dakshi is headed there too."

Goban scratched his cheek. "Must've crossed the river last night."

"Once across," began Tom, "they'd hafta take this path." He pointed. On the other side of the river, the map showed a trail heading into the Deathly Bog.

Avani nodded. "So they've gotta be somewhere between the ferry landing and the spot where Naagesh is now."

Devraj stared blankly at the raging current. "We must cross the river."

"Bellchar," said Tom.

The troll groaned. "Oh. It you."

Max walked over and licked the troll's face. Bellchar frowned, pushed himself up onto one knee, then stood. Devraj and Goban trained their weapons on him.

Tom glanced at the far shore, then at Bellchar. "We gotta get across."

"Ferry broken."

"We know," said the prince. "We saw!"

Bellchar gave Devraj a disinterested stare. "Why help you?"

Devraj raised his sword. Goban his axe.

Bellchar snorted. "Troll not afraid a dose puny weapons."

Chloe raced over and skidded to a stop beside Bellchar's leg. A panel flipped open and a long tubular arm extended toward the troll. From the tube's tip, a drill bit extended and began spinning. A high whine rose in pitch as the drill picked up speed.

Bellchar eyed the instrument warily. Chloe extended her arm.

"Chloe, stop!" shouted Tom, reaching out.

Bellchar leapt back, whipped his club off his shoulder and raised it above the robot.

"NO!" cried Tom. But before Bellchar could clobber Chloe, magic engulfed the club. Bellchar's hands, where he held his weapon, began to smoke. The club burst into flames. Avani flicked her wrist, and the club launched out, spinning over the river. There was a faint *plunk* followed by a hissing noise as the charred timber bobbed off downstream.

Chloe's whirring bit wound down, and her mechanical arm withdrew. Tom stared at her in shock. She gave a forlorn series of beeps.

Tom shifted his gaze to Bellchar.

"Shallows. Below falls," said the troll.

"We can cross at the shallows?" asked Tom, "where there's less current?"

Bellchar nodded.

"Falls?" Avani's eyes shot open. "Malak and Chatur!"

171

Goban laid his hand on her shoulder. "They're not stupid. They'd a jumped off afore the falls."

No one spoke.

"Well—not that stupid," Goban insisted.

"We've gotta find em!" said Avani.

Devraj faced downstream. "But that route leads through the heart of the Deathly Bog."

"Only way," said Bellchar. They all fell silent.

There was a flash of light behind them. Only Kiran seemed to notice. He walked to the edge of the trees.

The rest stared at Tom expectantly.

"What other choice do we have?" Tom asked. "The current's too strong here to cross. We can't go north, cause of the trolls." He glanced at Avani. "And on the way, we can look for Malak and Chatur. Besides, we know Naagesh is in the Bog and that's where your dads and my mom's headed." He walked off downstream. "Come on."

"Wait!" shouted Avani. "What'll we do with the troll?" Tom turned back.

"We can't trust him, he's a troll," said Goban. "If we let him live, he'll warn Phawta. Tell em our plans."

Devraj aimed his sword at Bellchar's chest. "We should kill him."

Goban hefted his axe.

"No!" shouted Tom, running back. "Bellchar saved our lives once, remember?"

Devraj shoved Tom aside.

"Goban no!"

"He's a troll!" shouted Goban. "They're almost as bad as giants!"

Tom ran in front of Bellchar and spread his arms. "He could help us."

"Help us?" Devraj said skeptically. "A troll? Probably betray us first chance he gets."

"Bellchar?" Tom began. "Can you show us a safe path into the Deathly Bog?"

"Bellchar know da way. But Bog not safe."

"See!" shouted Tom. "He's useful already." Without waiting for a response, Tom grabbed Bellchar's huge hand in his tiny one and pulled the troll along. "Show us the way, Bellchar."

# Tom and Bellchar

*Wish we coulda kept the horses.* Tom blinked. *What am I thinking? I'm afraid of horses.* Anyway, Devraj said horses couldn't navigate the steep, narrow trail beside the waterfall, and even if they could, they'd soon head into the Deathly Bog where the heavy animals would be useless on the soggy ground.

Bellchar trudged along directly in front of Tom. A rope tied around the troll's waist led ahead to Devraj. The prince had insisted.

Tom hurried up to Bellchar. Besides his rope leash, Goban had tied the troll's hands. "Hi Bellchar."

The troll just stared straight ahead.

Tom sighed. Their trail headed down steep switchbacks beside the waterfall. Off to his left the rumbling falls plummeted downward and slammed into the rocky riverbed below, launching up a cool mist that blanketed everything, themselves included, in sparkling droplets. A rainbow appeared in the mist.

They'd almost made it down the steep switchbacks beside the waterfall.

Tom tried again, "Bellchar, it's me. Tom."

This time, the troll glanced down.

"Long time no see." Tom smiled.

"Bellchar even."

"I know. I saved you from drowning. You didn't turn me in to the ogres."

"Bellchar even," he repeated.

173

The switchbacks ended, and the trail flattened out, changing from rock slabs to cobblestones, sand, and driftwood. White-capped rapids crashed down loudly to their left. It was hard to talk over the roar of the rapids.

"How far till the trail into the Bog?" asked Tom.

"Why you go to Bog? Bog dangerous."

"We hafta warn King Dakshi and my mom."

Bellchar gazed down at him.

"Naagesh's gonna open a portal to the forbidden planet and let the creatures loose. If he does, the creatures'll suck the life-force outta every living being on this world. Including trolls."

Bellchar blinked dully.

"Naagesh has a device," explained Tom. "A remote. If we can take it from him, and get it back to the Citadel in time, we can stop the portal from opening."

Bellchar didn't respond.

"It's our only chance of saving this world! Including trolls."

Bellchar just kept staring at him.

Tom's shoulders sank. "Naagesh is crazy."

"Wizard crazy," agreed the troll.

Tom brightened. "Will you help us? Help us stop Naagesh so we all survive?"

Bellchar looked straight ahead. "No one survive Bog."


The two continued walking beside one another, smooth, rounded cobblestones clacking underfoot.

Tom picked up a flat stone. "Ever skipped a rock?"

Bellchar glanced down.

Tom drew back and let fly. Sailing across the water, the rock clipped the top of a wave, skipped up, skipped again, hit a wave and sank.

"Four skips is my record. Sometimes I can't even get one, though," Tom admitted. Bending down, he picked up another much larger stone and held it up. "Here you try."

Bellchar stopped. The rope around his waist snapped taught, jerking Devraj off his feet. He fell, leapt back up swearing.

"It's OK," Tom took the rope from Devraj and held it limply in his hand. "I got this." Devraj glared at them both, then walked on.

Tom gazed up at Bellchar. "Try it." He motioned to the rock in the troll's hand.

Bellchar stared at the stone.

"Like this." Tom pretended to hold a rock. "You hold it in yer hand, between yer thumb and first finger like so."

"You no have stone."

"I know. Just pretend I do." Again, Tom held his mock stone. Bellchar leaned to the side, his arm cocked awkwardly, matching Tom's stance.

"That's it! Now tip your hand so the stone's parallel to the river's surface. Good. Pull back your arm and coil your body." Tom assumed the pose. "That's it. Now whip around and release your fingers when you're aiming straight for the river." Tom spun around and released his non-existent rock. His head bobbed up and down, visualizing his virtual stone skipping across the water.

Tom watched Bellchar expectantly.

Bellchar glanced from Tom to the stone to the river. He cocked his arm and twisted his muscular body.

"Now!" cried Tom.

Bellchar let fly. The stone arched up, then fell. *Plunk.* Bellchar frowned.

"Good first try!" Tom handed Bellchar another stone. "This time bend farther over and make sure you hold it flat. Throw it hard, so it skims just above the water before it touches down."

Bellchar flipped the stone over in his palm.

"Aim for the riverbank on the other side. In your mind's eye, see the stone skipping all the way across."

Focused on the far shore, Bellchar bent over, twisted back, whipped around and released. The stone whizzed out, hovering just above the river. Halfway across, it grazed the water, skipped, skipped again, skipped a third time, a fourth, a fifth. The stone ricocheted off a boulder on the far shore and hit a tree. *Crack.* The tree fell over.

Tom grinned up at Bellchar. Bellchar grinned back.

"Beats my record by a mile!" Tom raised his arm, palm outward, trying to initiate the hand bump.

Bellchar just stared at him.

Tom lowered his arm. "Come on. We gotta catch up."

Avani bit her lip. "No sign of em." She cupped her hands and yelled, "Malak! Chatur!" Nothing.

They'd left the waterfall and the rapids far behind. The thundering roar had long since given way to a gentle gurgling. Here the river stretched wide, with low grass-covered mounds dotting the river all the way across.

Avani tried again, "Chatur! Malak!" No response.

"Maybe we missed their tracks," Tom said hopefully.

"If they'd turned back, we'd of met em."

Goban knelt and studied the shoreline. "Downstream?"

"There is nowhere for them to go in that direction," said Devraj.

"What about Lake Elsar?" Kiran argued.

"Do not show your ignorance, boy. The lake is kiloters from here."

Avani ran in front of Devraj. Stood on her tiptoes and leaned forward. "Stop it, Devraj! We've had enough of your continual bad temper! Quit your sniveling and do something useful for a change!" Her face flushed with anger, she added, "Goban's a prince too, but you don't see him treating everyone like peasants, every chance he gets!"

Wide eyed, Devraj glanced at Goban.

"She's got a point," Goban agreed.

Devraj shifted his gaze to Tom. Tom just stared back at him.

Returning his attention to Avani, Devraj said, "I am sorry. I will try to act more like a *peasant* in the future."

Goban half-snorted.

Avani stared at Devraj, her face softening.

"Anyway—" Goban changed the subject. "No tracks head downstream either. Knowing Malak and Chatur, they'd a left tracks an ogre could follow."

This time, Bellchar snorted.

Goban gazed up at Bellchar strangely.

"Look!" Tom pointed. Fifty yards downstream, at the next riverbend, something large bobbed near shore.

Running to the spot, Avani picked up a torn piece of cloth. "Chatur's shirt." Tears welled up in her eyes. Tom walked up, hesitated, then took her hand. She hugged him, buried her head in his shoulder, and wept. Tom glanced uneasily at Goban, at Kiran, then at the prince. Devraj looked away.

Tom smoothed a snarled tangle from Avani's hair. "Maybe they swam across. To the other side."

She sniffled. "They can't swim."

* * *

"Where are we?" asked Chatur, glancing at the wide expanse of calm water. Wherever he looked, Chatur couldn't see land, only water.

Rising and falling as gentle waves washed under them, the two lay on their backs, on a tiny scrap of wood and rope, all that remained of the ferry.

Chatur wiped his face on Malak's wet sleeve. "River musta dumped us into the ocean."

"There's no ocean near Elfhaven, dummy!" Malak chuckled, which sent him into a coughing fit. "It's Lake Elsar, you idiot. Didn't you learn nuttin' in geography class?"

"I'd smack you," said Chatur, "but I ain't got the strength." He flopped his head over onto his arm. "Hey? What's that?"

"Where?"

Chatur tried to point, but his arm wouldn't move.

Malak squinted. In the distance, something big and dark seemed to rise from the deep. The apparition grew.

"Sea monster?" Chatur suggested, too exhausted to care.

"Don't be ridiculous!" replied Malak. "Lakes don't have sea monsters."

"Lake monster, then?"

As the thing neared, a deep groaning, creaking filled the air, followed by a sharp cracking, flapping like some giant flying predator, larger even than a dragon, had landed on the water beside them. Bigger waves lapped against their meager float.

Whatever it was, the monstrous thing towered above them, blocking out the sunlight. The pair squinted, shielding their eyes and gazing upward, trying to see what manor of catastrophe they'd managed to get themselves into this time.

## Gifts shared

Devraj jerked the rope from Tom's hands. "My turn to guard the prisoner." He tugged the rope. Bellchar didn't budge. Resting his hand on his sword's hilt, he tugged again. This time the troll grudgingly started moving.

Waiting for Goban, Tom watched Bellchar tromp down the path. Bellchar glanced back at him.

Once the dwarf arrived, Tom walked with him.

"What was that about?" Goban asked.

"Whaddaya mean?"

"You was talkin' to a troll."

"So?"

"So—what could ya possibly talk about?" Goban said. "You're smart. He's dumb."

"'Cause he's a troll?"

"Exactly!"

Tom studied his friend's face. "Why do you hate trolls so much? And ogres and giants, for that matter?"

Goban sounded taken aback, "Their trolls, ogres, 'n giants!"

"Bellchar was bullied as a kid," began Tom. "Same as me."

"He told you that?"

Tom nodded. "He's still bullied. You saw the way Phawta treated him."

Goban stared at Tom like he'd gone mad.

"And you and Devraj treat Bellchar the same." Tom paused. "Course, Devraj treats everyone that way."

Goban half-snorted, then stared at the huge troll's back.

"Hey. Wait up!" Avani called. Tom and Goban slowed. Avani grabbed Tom's arm, stopping him. "What's that?" She motioned to his waist.

A light shone from beneath his hoodie. Tom hiked up his sweatshirt. His dagger's gemstone glowed jade green. "That's weird. I forgot I had it."

"Is that the dagger Zhang gave you?" asked Avani. Tom nodded.

"Can I see it?"

Tom pulled the dagger from his belt and held it up.

Avani reached for it. As her hand neared the blade, purple lightning lanced from the dagger and struck her hand.

"Ouch!" She leapt back and shook her hand. "You have a magical weapon?"

Nearly dropping it, Tom held the knife gingerly as if it might bite him. "I—I didn't know it was magical."

Tom studied the blade. The gem continued to glow. "It's strange—"

"What?"

"Just before the bullies attacked—"

"On Earth?"

"Yeah. I noticed it glowing red."

"Red?" said Goban. "When the bullies attacked?"

"Yeah." Tom flipped the blade over. "Now it's green."

Avani leaned over, careful not to get too close. "Looks ancient."

"Zhang found it in an ogre armory in Ogmoonder. Said it looked more like a troll ceremonial blade than an ogre dagger."

Avani studied the weapon. "Trolls don't use magic. Nor ogres." She pointed. "Those runes on the handle. I don't recognize them."

"If you don't recognize em," began Tom, "They must be ancient," adding, "Long ago, trolls used to live in peace with the other races, right? Maybe it was a gift from some magical race?"

"Perhaps," she said thoughtfully. "Its magic attacked me. It doesn't affect you?"

Tom shook his head.

"Interesting." She rubbed her hand. "The magic felt foreign, somehow. Like the magic in the Realm of the Fairy, remember?"

"How could I forget?"

"You forgot several times." Goban pointed out.

Avani chuckled. "We all did."

"Yeah," said Tom. "I guess we did."

"Oh!" said Avani. "Speaking of the Realm of the Fairy." She pulled a long silver chain from inside her tunic. Suspended from the chain hung a small stone pendant with a wide face engraved on its surface. A hint of golden light flashed across the amulet's surface as it rotated.

Tom leaned close. "What is it?"

"Mab gave it to me."

"The fairy queen?"

Avani nodded.

"I thought that face looked familiar."

"It was a parting gift. The day she released us from the Realm of the Fairy."

"It's pretty," remarked Tom. "Does it do anything?"

"I asked Mab that same question. All she said was, *'When the time comes, you will know'.*"

Tom half-laughed. "Mab. Cryptic as ever."

"Cryptic?"

"Intentionally making things hard to understand."

"She's definitely cryptic then," Avani agreed.

"We must hurry," Devraj called from up ahead.

Bellchar stopped. "Dis da place."

The trail they'd been following continued downstream.

"You positive?" asked Devraj. "This is the way into the Bog?"

Bellchar nodded.

Goban watched the troll intently. He'd been watching him for some time.

Here the river stretched wide and the raging rapids gave way to a trickle.

Several clumps of soil, too small to be called islands, were lined up and equally spaced across the wide expanse of water. The far shore lay cloaked in swirling mist. For an instant, they glimpsed long strands of moss hanging from stunted, scraggly trees. Just as quickly, the vision vanished, swallowed by the fog.

"Charmin' place," said Goban.

"Still no sign of em." For the umpteenth time Avani called, "Malak! Chatur!" And for the umpteenth time there was no response.

"If you ask me," said Devraj, "we are better off without the troublemakers."

"How could you say that?" Avani shouted. "Have you no feelings? Haven't you ever lost someone you cared about?"

"No."

"What about your mother?"

Devraj's eyes clouded. He turned away.

Letting out a heavy sigh, Avani laid her hand gently on his shoulder. "I'm sorry. I shouldn't have said that."

The prince jerked loose, then slowly faced her. "No. I—I deserved it." He paused. "I am sorry you lost your friends. But there is nothing we can do for them now. If we hurry, however, we may yet save my father, Goban's father, Tom's mother, and your favorite wizard."

"There's only two wizard's left." She sniffled. "Not a tough choice."

Devraj half-grinned. "Soon, you'll make three." Avani blinked. She returned his grin with a shocked smile of her own.

Tom faced Bellchar. "How do we get to the other side?"

Bellchar pointed.

Devraj walked into the stream, sloshing through the shallows toward the first grassy knoll. Bellchar shuffled along behind, though it was obvious the troll hated being wet.

Goban ventured next.

There was a flash.

"What was that?" whispered Tom.

Avani scanned the forest behind. "Not sure."

"Coming?" called Goban. Avani took another look. She motioned to Max and Chloe. "What about your pets?"

"Max can swim if it's too deep to walk. But I forgot about Chloe."

"Hey Goban? Come back. We need to carry Chloe across."

Chloe's motors whined, and she just rocketed off, her oversized balloon tires throwing up jets of water.

"No!" cried Tom, stepping forward. His robot picked up speed, hydroplaning like a pro water skier and drenching Goban on her way past.

Chloe rolled up onto the first mossy knoll and stopped. Her platform slowly rotated to face them.

"That was amazing!" said Avani.

Goban stood frowning in the middle of the stream. Using his sleeve, he wiped water first from his battle axe Aileen, then from his face.

"Did you know Chloe could do that?" asked Avani.

"No." Tom blinked in surprise. "Well, theoretically. There's enough flotation in her tires, but I didn't program her to—"

"Come on." Goban sloshed off after Devraj. "Ya kin figure it out on the way."

# It takes a wizard

Larraj stepped foot onto a small island. The light was getting dimmer. Though fog obscured the sun, he knew dusk was fast approaching.

The swamp noises they'd grown accustomed to: insects buzzing, the rasping, croaking squawks of swamp toads, the short-lived cries of small animals falling prey to larger ones, all fell silent.

Larraj squinted. With the fog and the fading light, it was impossible to see what lay ahead.

The elf and dwarf kings walked up beside him. The others fanned out to either side, causing the island to bob gently. Floating like the other islands they'd crossed, this island lay shrouded in mist, its surface barely above the mire. The area smelled of mold and decay and a strange sour stench Larraj couldn't quite identify.

A sudden chill replaced the hot, muggy air they'd experienced since they'd entered the Bog.

Larraj tapped his staff to the soggy soil. "Careful," he warned. "I sense something…"

Wet sloshing footsteps sounded, growing louder. The fog swirled. Out of the mist stepped a dark figure.

"I thought we had guests."

"Naagesh." Larraj scanned the clearing. "You said *we* had guests."

Naagesh snapped his fingers. A dozen hideous stooped and twisted beings crept from the shadows.

"Goblins," spat King Abban, grabbing his axe. Swords rang out and bow strings creaked as elves trained their weapons on the beasts.

"Halt!" shouted the elven king. His soldiers froze.

"King Dakshi." Naagesh gave the slightest of nods. "I'm honored. And King Abban as well. To what do I owe this pleasure?"

Larraj studied the wizard carefully. "For a start, you stole books on dark magic."

"Stole?" Naagesh looked taken aback. "It's my understanding the great library was meant for all. Am I mistaken?" He tapped his finger thoughtfully against his cheek. "In any case, I merely—borrowed them. That's the function of a library, isn't it? Lending books?"

"The Citadel Manual," added Larraj. "Only a Keeper may view that text."

Naagesh stared at Larraj.

"It matters not," said the king. "You will come with us. I have prepared a nice uncomfortable *cell* for you in my dungeon."

"For borrowing books?" Naagesh sounded aghast. "My, my, but this has gotten to be a strict authoritarian regime under your rule. This is how it always begins. First you ban the reading of books. What's next? Forbidding people from going out beyond the barrier after dark?" He clucked his tongue shamefully.

"The barrier is down," Larraj reminded him. "You shut it down."

"Did I?" Naagesh pursed his lips. "Must've slipped my mind. Oh well! If you're the paranoid type, you can just build an old-fashioned wall. No, wait! You already have one. The shield wall!"

King Dakshi glared at the wizard.

"Keeps out the riff raff." Naagesh nodded knowingly. "Isn't that the usual excuse?"

"Twice in the past two yaras you have laid siege to my kingdom," charged Dakshi. "We will always fight you. You will always lose." King Dakshi raised his hand and his soldiers surrounded Naagesh's meager forces. The goblins extended their claws and crouched lower, preparing to pounce.

"There, there," soothed Naagesh. "Don't worry, my pets." He patted the knobby head of the nearest goblin.

"You've caught us." Naagesh stepped forward. "As you can see, we're vastly outnumbered. I fear surrender is the only prudent course."

"What?" hissed a goblin. "No!" The beast bared its claws and sprang at the king.

Sannu drew his sword, but before he could strike, emerald lightning lanced from Naagesh's hands and the goblin blasted sideways, disappearing into the fog.

Naagesh raised his wrists meekly. "As I said. It's over."

## Into the Bog the hard way

Tom raised his foot and froze mid-stride, his foot hovering above the soggy, moss-covered shore of the Deathly Bog. Goban and Avani sloshed up beside him. A swirling fog cloaked the trail ahead in mystery.

"What's wrong?" whispered Avani.

Tom withdrew his foot. He glanced back the way they'd come. They'd crossed six fingers of shallow water, separated by five grassy tufts.

During the crossing, it had been warm, and there'd been plenty of light. Now, poised to take his first step into the Bog, Tom felt a chill and a deep sinking feeling. Wasn't just the sudden change of climate, from warm and sunny to cool, damp and dark. It was something more. Something sinister. Like he was being watched, as if the Bog itself was alive, watching him, waiting for him to make a mistake. The Bog didn't want him here, he could feel it. He didn't belong here. It wasn't safe.

Tom tried to calm his mounting fear. "Wasn't expecting it to be so—"
"Cheery?" said Goban.

"Inviting?" suggested Kiran.

Tom shivered. "Dreadful."

Avani gazed ahead. "Where'd this fog come from?"

"This is not a natural fog," warned Devraj, sloshing up beside them. He lowered his voice, "As we enter the Bog. Stay close. Never lose sight of the one in front of you. Not even for a moment." He yanked Bellchar's leash.

Bellchar grunted.

The prince stepped onto shore and into the mist, Bellchar trudging along behind.

"Into the Deathly Bog," said Tom. "Ready?"

Tom zipped up his hoodie.

Avani patted her satchel.

Goban pulled Aileen from his shoulder and kissed her.

The other two winced in disgust.

"Hurry up!" called Kiran. Tom glanced over his shoulder. Kiran, Max and Chloe stood on the last grassy knoll twenty feet back, waiting for them to get out of their way.

The mist grew thicker the farther they trod down the moss-covered path. The sickly sweet smell of decay lay heavy in the stale, humid air of the swamp.

With each step, ghostly sentinels leapt from the mist, long dead trees, their silver-gray limbs cracked and twisted, draped in shawls of moss which hung nearly to the ground. Turning back, Tom watched the specters melt back into the fog.

In the distance a deep croaking preceded a rasping, screeching noise, then silence.

# To catch a wizard

Naagesh's defeat hung heavy in the stagnant air. Larraj studied Naagesh. His slumped shoulders, his down turned eyes. Larraj took in the triumphant looks of the elves and the goblin's angry looks of betrayal. Returning his gaze to Naagesh, the evil wizard raised his eyes and met his.

King Dakshi drew a stout cord from his belt and strode toward his prisoner.

"Wait!" cried Larraj. "Naagesh would never surrender this easily."

A thin smile seemed to crack across the wizard's stone hard face. Naagesh squared his shoulders and dropped his arms. "Ah, but you are correct, my *dear*—old—friend. We've not yet discussed the terms of surrender."

"There are no terms," said Dakshi. "You are coming with us."

"Oh? But you're mistaken. I didn't mean the terms of *my* surrender." Naagesh extended his arms to the sides, emerald magic arcing between ridged fingers.

Their surroundings darkened. Naagesh floated upward, seeming to grow larger. "I was referring—to the terms of *your* surrender."

Hovering above the ground, Naagesh's eyes turned to coals. At that same moment, his emerald magic darkened, and black sparks tinged with silver rocketed away from his hands. Lightning struck a tree behind him, then another.

The evil wizard's meager goblin forces surrounded him. Grinning wicked grins, exposing chipped, jagged teeth, the goblins crouched low, extended their hooked claws and hissed at the elven soldiers.

The elves held their weapons at the ready, glancing from the beasts to their king.

Dakshi watched Naagesh cautiously, his raised hand poised to signal the attack.

Reaching inside his cloak, Naagesh pulled out a small dark object. At his touch, two symbols lit up on the device, one blue, the other red. Raising the device, his thumb hovered above the glowing red symbol.

"I have something for you, King Dakshi. Consider it a gift from my dead father." His thumb dropped. From the remote came a calm female voice, "Voice authentication required for remote portal activation."

Through gritted teeth he shouted, "Naagesh! Wizard! Master class!"

"Voice authentication confirmed." A powerful whine came from the remote. "Commencing charging cycle," said the voice. The whine grew louder, higher pitched.

"Come on!" screamed Naagesh.

"Energy level at fifty percent."

King Dakshi dropped his hand. "Stop him!"

The elven guard charged.

The goblins sprang!

Swords slashed. Claws raked. Elven battle cries played counterpoint to howling goblins; the battle noise grew.

"Energy level at seventy percent."

Naagesh slammed his thumb down repeatedly.

\* \* \*

"Look out!" shouted Zhang to Larraj. The wizard leapt sideways. A goblin's claws slashed the mossy ground right where he'd stood. A blast from his staff sent the beast hurtling away. He fired another blast. Two more goblins tumbled away.

"Zhang!" shouted Larraj, pointing. "Over there!" Behind the monk, goblins had surrounded a lone elf. The solder fought well, but the beasts kept coming. The monk leapt, spinning through the air. His swords flashed. Two goblins fell before Zhang even landed.

\* \* \*

The two kings fought side-by-side, slowly inching their way toward the center of the clearing.

The dwarf swung his battleaxe. A goblin leapt back, barely avoiding being chopped in two. "What just happened?" Abban asked.

Dakshi flicked his sword, and a goblin howled. "I believe an unfortunate turn of events has occurred."

"And things were going so well." King Abban kicked a passing beast. Abban leaned back, a leaping goblin's claws narrowly missing his face. He blinked in surprise. "That twere a close one."

"Your beard was getting a bit scraggly," Dakshi confided. "Tis better for the trim."

The dwarf snorted and spun his axe again. "Takes me back to when we was but lads. Member the day we first fought together?"

"The ogre rebellion." Dakshi nodded. "Just outside Deltar, as I recall. Those were the days, my friend. On your right!"

Abban leapt left and raised his axe. The flat side slammed into a goblin's head, knocking him senseless. "Take that, ya' gnarled twit!"

"Remember earlier—" King Dakshi slashed left, then right. "—when I said I was getting old?"

"Uh huh."

"Well, I am not feeling so old anymore."

King Abban nodded. "Nothin' like a good fight, ta get the ol' heart a pumpin'." He hummed an uplifting dwarvish battle tune and continued on.


Once they'd fought their way close enough to be heard over all the ruckus, King Dakshi called out, "Naagesh! A dozen goblins are no match for trained elven soldiers. Surrender!"

Naagesh glanced down at the remote. It was not yet ready. "You think me a fool?" shouted the wizard. "To bring this few?" Naagesh motioned to the right, then to the left. "Now!" Out of the mist leapt hundreds of goblins, far outnumbering the surprised elves.

"Run!" screamed King Dakshi.


# Bellchar


Avani felt tense and wasn't sure why. They'd just crossed a string of small islands separated by narrow slivers of swamp grass, barely wide enough to walk on. At one point she had to hop from tuft to tuft, carefully picking her way over slick moss-covered stones, till the trail finally became solid.

At times, the mist parted, providing a glimpse of tiny islands dotting a vast sea of stagnant water.

Here, dead snags lined the trail. The Bog seemed to close in upon her, making her feel exposed, trapped, vulnerable.

*It's getting darker. The sun must've set.* Though, with the dense fog, it was hard to tell.

Devraj screamed.

Avani ran toward the sound. "What's wrong?" The prince stood gazing out into the Bog. Hidden in the fog, the whirring wings of swamp bats darted by unseen overhead.

Bellchar swatted at the fog without effect. A moment later, Tom and Goban hurried up, Max and Chloe close behind.

Goban yanked Aileen off his shoulder. "We under attack?"

Devraj pointed down. There was nothing there.

Tom wrinkled his forehead. "What is it?"

"The path," said Devraj.

"Don't see no path," said Goban. Nothing but stagnant swamp lay ahead.

"Exactly," Devraj confirmed. "We must have taken a wrong turn. We have to go back."

Goban re-slung his axe. "We haven't seen another path—"

"In the last hour," Tom finished.

Avani gasped. "Where's Kiran?" She spun around, searching frantically. "Kiran!" She started back.

"I'm OK," came her brother's voice. Avani stopped, unsure which direction the voice had come from. "Where are you?"

"Back here," Kiran called. "Behind you."

Squinting, she could just make out her brother's outline, twenty paces back.

"Guys!" he called again. "Something's coming."

"Which way?" They started inching their way through the dense fog.

"There!" Kiran threw out his arm. The mist thinned. Far across the Bog, ripples disturbed its otherwise still surface. The ripples were heading their way. There was a faint gurgling. The fog returned, and they lost sight of the churning waters, but the gurgling remained.

"Kiran!" shouted his sister. "Come here this instant!"

A flash of light came from a different direction, from back the way they'd come. Another flash. This time closer.

"What was that?" whispered Devraj. He drew his sword.

Another flash. Closer still. It came from a small island off to the left. Meanwhile, the gurgling to their right grew louder.

A third flash. The gurgling continued. Devraj flicked the tip of his sword back and forth, aiming first at the flash, then at the sound, then back. "Are there one or two of them?"

"One or two what?" whispered Tom.

"Kiran!" shouted Avani, inching forward, heading in the direction she'd last heard his voice. "Get back here now!" The others followed her.

Slapping, splashing noises added to the gurgling.

Finally, Avani spotted her brother, twenty paces ahead.

Kiran turned to run, but one last flash flared directly in front of him. As the light faded, a giant spider stood between Kiran and the rest. The spider hissed, clicking its pincers hungrily.

At that same moment, a massive brown tentacle with pink suckers rose from the Bog. The wriggling tentacle whipped out, suction cups fastening tightly round Kiran's waist. Another tentacle gushed up, grabbing his leg. The thrashing tentacles drew back, dragging Kiran toward the swamp.

"Help!" Arms flailing, Kiran slapped the marshy soil, searching for something solid to grab hold of.

Avani yelled an incantation. Light flared from her satchel. But the magic faltered, flickered, faded.

"NO!" A horrified look crossed her face. *Not again. Not now!*

Hefting his battle axe, Goban raced past the giant spider, heading for Kiran and the swamp monster. A blinding flash and the spider re-materialized directly in front of Goban, causing him to screech to a halt.

The huge arachnid lowered its bulbous body and hissed at the dwarf. Goban leapt back. The spider pivoted and raced toward Kiran. Devraj ran up, tried to get past, but the spider blocked him too.

"Help me, Avani!" Almost to the water's edge, Kiran's fear-filled eyes pleaded for his sister to save him.

She tried again. Focusing harder yet trying to relax. This time the magic didn't stop. Raising her arms, she took aim, sending an arcing bolt of magic at the swamp monster, but the bolt missed, striking instead, a tree on the next island over. The tree burst into flames.

"What?" She bit her lip, yelling the incantation once more. The magic didn't respond. "NO!"

Meanwhile, Chloe's laser rose from her chassis, folded out and latched into place. Her motors whined. The robot rocketed past Goban and Devraj, underneath the spider and up to Kiran and the swamp monster. Her laser pulsed. A suction studded arm splashed down and flopped around in the muck. Another arm wrapped around Chloe and lifted her up. High energy sparks arced across the robot's body as Chloe electrified her frame. The monster dropped her. Chloe landed upside down in the mud, her laser buried, her wheels spinning uselessly.

The monster dragged Kiran kicking and screaming. Behind him, the spider grabbed Kiran's shoe in its pincers and leaned back. Eight deep furrows in the muck formed as both Kiran and the spider were being dragged toward the swamp.

Kiran's shoe slipped off, and the spider stumbled backward.

As Kiran's feet entered the thick, oily water, the boy grabbed hold of an exposed tree root. "Help!" The tentacles tightened. Kiran screamed, but didn't let go. His eyes met his sister's.

Her own eyes wet with tears, Avani just stood there, hands trembling, her satchel dark.

The spider chittered, then raced forward, thudding to a halt directly over Kiran.

Long strands of gooey slime oozed from the spider's mouth, the wet soil sizzling where each drop struck the soil beside Kiran's head.

Kiran struggled to hold the root with one hand while raising the other to ward off the spider.

The spider's large, dark, multifaceted eyes gazed down at him. The spider lowered its bulbous body, its pincers reaching for the boy.

Kiran let go of the root and raised both hands, covering his face. The swamp monster jerked. The spider pounced, snapping onto—nothing but moss.

Kiran's fingers cleaved deep gouges in the mud till they disappeared at the water's edge.

The spider raced after its stolen prey, clumps of mud flying.

"NO!" screamed Avani, running forward.

Screeching with rage, the spider bolted into the water. A wriggling tentacle breached the surface and wrapped around one of the spider's legs. A second tentacle grabbed another leg. Then a third.

The spider faltered, tipping sideways, its legs buckling from the strain. Thrashing and splashing, the spider kept sinking lower till at last its head disappeared underwater.

The Bog's surface boiled for a few moments, then grew still.

Avani covered her mouth, tears gushing down her cheeks. Max ran up beside her, whimpering.

Suddenly, Kiran's head burst the surface. Max leapt in and swam to him. Kiran looped his arm over Max and Max dog-paddled back toward shore.

Goban, Tom and Avani ran out to meet him. Goban grabbed an arm, Avani and Tom the other and they dragged Kiran's limp body ashore.

Kiran coughed up a lung-full of foul-smelling water.

Avani hugged him tight.

There came a flash behind. Everyone turned. Water dripped from the spider's body, pieces of flopping tentacles still clinging to its legs.

The spider raced forward, spreading its pincers wide.

Goban and Devraj raised their weapons.

Bellchar wrenched a large tree from the ground, roots and all. Mud and moss flew as the troll whipped his make-shift club back, coiling his powerful body and released. As the tree struck the spider there was a loud *crack*. The spider sailed out over the bog, landing with a satisfying *plunk*.

Three sets of ripples, from three separate directions, converged on the spot where the spider sank. The water boiled furiously, then once again became still.

Everyone held their breaths but saw no more signs of either of the monsters.

"Nice hit!" Tom told Bellchar. "You should try out for the Cubs." Tom ran to Chloe and groaned, trying to right her. Goban came to help. While Tom scraped mud from Chloe, Goban stared up at the troll.

Bellchar released his grip, and the tree thudded to the ground, rocking the island.

Kiran coughed again and rose unsteadily to one knee. He stared at his sister. "Why didn't you save me?"

Avani swallowed, tears welling in her bloodshot eyes. She opened her mouth, but no words came out.

"If you are through playing with the local wildlife," said Devraj, sheathing his sword. "We still have to find our way."

## Sannu

King Dakshi's warning came an instant too late. Before his soldiers could retreat, they were completely surrounded. The battle suddenly shifted from mopping up the last few goblins and securing Naagesh to a race for their very survival.

The elven guard fought hard but were steadily being crowded together in an ever-tightening ring around the two kings.

Goblins pounced and slashed.

Soldiers thrust swords and fired arrows, but their fate was dire.

A soldier cried out and fell. Another. The ring of guards, led by Sanuu, tightened further.

"Watch out!" shouted Sanuu. A soldier to his right leaned sideways, barely avoiding being mauled by raking claws. "On your left!" Sanuu shouted again.

Another guard screamed, his sword falling from his limp, injured hand…

The elven forces were faltering. Soldiers fought. Soldier fell. Forced back, till they couldn't cram together any tighter.

Zhang strode through the goblin horde, his swords a blur of flashing steel. Realizing their fate, should they stray too near of the warrior's deadly blades, the beasts opened a path for the crazed monk.

Zhang quickly joined Larraj.

Larraj held his staff pointed outward. Fire from the golden owl perched atop his staff, forcing the goblins back.

Across the clearing they could just make out the voice from Naagesh's device. "Charging cycle complete. Remote is now operational. You may commence establishing portal conduit to the forbidden planet."

"The forbidden planet?" said Zhang. "What is that thing?"

Larraj shook his head. "Naagesh has the Manual." He frowned. "That device must be able to open a portal."

The monk stared at Larraj. "The forbidden planet."

Larraj nodded. "Naagesh found a way to open Pandora's Portal."

The female voice sounded, "You have thirty sectars to engage portal event sequence."

"We've got to stop him." Zhang crouched, preparing to spring.

Larraj aimed his staff.

Naagesh raised his thumb.

A blast of golden magic struck Naagesh in the chest, spinning him in mid-air. The remote went flying.

"I'll retrieve the device," Larraj told Zhang. "You get the kings safely away from here."

"I will not leave you."

"I can handle the goblins."

"And Naagesh?" The monk stared at his friend. "You saw his heightened powers."

"I can handle him too."

Zhang continued to stare.

"If something happens to Dakshi. Who would defend Elfhaven, should Naagesh succeed in freeing the creatures?"

Zhang paused. "The boy."

"Go!" Larraj rested his hand on his friend's shoulder. "I'm depending on you. King Dakshi is our only hope. You must protect him."

"You will not survive this," Zhang said.

Larraj stared at his friend. "Go."

Zhang stared back, then turned and sprinted off.

Watching the monk go, Larraj mumbled an incantation and Zhang's swords glowed faintly for an instant. The monk didn't seem to notice.

"A parting gift, my friend," Larraj whispered. "You shall need it."

# A failed promise

Night had fallen. Tom wore his headlamp. Goban and Devraj lit torches. Even so, in the dark and the fog, it took nearly an hour to retrace their steps, before they discovered a small trail, barely rising above the swamp, leading off to their left. Tom stopped and waited for Avani.

"What happened back there?" Tom asked, concern in his voice.

"What do you mean?"

"With Kiran? With your magic?"

Avani faced Tom. Her eyes looked distant. "My magic failed. It's been failing more and more."

"Magic failed you? But—but you're the chosen one? Chosen by the magic crystals."

Her head dropped. She stared at her feet.

"Wasn't your fault," said Tom.

Avani pulled a magic crystal from her satchel and laid it in her palm. The crystal gave off a faint purple glow. "When dad left during the great troll rebellion and never returned—" She gazed at the gemstone. "—he charged me with protecting my little brother, my whole family, everyone I love, everyone I care about."

"You tried your best."

She stared at the now dark crystal in her palm. "Larraj said something's holding me back. Causing me to fail." She sighed. "I thought I was ready— thought I could be a real wizard, but—" Her voice caught. "People could die. You could die. And it would be my fault." Her eyes misted over. She turned away.

Tom laid his hand gently on her shoulder. "You've got my back."

Wiping her nose, she gave Tom an odd look, then leaned around and looked at his back.

"No." Tom frowned. "It's an expression."

She scanned his face. "Studying wizardry takes too much time. It's a distraction. How can I protect Kiran when I'm off studying magic?"

Tom didn't answer.

Her shoulders sank. "My magic failed, again. I should give it up."

"You love magic!" said Tom. "You wanna be a wizard more than anything." After a moment, his eyes lit up. "I bet fear's your problem! Fear of failing. Failing your family, failing your father. That's what's holding you back. Your fear of letting down your father is somehow blocking your magic. Just trust yourself. I do. I trust you with my life."

Tom grabbed her shoulders. "Avani, you're incredible! You're the most incredible person I know." He waited for his words to sink in. "There's no better way of protecting your family than with magic. You're the chosen one! Let go of fear. Unleash your power! Unleash your magic!

Avani gave Tom a weak smile, but then her shoulders sank. "Here." She thrust out her hand, offering Tom the magic crystal.

Tom gasped. "No way!"

"You're the only other person who can touch them, besides me."

Tom didn't respond.

"Larraj says your magic's even more powerful than his."

"He did? That's crazy. Remember what happened in magic class, with the green slime?"

She chuckled. "Kids jumped up onto their desks in panic."

"Not funny. I nearly destroyed the school!"

"But didn't you see how the other students looked at you after that?"

"Yeah. In fear."

"They looked at you in awe." She tipped her head to the side. "And a little fear."

"Thanks. Nice pep talk."

"Here. You should have them." She extended her arm. "They're no longer working for me."

"Are you crazy?" He stared at the gem in her hand.

"They worked for you before," she argued. "When we called the dragon, near Naagesh's lair."

"I just barely touched one! You were holding em. You did the spell. You were the one controlling em!"

She held the magic crystal in front of his nose. "Take it."

With a trembling hand, Tom reached out and poked it. The gem lit up. He jerked his hand away, and the magic faded. Avani grabbed his hand, slapped the crystal in his palm and folded his fingers around the gem. Light shot out from between his fingers and his eyes grew wide.

Thousands of voices sang in his head. *Who awakes the crystals?* chimed a voice. *This is not the chosen one?* replied another. *What is it?* said a third. *Destroy the crystal! What of the Prophecy? Destroy him!*

Tom's hand shook. His body shook. Brilliant purple magic blasted from his hand. Avani leapt aside. The tree right behind where she'd been standing exploded. Another bolt struck an island nearby. The island sank. Tom dropped the crystal and jumped back. The crystal struck the soggy ground, cracked, flashed, its magic quickly fading.

"I'll never touch one of those again! Coulda killed me." Tom stared at her. "Coulda killed you!"

Tom nudged the shattered crystal with his shoe. "I heard voices. They were arguing. Arguing about me."

"What?"

"Don't you hear em? When you use the crystals?"

"Ahhh? I hear distant voices. Singing, mostly. But I can't understand them." Avani paused. "Still, I know they're there. I can feel their magic mixing with mine. Adding to it. The magic within me seems to act on its own. As if it's alive." She scanned his face. "But that was before. Haven't heard the voices since my magic started failing."

The two stared down at the broken crystal in silence.


## Zhang and Sanuu


Zhang dropped to one knee as a goblin leapt for his face. The startled beast looked down just as the monk's sword thrust upward. Zhang jumped to his feet and started running. As he picked up speed, so did his swords. And as before, his blades blurred and began to hum.

As he neared what remained of the king's party, the smarter goblins leapt from Zhang's path. The dumber ones—weren't around to learn from their mistake.

"Signal the retreat," Zhang ordered Sanuu.

"Retreat?" said Sanuu. "What do you think we're trying to do?" He shook his head. "There are too many goblins."

"I'll clear the way," replied Zhang. "You and your men guard our flank."

"Where's Larraj?"

Zhang glanced back. "He trades his life for the kings'."

Sanuu's jaw dropped. He looked to his liege. King Dakshi nodded gravely.

"Make good our retreat!" shouted Sanuu.

Zhang ducked beneath archers' bows, as a barrage of arrows pushed the goblins back. The monk darted around to lead the way.

Pulled out a magical throwing star, Zhang tossed it ahead, warning, "Cover your eyes!" The star exploded, launching goblins into the Bog and causing their floating island to rock violently.

"This way!" Zhang charged ahead. Within moments, the way stood clear. He led them across the narrow soggy path to the wider, firmer ground beyond. "Hurry!"

Zhang felt frustrated. It was slow going. Far too slow. And it was dark. Without Larraj's magic lighting the way, they were forced to stop and light torches. Plus, soldiers were injured. Others helped them, which slowed their progress further.

"We must go faster!" urged the monk. "Larraj won't last long."

A soldier moaned. Someone else fell, plopping to the moist ground. Zhang grabbed a torch and hurried to him. When he rolled the elf over, his face was deathly pale. It was Sanuu. He coughed. Tried to speak.

Zhang leaned close. "What?"

"The king," he rasped. "Save him."

The monk stared at Sanuu's haggard face. "King Dakshi!" shouted Zhang.

Sanuu grabbed the monk's arm. "Promise me you'll protect the king."

Zhang clenched his teeth.

Sanuu coughed again. "Promise me!"

Zhang nodded. "I promise."

By the time King Dakshi made it back, Sanuu had already passed.

# Larraj

Larraj swiveled. Naagesh was still running around searching for his lost device.

As he headed for Naagesh, a host of goblins spotted Larraj standing alone and stormed him. Slamming his staff to the ground. A circular wave formed in the soggy ground at Larraj's feet. The wave flashed outward, growing larger each sectar, blasting the goblins back.

As the wave passed harmlessly underneath, Naagesh looked up. Their eyes met. Naagesh stared at Larraj a sectar longer, then redoubled his search.

Larraj glanced over his shoulder. Zhang had led the king's party nearly to the island's exit trail. But a throng of angry goblins were charging ahead, threatening to cut them off.

Larraj thrust out his staff. Magic flared. A bolt of white-hot energy lashed out. "You shall not leave this island!" thundered the wizard. Just ahead of the charging horde, a glowing wall began to materialize. A few goblins made it past before it solidified. Most slammed into the glowing wall full speed, collapsing in a heap.

Larraj's cloak flew as he whirled and sprinted toward Naagesh.

# Naagesh

Naagesh stomped around searching for the lost device, his goblin servant scampering beside him. "Find it!" screamed the wizard.

"Fifteen sectars left to initiate portal event," came a muted voice off to their right.

"This way, Master!"

"Five sectars left before portal initiation sequence is terminated."

"Master! I found it!" The horned goblin held the device up triumphantly, thick clumps of mud falling from its once polished surface.

"Portal initiation sequence terminated," said the device. A high-pitched whine wound down. "Portal safety re-engaged."

"NO!" shouted Naagesh and his servant.

The horned goblin thumped the device. "Voice authentication required for remote portal activation," chimed the device. The goblin thumped it again. "Voice authentication required for remote portal activation," it repeated.

"Give that to me, you fool!" Storming over, Naagesh snatched the unit from him.

"Restart the sequence, Master! Release the creatures!"

Naagesh glanced over his shoulder. The island now lay clear, save for an enormous pile of moaning goblins... And an angry wizard storming his way. The king had escaped.

"No." Naagesh clenched his fist. "Phawta's army waits at the ferry crossing. There's nowhere for Dakshi to run."

"But—"

"Silence!" screamed Naagesh.

Larraj stopped ten paces away. He stared at Naagesh's servant. The goblin slunk away into the mist.

Facing his rival, Larraj demanded, "Naagesh! Give me the device!" Larraj's staff lit up. "Or I shall destroy you."

"I think not."

Larraj's staff's golden owl opened its metallic eyes and beak. From them, shot a blinding white light, aimed straight for Naagesh's heart. Squinting slightly, Naagesh raised his hand, palm outward. Just before the white magic struck, swirling dark magic met the white, stopping it. Naagesh took a step forward. The white was forced back.

"Time you learned the power of the dark," said Naagesh. He twisted his wrist, and the dark lashed out, driving the white back inside Larraj's staff. The staff glowed brighter. Larraj dropped it. Before the staff even touched the ground, it blasted apart, scattering glowing embers across the clearing where they landed, hissing, and steaming in the muck till their magical energy finally snuffed out.

The golden owl spun, sailing through the air, landed in the swamp and immediately sank.

Larraj gasped. He glanced from his hands to the fragments littered about him.

Naagesh muttered an unfamiliar incantation. The ground began to shake. There came a sickening wail. Naagesh raised his arms yet further. Transparent bodies of the long dead rose from the marsh, their hollow eyes fixed upon Larraj.

The wailing swelled into shrieks, the shrieks to screams. Larraj clamped his hands over his ears.

Gazing skyward, Naagesh mouthed another spell. A thunderclap rocked the area. The spirits sped toward Larraj.

Larraj cried out in agony as a seething mass of tormented souls engulfed him.


# Of mist and monsters


Ten minutes later, the path widened and continued across a small island. No longer forced to walk single file, Avani hurried up beside the others. "Did you hear that?" she asked.

Tom shook his head.

"I heard somethin'," said Goban.

Tom glanced from one to the other. "What'd it sound like?"

"Moaning shrieks." She shuddered. "Like tormented souls, crying out in pain."

Goban glanced around uneasily, "Never heard the like."

"Sounded nearby," she said. "Though it's hard to tell out here."

Suddenly, a pair of large glowing blue eyes appeared, staring down at them. Another set appeared, then another. Within moments, the entire island lit up with sapphire eyes.

"What now?" Devraj grabbed the hilt of his sword. "What manor of beast are these?"

There was a blue flash and a tiny critter stood right in front of Avani. Huge glowing eyes extended on thin stalks, its eyes nearly as big as its plump, ball of fur body.

Max sniffed and started forward. Kiran grabbed his collar.

Devraj drew his blade. The critter disappeared, then reappeared on the other side of Avani, away from the prince and his sword.

Avani touched Devraj's arm lightly, then squatted down in front of the animal, smiled and extended her hand.

The thing sniffed her fingers, then rubbed its furry body against her hand and cooed. "They're called fluff monsters. They're harmless. Make great pets." She reached out to stroke its fur. The thing disappeared and reappeared behind her. "'Cept they're hard to keep track of."

Max whined. Kiran let him go. Max walked up. The creature blinked. They just stared at each other.

Tom knelt and offered his hand. "They're cute." The thing sniffed, jerked back, its eyes staring at Tom like he had two heads. "I must smell weird."

"Well, you are an alien," Avani pointed out.

The temperature suddenly plummeted. Frost formed on the moss, the trees, and the ground itself. Tom stood up. "Are these things causing—"

"No," whispered Avani.

The cooing stopped. The fluff monster at their feet disappeared. All across the island, eyes winked out.

"Uh oh," said Tom. "I remember this feeling."

Max growled. The mist swirled.

"Dangerous or not dangerous?" whispered Goban.

"Definitely dangerous," Tom said.

"What?" Goban slipped Aileen off his shoulder. "Another spider? A bog monster?"

"Worse," Tom whispered. "Far worse."

Dense wisps of mist rose from the Fog. Dangling strands grew denser, more solid, with each passing second. Wispy *arms* formed to either side of churning bodies. Featureless, transparent heads materialized.

"Mist wraiths!" Devraj drew his sword, though weapons were of no use against wraiths. Avani stepped in front of her brother, shielding him. Bellchar stepped back.

The wraiths floated forward. Avani hesitated, then set her jaw. Magic burst forth from her out-thrust arms, but quickly winked out. "No!" she screamed. Forcing herself to relax, she focused again. This time, golden magic ignited round her hands and brightened.

Everyone braced for the attack.

Tom leaned toward Avani, her magic now seething around her hands. "Will magic work against wraiths?"

"Don't think so," she whispered.

The wraiths drifted nearer.

"If they touch us, we're dead!" warned Kiran.

Avani's hands began to shake. Gritting her teeth, she raised her arms, but her magic faded.


# Trapped

Covered in sweat, Larraj trembled from the pain. The more he used magic to try and free himself, the quicker his magic reserves were depleted.

"Naagesh! You fool! There aren't enough wizards left to contain the creatures if you free them. Once they've devoured the life force of every living being on this world, they'll come for you."

"I'm now the most powerful wizard that ever lived."

"Perhaps so. But even you have to sleep sometime."

"Hmmm." Naagesh pulled out the device. Red light from Larraj's spirit prison reflected off its black surface. "Perhaps you're right."

"Throw it away!" said Larraj. "Far out into the Bog where it'll never be found."

Naagesh shook his head. "Sadly, that wouldn't help."

"What?"

"When I synced the remote to the forbidden planet, I started a failsafe timer."

"A what?"

"Tomorrow at midnight, on the eve of the royal wedding, when the elves and dwarves will be most distracted, the portal will open."

"Shut it off."

"It can't be shut off," Naagesh lied.

Larraj gritted his teeth against the pain. "Then destroy it!"

"It's technology from an advanced civilization," began Naagesh. "I haven't the physical strength and even with my vast new powers, my magic wouldn't be enough." He gazed thoughtfully at the device in his hand. "Unless—"

"Unless what?"

"There is a way," began Naagesh. "If you were to use the Transferrem Potestates incantation, you could temporarily lend me your powers. With the combined might of both our magics, I could destroy the device!"

"I'm no fool."

"It's been done before," argued Naagesh. "Wizards lending their powers for the greater good."

"Yes, but those wizards were allies, combining strengths to defeat a common foe. You and I are not allies. Besides, it was your plan to free the creatures. I couldn't have swayed your mind this easily."

"Ah well," Naagesh said wistfully, "It was worth a try." Naagesh pivoted on his heel, preparing to leave.

"Wait!" cried Larraj.

Naagesh sighed. Turned back.

"At least tell me why? Why do you hate me so?"

"I've already told you. When we were students, you left me to die at the hands of that dragon."

"That's not true," Larraj insisted. "It's about your father, isn't it?"

Naagesh didn't respond.

"And your sister's death."

Naagesh clenched his fists. "You killed her."

"What? No! I tried to save her."

"Lier!" Naagesh grabbed Larraj's arm, and they both disappeared.

# Back to school

"Where are we?" Larraj asked. No longer bound, he felt no pain. There were no swirling spirits. No swamp. No mist. In fact, the entire island had vanished. Here it was warm and dry.

A long, narrow hallway stretched before them, softly lit from candles magically floating above. Tall windows with arched tops lined each wall, and a high-arched ceiling, laced with crisscrossed wooden beams, capped the hall.

The pair hovered just above the hallway's polished marble floor.

"Where are we?" Larraj repeated.

"You don't recognize your alma-mater?"

"Dragon Hollow School of Wizardry?"

Naagesh nodded.

"The east wing near the lecture halls?"

"Yes. We'd just finished Professor Zangar's third period lecture."

"'Carnivorous Plants - Proper Care and Usage'?"

"YES! THE 'CARNIVOROUS PLANTS - PROPER CARE AND USAGE' LECTURE!"

Larraj faced him. "Why have you brought me here? What has this to do with me?"

"You told Headmaster Septus, my father was torturing my sister."

"I—"

"I heard you! I was there, hiding behind the statue."

"Statue?"

Naagesh gestured to a large marble statue at the end of the hall. "There."

"Go on," said Larraj.

"I overheard you and the Headmaster speaking."

"You—were spying on me?"

"Yes—NO!" Naagesh hissed. "I was on my way to class." Naagesh let out a deep sigh. "I remember as if it were yesterday. Observe." Naagesh flicked his wrist, and they glided down the hallway.

As they floated past a window Larraj pointed at a small courtyard on their left. "We used to play wizards and dragons behind that fountain."

Naagesh glanced over.

"The other students used to call you *Beety*," remarked Larraj, trying to draw him out, "short for Beetle Book, cause you were always scurrying about the library in search of some long-forgotten spell referenced in some obscure dust-covered text."

Naagesh didn't respond.

"And I was called *Dreamer.*"

"From that time you were caught snoring during Professor Litewort's lecture," Naagesh responded.

Larraj appraised his rival with a sidelong glance. "You must admit his lectures were boring."

"He was a self-absorbed twit," agreed Naagesh.

The two drifted along in silence, lost in their own distant memories.

Up ahead, the hallway intersected with two more. One veered off to the left while the other made a sharp right. Just before the intersection they saw a boy hiding behind a white marble statue depicting a wizard valiantly wrestling a giant iceworm. Light reflected off the monster's circular mouth and its glistening knife-like teeth as it towered above the courageous wizard, threatening to slice him to shreds.

"That's you, right?" Larraj motioned to the boy.

Naagesh nodded.

Not far down the left hallway, another young student stood conversing with an elderly elf. The adult had a wrinkled face, yet his eyes shone bright and clear. The man wore a faded blue gown with a matching pointed hat that bent over precariously near its tip, threatening to topple off the wizard's ample balding head at any moment. The boy's mouth hung open, frozen in time.

"And that's me," said Larraj. "When I was a student."

Naagesh snapped his fingers, and the pair before them began to move.

"Can they see us?" whispered Larraj.

"No, nor hear us. Listen."

*"Professor,"* said student Larraj. *"Headmaster, sir. Come quickly!"*

*The headmaster pulled up his long draping sleeve and glanced at a small magical sundial strapped to his wrist. Whichever way he moved, the rays of sunlight shining through the hall windows, bent to show the correct time. On the professor's forearm, just above the sundial, a simple line drawing tattoo of a wizard's hat and magical wand were clearly visible. The Mark of the Wizard.*

*The headmaster tapped his sundial and frowned. "What is it, Larraj? I have only half an oort before my next lecture, Magical Insects-Proper Care and Usage. I really must prepare."*

*"Sir, it's important. Beety's sister is in danger!"*

*"Beety?"*

*"Ah—Naagesh, sir. His father. Professor Valdor." The young Larraj appeared on the edge of panic. "We must hurry. Please!"*

*"Calm down, son,"* Septus urged. *"First it's Naagesh's sister, then it's his father. Which is it, boy?"*

*"There's no time. Naagesh's sister's trapped in her father's lab! Professor Valdor's gone mad! He summoned a seventh level—"*

*"This is a serious charge, Larraj! Is this some sort of freshman prank?"* His eyes narrowed. *"How do you know this?"*

Young Larraj lowered his head. *"I—I left my papers in Professor Valdor's lab. I needed them to study."*

The headmaster's glare intensified. *"You broke into a professor's lab with the intention of stealing papers!"*

*"My papers—sir."*

*"If this is a hoax, Larraj, you shall face stern punishment!"* Grabbing the headmaster's sleeve, Larraj tugged, trying desperately to get him to follow.

The headmaster jerked free. Larraj raced off. Clucking his disapproval, the headmaster traipsed after the boy, around the corner and down the hall to the entrance to Naagesh's father's lab. The headmaster glanced at Larraj, then grudgingly placed his ear to the door and called out, *"Professor? Professor Valdor? It's Headmaster Septus. May I have a word?"*

No reply. The headmaster rapped his knuckles on the door. *"Professor?"* Still nothing.

Grasping the door handle, his hand flew back. *"Ouch!"* He stared in shock at the doorknob. The knob glowed red hot.

The headmaster blinked. *"Larraj! Activate the EBS!"*

*"Sir?"*

*"The Emergency Broadcast System! Hurry!"* He thrust his arm out.

The boy dashed off. Not far down the hall, a stout rope with a long red tassel dangling beneath it, hung suspended in mid-air. Oddly, it just hovered there, attached to nothing. On the wall, directly behind the rope, a placard stated: Emergency Broadcast System. Warning: if you wish to protect your sanity, as well as your hearing, COVER YOUR EARS!

Larraj yanked down on the cord, then slapped his hands over his ears. Suddenly, all along the hallway walls, floor and ceiling, a gaggle of howling, *shrieking ghosts burst forth and flew about in panic.*

*"Go!" cried the boy. "Sound the alarm! Bring help!"*

*The ghosts paused, staring bug-eyed at young Larraj, then darted off in all directions, screaming their frantic alarm.*

*Within moments, a dozen professors, in long flapping robes, raced down the hall and screeched to a stop beside the headmaster, staffs and wands at the ready.*

*"What is it?" cried one.*

*"Where's the threat?" shouted another.*

*Headmaster Septus hurriedly appraised them of the situation.*

*"Perhaps a snake-toothed cave bat broke into the school again?" suggested an instructor.*

*A white-haired wizard tipped his head to one side, scrunched up his face whilst twirling his wand in his ear. "Haven't seen a snake-toothed bat since the time of mad king Bandhu." He glanced at his wand and wiped a rather large glob of yellow-green earwax onto his sleeve.*

*"I believe you'll find King Bhupati was the mad king," his associate corrected, gazing with disgust at his friend's earwax stained wand. "Bandhu was not truly mad, just a bit dingy. Had quite a sense of humor, though."*

*"Oh? I could have sworn—"*

*"Focus!" snapped the headmaster. "We don't know what we shall find inside. Break down the door. Be prepared to act quickly!"*

*Twelve strands of magic launched from staffs and wands and attached themselves to the door. The door bowed outward, then exploded. The wizards leapt aside as flames burst from the lab, hungrily licking the hallway wall where they'd just stood.*

The elder Naagesh snapped his fingers, and the scene stopped, wizard's frozen in mid-leap, motionless flames licking at their heels.

Naagesh snapped his fingers and again the two stood in the cool dampness of the Deathly bog, mists swirling round them. And Larraj was once more trapped in the painful writhing prison of the dead.

"See!" Naagesh shook with barely contained rage. "Father was in the midst of a highly sensitive experiment. When the other professors broke in, it triggered the explosion."

"You didn't see what happened before—" Larraj insisted, "—inside his lab." Larraj struggled with his bonds. "Your father performed forbidden rites of dark magic! He'd conjured up a seventh-level—"

"No!" screamed Naagesh. "You robbed me of everything!" Naagesh's face reddened. He leaned forward, clenching his fist. As he did, his hand dissolved into black, inky smoke.

"You're showing signs of dark magic poisoning," warned Larraj.

Naagesh glanced at his hand. He relaxed his fist. The swirling blackness withdrew, and his hand returned to normal.

"Your father was insane," said Larraj.

"Enough!" Naagesh whirled and stormed away. He snapped his fingers and from out of the mist, crept the horned goblin, scampering at the wizard's heels.

As Naagesh neared Larraj's still shimmering magical wall, hundreds of hissing goblins pushed and clawed uselessly at the obstruction. Without stopping, Naagesh thrust out his fist and the wall exploded in a spectacular display of whizzing golden sparks.


Larraj watched Naagesh's retreating form till he and his goblin forces left the island and disappeared into the fog.

His jaw taught, his brow covered in sweat, Larraj fought the pain, twisting his neck to scan the clearing. Focusing intently, his lips twitched, mouthing an incantation. All across the island, pieces of his staff flickered. The largest one, the length of his forearm, began to twitch.

Larraj strained, flexing his fingers, pointing at that larger piece. The fragment glowed brighter, started to slide.

Extending his fingers farther. The staff slid faster, heading his way. His finger brushed the edge of his seething crimson prison. Screaming in agony, he jerked his hand away.

The hunk of staff stopped moving. All the separate, scattered pieces faded to black.

Larraj's head drooped.

## Trapped as well

Max leapt between the wraiths and the kids, barking ferociously. Chloe's laser latched into place. She spun around and fired. The beam passed through the wraiths without effect.

"Stop!" cried Tom. Max stopped barking. The laser beam stopped.

Tom faced the wraiths. "Hi." He raised his hand. All save one of the wraiths, stopped. The one glided to within a foot of Tom. Wisps of mist trailed from the spectral form's limbs and torso, fluttering in a non-existent breeze.

"I'm Tom—Thomas Holland." Nothing. "The boy from the Prophecy?" Still nothing.

Tom glanced nervously at his friends. "Ah—we're trying to warn King Dakshi. Naagesh intends to release the creatures. We've gotta stop him." The only movements were the eerily flapping ribbons of mist.

Tom coughed nervously. "We're friends of the wizard Larraj. He—"

The wraiths seemed to become agitated and resumed floating toward them. Tom whipped around. Wraiths materialized in front of him. He turned to the side. More wraiths. Everyone huddled tight as the wraiths closed in.

Two feet away, the wraiths stopped. Tom and his friends were trapped; encircled in a deadly ring of spectral forms hovering inches from their bodies.

"Nice job, Thomas," whispered Devraj.

As one, the wraiths began moving, forcing everyone to shuffle along with them, desperately trying to stay away from the deadly wavering strands.

Instead of continuing down the main trail, the wraiths veered right onto a narrow, marshy strip of grass and moss, barely wide enough to walk, forcing everyone to watch their step, knowing that slipping and falling into the bog or into a wraith meant instant death.

"Where are they taking us?" whispered Avani.

Tom shivered. "Not sure we wanna know."


## Zhang


Zhang glanced around. Of the remaining troops, nearly half were injured. They had to reach the horses before Naagesh caught up with them, or else…

He forced his attention back to the task at hand. To the left side of the mossy trail, there were strange ripples in the Bog.

*Something's tracking us. Something big.*

Whatever it was, it had been following them ever since they'd left the island.

The ripples drifted closer. A second wake joined the first, then a third. Three spiked and tattered dorsal fins broke the Bog's bubbling surface.

From his coat, Zhang pulled out a throwing star. At his touch, the weapon glowed, seething with barely contained power. Suddenly, the path widened, and they stepped onto a small island. The fins sank into the Bog, retreating into the depths. A deep gurgling, thrashing ensued, belying the monsters' frustration at being robbed of their prey.

Zhang put away his star.

A fitful half-oort later they arrived back on solid, reassuring soil of the main path. Elves rushed to the horses, gathering medical supplies and tending to the wounded. Others stood guard; their bows aimed back the way they'd come. As yet, they'd neither seen nor heard anyone pursuing them, but it was only a question of time till Naagesh and his goblin forces arrived.

The soldier who King Dakshi had ordered to stay behind with the horses, handed Dakshi his reins, likewise King Abban. The pair mounted. More torches were lit and passed around. The king's each took one.

"What happened?" the soldier gasped, staring at the wounded.

"It was a trap," Dakshi sighed. "My fault. I should have anticipated. Brought more troops."

"Where's Sanuu and Larraj?"

Dakshi sighed. "Gone."

"Gone?"

"Hurry," urged Dakshi. "Help the wounded to their steeds."

The swamp remained dark and dreary, matching everyone's mood.

Once those who could ride mounted their horses, and those who could not were strapped to the back of someone who could. King Dakshi lifted his reins, preparing to leave. He glanced at King Abban. "What, my friend? No witty retort to send us off?"

The dwarve's grim face told all.

King Dakshi sighed. "My sentiments exactly." Digging in their heels, the pair galloped off, the others keeping up as best they could.

The king's party had ridden for less than an oort when King Dakshi suddenly brought his steed, skidding to a halt. King Abban and Zhang Wu stopped beside him, the rest behind.

"What is it?" said Abban. "Are we under attack? Not sure we can survive another."

Dakshi pointed ahead.

"I haven't yer keen elven eyesight."

"It's Tappas." Dakshi dismounted, as did King Abban and Zhang. "Watch our flank!" the king ordered. Soldiers leapt from their horses, drew their weapons and fanned out.

King Dakshi grabbed a torch from one of his men and strode up the trail, Abban and Zhang beside him.

Ahead, two people hobbled slowly toward them, one supporting the other's arm over their shoulder.

"Tappus?" cried the king. "What happened? Did you—" Dakshi froze mid-sentence when he recognized the person helping him.

"An explosion," Juanita explained, "The horses spooked. Tappus fell and dislocated his shoulder."

"My lord!" began Tappus. "We came to warn you. Naagesh intends to—" he gasped. "—release unspeakable monsters from the forbidden planet."

"We know."

Tappus gasped. "Did the evil wizard already—"

"Not yet," Dakshi assured him. He motioned, and a soldier relieved Juanita of her burden.

Tappus slumped. He scanned the soldier's exhausted faces. His lips moved slightly, counting. "So few left?"

Dakshi nodded. "And half are injured."

"Yet you somehow managed to survive."

"Larraj—" The king glanced back at Zhang. "There is much to tell. But not here. We have need of our army." He glanced at King Abban. "And the dwarf army, as well." Abban nodded.

Dakshi continued, "We must reach Elfhaven before Naagesh releases the creatures. Without our army…"

He gestured to his men, "Help Tappus onto a horse."

"Where's Sanuu?" Tappus asked.

The king's face paled. "Tappus. It is with a sad heart that I inform you— you are now *sole* Captain of the Palace guard, and I hereby promote you to Right Hand of the King."

Tappus sat motionless.

"Mount up!" cried Dakshi. He did the same. "We must hurry! If Larraj should fail, we must cross the ferry before Naagesh catches up."

The king glanced down at Juanita, then back at the line of troops. There were no free horses. He offered Juanita his hand. "Sorry, my lady, but horses seem to be in short supply. Would you do me the honor of riding with me?"

"Who's driving?" she asked.

King Dakshi half-snorted and grinned, despite the dire circumstances. "Perhaps we shall take turns."

Matching his grin, she grasped his hand, vaulted up behind him and wrapped her arms firmly around his waist. "Your turn first then, I take it?"

His hearty laughter seemed discordant with the otherwise gloomy mood of dread.

## The Grapes of Wraiths

In the company of the wraiths, all sounds of swamp life ceased: the buzzing of insects, the sandpapery slithering of reptiles, the soft whoosh of swamp bats whizzing by unseen in the mist. Only their own breathing and their glopping, sloshing footsteps, disturbed the otherwise total silence.

With each passing moment, more wraiths appeared: ahead, beside, and behind.

"Guess we got no choice," Goban whispered.

"Look," said Tom. An eerie red glow highlighted faint outlines of trees in the distance.

As the trees neared, Tom slipped his night vision goggles from their pouch, slid them on and flicked the switch. The usual satisfying hum sounded as the world around him burst into various intensities of green.

"The light's coming from the center of the island up ahead." Tom adjusted the focus. "Can't make out the source but—" He shoved his goggles up onto his forehead. "The hairs on the back of my neck are standin' on end." His eyes locked onto Avani's. "Either something's giving me the creeps—or—I'm sensing magic."

"It's magic," she replied. "And strong. But the magic feels dark—evil."

The path led onto a larger island than they'd seen before. Nearing the light's source, Tom ducked underneath a branch, brushed aside strands of hanging moss, walked into a wide clearing, and stopped.

The wraiths fanned out, forming a circle facing inward. A figure stood in the center of the ring surrounded by a swirling, seething, dark red mass.

"Larraj!" Avani ran to him.

"STOP!" shouted the wizard, a pained look gripping his sweat covered face.

Avani screeched to a halt in front of him. "What happened? Who did this?"

"Naagesh," he rasped. "Used—dark—magic."

"What can I do? Is there a counter spell?"

Larraj gestured to pieces of his staff littered about the clearing.

Avani gasped. Larraj wiggled his finger, pointing toward the largest hunk.

Avani hurried over and stopped, her eyes flicking cautiously from the shattered fragment of staff, to the wraith, just beyond. Wavering strands hanging beneath slowly undulating arms of fog.

Avani swallowed. Keeping her eye on the wraith, she reached down and slowly picked up the charred hunk of wood. Golden bands of magic sprang from the wood, encircled her hand, moved up her arm and spread across her body. Avani dropped it and leapt back.

"It's all right," Larraj assured her. "It won't hurt you. The staff is just sensing you, testing you, learning who and what you stand for, and lastly, aligning its magic with your own."

Avani glanced at Tom. "Like with my crystals."

"Similar," the wizard agreed.

Avani took a tentative step forward, reached out again, her hand poised over the splintered staff.

"Go on," Larraj encouraged.

Inhaling deeply, she clutched the remnant firmly and lifted it. Magic engulfed her body once more. She gasped but held on. The light slowly faded.

"Good. Now bring it here. Careful not to get too close. There, that's it. Stop!"

Avani stood just beyond the swirling mass of tormented souls.

"Now point it at me. Good, now slowly, carefully push the end through the swirling mass." He opened his fist, raising his hand toward the shattered staff, ever-so-slightly.

Inching the shard forward, when it neared the edge of crimson glow, the spirits' moans intensified, sped up, circling Larraj's body faster. She jerked the staff back.

"Don't worry," gasped the wizard. "If you don't touch the souls yourself, you should be safe."

Avani glanced at Tom. He gave her a thumbs up. Swallowing, she repositioned the splintered staff, aiming for the center of the crimson prison.

"Now!" cried Larraj.

Avani slammed the shard into the heart of the writhing mass. A blinding flash sent her and the staff hurtling away. Avani landed hard on her back.

Tom rushed to her side. "You OK?"

Devraj shoved Tom aside. Tom landed seat first on the soggy ground. Tom glared at the prince, then stood and brushed wet moss from the seat of his jeans.

"Avani. Are you hurt?" asked Devraj.

Still moaning, the spirits imprisoning Larraj slowed their frantic rotation.

"It's no use," Larraj said. "The dark magic's too powerful."

"Avani you OK?" Tom repeated, ignoring the prince's glare.

Avani nodded, groaning as she sat up. Tom grabbed an arm, Devraj the other, and they helped her to her feet.

"Gonna try again?" Tom asked.

"You heard Larraj," she said sadly. "It's no use."

Tom paused, then suddenly spoke up, "What about that spell?"

"Spell?"

"The one you learned from that vision."

She tipped her head to the side.

"The vision of that ol' geezer wizard," he reminded her. "Last year at the Library of Nalanda."

"So?"

"He taught you a spell. You used it to bore a hole through the magic, remember?"

"The Library's protection magic!" Avani's eyes darted back and forth. "The spell opened a hole."

"Yes!" cried Tom. "And the gremlin went through the hole into the library. If you could open a hole, maybe you could pass the staff through it?"

She glanced back at the swirling mass.

"Won't hurt to try," Tom winced. "Or—maybe it will."

"Your magic is failing you," warned Devraj. "You could get seriously hurt."

"We need Larraj's help," Avani argued. "We'll never be able to retrieve the remote without him." Dusting herself off, she stared at her mentor, his face masked in pain.

"You saw what dark magic can do," said Devraj. "It is too dangerous."

"The prince is right," gasped Larraj. "It's no use. The dark magic's too strong."

"But Tom reminded me of a spell—"

"I heard. That was different. White magic protected the library. This is dark, and far more powerful."

"You told me white magic is as powerful as dark, and that my crystals are pure concentrated white magic. Nothing can stand against them, you said."

Opening her satchel, she grabbed a handful of crystals; they glowed softly, responding to her touch. Bending down, she picked up the piece of staff. This time the staff didn't react, apparently recognizing her touch.

Avani brought her hands together and both staff and crystals glowed brighter. She walked across the clearing, Tom at her side. Again, she aimed the shard at the seething crimson mass.

"Don't," Larraj said. "It could kill you."

Ignoring his warning, Avani started chanting and her crystal's magic swirled round her hand and around the splintered staff, mixing with the staff's power, growing ever brighter.

Strands of multi-colored energy began to spin, then shrink. Tightening, spinning faster, forming a focused beam of intense energy; a drill with a whizzing, blinding magical laser for a bit.

Avani slammed the staff into the heart of the dark red mass. The wails of the tormented souls, racing around Larraj's body at enormous speed, became deafening.

The wizard gritted his teeth, waves of pain washing across his face. Avani's hair and cheeks blew back, as if facing hurricane-force winds. Yet Tom, standing beside her, felt nothing.

Avani's face drained of color. She shook, her body on the verge of collapse. The spirits moved so fast they became a red blur. Multi-colored sparks whizzed off, away from the contact point, but still it couldn't break through.

Impulsively, Tom slapped his hand down on top of Avani's. She pressed his thumb against a crystal. Everyone shielded their eyes from the sudden brilliant light.

A hole opened in the swirling mass. Larraj reached through and grabbed his staff.

There was a brilliant flash and a soundless explosion. Tom and Avani leapt back.

# Wizard rising

Crimson magic blasted from the clearing. "I release you," Larraj called softly. The howls of the dead receded as the freed spirits flew away, disappearing into the mist.

Still holding the hunk of staff, Larraj collapsed to one knee.

After a moment, he drew himself back up. "You two all right?"

Speaking over one-another, she said, "I'm OK," while Tom said, "I'm good." They glanced at each other but said nothing.

Larraj gazed at the shard of his staff still clutched in his hand. He tossed it to the ground.

Avani reached out. "But—"

Larraj stopped her. "Shattered, its magic drains away." He shook his head. "It was only a tool. A focal point. Some might say a crutch." He drew in a deep breath. "I don't need it anymore."

Devraj addressed Larraj, "Where is my father?"

"Naagesh tried to open a portal to the forbidden planet. He nearly succeeded. King Dakshi ordered a retreat."

"The coward!" said Devraj.

Avani gasped. Her eyes met Larraj's.

"I told Zhang to get the kings to safety. My intent was to stop Naagesh, or at least slow Naagesh down, giving the king time to escape."

"Father should have stayed and fought!"

"Larraj is right," agreed Tom. "If the king had died, then—"

"Then I'd be king, and things would be different."

"Devraj!" shouted Avani, her face a mask of shock and horror. "How could you say that?"

Tom asked Larraj, "What happened?" He glanced around nervously. Larraj hurriedly told them what had happened, and they told him what they'd learned from the Guardian.

"Our only hope," said Avani. "is to take back the device and get it to the Citadel before the portal opens."

Larraj shook his head, wearily. "Naagesh said the timer cannot be stopped."

"He lied," said Tom. "Only problem is, we don't know when he set the failsafe timer to go off."

"The portal will open at midnight tomorrow." Larraj glanced from Avani to Devraj. "On the eve of your joining ceremony."

Avani's face blanched. No one spoke.

Larraj shifted his attention to the mist wraiths, waiting silently, still hovering near the clearing's edge. One of the wraiths drifted forward.

"Yet again, I owe you a great debt," said Larraj. "And I fear, this won't be the last."

The wraith remained motionless, save for the wavering strands at its sides. Though it didn't utter a sound, the wizard nodded agreement. The wraiths hovered a moment longer, then as one, sank into the mist and disappeared.

# The missing ferry

By the time the king's party arrived at the ferry crossing, and found the ferry missing, the sun had risen.

Tappus sent out two scouts: one back down the trail to the Bog and another upriver.

King Dakshi stared across the raging Icebain River. One of his soldiers pulled the ferry's main rope from the frigid waters and held up the frayed end, dashing their hopes yet again.

"Naagesh?" suggested the dwarf king.

"How could he?" argued Zhang. "He was ahead of you."

"The ferry was still here when we arrived," Tappus pointed out.

"What do we do now, sire?" asked Tappus. "With the ferry gone, we cannot cross the river here. The current's too swift."

"Might the horses swim across?" said Abban.

"Unlikely," Tappus replied. "Certainly not with us on their backs."

"There's a bridge five kiloters upstream," said the dwarf king.

"The trolls have an outpost there," argued Tappus. "It'll likely be heavily guarded."

"It's our only chance," replied Abban.

Everyone stared at King Dakshi, awaiting his decision. His gaze rose to the signpost.

Suddenly, the two scouts came charging back. "Trolls! Thousands of them. Headed right for us," said one.

"How soon until they arrive?"

"An oort. Maybe sooner."

King Dakshi faced the second scout. "And Naagesh?"

"We've only myntars, my lord."

"We're trapped," said King Abban.

"What are your orders, sire," asked Tappus.

"If we are captured or killed, Elfhaven will fall."

"The whole world'll fall," Abban reminded him.

King Dakshi addressed Tappus, "Choose your best scout. Tell him to hide upriver. Once the trolls have passed. Have him make his way to Elfhaven. Alert General Kanak. Tell him to bring the army to our aid."

"What of the ogres?" Tappus asked. "Since you left, our scouts report the entire ogre army is now on the move, headed for Elfhaven."

Dakshi grimaced.

"The ogre commander," said Abban, "wouldn't dare attack Elfhaven without the evil wizard's order."

"Let us not tempt Lardas," King Dakshi sighed. "If Elfhaven were left completely unprotected..."

"Send another scout to Deltar," Abban suggested. "Order the High

Council, in my name, to send the dwarf army to Elfhaven."

Dakshi nodded. He faced Tappus. "Send two scouts. One to Elfhaven, one to Deltar. Have the general send half the elven army to our aid, while the other half remains in Elfhaven, awaiting the dwarf army."

"We're trapped here, sire?" asked Tappus. "By the time Kanak arrives, it'll be too late."

"There is a way we can purchase time for help to arrive, with the dual purpose of leading Naagesh and the trolls away from Elfhaven." Dakshi motioned to the third sign.

King Abban's jaw dropped. "You can't be serious…"

# Naagesh

Naagesh stormed onto the beach at the ferry landing. Goblins spread out, milling about the clearing. The rest had to wait, backed up on the trail from the Bog.

Naagesh clenched his fists. "Where's King Dakshi?"

"Don't know, Master," said the horned goblin.

"Wasn't asking you!" snapped the wizard. "It was a rhetorical question."

He scanned the beach, taking in the raging river, the absent ferry, the slack rope. As he spun round and studied the trailhead signs, the remote fell from his pocket. Naagesh picked it up and brushed it off.

The goblin stared at the device. "Open the portal now, Master."

"The king's not here."

"So? The creatures will find him. Wherever he's gone."

"I wish to see his face, the moment the portal opens. See the fear in his eyes when the creatures burst forth!"

Naagesh squeezed the device in his fist. "And where's Phawta and the troll army? Phawta was supposed to capture Dakshi if he got away from me."

A fight broke out behind them. Naagesh turned. Impatient goblins had pushed their way onto the already overcrowded beach.

Naagesh stuffed the remote into his cloak and stormed across the clearing, goblins leaping out of his way, the horned goblin scrambling to keep up.

"Where's Phawta?" Naagesh spat.

"Perhaps your spell of obedience wore off," suggested his servant.

Naagesh stopped. "What did you say?"

Gazing up meekly, his servant replied, "Mustn't lose control, Master. Not when we're this close to—"

"My spell worked perfectly!" Emerald flames burst from the wizard's hands, painting trees, driftwood, and even the goblin's face with a flickering green tint. "And I—am—*not*! Losing control." Emerald sparks cascaded down from Naagesh's fists. Wherever a spark landed, bits of sand blasted into the air. All but the horned goblin backed away. The green flames darkened.

"Master, your arms!"

Naagesh glanced down. Below his elbows, there was nothing but swirling, black smoke. Unclenching his fists, the smoke sucked back in, solidified, becoming arms once more.

He spun in a complete circle. "What happened here? Where's the king? And where are the trolls?"

The goblin raised its head and sniffed. "Perhaps the ogre knows."

"What?"

The horned goblin raised a spindly finger and pointed at a small grove of trees.

"Dumerre!" shouted Naagesh. "I know you're in there. We can smell your stench."

# Juanita

Once they'd navigated the last bend of the trail through the Weeping Forest, so named for the chilling sound the tree's thin, reed-like leaves made, the trail dumped them at the edge of a vast desert of parched, deeply cracked soil.

Beyond that, maybe a half mile ahead, sand dunes stretched for kiloters. Scattered amongst the dunes; tall, leaning towers of blueish rocks jutted up from the dunes, angling upward, all at the same angle and all pointing in the same direction. Here and there, dark circular patches stood in stark contrast to the tan-colored sand and the blue stones.

It was hard for Juanita to make it out but, far off on the southern horizon, strange bulbous spheres swayed gently in the wind; long strings of huge black pearls, only hanging upward instead of down.

King Dakshi stopped their horse and dismounted. This time Juanita accepted his hand. A soldier ran up and took the reins.

The trees behind began to sway. Juanita felt the ground shudder beneath her feet. Far ahead and to their right, a large section of sand shimmered, then just disappeared, followed immediately by a pillar of dust and sand.

She glanced at King Dakshi. "Welcome to the Plains of Illusion," he said.

A soldier ran up. "What of the supplies, sire?"

"Take what you can carry: weapons, food, water. Especially water. Bury the rest. I will not supply Naagesh's forces."

"And the horses?" asked Juanita.

The king scanned her face. "These horses were bred for intelligence and are highly trained." He strode to his horse, grabbed its bridle and looked it square in the eyes.

"War Hammer, lead the herd deep into the Weeping Forest. Remain silent until our enemies pass, then make your way back to Elfhaven, however you can." The horse whinnied, pawed the hard-baked soil twice, and nodded. King Dakshi rubbed the animal's broad forehead.

Juanita watched the king until he came back to her.

"The horses have a far better chance of surviving than we."

# The Plains of Illusion

Having arrived at the ferry landing, Larraj studied footprints while Max lapped water at the river's edge. Tom and Kiran followed him. Goban and Devraj gazed up at the trailhead signpost.

Avani stood by a group of trees at the clearing's edge. "There's something…" She touched a branch. The entire tree shimmered for an instant. "Something odd about these trees."

"I sensed that earlier." Larraj stood. "Tried the spell to reveal truth." He shook his head.

Avani continued to stare.

"These tracks." Goban knelt. "They lead into the Plains of Illusion."

"Elves and horses," agreed Devraj. "Why would Father go there?"

"He's not the only one," said Goban. "Look. Goblin prints. Hundreds of em."

Larraj strode over. "Naagesh followed the kings."

"But why would Father go into the Plains in the first place?"

"I agree," said the wizard. "Why not head upstream?"

"Quiet. Listen," said Goban. Barely audible over the raging river, came the faint sound of rocks clacking.

"Look!" Kiran pointed upriver. Far up slope, maybe a kiloter away, the trees swayed.

"What is it?" asked Tom. Through a slight gap in the trees, they saw movement, far upriver. A long line of tall, stalky figures was heading their way.

"Trolls," said Devraj.

Goban nodded. "The whole troll army, by the sound of it."

"The king must've known they were coming," Tom reasoned.

"He had no choice," said Larraj. "Trapped between the river, Naagesh, and the troll army, his only option left was the Plains."

"Phawta!" cried Bellchar, waving his arms. "Dey here!"

Devraj drew his sword, Goban his axe. Bellchar fell silent. Everyone listened but heard no response to Bellchar's outcry.

"They will be here within myntars," said Devraj.

"Quickly!" Larraj urged. "Into the Plains of Illusion!"

# Phawta

From the rocky forest trail beside the Icebain river gorge, trolls trudged into the light. Phawta raised his hand and the troll army stopped behind him.

A section of trees sparkled and out stepped an ogre.

The troll commander eyed him suspiciously.

"You late," said Dumerre. "Wizard, not happy."

Phawta leaned over the ogre and bared his teeth.

Dumerre hurriedly continued, "Naagesh say, 'have Phawta follow me into da Plains'."

"Da Plains?" spat Phawta. "Spose ta meet wizard here."

"Cause you late, King escape into Plains. Wizard follow."

Phawta glared at him.

"Oh. And King sent two spies upriver to warn Elfhaven."

"We know," huffed Phawta. "Dey won't be warnin' anyone."

After the last trolls slogged off into the Plains, Dumerre stared across the river. Naagesh had given him an important message to relay to Lardas his commander. Lardas and the ogre army were camped outside Elfhaven's north gate, awaiting the wizard to signal the attack.

With the ferry gone, that meant Dumerre would have to climb the steep, rocky trail, the same tough route the trolls had just come down.

Dumerre snorted. The upper bridge was a good five kiloters upriver, at least half a day's walk. He'd then hafta cross the bridge and walk all the way back down the other side.

Dumerre scratched his fat belly and studied his surroundings. He glanced again at the raging waters, groaned, and headed off up the river trail.

## Illusions?

Tom wiped sweat from his forehead. He estimated they'd traveled a couple of miles into the Plains, maybe more. The sun shone well past its zenith and the temperature continued to rise. Not far back, the cracked, sun-backed soil gave way to sand, then dunes, and more dunes.

As he slogged along, Tom's sneakers kept disappearing beneath the dunes, sand cascading round his ankles, then breaching the surface like sand trout, trailing a wake of fine-grained particles only to dive once more.

Here and there, jagged outcroppings of blueish stone thrust upward, all aligned in the same direction and at the same angle. Some towered nearly fifty feet above him.

Walking past a particularly tall stone, Tom let his hand slide across its cool, rough surface. *Odd. Feels cool. And it's in the desert.* Gazing up, he studied the stone's jagged, powerful pose. *Looks like a blue lightning bolt thrown by Thor and turned to stone when it slammed into the dunes, half buried by the force of impact.*

Tom grinned at the thought, then hurried to catch the others. As he passed Bellchar, Tom glanced up, smiled and waved. If the troll noticed, he pretended not to. Tom slowed to walk beside the prince. "You didn't mean what you said back there in the Bog, did ya?"

"What?"

"That you could've done better than yer father."

Devraj's jaw tightened.

"It's just that," Tom blurted on. "Maybe you could've. It was a tough decision, though. Responsible for all those lives, not just his guards, but everyone in Elfhaven. If he failed, people would die. He couldn't just—"

"I would not have failed."

"I know you're brave. I was glad you were there in the Bog when the monsters attacked, but—" Tom hesitated. "Uncle Carlos says leading takes more than bravery. It takes experience. Cool, level-headed—"

"Silence!" Devraj's hands clenched into fists. "I wish to walk alone."

Tom stopped, staring at the prince's back as he trudged ahead. Beside him stood another tall blue stone. Still watching Devraj, Tom leaned against the monolith.

A minor tremor shook the area. Dirt and pebbles rained down on Tom from the stone above. Stepping away, he glanced back. *Still no sign of the trolls.* Goban plodded through the sand. Tom waited for him.

"What was that all about?" asked Goban.

"Ya mean with Devraj?"

Goban nodded.

"The usual."

"He's got issues," the dwarf said.

Tom raised his brow and grinned.

"Whadaya mean by that grin?" Goban said suspiciously. "I don't have issues."

"Me neither," agreed Tom. They stared at each other, then laughed.

A hot, dry wind sent fine-grained sand skittering across the dunes.

"The tracks," called Goban. "They're disappearing."

Larraj knelt. The goblin footprints they'd been following were steadily being filled in. Moments ago, hundreds of clear goblin prints, some even showing claw marks, pointed the way. Within moments there was nothing left to follow, only dunes blanketed with shifting sheets of drifting sand, rasping softly as they flowed across smooth unbroken dunes.

"How can we follow the wizard now?" asked Kiran.

Larraj started raising his sleeve, the hint of gold sparkling in the sunlight.

"Chloe," began Tom. "Locate Naagesh."

A 3-D map appeared. "Naagesh located." The view zoomed in. A flashing red dot shone on the map.

Larraj blinked in surprise.

Tom explained, "One of the Guardian's nano-droids stowed away in the wizard's boot."

The wizard looked confused.

"The droid has a radio transponder inside," added Tom. "Chloe. Where are we now?" A blue dot appeared, not far from the red flashing one. "How far away is the wizard?"

"2.675 miles or 3.258 kiloters."

Tom pulled out his compass.

"What's that?" asked Goban.

"A compass. Your planet has a magnetic field generated by flowing currents in its molten core.

"Molten core?" Goban stared at his feet. "What make's ya think that?"

"You live on a volcano don't you?"

Goban's eyes widened.

Tom continued. "The compass needle is a magnet. It's attracted to the planet's magnetic field." Tom held the compass out and glanced from the needle to the red dot. "Looks like Naagesh is heading south. Toward those hovering thingies in the distance."

"The Floating Mountains," said Larraj.

Tom tapped his compass. "Won't stabilize. Keeps shifting."

"What's that mean?" asked Avani.

"Something's interfering with the planet's magnetic field." Tom slapped the compass against his palm.

"Hey guys, come look at this," called Kiran.

A hundred paces away, Kiran stared down at one of the dark patches of sand. The others walked over.

"They're not dark patches of sand—" began Tom.

"They're holes," said Goban.

"Sinkholes," Tom added.

Kiran frowned. "Stink holes?"

"Sinkholes," Tom corrected him. "Fifty feet across, I'd guess. And almost perfectly round." Tom gulped in a deep breath, grabbed Goban's arm and leaned over the edge. "Too dark. Can't see."

Kiran kicked a pebble. A brief pause. Then a soft *plunk*.

"Water?" said Goban.

"In a desert?" Tom grabbed two glow sticks from a belt pouch, held them firmly between his hands and *snapped*. Quickly brightening, the sticks gave off a soft lime-colored light.

"Magic!" cried Avani.

"Chemistry actually." Tom shrugged. "But—close enough."

Everyone crowded round.

"How's it work?" asked Goban.

"Ya break the thin barrier between two chemicals. The chemicals mix, creating an exothermic chemical reaction."

Goban looked puzzled.

"In chemical reactions you get either an endothermic or an exothermic reaction. Endothermic absorbs energy, exothermic releases energy. In this case, the reaction releases energy."

Goban's puzzled look morphed to one of excitement. "Go on."

"Can we get on with this?" rasped Devraj.

Goban fired back, "I just wanted to learn—"

"Devraj!" snapped Avani. "Must you always—"

Tom thrust his arm out over the sinkhole and opened his hand. "Check this out!" Everyone stopped arguing and peered over the edge.

As the sticks fell, their faint green light gave a glimpse of a rock grotto; a large bowl curved back at least a hundred feet underneath the area. An instant later, they struck the surface of a small lake. The stick's glowing image wavered, drifting back and forth, finally settling on the bottom.

Tom stepped away from the edge. "Definitely a sinkhole."

"What are they?" asked Avani.

"Back on Earth there're places where the ground just suddenly opens up, swallowing whole houses, sometimes."

Avani's eyes blossomed. Everyone inched away from the edge.

"In the Amazon basin, there's a network of sinkholes, caves, and underground rivers. The subterranean network flows for hundreds of miles, er, kiloters, eventually reaching the sea. It's like a whole 'nother world."

"How very exciting," began the prince. "And how exactly does this— amazing basin help us here?"

Devraj leaned toward Tom, opened his mouth to speak, but another quake rocked the area, stronger than the last.

Tom said, "Did you hear that?"

"The quake?" rasped the prince. "Kind of hard to miss."

"No. This was different. Like distant thunder only—" He turned. "It came from behind." Everyone gazed back the way they'd come. A cloud of dust covered the horizon.

"What is it?" asked Goban.

Avani squinted. "Too far away."

"Probably a sandstorm," said Devraj. "We should continue on. If the storm reaches us before we find Father..." He slogged off through the blowing sand. The others followed, except for Tom.

Tom continued to stare at the billowing dust cloud in the distance. "But the wind's blowing from the other direction, from the south. Storms come from upwind." He turned back. The others had vanished over the dune, their footprints quickly filling in. "Hey! Wait up!"

# A stowaway

After wading through a deep dune, Naagesh stopped beside a blue stone, pulled his left boot from the sand, frowned and shook his leg.

"Master. Back at the river," shouted the wizard's servant over the howling wind. "Why d'you trust that ogre? He's an idiot."

Naagesh studied their surroundings. Beside him, three blue stones jutted skyward near the edge of a gigantic hole. A sea of grumbling goblins huddled behind the stones, seeking shelter from the blasting sand.

"Dumerre is none of your concern." Naagesh leaned against the nearest stone, jerked off his boot and flipped it upside down. Sand drained from his shoe.

"Master there's a—"

"Silence! Dumerre was all I had! I will not tolerate your constant—"

"Not the ogre, Master. There's a sandstorm. It's headed this way."

Slapping his palm against the heel of his boot, more sand fell. "From which direction?"

"From behind."

Naagesh slapped his boot again and this time, a tiny, gray object tumbled out, half burying itself in the sand. "It's not a storm, you idiot." Naagesh reached for the item. "It's Phawta, bringing the troll army, as I commanded. Which means—" Naagesh paused, his skeletal fingers poised over the object. "*You* were wrong. My *spell* worked on Phawta. Guess I'm not—*losing control*, after all."

The goblin didn't respond.

"Wait for them up there." Naagesh gestured to the crest of the next dune. "Hurry Phawta along. I have need of his army."

"As you wish, Master."

Naagesh plucked the piece from the sand, dusted it off and held it up into the sunlight. "It appears the Guardian left us a present."

"A what?"

"A spy. A tiny—little—spy." Naagesh glanced back. "Someone's following us. I've sensed them for some time."

"Phawta?"

"Not the trolls! Someone else!" He gazed down at the tiny device.

"Why would anyone—" The goblin froze. "The device! They're after the device!"

"It's keyed to my voice. No one can use it but me."

"Destroy the tiny spy!"

"Yes." Naagesh rolled the nano-droid between his fingers. "I could do that." His eyes flicked to the dunes, the blue stones, the sinkhole.

# Avani

"Can't see anything," said Avani.

"I know. The wind's really picked up." Tom scanned the area. Tom, Avani and Goban stood in a deep trough between dunes.

"Let's wait over there," Goban suggested. "Behind those three stones. Outta the wind." Wallowing through knee deep sand, Goban headed over to nearest of three blue stones standing beside the lip of a sinkhole. Tom and Avani followed him.

Avani bent over and shook sand from her hair. "Least we're out of that stinging sand."

"If the wind keeps picking up," reasoned Tom. "We'll hafta find shelter soon."

"If there is any," Goban replied skeptically.

Avani glanced back. "What's taking em so long?"

Squinting, Tom gazed back up the steep dune they'd just half waded, half slid down. Bellchar's head crested the dune first, followed by Devraj, then the others.

Kiran didn't seem to be having much trouble. Max, at Kiran's side, bounded like a dolphin, leaping up from the sand, then diving back down.

Tom smiled. *Looks like Max is havin' fun.*

Chloe sped down the dune with ease, sand churning from her oversized tires. The prince seemed to be struggling. Weighing the most, Bellchar sank deepest, but being the strongest, the sand didn't slow him down much. Larraj, however, walked as if on solid ground, leaving tiny mounds in the wake of each gliding step.

Leading the pack, Chloe stopped beside Tom.

"Where's Naagesh now?" asked Larraj.

"The nano-droid's locater beacon," Chloe began, "places the wizard's position at 23.427 meters from our current location."

Chloe's platform rotated. "Down there."

"What?" Tom said. "In the sinkhole?"

"Affirmative."

"Ah—moving or stationary?"

"Stationary."

"For how long?"

"2.175 hours, approximately."

Tom stepped cautiously to the edge. Goban stepped beside him. "Got any more of those fire twigs?"

Tom handed Goban a glow stick.

Goban snapped it and tossed it in. *Plunk.* Its light wavered and settled on the bottom. "Another lake."

"I cannot see," complained Devraj. "We need more light."

Avani opened her palm and muttered an incantation. Nothing happened. She glanced sheepishly at Larraj. Bending forward, he blew across her palm and a half dozen magic glowing orbs floated out and down.

The sand started shaking. Everyone turned at a hissing noise behind them. The dunes to either side shifted. Twin avalanches of sand cascaded down the face of both dunes. When the two waves collided, the combined torrent flooded down the trough straight for them.

"Grab onto the stones!" cried Larraj. "Hold on tight!"

Once the flooding sand slowed to a trickle, Max barked, dug himself out, and barked again. Half buried and still clinging to the rocks, the others stood and brushed themselves off.

"Everyone all right?" asked Larraj.

From beneath a deep drift, came the muted sound of motors revving. The sand shifted. Max dug, throwing sand behind him, exposing Chloe's mast buried just a foot from the lip of the sinkhole. Tom and Goban rushed over, pulled Chloe out and dragged her away from the edge.

Tom sighed. "That was close."

"Ah—guys," said Kiran. "Wasn't a storm behind us." Tom peered around a stone. At the crest of the dune behind, a wall of dark heads appeared. Rising farther, the heads were stacked upon broad shoulders, and beneath those, rock-hard muscular bodies.

"Trolls," whispered Devraj. "Stay hidden behind the stones."

## Phawta

Phawta stopped in a deep trough between dunes. Fifty paces away, at the end of the trough, three blue stones jutted skyward. "You hear somethin'?" he asked his lieutenant.

"No."

Suddenly, a troll stepped from behind one of stones with a rope tied around his waist. He jerked the rope and a young elf flew out from behind the stone, landed on his face, jumped up and drew his sword.

Phawta huffed in shock. "Bellchar? You capture another elf?"

"I captured Bellchar, actually," Devraj called back.

Phawta trudged over. "You alone?"

"Yes," said Devraj. "No," said Bellchar.

Bellchar glanced at the stones.

"I said we were alone!" Devraj aimed his sword at Phawta's chest. Trolls immediately surrounded him.

Bellchar grabbed the prince's arm and squeezed.

Devraj dropped his sword. Trolls grabbed him.

Phawta nodded to his lieutenant. The soldier checked behind the stones. "No one there."

"What?" Bellchar trudged over. "Dey was here!"

Phawta's lieutenant chuckled gruffly. "Bellchar caught by a single elf runt." Laughter spread through the troll ranks.

Bellchar slogged back to Phawta. "Dey was here," he insisted.

Keeping his gaze fixed on Bellchar, Phawta slipped his club off his shoulder, walked casually behind the first stone and slammed it to the ground. He glanced at Devraj, then moved on to the next.

"You are wasting time," said the prince. "Bellchar's an idiot! I captured him all by myself."

Phawta tipped his head, considering. "Bellchar is an idiot. Still…" Sand bounced when he slammed the club down a second time. He stepped to the third stone.

"I told you!" shouted Devraj. "There is no one—"

From out of nowhere, a furry animal leapt forward and started barking.

"What dis?" Phawta raised his massive foot over the critter.

The area behind the animal shimmered. The shimmer faded. A wizard and four kids appeared: two elves, a dwarf and a human, plus a strange tin box with eyes.

Goban raised his axe.

Chloe's laser folded out and *clicked* into place.

Max growled.

"If you leave now," said Larraj. "We will not harm you."

* * *

The horned goblin pressed its long, thin, claw-tipped hands against the hot crest of the dune and pushed itself up till its beady eyes hovered just above the dune. To the north, as far as he could see, the dunes darkened from buff to black as thousands of trolls awaited their leader's orders.

Shifting his gaze below, the goblin spotted the wizard standing amidst a small group of youngins facing off against the entire troll army.

"Larraj yet lives?" The goblin considered. "Mustn't let the wizard interfere with the plan."

## One wizard?

Phawta snapped his fingers and a hundred trolls surrounded Tom and the others.

The troll commander's face hardened. "Kill dem."

Max leapt in front of Tom and growled. Larraj reflexively tightened his grip, but his staff wasn't there. He blinked. Magic flared around his hands.

"Wait!" shouted Bellchar. Though oft made fun of, Bellchar was taller and more muscular than Phawta. The nearest trolls glanced from Phawta to Bellchar uncertainly.

Phawta noticed. He asked Bellchar, "Why wait?"

"Dey not after trolls. Dey after evil wizard."

"So?"

"Naagesh treat trolls bad." Several trolls grumbled agreement. Bellchar continued, "Wizard force trolls ta work with our enemies." He spat. "Da ogres." The troll's grumblings grew louder.

Phawta leaned forward. "You callin' me weak?"

"No. Wizard put spell on you. Make you his slave."

Phawta clenched his fists.

Bellchar looked to his brethren. This time, they remained silent.

Phawta's arm shot out, pointing at their captives. "Kill dem!"

Trolls roared and charged. A wall of sparkling golden magic blasted the first row of trolls backwards, taking out the next two rows like dominoes.

"Stop!" cried Larraj, stepping forward.

The trolls halted. Phawta gazed coolly at the wizard.

"We have no quarrel with you," began Larraj, "You saw what the power of my magic can do. My offer stands. If you leave now, we will let you live."

Phawta studied the wizard's face. "You have powerful magic." He gestured to the dark sea of muscular bodies behind and grinned. "Tink yer magic kin beat five thousand battle-hardened trolls?"

Larraj scanned the nearest troll's faces. "You're right," he conceded, "I haven't the power to kill five thousand trolls. But," he paused. "Trolls follow their leader's orders." Larraj scratched his chin, thoughtfully. "So, I only *need* to kill one."

Phawta's grin dropped.

Golden lightning arced between Larraj's hands. Phawta stepped back.

"Wait!" cried Tom. "Phawta? Naagesh intends to open a portal to the forbidden planet."

"So?"

"Naagesh is going to release creatures. Horrible creatures that will suck the life force outta every living thing in this world, including trolls."

"Lies," laughed Phawta. "Boy tink Phawta stupid."

"Tell him, Bellchar. Tell Phawta it's true."

Bellchar hesitated. "Boy, speak truth."

Phawta snorted. "What Bellchar know? You stupid." He stepped face-to-face with Bellchar. "'Sides. Trolls not afraid a creatures. Trolls not afraid a nuttin'!" He looked at this army. A few mumbled agreement. Others, not so much.

Phawta pursed his thick lips. "Hmmm. Need ta think." He pivoted on his heel. Troops stepped aside as Phawta strode through their ranks. Ten rows back he faced Larraj. "Not so easy ta kill me now, is it wizard?" He thrust his fist skyward. "Kill dem all!"

## Against five thousand trolls

Max barked.

Tom watched the trolls attack as if viewing a slow-mo, 3-D vid. It didn't seem real.

Larraj sent trolls flying. Blast after blast, trolls were bowled over like sticks. Yet the trolls kept coming. By the tenth blast, only half as many trolls fell. The next blast, only three. And those stood right back up.

Tom glanced to his right. Somehow Devraj had retrieved his sword and he and Goban swung their weapons furiously, forcing trolls back. To his left, Avani's magic failed twice, but on her third try, arms of sand rose from below, grabbed a troll and jerked it down beneath the dune.

Flashes of laser light from Chloe, forced trolls to leap and hop, dancing around wildly, occasionally crying out when her laser grazed a troll's tough hide.

Max barked again.

"I know," said Tom. "We're hosed."

Ten feet away, Bellchar just stood there staring at him.

"Help us, Bellchar!" Tom's eyes watered. "Please."

Max barked a third time.

"Barking won't help, Max." Tom glanced down at his dog. "We can't fight this many…" He stopped mid-sentence. Max wasn't barking at the trolls. Max was barking at him.

A bright green glow shone from beneath his hoodie. Lifting his sweatshirt, his dagger's gemstone glowed brighter than Tom had ever seen. Bellchar noticed too. The troll stood frozen at the sight.

Drawing the blade, Tom aimed it shakily at the charging trolls.

"STOP!!!" thundered Bellchar. All fighting ground to a halt.

Tom blinked.

Bellchar faced Tom, dropped to his knees and bowed. Across the face of the dune, trolls stared first at Bellchar, then at Tom.

"All hail Tom!" cried Bellchar. "Lord of Trolls!"


# The King and I


Heading ever deeper into the Plains, Juanita kept noticing King Dakshi stealing glances at her.

*He doesn't think I noticed.* She smiled. When he looked again, she stared back at him. Whipping around, he pretended to study the horizon. She followed his gaze. With the steadily increasing wind the Floating Mountains, though closer, kept disappearing, cloaked by a curtain of blowing sand.

"Haven't seen any illusions," she remarked. "Jutting stones. Ok, unusual that they're all pointing in the same angle and direction. The dark patches of sand could be rock or some harder material."

"And the rumblings from the deep? The underworld swallowing whole dunes in a single gulp?"

She laughed. "The quakes are likely the result of plate tectonics or volcanism."

"And the underworld swallowing dunes?"

"Sink holes, no doubt. We haven't got close enough to one to see."

He glanced at her with a perplexed look. "And what of the Floating Mountains?"

Juanita turned and squinted. On the southern horizon, strands of beads, giant dark pearls, waved gently in the wind. She shook her head.

They continued walking. King Dakshi tried to steal another glance.

"What is it?" she asked before he could look away. "You've been wanting to ask me something ever since the Deathly Bog."

"Ahhh—"

"Yes?" She raised an eyebrow expectantly. "You're not usually this tongue tied."

He gave her a puzzled look. Bulges appeared in his cheeks, his tongue exploring the inside of his mouth.

"It's just an expression," Juanita explained, "from Earth." When he didn't respond she added, "I'm still waiting."

He sighed. "Juanita, you should not have endangered yourself coming all this way to warn me."

"That's what you've been struggling with all this time?" She raised her brow skeptically. "OK, I'll play along. So—by '*I shouldn't have come all this way*' did you mean—the billions of light years from my universe to yours or the few kiloters from Elfhaven to the Deathly Bog?"

He grinned.

Caught off guard by his unexpected reaction, Juanita stumbled over her words, "Did—did you—ahhh—are you implying you think it's too dangerous for a *woman* to be traipsing about in the wilderness? If so, might I remind you I wasn't the one who dislocated my shoulder."

Dakshi winced and glanced at Tappus, scouting ahead for signs of trouble.

"Besides," she argued, "you should know me better than that. I'm not afraid of a little danger, or a fight."

He grinned again. "As I recall—" His eyes sparkled in the midday sun. "—you know your way around a sword quite well. Where did you learn to fight like that?"

"Thought you knew. In my spare time, I'm a Wu Shu instructor. It's an ancient Chinese martial art." She flicked sand from her blouse. "It's a pleasant diversion. Helps me quiet my over-active scientist's mind. Keeps me in shape."

"Your shape looks good."

Juanita chuckled. "Another expression. Means staying fit. Keeping one's muscles toned."

"Ah! Nice tone then."

She blushed, shocking herself.

He looked away awkwardly. For a time, they walked in silence.

"I—" they both said in unison.

"You first," she said.

"I—It has been a long time since last I saw you," the king began.

"Nearly a year, er—a yara."

"Quite so."

"Go on."

He inhaled deeply. "It is just that—well, I have been thinking about you quite a bit this past yara, ah—year."

"Yes?"

His right eye began to twitch. "It is troubling to admit—but I seem to have acquired *feelings* for you."

"Feelings?" she said casually.

King Dakshi coughed awkwardly. "You are not making this simple."

"Sorry. That was cruel of me. To be honest, I've been thinking of you as well."

"And?"

She glanced down at her hiking boots, then up at him. "And I guess I have *feelings* for you, too."

"You guess?"

"I have."

"So, what shall we do about these—*feelings?*"

She laughed. "What can we do? You're a king. An elf king at that. You live in an alien world far from home. I'm a human and a scientist. I live in a world of science and technology. You live in a world of magic and monsters. We are universes apart, both literally and figuratively."

"We have the Citadel—" he pointed out, "—built by beings from beyond."

"Which you thought was powered by magic until Tom discovered otherwise."

Again they walked in silence.

"Is it the class difference?" began King Dakshi. "Me being of royal blood and you a commoner?"

"A what?"

He stopped. She stopped.

"I don't consider myself a commoner!"

"Because if that is all that stands between us," Dakshi hurried on, "then we could close the class gap by a joining ceremony."

"Class distinctions on Earth were stamped out back in the late twenty-first cent…" Juanita froze. "Wait? What did you say?"

He shrugged. "If you were my queen, the class difference would no longer exist."

Juanita's jaw dropped. "Did—did you just propose to me?"

"If to propose means—offering to make you my partner, my wife, my queen, then no. I was speaking hypothetically."

Her jaw snapped shut. "You were just—*brain-storming* possible solutions to our—*problem*?"

"A storm?" He frowned. "In my brain?"

"It's just—"

"Another Earth expression?"

She nodded.

They resumed trudging along. "But if I *were* to propose to you, would you accept, hypothetically speaking, of course?"

Juanita stopped again and stared at him. "Are you crazy? We're from different worlds, different cultures. We're not even of the same species!"

"Yet we each have feelings for one-another."

She continued to stare. The soldiers behind stopped and began murmuring to themselves. The king glanced over his shoulder. The guards fell silent.

He touched her arm lightly, and they moved on.

She glanced back; the soldiers maintained a respectful distance. "True," Juanita whispered, "we have feelings. Putting aside the obvious ludicrousy of the idea, I'm currently waiting to hear if I won the Nobel prize, a scientists' greatest honor. It's been my life's goal, ever since I was a little girl. Plus, there's so much more to be done on our project: publish our findings, fund raising for future research, lead my team of scientists."

"Others can do that work, can they not? Your brother Carlos, for one. He seemed competent enough." His eyes found hers. "You have already proved yourself, Juanita. What more accolades do you need?"

"I—I can't believe we're even having this conversation!" She tried to collect her thoughts. "There's also Tom to think about."

"Tom?"

"Tom has his entire future ahead of him. He'll become a scientist or engineer. Might even start a successful company or find a cure for cancer."

"Cancer?"

"It's a disease. Oh, that's right. You don't have diseases here."

Dakshi took her hand and squeezed it. "You once said Tom was not well liked on your world."

"True, he's bullied a lot." She stared at their clasped hands. "He's small for his age and smart. Others make fun of him because he's smart."

"He has friends here in Elfhaven," the king pointed out. "Tom is famous here, due to the Prophecy. Plus, Tom is a hero!" The king paused. "And I would be proud to call him my son."

Juanita's eyes began to water. She turned away. When she finally spoke her voice cracked, "I'm honored. Really." She turned back and scanned his face. "It can't work. The idea is ludicrous, but—"

"But?"

"But I shall consider your offer."

"I did not propose," he reminded her. "I said '*hypothetically speaking*' remember?"

She choked back a laugh.

King Dakshi grinned anew.

# Lord of Trolls

The trolls, near enough to see, stared at Bellchar, at Tom, at the blade.

"What's happening?" Tom asked Bellchar.

Trolls grumbled as Phawta shoved them aside on his way back down. "Bellchar! What are you doing, you fool? Stand up!"

Bellchar grabbed Tom, hoisted him onto his shoulder, stood and faced the troll army. "He has da Acutis Lignum Unum! Da sacred blade. Boy, Lord of Trolls!"

Chuckles burst forth, faltered, morphed into murmurs of disbelief.

"Raise da Lignum Unum," urged Bellchar.

"The what?" Tom's heartbeat raced like a CPU's clock speed pushed beyond its design limit.

"Dagger! Hold up dagger!"

Tom glanced at Avani. She looked as shocked as he felt.

Swallowing hard, Tom slowly raised the blade over his head.

Gasps swept through the troll ranks.

The dagger's gemstone suddenly blazed with light. A brilliant, crackling storm of orange magic lanced out, striking tens, hundreds, thousands of trolls, until all felt the power of its magic. One last flash and the gem's light faded.

Tom opened his hand and stared at the magical artifact in his trembling palm. The dagger tipped, slipping from his hand. His other hand shot out, grabbed for the handle, but that only started it spinning.

His friends gasped in horror.

Tom snatched the dagger and clutched it tightly, then gave his friends a sheepish grin.

Tom looked up at the sound of thousands of deep voices inhaling. Here and there, trolls began to kneel. Then more. Within moments, a waving black flag settled to the dunes. As far as Tom could see, the vast troll army knelt before him. All except for Phawta and Bellchar.

Bellchar sat Tom down gently, then he too knelt.

The only ones left standing were Tom and his friends and the troll commander.

Phawta scanned his kneeling army. "Get up, you fools! All of you stand up!" No one moved.

"Dis—ting!" Phawta threw out his arm, pointing at Tom. "It not a *troll!* Only *troll* can be Lord of Trolls!" He thrust his club skyward. "Get up! Dat an order!" A few stood. Most remained kneeling.

Phawta clenched his teeth. "I da rightful leader! I should be Lord of Trolls!" Faster than Tom could believe a troll could move, Phawta leapt for the dagger. As his hand neared the blade, a flash of orange magic hurled him backwards violently, bowling over dozens of trolls, coming to rest on top of a tall mound of squirming bodies.

Climbing off the cursing pile, Phawta brushed himself off and stormed back over to Tom. Phawta's hands tightened into fists, eying the dagger cautiously.

Bellchar rose and stood beside Tom. Phawta glared at Bellchar. Drumming his fingers lightly on his club, Bellchar returned his commander's icy glare with a calm look.

"What just happened?" Tom asked Bellchar. "Why couldn't Phawta take the dagger?"

Keeping his eyes on Phawta, Bellchar bent over and whispered in Tom's ear, "Acutis Lignum Unum can't be taken. Only given." Bellchar stood up straight. "You da Supreme Leader. Troll army await yer command."

Tom slowly pivoted, taking in the sea of mostly kneeling trolls. "What should I do?" he asked his friends.

Devraj stepped forward, whispering, "Have them capture Naagesh, and kill his goblins. But make sure they do not destroy his device," Devraj reminded him. "It is our only hope."

The prince stepped back. "Go ahead," he urged.

Tom stared at him, then glanced at Larraj. The wizard nodded.

Tom faced the troll army. His army. Tom's heart pounded, louder in his ears than the faint hissing sand blowing across the dunes. Thousands of dark kneeling forms, their gazes fixed on him, awaited their new leader's orders.

"Rise!" Tom shouted. The dune shifted as a wave of dark bodies stood.

"Capture Naagesh! And his goblins." Tom glanced at Devraj. The prince hesitated, then nodded.

Nothing happened.

Tom asked Bellchar, "Why aren't they moving?"

"Louder," Bellchar instructed. "Raise blade. Deeper voice. Sound more like troll."

Tom squared his shoulders, thrust the dagger skyward, and in the deepest voice he could muster yelled, "Capture Naagesh and his goblins!"

Thousands of trolls slogged southward.

"Stop!" cried Phawta. The army ground to a halt. "I said—" Again Phawta pointed at Tom. "It—not a *troll*. So *it* not Lord of Trolls. I your commander. I order ya ta kill phony Lord and his friends!" Phawta waggled his club above him.

A murmur passed through the troll ranks. A few continued south, as the Lord of Trolls commanded. Others moved to stand with Phawta. Most, however, just stood there.

Trembling from the strain, Tom raised the dagger once more and shouted, "Whoever holds this blade is the Lord of Trolls. I hold the blade." The dagger felt slick in Tom's sweaty hands. Tom faced Phawta.

"If Naagesh wins," pleaded Tom. "We all die." Phawta looked like he might explode from anger.

"Save the world! Capture Naagesh!" Tom thrust the blade skyward once more and took a step up the next dune. Behind him came more murmurs followed by heated arguments. This time, none of the trolls moved.

Tom turned and whispered to Bellchar, "What's wrong? Why won't they follow me?"

"Phawta have point." Bellchar's dark eyes scanned Tom's wimpy body. "You no troll. Too small 'n sickly."

"But the dagger!" Tom insisted. "The Acutis Lig—whatever. They should be following me!"

Phawta nodded to his loyal followers, and a dozen trolls advanced on Tom and his friends. Larraj spread his now glowing arms apart, the magic building.

Bellchar gazed down at Tom. "You right. You have Acutis Lignum Unum. You Supreme Leader." Bellchar stepped between Tom and Phawta and slapped his club down hard onto his outstretched palm. *Thwack.* The advancing trolls stopped.

Bellchar whispered to Tom, "But you still no troll."

Sweat dripped from Tom's forehead. He asked Goban and Avani for guidance. Neither spoke.

Tom took a deep breath. "You said *'the dagger can't be taken, only given'*, right?"

Bellchar grunted.

Tom faced Phawta. "Naagesh intends to open Pandora's Portal."

"You said dat."

"If Naagesh opens the portal and releases the creatures, the creatures'll destroy all life on this planet, including trolls."

"You say dat too."

"The only way to stop him is to take the device he's carrying back to the Citadel before the portal opens."

"So?"

"So, if I give you this dagger and make you Lord of Trolls, will you promise to help us stop Naagesh?"

A broad grin slowly spread across Phawta's face. "Course I will."

"No!" cried Devraj.

Tom said, "Cross your heart and hope to die?"

Phawta tipped his head uncertainly, then slapped his arms across his chest. "Troll's honor."

Tom clenched his jaw, staring at the blade. He glanced at his friends, their faces masked in horror.

Tom opened his palm and raised the blade. Phawta's leaned down, his grin widening. Tom hesitated. Closing his hand he asked Bellchar, "Can I trust Phawta? Will he keep his word?"

Bellchar eyed Phawta critically. "No."

Phawta growled.

"Then here." Tom offered Bellchar the dagger. "You take it."

Bellchar stumbled back. "No!"

Tom grabbed Bellchar's huge hand, twisted it over and slapped the dagger's handle into Bellchar's palm.

"NO!" cried Phawta and Devraj.

Phawta lunged for the blade, but it was already too late; a cyclone of powerful magic encircled Bellchar's body, then flashed, encasing him in a brilliant tangerine glow. Everyone froze. The glow faded.

Bellchar blinked, turned slowly as if in a daze. His eyes slowly cleared.

Bellchar leaned toward Phawta. "When I commander den I make da rules." Upon hearing his own words spat back at him, Phawta's eyes widened.

Bellchar thrust the dagger skyward. As with Tom, the magic lanced out, touching troll after troll. Again, the troll army thundered to their knees.

Phawta bared his teeth and lunged for Tom's neck. Bellchar grabbed Phawta's arm.

"Phawta my prisoner!" shouted Bellchar. Trolls grabbed him. Phawta struggled but couldn't break free. The ex-commander glared at Bellchar, rage burning deep within his eyes.

Bellchar waved his hand dismissively. Phawta cursed as troll warriors dragged him away.

Bellchar thrust the dagger skyward once more. "I Bellchar, Lord of Trolls!"

A thunderous roar erupted across the dunes as thousands of trolls leapt to their feet.

"Sweet!" Tom grinned up at Bellchar. "Now help us stop Naagesh."

Bellchar stared down at Tom. Then just strode off up the dune, heading back the way they'd come, thousands of trolls in his wake.

"No! Wait!" cried Tom. "You're goin' the wrong way. Naagesh went that way."

Bellchar didn't even look back.

# Lord of nothing

Larraj's magic faded. Goban and Devraj put away their weapons, Chloe's laser withdrew. Max barked at the retreating trolls.

The wizard watched the tall dark backs till they crested the dune and disappeared, their tracks already drifting in.

Devraj stormed over to Tom. "You fool! You idiot! What have you done? If you would have just done what I told you!"

"I—I tried," Tom's voice faltered. "I thought—"

"You thought!" snapped the prince. "You had command of the troll army! You just threw away our only means of defeating Naagesh!"

Tom's eyes pleaded for his friends' support. Kiran stared at his feet. Avani remained silent. Chloe gave a forlorn chirp. Max whined.

"Told ya not to trust a troll," said Goban. "Almost as bad as giants."

"Goban's right!" shouted Devraj. "Bellchar just gave us away! We should have killed him when we first found him!"

"Bellchar led us into the Deathly Bog," Tom argued meekly. "And saved us from the giant spider."

"Least Bellchar let us go," Kiran pointed out. "Phawta woulda killed us."

Spittle flew as Devraj shouted, "If your mechanical pet had not delayed us here!" His arm shot out, indicating the sink hole. "With that ludicrous notion that Naagesh is hiding in that pit!"

"But the nano-droid," Tom insisted. "It says—"

"Why would the wizard hide down there, instead of going after Father like we should be?" Devraj scanned the other faces. "Well, I for one have had enough of this. Enough of this *self-appointed leader* who's plans keep failing. Face it! Tom is inept and a weakling. His *brilliant plans* and useless science lectures have brought us no closer to finding my father or retrieving the remote! And the watch tower's hands continue to rotate.

"In fact, his actions have been nothing but distractions!" With barely contained rage, Devraj rasped, "The Prophecy is unclear. Perhaps you will bring about the destruction of our world instead of saving it, hmmm?" The prince leaned in close, his voice now quiet, "Perhaps that was your goal all along."

Tom's lip began to quiver.

Devraj stood tall. "I am leaving. Who is coming with me?" No one moved. He slammed his arm down, pointing at his feet. "Avani come here!"

She sighed. "Devraj please. We need your help and we'll all be safer together."

Devraj screamed and strode off.

Avani watched the prince disappear over the next dune crest. "We should go after him."

Larraj started up the dune. "Wait here."

Avani bit her lip. "But—"

"Give him a moment to calm down," Larraj called over his shoulder. "I'll bring him back, then use the seeker to verify Naagesh's whereabouts."

Chloe sped off after the wizard.

"Chloe no!" shouted Tom. Chloe stopped halfway up the dune. She gave a forlorn chirp.

Tom walked to the edge of the sinkhole. His shoulders sank. He gazed down dejectedly into the gloom.

Goban walked up beside him and rested his hand on Tom's shoulder. "Hey. We don't have em, but neither does Naagesh."

Tom raised his head and stared into his friend's eyes.

"The troll army, I mean."

Once Larraj disappeared over the dune, Kiran, Max and Avani joined Tom and Goban.

Avani studied Tom; his lowered head, his drooped shoulders. She finally spoke, "So—Chloe said Naagesh is down there, huh?"

Tom nodded.

Avani relaxed, her face adopting a distant look. She leaned over the edge, focusing. "Don't sense magic. Not from down there." She straightened up, her gaze shifting to the crest of the dune ahead.

## The horned goblin

From the top of the dune, amidst howling wind and blasting sand, the horned goblin watched the scene below with interest. It had witnessed many strange turns of events from the moment the troll army arrived, up until the underworld opened its glorious mouth wide and swallowed the sniveling brats whole!

The goblin was about to leave when suddenly, the ground started shaking.

"Another quake!" cried Earth boy from down below. "Look out!"

The goblin watched till the last grains of sand stopped flowing and the massive blue stone, that teetered at the edge, came to rest.

The children had struggled, trying to avoid the inevitable, but were now gone, swallowed up by the sea of flooding sand.

The goblin waited a long time, but nothing moved and there were no cries for help from the pit.

Turning to leave, the goblin hesitated, tipped its knobby head to one side and turned back. Raising a spindly arm, it flicked its spindly wrist.

The blue stone, perched precariously over the edge, started wobbling. The goblin grinned a wicked grin, then scurried off across the dunes on all fours, heading in the direction the prince had gone.

# The sinkhole

Tom half fell, half slid down the torrential flood of sand, like the scariest water-slide ride Tom had ever taken—only drier. When the tons of sand struck the floor of the sinkhole it angled toward the underground lake, taking a struggling Tom with it.

"Aaaah!" Tom tried swimming against the rushing, swirling current of sand.

Glancing over his shoulder, the lake was fast approaching. Tom screamed. Splashes echoed throughout the cavern. A moment later, the avalanche trickled to a stop.

Buried up to his neck, Tom spit out a mouthful of gritty, salty grains. It took several minutes to dig himself free.

"Where are you guys?" he yelled. "Everyone OK?" No one answered. "Say something!"

Kiran's head burst from the sand to his left, gasping for breath. A second later, Avani popped up, then Max.

"Where's Chloe?" asked Kiran.

"She was halfway up the next dune," Tom replied. "She's probably still up there."

Tom wallowed over to help Avani. By the time he reached her, she was already standing.

Avani shook, sand flying from her hair. Holding out the bottom of her tunic, sand drifted down. Flicking the garment's hem, yet more sand flew. She stopped abruptly. "Where's Goban?"

Tom slogged around, making a full circle. "Goban?" he called. Avani joined him, "Goban!"

Max bounded across the sand pile, barked, and started digging. The others ran over. Max's efforts exposed an arm, then a leg, then another arm. Each grabbing a limb, they pulled Goban from the sand.

Goban's eyes were shut. Avani put her ear to his face. "He's not breathing!"

"We've gotta do CPR!" cried Tom.

"What?"

Tom bent over and started pumping Goban's chest. "Kiran! When I release pressure on Goban's stomach, you blow air in his mouth."

Kiran's face wrinkled in horror. "I'm not gonna kiss him!"

Tom stared at Avani. She looked almost as horrified.

"I can't do both!" said Tom, still pumping Goban's chest. "Avani!"

She hesitated. Leaned over the dwarf. Glanced nervously at Tom.

"Do it!" Tom shouted.

Avani bent down and closed her eyes. Her lips touched Goban's. His eyes popped open. Avani jerked away. Goban coughed. "Did you just—"

"NO!" shouted Avani, blushing.

"We were trying to save yer life," explained Tom.

Goban looked disgusted. "Did you kiss me too?"

"NO! I—" Tom grimaced. "Come on." He motioned to Avani and Kiran. "Help me lift him."

They grabbed Goban's arms and pulled. "Ouch!" cried Goban.

"My arm!" Goban winced. He turned his left arm over. On the underside was a deep gash with a large shard of chipped stone jutting out. Blood oozed from the wound. Tom gagged and turned away.

"Cool!" said Kiran, staring at Goban's wound.

Unable to watch, Tom walked away and scanned the area, searching for a way out. He heard gushing water off to his right. Across the lake, there was a pile of sand, rocks and boulders reaching nearly to the sinkhole's lip.

Avani took off her cloak, tore two long strips from the hem. Using one, she dabbed at the cut.

"Ouch!"

"Quiet," she scolded gently. "It's only a scratch."

Kiran reached for the shard. "Can I pull it out?"

"No!" shouted Goban and Avani. She gave Goban a reassuring smile, grabbed the shard and jerked.

"Aaahhh!"

Tom looked back, wished he hadn't, looked away.

Avani handed the bloody shard to Kiran. He glared at her, studied the shard intently for a moment, then tossed it away.

Using the second strip of cloth, Avani wrapped it around Goban's arm and pulled, tightening the makeshift bandage around his arm.

Goban winced again.

"Baby," she said, tying the ends in a knot.

"Hurts," he insisted.

She cinched it down tight. "There. How's that?"

Goban flexed his hand and smiled weakly.

"There's running water at the far end of the cavern," called Tom. "Might be a way out." He pointed across the lake. "Or maybe we could climb out over there."

Kiran bolted to the water's edge, shouting, "Something's happening!" Ripples formed on the lake.

"Another quake!" cried Tom. A rasping, cracking noise caused him to glance up. The blue stone hanging over the edge above them, began to tip. "Run!"

"Run where?" shouted Goban.

Tom wallowed through sand as fast as he could, heading in the direction he'd heard rushing water. "This way!"

Goban leapt aside just as the massive stone crashed to the cavern floor, right where he'd been standing. Which—started another avalanche.

"Run!" repeated Tom.

Max barked. Tom craned his neck back as he ran. Ten feet behind, Max bounded along, the roiling avalanche of sand nearing his hind legs.

"Faster Max," urged Tom. "You can do it!" Stretching farther with each stride, Max barely kept ahead of the thundering torrent.

The farther he went, the sound of gushing water grew nearly as loud as the avalanche.

Tom screeched to a stop at the end of the cavern. The tunnel he'd hoped for wasn't there. Water rushed toward the wall and just disappeared!

*Must be an underwater tunnel.* Tom glanced back. A massive wave of sand and rocks bared down upon them.

Tom leapt. "Jump!" he cried and disappeared beneath the turbulent waters.


# Larraj

Larraj squinted into the continually building wind. Beyond the dunes, beyond even the Floating Mountains, ominous clouds blanketed the horizon. A massive storm was headed this way.

The wizard bent over, pulled his hood down low, shielding his eyes from the blistering sand.

Devraj's tracks had almost disappeared.

Even before he heard the *boom*, Larraj felt the dune shudder. He turned back. A plume of dust shot skyward.

*Something's happened.*

Larraj looked down. The prince's footprints were gone.

# A glowing reception

Swept along in the strong current, Tom held his breath.

The submerged stream veered left, right, another quick left. Completely filled with churning water, the narrow underground stream provided no air pockets to breathe. If the tunnel didn't end soon, he'd drown.

The moment Tom realized he couldn't hold his breath any longer, the tunnel abruptly ended, spewing him out along with tons of bubbling, effervescent water, into the chill, humid air of a small cavern.

He gasped for breath. Arms and legs flailing, twenty feet below, a tiny lake's surface rushed up to meet him. *Splash!* With the force of water pounding upon him, the current dragged him down and rolled him across the lake bottom.

Feet kicking, arms waving, a detached part of his mind noticed that each time he moved, the water surrounding his body glowed neon blue. And that the quicker he moved, the brighter it glowed.

He heard muted splashes behind.

Tumbling along the bottom, Tom felt the downward pressure stop and the current ease. Preparing to head for the surface, Tom spotted a tiny oblong object rolling past in the now gentle current. He scooped it up along with a handful of sand and kicked off from the bottom.

He gasped again when his head burst the surface. As his ears drained, he heard the muted sound of the distant avalanche that had nearly killed him.

Treading water, Tom spun in a tight circle. The churning water glowed faintly, dimly illuminating the small cavern around him. A narrow ledge stood to the left of the gushing tunnel he'd entered through.

Avani's head popped up beside him, then Kiran. Max burst the surface and dog-paddled to shore.

Treading water, Avani stared in awe at the blue glow surrounding them.

"The water glows! Magic?"

Tom cupped his palm and raised it above the lake. Bright neon blue flecks squirmed around in his hand.

"They're tiny organisms called dinoflagellates. They're naturally bioluminescent. Awesome, huh? Uncle Carlos took me to Jamaica once. There's a lagoon there that's loaded with em. At night we could see the wake from our boat, fish swimming by, and even a ray, its wings glowing blue each time it flapped."

"How can rays have wings? Rays of light?"

"No. Rays are like fish. Only flat. Ah—with wings."

"Where's Goban?" called Kiran.

A soft clacking noise caused them to turn. Goban burst from a small dark alcove, followed by a cloud of dust and rocks.

Lurching to a stop, dust settling at his feet, Goban bent over, rested hands on knees and coughed. Within moments, the distant muted rumble of the avalanche fell silent.

Swimming ashore, Tom and Avani crawled onto the ledge, sparkling blue water draining from their clothing. Kiran and Max climbed up next. Max shook, sending shimmering droplets flying.

Tom stared at Goban expectantly.

"I was too far behind," he explained. "Wasn't gonna make it to the stream. I spotted a hole in the cavern wall and ducked inside. Turned out to be a tunnel."

Goban grinned. "If you'd followed me, ya wouldn't a needed a bath."

Kiran sniffed the dwarf, then recoiled in mock disgust. "Maybe you shoulda followed us." Goban frowned.

Taking off his adventurers' belt, Tom flipped it upside down, draining the compartments. As he did, a glob of wet sand fell from his hand. There came a soft *clink* when it struck the ledge.

Cinching up his belt, Tom scanned his friends: three of them, himself included, looked like drowned rats. Goban, however, looked like he'd been playing King of the Mountain on a dirt pile—and lost.

Kiran tipped his head sideways. Water drained from his ear.

Avani's clothes, like Tom's were plastered to her slim elven body. Rivulets of sparkling blue water dripped from her clothing. Combing her hair with her fingers, she wrung out water. Then she moved on to her drenched tunic, wiping it down, flicking water from her hands as she went.

Looking up, Avani noticed Tom staring and flicked water in his face.

"Hey stop that!"

She flicked again.

Tom rubbed his hands on his jeans and flicked back.

Avani squeezed the bottom of her tunic, reloading for her next attack.

"Would you two stop flirting," said Goban. "We gotta find a way out."

Tom blushed. "We weren't—I wasn't."

Avani giggled, spun around, sending a barrage of droplets flying from her outstretched hair, peppering both Goban and Tom with sparkling water pellets. The pair jumped back.

Stopping abruptly, Avani's hair slapped across her face, then fell limply over her shoulders. Brushing hair from her eyes, she flashed them a broad smile.

Goban walked back to the tunnel he'd just escaped through. "It's completely blocked. Hafta find another way."

Max barked.

Kiran walked over and picked up a tiny gray, oblong object and handed it to Tom, flecks of neon blue sparkling across its wet surface.

"I forgot." Tom held it up. "Found this at the bottom of the lake." Everyone stared at it.

Avani leaned in close. "What is it?"

"It's Naagesh," replied Kiran.

"Wow!" Tom remarked. "Kiran's right."

Goban nodded.

"What?" said Avani.

# Devraj

An oort had passed since he'd stormed off and left the others behind.

Devraj relaxed his tense shoulders. *It was their own fault. They left me no choice. If I had stayed any longer, I would never find Father in—*

He stopped. *There it was again. That feeling.* He scanned the dunes and as before and saw nothing.

*Nothing, save this accursed blowing sand.* Yanking his leg from the dune, the action flipped up sand which immediately blew back, peppering his face with stinging particles.

"Aaaah!" Frowning, he spat and resumed his march. The sandstorm had not only wiped away all trace of Naagesh's passing, the foul storm had increased its rage to the point where he could no longer see the sun. He wasn't even sure which direction he was going.

*I know I am being followed. Being watched.* With each passing myntar, his sense of unease grew.

*But there is something more. I sense—magic.* He grinned. *Larraj. Hah! The wizard must have come to his senses and decided to go with me.* His grin faded. *Else he intends to bring me back.* Devraj clenched his teeth. *Well, I shall not go back! No matter how hard the wizard tries to—*

There it was yet again! He whipped around. Through the blasting sand, he thought he glimpsed something drop below the dune's crest.

"Larraj! I know you are there. Stop lurking about like some stalking beast."

A gnarled, ugly head rose above the dune, followed by an equally grotesque, misshapen body.

Devraj reached for his sword, but his scabbard was empty.

The horned goblin raised the prince's sword and grinned.

# The seeker

"Chloe. What happened?" Larraj studied the area. The sink hole was much wider, and one of the three blue stones was missing.

"There was a quake," explained Chloe. The dune collapsed into the sinkhole."

Larraj leaned over the edge. "Avani?" No response. "Tom? Goban?" He paused. "Kiran?" Nothing.

Pulling up his sleeve, exposing his bracelet, Larraj uttered the seeker's invocation spell. The eye in the vortex opened, and the swirling blue cloud hovered above his arm.

"Show us Avani and her companions." The roil quickened, and the cloud parted. The vision seemed to dive, darting around in the dark, finally popping out into a dimly lit cavern. The image ground to a halt above a glowing sapphire pool in a small cavern.

"Rotate slowly. There! Closer." The view moved in. Avani and Kiran stood staring at something Tom held. "Closer. What's he holding?" Zooming farther in, Tom held a tiny gray object, no bigger than a grain of cirrus wheat.

"It's the Guardian's nano-droid from Naagesh's boot," replied Chloe. "The one I've been tracking."

"Well, at least we know Tom and the others are alive. They should be safe enough for the time being, long as they stay put. Seeker," Larraj commanded. "Show me Prince Devraj."

The vision blasted up from the ground, angled sideways, racing just above the dune crests, heading deeper into the Plains. The vision picked up speed, dunes hurtling by faster and faster. Finally, the image slowed, then stopped.

"It appears—" began Chloe.

"Devraj has been captured." The seeker showed the prince slogging through deep sand, a sword aimed at his back.

"And by a single goblin," remarked Chloe.

# A red herring

"More accurately," Tom explained to Avani, "it's the Guardian's nano-droid."

Goban strolled down the ledge.

Avani took the object from Tom and stared at it. "Naagesh sent us on a wild zapterchick chase…" She dropped the tiny robot. *Clink.*

"And now we're trapped," said Kiran.

"Hey!" Goban waved from down the ledge. "Think I found a way out."

Tom picked up the nano-droid, brushed it off, and shoved it into his pocket.

Goban had found a wide crack in the cavern wall, partially hidden behind a rockslide.

They all tossed stones aside. Soon they'd exposed a narrow horizontal slit. Slithering on their bellies till the crack widened enough so they could walk hunched over, they then walked single file down a rocky passageway; sometimes on a narrow ledge, sometimes across slippery stone slabs and sometimes; when there was no bank, wading down the sapphire-blue stream.

Tom had fallen behind. At the point where the stream veered away to the left, Tom stepped from the water onto a ledge. Up ahead, his friends crowded together at an entrance to a tunnel, staring down at something.

Tom pulled out his headlamp. "What is it?" he said as he walked up. They stepped aside.

Tom gasped.

An enormous square stone, about three feet per side, half-blocked a narrow passageway. What held their attention, though, were the two skeletal feet, facing downward, protruding from beneath the stone.

Tom stood frozen, unable to take his eyes off the gruesome sight. The others scooched between the stone and the cavern wall. Tom continued to stare.

"It's an elf," Avani called. "Probably male."

"Poor guy," Goban added. "Horrible accident."

Tom inched his way sideways, following them.

On this side, the upper torso of the skeleton lay face down, jutting out from beneath the rock. The unfortunate victim's head twisted sharply to one side and his right arm stretched outward as if reaching for something while his other arm lay folded by his side, his hand barely extending beyond the stone.

"How d'ya know it's an elf?" Tom asked, "let alone a guy?"

Avani knelt. "See this curved bump?" She touched the skull. "It supports the larger elven ears. And his jaw—" She tapped it. "—is larger than a female's." Laying down, she placed her head beside the skeleton's, twisted her head and jutting out her jaw to match the skull's. "See?"

Tom grimaced. "Gross! Now I'll have that image stuck in my mind forever."

"Hey!" Kiran piped up. "The dead guy's holding something."

Tom leaned forward. There was something clutched tightly in the skeleton's right hand. Kiran grabbed hold of a finger and tugged.

"Kiran no!" scolded Avani. He gave her a defiant look but let go.

"Picked the wrong time to walk by," said Goban. "Wonder who he was?"

"His friends called him lucky," said Kiran.

Goban strolled off.

Tom shone his headlamp on the top of the stone. A stout metal spike protruded upward from the rock. Attached to the spike was a thin metal cable. Tom tipped his head back, shining the light higher. The cable ran through a pulley attacked to the cavern ceiling. "Don't think it was bad luck."

Tom leaned around the stone, stared at the feet once more. Something sparkled in his headlamp beam. A thin wire was stretched taut against the skeleton's ankle bone.

"Hey look at this," called Goban.

Max barked.

"Goban stop! It's a tripwire! There may be—"

From above came a grinding noise.

"Goban look out!" cried Tom.

Max bounded forward and leapt.

Goban glanced up as another slab fell.

Max slammed into Goban's back.

Avani screamed.

The rock crashed down. The tunnel shook, dust slowly settling.

"Max!" cried Kiran. "Goban!" cried the others.

The three scrambled around the massive stone. Goban lay face down, his feet barely an inch beyond the rock.

Goban coughed. Max wagged his tail and licked the dwarf's ear. Frowning, Goban pushed himself up to his knees.

"You Ok?" said Tom.

Goban wiped his nose and stared at his blood-stained hand. "Bloodied my nose is all." Smiling, he ruffled Max's furry head. "Thanks Max." Max raised his paw and Goban shook it.

Tom shuddered. "That was close."

Avani asked Goban, "What were you saying before?"

"Before you almost got squished," added Kiran.

Goban grabbed Tom's arm for support and stood. He gestured ahead. Avani opened her palm and muttered the light globe incantation. Nothing happened. She tried again. Still nothing.

Kiran spoke the same incantation. Instantly, a glow orb hovered above his palm. His face burst into a huge grin. Kiran waved his hand and the orb obediently drifted forward, its dim light reflecting off something big, dark and solid.

Avani met Tom's gaze, an embarrassed look in her eye.

"Think they're any more of those—" Goban glanced around warily. "—whatchamacallits?"

"Tripwires," repeated Tom. Swinging his headlamp slowly back and forth, Tom inched his way forward, Kiran, Max and Goban close behind.

Avani just stared at her empty palm.


"It's safe," called Tom, standing in front of a solid, rust covered metal wall. "At least there are no more tripwires." He patted the wall's, cool surface. "It's some sorta barrier, sealing the tunnel."

Goban lowered his voice, "Is it supposed ta keep people out? Or keep something inside from escaping?"

Tom pointed to the stone resting atop the skeleton. "Someone's try'n pretty hard to discourage people from going further."

Avani walked up.

"You OK?" asked Tom. "You look shook."

"My magic. It—it's getting worse." Tom placed his hand lightly on her shoulder. She managed a weak smile.

Goban walked over and studied a circular depression in the barrier wall. "There's an indent in the wall. With geometric shapes inside." Goban moved over. Tom focused his headlamp on the spot.

"Any idea what the shapes mean?" Avani asked.

Tom drummed his fingers on the metal surface. "Maybe it's a gate, not a wall." He stared at the indent. "Might be some sorta lock." He felt inside the recess. "Don't feel a release mechanism."

Goban pulled his axe off his shoulder, flipped it over so his axe's flat metal side faced the wall, and drew back.

Max barked. Tom leapt back. "Goban? I wouldn't do—"

Goban slammed the axe against the barrier. Tom dropped face down on the floor. *Bong. zing, zing, thunk.* Everyone else leapt back as a barrage of deadly needles launched from the left and ricocheted off Goban's axe. When the barrage finally stopped, Tom stood up. The floor lay littered with tiny glistening spikes.

Tom motioned to Goban's axe.

"Ahhhh," moaned Goban, yanking two spikes from Aileen's handle. "That twernt nice."

Tom studied the indentation once more. "If it's a lock, there must be a key."

"How about this?" said Kiran. Everyone turned. Kiran leaned over the skeleton and again grasped a finger.

"Kiran?!" warned his sister.

*Crack!* The finger snapped off. Tom winced. Kiran snapped another. Tom winced again. A dark gray ball rolled free from the skeleton's hand, stopping at Kiran's feet.

Kiran handed the object to Tom. It was heavier than Tom expected.

A half sphere, carved from a marbled blue and white stone with brass lines inlaid into its surface, the object had a dragon's head engraved into its rounded side. Flipping it over, the other side was flat with a brass ring encompassing a series of squares, triangles, and circles etched deeply into its surface.

Tom rolled it in his hands till the dragon's face stared up at him. Light from Kiran's magical orb shone through three triangular holes, where the dragon's eyes and mouth should be.

Goban gestured to the barrier's indent. "Worth a try."

Tom held the object near the recession in the wall. The geometric pattern engraved into the object's flat side matched those in the wall perfectly.

Tom glanced at the others, took a deep breath and shoved the object into the receptacle. *Clunk.* Triangular metal rods extended all the way through the dragon's eyes and mouth and clicked into place. Tom jumped back.

Everyone watched the walls, floor and ceiling warily.

Tom stepped up and grabbed the object.

"Wait!" cried the others.

"It's gotta be a lock," reasoned Tom. "And this has to be the key."

Avani asked, "So what do we do?"

"Surrounding the lock are three sets of grooves separated by three flat rings. My guess is we hafta rotate the key three times, reversing direction each time."

"But which way first?" asked Avani. "Right or left?"

Tom stared at her.

"If we turn it the wrong way—"

"We'll spring another trap," Tom nodded. "Do we have a choice?" No one answered. "OK. Who votes for left first?" Kiran raised his hand. "Right?" Goban raised his hand. "Avani?"

"Go ahead," she said. "You cast the final vote."

"OK. Right! Seems logical." Tom grabbed hold of the dragon-head key. He hesitated. "Maybe too logical?" His hand started shaking. "Left it is!"

"Wait!" shouted Kiran. "There's something in the dead guy's other hand."

Tom exhaled and turned to watch Kiran wrestling yet again with the skeleton. This time, the unfortunate fellow's whole wrist broke off.

Tom gasped.

*Snap!* Kiran tossed a finger bone to the ground.

Tom winced again. "Kiran. Do you hafta—" *Snap, snap.* Two more fingers clattered to the floor.

Kiran held up a folded sheet of dry, crinkly parchment. Releasing the finger bone, it bounced off the skull; the skull twisted and its jaw dropped open.

Tom leapt back. Max hunkered down and barked at the skull, then inching forward, he sniffed first the skull, then one of the finger bones. Max turned to face them, a finger bone sticking out of his mouth.

"Max no!" Tom wrinkled his face in disgust. "Spit that out."

Max gazed up at Tom with his sad brown eyes.

"Now Max!"

Reluctantly, Max opened his mouth, and the bone clattered to the floor.

"Kiran, whadja find?"

Max pawed the now slobbery bone and whined.

Kiran flipped the paper over. "Looks like a map." He raised the page. "Hey! It's signed—" He squinted. "—by Kila Brasscouldron."

"Who?" Avani peered over his shoulder. "It can't be!"

"What is it?" asked Tom.

Avani blinked. "Remember that book you guys found?"

"Book?"

"The one from the Elfhaven library. You showed it to us at Nadda and Nanni's house."

"Yeah. So?"

"It was written by Kila Brasscouldron."

"Oh, yeah!" Goban blurted. "The guy what claimed he found a lost world."

"Nadda said he was insane," said Kiran.

"Was he?" Tom stared at the skeletal hand.

Goban followed his stare. "Guess we know what happened to him."

Kiran picked up a slimy finger bone. "Guess so."

"What was his name again?" asked Tom. "Chester Copper—"

"Kila Brasscouldron," Avani corrected.

"Right." Tom stared at the dragon face key protruding from the wall. "Remember that secret compartment in the center of the book?"

Goban nodded.

"How big was that hole?"

Goban made a fist.

"'Bout the size of that key?"

"Exactly that size!"

Avani snatched the paper from Kiran. "There was a page torn from the book, remember?"

"Part of a page," said Goban. "All that was left was the lower left corner."

Avani held up the page. The lower left corner was missing.

Goban's eyes lit up. Slipping off his knapsack, he rummaged through it, and lifted a crumpled scrap of paper. Smoothing it on his sleeve, he handed it to Avani.

She held the two pages side-by-side. The edges sparkled and the two halves welded back together. Startled, she dropped the page.

# Right or left?

"Did you do that?" whispered Tom. "Ahhh—repair the page?"

Avani shook her head.

"Can you read it?" Tom asked.

She waved her hand at the light globe. It didn't respond. Kiran waved, and the light glided closer. Avani picked up the page, pretending not to notice.

"Kiran's right," she said. "It's a map. There're lots of squiggly lines, paths? Most end at circles. Caverns? There are drawings of lakes and streams, but one path—" The parchment crackled as she stabbed her finger onto the page. "—is highlighted in red."

"Could be important," said Tom.

"Where are we?" asked Goban.

Kiran pointed at the ground beside him. "Right here."

"On the map," moaned Goban.

Avani scanned the page. "There. At the lower left there are two bold lines crossing the path. Beside them there's a sketch of this same lock and key," she said excitedly. "Tracing the line backwards, there's a small lake."

Tom piped up, "Where we found Naagesh's nano-droid." Avani nodded.

"Any instructions?" Goban gestured to the metal wall. "Like which way to turn the key?"

"Without getting killed?" added Tom.

Avani ran her fingers lightly across the page. As she did so, words appeared hovering above the map. She blinked in surprise, then continued, sliding her finger over the symbol for the barrier. The previous words faded, and new words appeared.

Tom peeked over her shoulder. "What's it say?"

"It's an ancient elvish script written in cursive. No one's used cursive in hundreds of yara." She leaned in close. "I can only make out a few words."

"Like what?"

"Danger—or—beware." She scrunched up her face. "To begin, no—to *enter* the world of past and future—" Her frown deepened. "Something, something—must pass three tests. 1st: A wrong step. No! A *false* step... something, something—a weighty death awaits." She nodded at the stone resting atop Kila.

"Coulda found this map sooner!" Goban told Kiran.

"Go on," urged Tom.

"For the impatient—" She stared pointedly at Goban. "—needles of death."

"Seems to be a death theme goin' on," said Tom. "And the third challenge?"

"Yeah," Kiran chimed in. "How'll we die if we screw up this time?"

"Who cares how we'll die if we get it wrong?" said Tom. "We wanna know how to get it right."

"I'm kinda curious?" Goban admitted.

Tom faced Avani. "Just tell us which way to turn the darn thing so we *don't* die?"

"Beside the drawing of the key—" She motioned to the dragon-faced bulb fastened to the wall. "—are the words: the knives... No—the *swords* of time march to your doom."

Goban sighed. "Oh great. A riddle."

"Swords of time?" Kiran said. "Swords can kill."

Goban suggested, "Time marches on..."

"Killing all of us, eventually," added Avani.

Tom scratched his cheek. "Swords? Time?" His face brightened. "That's it! The hands on a clock! Remember the clock tower in Elfhaven? The hands on the clocks looked like swords."

"They are swords," said Kiran.

Goban's face lit up. "That's gotta be it!"

"Clock hands turn clockwise," began Tom, "meaning they rotate to the right. The riddle says, 'the swords of time marches to your doom.' Clockwise first will trigger the trap, bringing us to our doom! Tom grabbed hold of the dragon-head key, preparing to twist left.

Avani grabbed Tom's hand. "Wait!"

"Why?"

"You mentioned the Elfhaven clock tower?"

"Uh, huh?"

"The top clock is Elfhaven time. Last yara you figured out the second clock down was set to Earth time."

"Yeah. So?"

"The hands on our clock moves the opposite direction to your clock. Our *clockwise* is your *counterclockwise*."

Tom pictured the clock tower in his mind. "That's right! And the numbers were reversed."

Avani removed her hand from his.

"So—" Tom began to sweat. "Left means death?"

She nodded.

"Assuming we solved the riddle correctly," Goban reminded them.

Without taking his eyes off Avani, Tom swallowed, then rotated the key hard to the right. A deep *thunk,* then a grinding noise. Everyone scanned the room for signs of their immanent death. Nothing.

Tom faced the barricade. The dragon's face had rotated 30 degrees to the right, taking the closest metal ring with it. He cranked the key to the left. The first ring remained in place, while the next ring out rotated in sync with the key.

Another *clank*.

Holding his breath, Tom spun the stone to the right.

*Clang, clunk,* a whirring noise. The three rings spun. The wall started vibrating. Dust drifted down from above.

They all stepped back. The top layer of the metal wall split in half and withdrew inside the walls to either side. Inside the gate, wheels spun, gears ratcheted as more pieces of the massive door folded back inside the walls.

A faint light from the other side shone through the machinery. Within moments, the last few pieces of the mechanism withdrew inside the outer walls, leaving only a dimly lit passageway.

*Clunk.* The dragon-head key bounced off the stone floor. Kiran picked up it up.

"Come on!" Kiran's running footsteps echoed down the stone passageway, his magical light globe obediently bobbing along ahead.

# The path divides

Kiran sat, his back against the cave wall, waiting for them at the junction of three small tunnels. Each branch looked identical: four feet wide and perfectly round. Kiran yawned, his eyes barely open.

Goban glanced from tunnel to tunnel. "Which one?" said Goban. "They all look the same?"

Tom took out his compass. The dial spun even wilder than before. "Don't know what's wrong with this thing."

He glanced at Avani. Her eyes were shut. Tom nudged her. "Avani. We need the map."

Her eyes slowly opened. She seemed to have trouble focusing. "What?"

"Map?" Tom pointed at the tunnels.

"Oh. Yeah." She pulled it out and handed it to Tom, then walked over and sat beside her brother.

Tom and Goban huddled close, studying the map.

"Check for symbols that look like exits," suggested Tom.

"There's arrows," Goban said hesitantly. "Pointing up and down,"

"Maybe there's a legend," Tom said.

"A legend?"

"Maps usually have something that says what the symbols mean." Tom touched the bottom right corner. Words sprang up, hovering above the symbols. "Whoa!" he jerked his hand away, and the words faded.

Goban tapped the page. Nothing happened. "Guess Avani and Kiran aren't the only ones with magic."

Tom stared at his finger. "Avani?" he called. "There's magical hidden symbols on the map."

She didn't answer. Tom glanced over. Kiran's head rested on Avani's shoulder. His light globe, like a faithful sentinel, hovered above their heads. They were both asleep.

Tom yawned. "We've been walking for a day and a half. I could use some rest. How about you?"

"I'm Ok," replied Goban. "Besides, someone should keep watch." He tapped his temple, knowingly. "I've the eyes of a hawk and the ears of a fox."

"Gimli! Lord of the Rings. Good memory!" Tom folded the map and put it in his pocket, laid down and curled up. "Just need a nap. Wake me when you're tired and I'll take next watch."

Tom awoke with a start, at a deep, ghastly groaning. It was Goban. He was snoring.

Tom glanced at his watch. "Yikes!" He jumped up and shook the others. "We gotta go."

Avani yawned and stretched. "How long have we been sleeping?"

"Too long." Tom helped her to her feet, then pulled out the map. "Look what Goban and I found." He touched it. As before, glowing runes appeared floating above the page.

She took the map, her eyes now clear.

"We gotta choose," said Tom, gesturing to the three tunnels. "Can you read the symbols? We need to find an exit."

"Naagesh was heading south," Goban reminded them.

"Great. Are there any southern exits?"

Avani touched the page, and the words reappeared. "This symbol means—passageway. This means cavern. And this… might mean—a hole."

"Sink holes!" reasoned Tom. Kiran joined them.

Goban said, "Might be able ta climb out one of those."

"What's that symbol?" Kiran pointed.

Avani shifted her finger. "Shrine—or—statue."

"How about that one?" asked Tom. "The circle with an arrow through its center, pointing up."

"Out!"

"That's it!"

"Can ya spot any a those symbols on the map?" asked Goban.

"There's one!" cried Kiran.

"And there," said Avani.

Goban grinned, "There's another!"

Tom edged his way beside Avani and studied the map. "They're all far apart. Two of em look like we'd be back-tracking." Tom took the map from Avani. "Assuming up means north." He stabbed his finger onto the map. "This is the southernmost exit. Directly above it are squiggly lines with balls attached."

Avani blurted, "The Floating Mountains!"

"Makes sense," said Goban. "They're in the south."

Tom scratched his temple. "Where did you say we were?"

Avani squinted. "The skeleton was here beside the metal gate. Then we followed this path."

"The red line."

She nodded. "So we must be here, where the path splits three ways."

"Any of em lead directly to the southern exit?"

She shook her head no.

Tom frowned. "Which one's marked in red?"

She pointed. "The left one."

Avani and Kiran hurried down the tunnel. Tom turned on his headlamp and moved to follow, Goban grabbed his arm.

"What?" said Tom.

"These tunnels aren't like the others." Goban let go, and they started walking.

"Back there the caves were natural," Tom agreed. "Carved by water. Someone built these."

Goban agreed, "Everything changed once we got past the barricade." Goban slid his stubby fingers across the cold, smooth stone wall.

"Whoever built em," began Tom, "had impressive tunneling skills. Think dwarves built this place?"

Goban glanced ahead at Avani and Kiran, talking amongst themselves. Goban lowered his voice, "The tunnel's perfectly round and there're no chisel marks. A tad too perfect—know what I mean? Even dwarves, as advanced as we are—even *we* couldn't a built these."

Goban hiked up his pants. "Won't be long though, till we can."

Tom nodded soberly, struggling to keep from laughing.

Once they'd caught up with Kiran and Avani, Tom pulled out his compass. Kiran called excitedly from up ahead. Something about a pebble. Goban walked off to investigate.

"Wish Chloe was here," Tom told Avani. He tapped his compass and frowned. "She could tell us exactly where we are."

"She couldn't tell us where Naagesh is though," Avani reminded him. "He no longer carries that druid, remember?"

"Droid," Tom corrected. "Short for android. Basically, a robot." Tom reached in his pocket. The nano-droid was still there.

"A robot. Like Chloe?"

Tom smiled. "Only smaller." His smile faded.

"What's wrong?"

"Hope Chloe's Ok."

Avani squeezed his hand. "I'm sure she's waiting for you back at the sinkhole, right now."

He gave her a half-hearted smile.


## Larraj and Chloe

"This is the spot," Larraj squinted, gazing across the dunes. On the horizon, a towering wall of sand steadily grew larger, the leading edge of the storm.

Chloe's platform rotated. "My sensors show no trace of the prince's passing in either the visible or infrared wavelengths."

Larraj swept his hand over the sand. Two sets of footsteps appeared for an instant, an elf and a goblin's, then faded away.

"What now?" asked the robot.

"The goblin is Naagesh's servant. It'll lead us to him."


## Another surprise

"Look what Kiran found," said Goban, holding something tiny between his thumb and forefinger.

"What is it?" asked Tom. He adjusted his headlamp. "A pebble. So?"

Goban opened his fingers and the tiny stone just hovered there, spinning slowly.

Tom grabbed the pebble and rolled it between his fingers. He released it. The pebble hovered once more. Using his palm, he pressed the stone down a couple feet then jerked his hand away. The pebble rose back up to its original spot. "Cool!"

"There's more!" came Kiran's excited voice. "Come see!"

They found Kiran wide eyed, surrounded by floating pebbles. Kiran plucked one from the air and handed it to Tom. Tom grabbed another and tried pushing the two together. The stones resisted his efforts. Releasing them both at once, the two pebbles shot apart, then slowed and stopped, hovering a few feet away from each other. He tried again, with the same result.

"Interesting," said Tom.

"That's nothing," called Avani. "Look at this!"

Tom hurried around the next corner. Up ahead, soft light filtered into the tunnel from another cavern.

Nearing the end of the tunnel, the light brightened. Colorful flower-laden vines hung down across the cavern's entrance. Brushing aside vines, Tom stepped through, causing the swaying flowers to chime like bells. Goban, Kiran, and Max came next.

Tom stopped beside Avani, switched off his headlamp, and stared. By far the largest cavern they'd seen, they stood on a perfectly flat, wide stone walkway. The walkway appeared to go all the way around an enormous lake.

Five massive stone dragonheads, equally spaced around the lake, jutted out from the cavern walls just above the walkway. From each of the dragons' mouths, waterfalls gushed forth, their splashes echoing throughout the cavern. Here too, the water glowed blue, brightest beneath the waterfalls.

Directly to their right, ten rows of narrow wooden floats extended thirty feet out into the lake and were attached to the walkway by heavy iron rings.

"They look like piers." Tom scratched his head. "Only—no boats."

"And nowhere to go," said Goban. "The lake's not that big."

Gazing up, Tom took in the high, rough, gently arched roof half-covered in more of the colorful flowered vines.

"Look!" said Kiran. "More floating rocks." Tom hadn't noticed before, but stones hovered throughout the cavern. Most were pebble sized, some larger, a few the size of soccer balls. What's more, the bigger the stone, the higher they hovered.

Avani caught a pebble between her cupped hands. "think they're magic?"

"Don't think so. They act sorta like magnets, like the one in my compass, only—"

"Only what?" Goban asked.

"Only—with magnetism, like poles repel and opposite poles attract. These only repel and far stronger than magnets." Tom tapped his foot on the rock floor. "Must be a huge deposit of the same mineral buried beneath us, causing these stones to float."

"Or else their magic," argued Avani.

Tom shrugged.

Goban ran off around the walkway. "There's gotta be an exit somewhere."

"There's no way out," said Tom, stopping beside Avani and Kiran.

They'd spent the last half hour racing all the way around the lake and were now back where they started. Goban staggered up, gasping for breath. "There's no way out."

"We know!" said the others.

Goban gulped in a final deep breath. "So, whadda we do?"

Tom pulled out the map and handed it to Avani.

"The map shows five exits, plus the one we came from." She glanced around and frowned.

"There are five dragonheads," Kiran pointed out.

"We walked under em," said Goban. "Weren't any tunnels."

Tom considered. "We followed the red line here, right?"

Avani nodded.

"Where's it go from here?"

Avani studied the map again. "It doesn't!"

"What?" Tom took the page from her. "Where are we now?" She pointed.

Max barked.

"In a minute, Max." Tom slid his fingers across the map to their current position. Words appeared. "What's it say?"

Avani leaned close, a strand of her long golden hair brushing his cheek.

"To rise, you must sink.
A monster sleeps below.
Wake the monster!
Feed the monster!"

"Sounds like fun!" said Kiran.

"Whadya think it means?" Goban asked.

"To rise—" Avani scratched her head. "Back to the Plains?"

"The way out?" said Goban hopefully. He frowned. "But—we gotta sink first." He glanced at the lake. "Swim?"

"Swim where?" said Tom.

"What about the monster?" Kiran leaned over the edge, peering into the depths. "We need to wake it up."

"You crazy?" said Goban.

Max barked again. He stood pawing at something, half-way down one of the floats. Kiran walked over. "Hey," cried Kiran. "Max found something!"

"What is it?" said Avani.

"Come look!"

Avani sighed and walked down the gently bobbing float. The others followed.

"What is it?" she repeated.

Max pawed at a round indent in the walkway.

Tom knelt. "Another dragon face. Kiran, ya still got that—" Kiran handed him the key.

Tom studied the indent. There were no geometric shapes, like the lock on the barricade, but the rounded hole did have a dragon face like the one Tom held. He handed it back to Kiran. "Give her a try."

"Wait!" said Goban. "What about the monster?"

"Only one way to find out." Tom nodded to Kiran.

Kiran lined up the dragon carving with the indent and dropped it in and stepped back. *Clink.*

Nothing happened.

Tom let out a long, slow breath.

Three triangular spikes suddenly extended up through the holes in the dragon's eyes and mouth. There was a faint *click.* Bubbles erupted from the lake beside them, causing their floating walkway to wobble wildly. Tom could just make out something huge rising from the depths. Max barked.

"Hope yer happy," said Goban.

They couldn't back up any farther or they'd fall off the narrow float.

A giant fin broke the surface directly in front of them. They started to run back, but a hideous head with six enormous, bulging eyes breached the surface between them and the shore. Water gushed from several slits in the monster's hide, drenching the float.

"Yikes!" Pivoting to run the other way, Kiran collided with Goban, knocking them both down. Kiran looked up. A tall, spiked tail burst from the lake.

"We're trapped!" cried Kiran. "Git off me!" shouted Goban. The two scrambled to their feet.

Goban yanked Aileen off his shoulder.

They held their collective breath. Bobbing and rolling, the monster measured at least thirty feet long, its hide covered with long, slimy tendrils which dripped and oozed globs of goo.

Jutting out from its side, a long, hooked fin rested just inches from their legs. As water drained off its hideous body, they could see more clearly the monster they'd awakened.

Tom stretched out his hand.

"Tom no!" cried Avani.

He touched the fin.

"Tom don't!"

Globs of dark goo dripped from his fingers. Tom sniffed his hand, then wrinkled up his nose.

"What is it?" asked Kiran.

Tom leaned over the monstrous thing and raised his palm.

"You're gonna make it angry," warned Goban.

Tom slapped his hand down hard against the monster's side. The beast let out a deep booming moan. Behind them, its head split into four curving wedges which folded back, opening its hideous mouth wide.

"Now you've really done it," said Goban, raising his axe.

Tom sprinted down the bobbing walkway toward the monster's head.

"Tom stop!" cried Avani.

"Feed the monster!" he shouted, leaping into its mouth.

# A goblin bears a gift

Somewhat sheltered from the sandstorm, Naagesh and his goblin hordes waited impatiently in a narrow trough between dunes.

A commotion caused the wizard to turn. A lone goblin scampered down the dune behind.

"What kept you?" the wizard demanded.

"I've much to report, Master," replied his servant.

"Where's Phawta and the troll army?"

"Unfortunately, Master—" The horned goblin watched the wizard's reaction carefully. "—the trolls departed."

"What?!"

"It's a long and complicated—"

"Get on with it!"

The goblin sighed. Then recounted the tale, leaving out parts, while embellishing others.

"Bellchar?" said Naagesh in disbelief. "Bellchar led the trolls?"

The goblin nodded, then stared at Naagesh expectantly.

"Yes?"

"Master, I do not wish to offend but—"

"Just say it!"

"Well—since in point of fact, Phawta didn't follow your orders, *your* obedience spell may have failed after all so—"

"Silence!" Emerald magic crackled around Naagesh's upraised hand. "This time you've gone too far." The other goblins inched away. Naagesh aimed an arcing, crackling finger at the goblin.

"Wait!" The goblin bowed deeply. "Before you kill me, Master, you'll want to hear the rest of my tale."

"I may kill you anyway, afterwards."

His servant rushed on, "Suddenly, there was a glorious quake! The underworld opened its giant mouth and swallowed the youngins whole."

"All of them?"

"All but one. He'd already left, pursued by the lone adult."

"Adult? An elven soldier?"

The slightest hesitation. "A wizard."

Jade flames swirled around Naagesh's clenched fists. The flames turned to black.

"Good news though, Master! I caught up with the boy before Larraj did."

Through clenched teeth Naagesh managed, "How—is that—good news?"

The horned goblin whistled. From over the rise, a host of goblins pushed and shoved a struggling figure down the slope.

"I demand you release me at once!" shouted Prince Devraj.

## Swallowed whole!

"Tom?" Avani called softly. "Tom!"

Tom's head popped out of the beast's mouth and grinned. "It's not a monster. It's not even alive!"

Keeping as far away from the beast as possible on the narrow walkway, they crept cautiously up beside its head.

Tom jumped ashore. "It's a boat. A submarine, I think." Walking beside the craft, Tom scraped mud and pulled lakeweed off the hull. Tugging on a particularly stubborn weed, it finally pulled loose, the weed, a large clump of mud, along with a three-eyed fish, with spikey bones protruding from its fins, landed on the float beside him.

The fish flopped about on the pier. Tom leapt back. Avani wedged her shoe underneath the fish and flipped it into the lake, where it darted away.

Tom sighed. "Anyway. Come help me." Tom started scraping mud from the hull.

Wrinkling his forehead in disgust, Goban pulled off a slimy weed. The others chipped in too.

Within moments, the ship's chrome hull stood mostly exposed. Besides the fins and rudder, brass and copper devices of unknown function dotted the hull's otherwise smooth surface.

Tom patted the fin beside him. "This is a stabilizer fin. Its back-end control surface rotates up and down. It's called a fairwater. Similar to an aileron on an airship. It allows the sub to rise toward the surface or dive toward the bottom."

"Airship?" Goban said excitedly. "Can you draw me the plans?"

Tom walked to the end of the pier, chuckling. The others followed.

Half above and half below water, a giant brass corkscrew device, two feet wide at the stern, tapered down to a point six feet behind the craft.

"That's the prop." Tom pointed at the corkscrew. "The motor spins it. It pushes water. Moves the sub forward or back, depending which way the prop is spinning.

"And that," Tom gestured to the giant metal fishtail rising from the stern. "That's the rudder. Makes it turn."

"If it's not alive," began Kiran, "how come it has eyes?"

"They're portholes. Windows. Three on each side. Plus two on the stern, and six on the bow."

Tom strode briskly back up the pier, his friends trailing behind. On the way, Kiran grabbed the dragonhead key and yanked. A sucking sound, and the pins withdrew. Kiran picked it up.

Tom waited at the bow. "It's Ok. Follow me." He stepped into the mouth and disappeared.

"I'm waiting!" came his muted hollow voice.


Tom ducked through the hatch and entered a small cramped chamber. The walls and ceiling were just the inside of the circular metal tube that formed the hull.

Six feet back, a flat metal bulkhead, with an oval doorway, separated this chamber from the next. Various sized pipes, strapped to the walls and ceiling, snaked their way through the bulkhead heading aft.

As the others cautiously stepped aboard, the ship bobbed gently side-to-side, the metallic clomp of their footsteps echoing throughout the ship. Dim yellow lights suddenly switched on one-after-another. The light came from domed, frosted glass enclosures mounted just above their heads. Thick brass wires crisscrossed the enclosures.

The lamp directly above Tom, however, remained dark. Tom flicked the glass with his finger. A muted electrical arcing sounded. The light flickered, then lit up dimly, slowly growing brighter.

"That was odd," said Goban.

"Especially since—" Tom brushed his fingers across the nearest globe. A thick layer of dust drifted down. "—they probably haven't been used in hundreds of years."

Near the front of the cramped chamber and bolted to the floor, a small narrow chair sat facing a curved console. In the center of the console and surrounded by a plethora of switches, knobs, and dials, a large circular screen lay dark and silent.

"This is the bridge," Tom patted the seat. "Obviously the captain's chair."

Goban stared at six brass handles, three per side, attached to the chair. "A small—six-armed captain, then?" He started to sit.

"Uhhh." Tom hesitated. "No offense, Goban, but—don't think you'll fit."

Goban glanced at his backside.

"I can!" Kiran made a dash for the chair.

"Kiran!" Avani tried to stop him. "Don't you even—"

Twisting sideways to avoid her grasp, Kiran wriggled past the levers and plopped down in the seat. Three things happened in rapid succession: the instrument panel lit up. Two thick straps sprang out, wrapped around Kiran's chest and cinched him in tight. A deep shudder passed through the ship.

Avani yanked on Kiran's bonds. The map slid from her tunic and fluttered to the floor.

"Help me!" she yelled.

The sub's hatch began to close. Max's bark echoed metallically through the ship.

The four curved panels, like the monstrous mouth they'd envisioned, hinged together and snapped shut.

"Help me!" cried Avani.

Tom scrambled to her side. They strained together, pulling on the straps, but they wouldn't budge. "Goban! Your axe!"

"Axe?" said Kiran.

Goban slipped Aileen off his shoulder.

Kiran's eyes widened.

Goban raised his axe.

Leaning away, Kiran bumped one of the levers. The lever pivoted forward. A shrill grinding preceded a deep thumping noise.

"Uh oh." Goban looked back. Steam hissed. A shudder passed through the hull. There came a churning, gurgling sound from astern and the ship lurched forward.

"Stop!" cried Tom.

The sub rammed the dock, throwing them all forward. The bow tipped up, climbing the dock, throwing them backwards.

"Kiran! The other way!"

Kiran yanked back hard on the lever. The gurgling stopped, then immediately resumed, louder than before. Tom covered his ears from the grinding squeal as the metal hull scraped off the dock and splashed back down into the water.

Bobbing wildly, the ship picked up speed, heading backwards. Goban and Avani began frantically pulling levers. The boat bucked and pivoted sideways, scrapping along the pier beside them.

Another screech of metal, this time from the right side. Tom stared out the starboard porthole. The stabilizer fin skidded up onto the pier, grinding as it bent and twisted.

"You're destroying the ship!" cried Tom. "Let go of the levers!"

Everyone let go. All sounds slowly ceased and the ship ground to a halt, laying at an angle, its mangled fin resting on the pier.

"That was fun!" said Kiran.

Tom sighed, then bent over and picked up the map. It accordioned out along well-worn fold lines. He carefully folded, then unfolded it.

"What is it?" asked Avani.

Tom held the map flat so she could see.

"Yeah? So?"

"Where are we now?"

She pointed.

"And where's the red line go from here?"

"It doesn't. I already told you it ends—" Tom folded the left side of the map till it rested at their current location. Avani stopped mid-sentence. Another red line matched up from the fold and continued on. Goban crowded in to see.

"Hey." Kiran tugged on the straps holding him in. "I'm still stuck here."

Avani took the sheet from Tom and folded it twice more. "Wow!"

"That means—" began Goban.

"There must be a way out of this lake after all," Avani said.

Tom nodded. "And I think this ship is it."

"Doesn't someone have a knife?" Kiran asked. "'Stead of Goban's axe?"

## Maps within

Tom touched the fold of the map at the exact spot where they were. As before, runes appeared. "What's it say?"

Avani read,

> "Move not the levers, least disaster strike,"

"You made that up," said Kiran, still struggling with the straps.

Avani grinned at him, then read on,

> "Flat and broken, hope lost
> Folded mended, hope restored!"

Avani tapped her finger excitedly on the map. "When the map's flat—"

"The red line's broken!" shouted Goban.

"Folded. The line's mended," Tom finished. "Anything else?"

"The map's the key, it's touch and go
 Your destiny awaits, why so slow?"

"Cryptic as ever," Avani grinned at Tom. Tom grinned back.

"At least that clue rhymes," said Kiran, still tugging at the straps.

"Align the maps?" Goban grabbed the map and flipped it over. It was blank. "There's only one map."

"Here's one." Kiran stopped struggling and pointed at the console. The screen was now plastered with colored symbols. One of the symbols, a blue octagon, pulsed brightly.

Tom grabbed the map back from Goban. "That's the same symbol! The one on the map that shows our present location."

Avani snatched the map from Tom and folded it so the red lines matched up, then scanned the page. "The red line now stops here," she looked puzzled. "At this squiggly star."

Tom glanced from the map to the screen. "There!" He pointed to the matching symbol on the display.

"But the red line ends there." She studied the map once more.

"Ya sure?" Tom grinned.

Avani tried folding along well-worn folds. On her third try, the red lines again matched up.

"All we hafta do," began Tom. "Is figure out how to get from here to there."

Goban scratched a bristly eyebrow. "The riddle said, 'The map's the key'."

"It's touch and go!" Kiran leaned against his straps, trying to touch the screen.

"Don't!" Tom grabbed Kiran's hand. "Remember what happened when I told Malak and Chatur not to touch anything in the crashed spaceship and they did it, anyway?"

"Malak and Chatur are dead," said Kiran.

"Kiran!" gasped Avani.

Kiran's shoulders slumped. He sat back. "Guess you're right. Guess it's too dangerous." Tom released him. Kiran lunged forward and touched the screen. A warning siren blared, and the engines again roared to life. Levers began moving themselves. The ship lurched and shuddered, screeching loudly till its damaged fin slid off the pier and they glided backwards away from the dock.

Muted gurgling echoed throughout the ship. Outside, the water level rose above the portholes.

Max whined.

"Hope I was right," said Tom. "Hope this is a submarine."

"What's happening? I can't see!" complained Kiran. No one responded. They were all too busy, their faces glued to the bubble-shaped portholes, watching the frightening and yet exciting watery spectacle outside.

Tom and Goban ran back and gazed out the stern portholes at the wildly spinning corkscrew prop, propelling the ship backward, sending a churning torrent of bubbles past their windows.

Now completely submerged, they watched the mossy underbelly of the pier pass by above.

Upon reaching open water, a panel on the stern's vertical fin hinged right.

"Look," Tom slapped Goban on the shoulder. "The rudder's moving. We're gonna turn." Right on cue, the ship creaked and groaned, rolling slightly to port as its stern swung right. The rudder hinged back into place, halting their turn. The screw reversed direction, clearing bubbles from their view as the ship gained speed, gliding out into open water.

"Check this out." Tom yanked Goban's sleeve, pointing at the starboard stabilizer. The trailing edge of the fin swiveled down. Likewise, the sub's nose angled down and their craft dove, weaving strangely as they descended. A grinding noise sent the pair rushing to the viewport.

"Uh oh," said Tom.

"What's wrong?"

"The damaged stabilizer. It's having trouble moving into position."

"That's bad?"

"That's bad."

The fin moved in jerks and stops. Transmitted through the metal hull, they heard the fin pop, through the soles of their feet they could feel it grinding. Finally, the damaged fin stopped swiveling and the ship's dive smoothed out.

Descending farther, they plunged into darkness. The hull made eerie, muted, metallic creaks and groans.

Tom's ears popped. "Come on. Let's go back."


As Tom and Goban ducked through the bulkhead hatchway separating the central hall from the bridge, underwater lamps outside of the hull, switched on, sending beams of light lancing ahead, down and to the sides, illuminating a narrow swath around the sub with a soft yellow light.

When the pair walked up, Avani said, "Look."

Shadows receded, revealing Greek style columns in the dark murky waters ahead. They dove straight for them. The hull shuddered. The grinding, wobbling happened again, then the sub leveled out just above the lake floor, sending swirly ripples of silt upward, marking their passage.

Their ship glided along through what looked like ruins of a sunken temple.

"Whoa!" said Kiran, the straps momentarily forgotten.

Drifting smoothly past tall columns, the sub's lamps exposed their intricate details. Carved from stone, the columns depicted stylized trees with vines encircling their trunks all the way to the crown where the vines opened into flowers forming a wide base. Perched atop the bases rested yet more stone dragon heads, watching them as they glided past.

"Whoever built this place musta liked dragons," Goban remarked.

A moment later, the sub churned out of the sunken building, leaving the mysterious columns behind. Here, the lake bottom dropped off and the sub's lights weren't strong enough to pierce the murky depths. Now and then they glimpsed eerie shapes looming beneath them.

"Hey look!" said Kiran.

A tiny fish swam by the left side portals, swimming hard, zigging and zagging wildly, going in the same direction as they. Behind it, a larger horned fish with a long snout and spiked fins came into view, gaining on the little fish.

The larger fish opened its mouth. Light from the sub reflected off needle-sharp teeth as it swam by.

The smaller fish arched its tiny body, gazing back in terror at the large predator. Redoubling its efforts, it thrashed through the water in a courageous attempt to avoid the inevitable.

"Faster little one!" urged Avani.

Suddenly, an enormous fish, nearly half the length of their submarine, swam past. The behemoth swiveled a huge eye to regard the lumbering metal fish beside it, then the eye swung forward.

The monster's lower jaw jutted out and from it rose a pair of long curved tusks, parallel to its flat, bug-eyed face. Gaining on the others, it opened its mouth and a long, barbed tongue lanced out. Its attack missed the medium-sized fish and its tongue reeled back inside its mouth, its intended prey unaware of its narrow escape.

Meanwhile, seemingly exhausted, the little fish at the head of the parade slowed, then stopped.

"Of no!" gasped Avani.

The little fish's tiny tail suddenly split open, exposing a tooth-filled mouth on its back end. Exploding in size, the mouth sprang out, swallowing the middle-sized fish in a single gulp. The mouth shrank back inside the tiny fish.

Now wide-eyed, the enormous fish thrashed its fins, frantically trying to stop.

Too late!

Again the tiny fish's tail opened. Again the jaws pounced. *Gulp*!

And then there was one.

Its tail snapped shut. Bubbles rose as it lazily swam off into the murky gloom.

Avani covered her mouth in shock.

Kiran snickered.

The others stared at him.

"What?" Kiran tugged on his straps. "Can someone get me out of this?"

Goban drummed his stubby fingers on his axe handle.

Kiran shook his head.

"The sub's on autopilot," reasoned Tom. "When we arrive at our destination, the ship'll probably release you."

"Probably?"

"Arrive where?" asked Avani. "We're in a lake. Where can we go?"

"Mmm, guys," began Goban. "You should check this out."

Everyone turned. At this depth the sub's bow lights could only penetrate the murky gloom a short distance. Hazy details slowly resolved themselves.

A solid rock wall, the end of the lake, loomed ahead.


# A three-hour tour

"We're gonna crash!" shouted Kiran.

"Maybe. Maybe not," said Tom.

Though difficult to see in the watery gloom, a faint outline of a circular opening in the cavern wall appeared ahead.

"A tunnel!" cried Goban. He glanced left and right. "Look! More tunnels."

"The missing tunnels," Tom said. "All five, I bet. When we ran around the cavern, we didn't see em 'cause they were underwater."

"Under the waterfalls," said Goban.

Kiran glanced from one to the other. "So—we're not gonna crash?"

"No," Tom assured him.

"What about the bars?" asked Avani.

"Bars?"

"The metal bars blocking the opening."

Tom leaned forward. "Uh oh. There's an iron grate."

"So, we are gonna crash then?" asked Kiran. A siren wailed. Max howled at the siren.

"YES!" Tom grabbed the console, bracing for collision, and closed his eyes.

The deep whine of the engines grew louder. The craft picked up speed. Someone screamed.

Fifty feet.

Goban grabbed Tom and shook him. "Stop screaming and think of something!"

"That was me screaming?"

"YES!" screamed Goban and Avani.

Tom's eyes popped open. "Maybe there's a remote release mechanism."

"A what?" said Goban.

Tom's eyes scanned the instrument panel.

"What would it look like?" asked Avani, scanning the panel.

Tom smiled. "Something like this!" He leaned sideways and tapped a symbol of a grate with arrows pointing out to either side. The symbol flashed.

"It's working!" shouted Goban.

The grate split in two. Half sliding to the left, half to the right. A narrow opening appeared between, growing wider.

Thirty feet.

"We're not gonna make it," said Goban.

"We'll make it," Avani insisted.

Twenty feet.

Half the tunnel now stood open. The grate continued to withdraw.

Ten feet.

Kiran covered his eyes.

Five feet.

"We're gonna make it!" said Avani, but she scrunched up her face.

Kiran peeked out between two fingers. The upper and lower parts of the grate cleared the round opening, but the widest part at the center still had a ways to go.

One foot.

Everyone held their breath. The sub's bow glided smoothly into the tunnel.

Avani clapped. "We made it!"

A deep grinding sounded. The left side of the grate kept opening but the right-side ground to a halt, frozen, jutting six inches out into the tunnel.

"We're not gonna to make it," said Goban.

Tom ran to the starboard porthole. The already mangled stabilizer fin was on a collision course with the grate.

"Goban's right!" shouted Tom. "We're not gonna—"

They heard a muted bang. The grate resumed opening.

"Or maybe—" Tom paused. "Gonna be close."

The starboard fin struck the grate, pivoting the ship hard right and wedging the stabilizer firmly into the grate. A fierce rasping ensued. Continuing to turn, the bow struck the right side of the tunnel and the stern struck the left. The hull vibrated violently. Chunks of rock and torn, twisted metal bars spewed out from behind the spinning prop.

The engine's roar increased, sending yet more debris flying.

Massive stones, dislodged from the tunnel above, crashed down upon the hull, *clank, clank, thud.*

"The whole tunnel's gonna collapse!" yelled Tom.

# Larraj and Chloe

Barely visible through the blinding sandstorm, vague silhouettes of two unlikely companions materialized at the crest of a dune.

Hiking up his sleeve, the familiar swirling blue nebula materialized above the wizard's wrist. "Seeker," shouted Larraj above the storm. "Show me Naagesh."

Again, the image raced across the dunes, presenting a blur of images too quick to focus on.

"Wait!" ordered Larraj. "What was that?" The image slowed to a stop. King Dakshi clinging tightly, dangling from a stout, windswept vine.

"What?" Larraj frowned. "No. I said Naagesh." The image pulled back. "Wait!" The vision froze. From this vantage point he could see the king's party climbing between levels of swaying boulders.

"They're climbing the Floating Mountains." He paused. "Back up. Slowly." Once more, the image receded. In doing so, it passed through a swirling neon blue cloud.

Larraj gasped. "Stop!" The vision showed an arm, surrounded by an identical bracelet as his. Naagesh viewed the scene before him, watching King Dakshi and his party through his own seeker.

"Guess we know where the second seeker is," muttered Larraj.

"And there's Prince Devraj," said Chloe. "Behind Naagesh."

"Rotate right. Stop!" Fifty paces back, goblins held Devraj, struggling against his bonds.

A goblin stepped in front of the prince, blocking Larraj's view. The goblin walked straight forward till the goblin's face filled the whole image.

The horned goblin extended a spindly arm and poked a long, claw-studded finger at Larraj.

Larraj blinked. He waved his hand, and the vision retreated inside the seeker.

"Odd," remarked Chloe. "The goblin knew we were watching."

"So it would seem."

# That sinking feeling

A shrill metallic screech echoed throughout the sub. The ship lurched forward, then stopped.

Everyone watched in horror as the stabilizer fin began to rip loose from the hull. The tear widened. Dents formed overhead as chunks of the collapsing tunnel smashed against the hull. A violent shudder passed through the ship, accompanied by a loud *boom*.

Five squashed noses, attached to five wide-eyed faces, stared out five portholes as the stabilizer broke free and zig-zagged its way to the bottom. Water gushed through the resulting gash in the hull.

Free at last, the ship surged forward, but with the loss of its stabilizing fin, the sub turned too fast. Picking up speed, the seemingly possessed craft struck the left side of the tunnel. *Boom!*

Everyone screamed! Except Max, who barked.

The bow careened off the left tunnel wall and struck the right. *Boom!* A steam pipe burst, hissing and spewing hot mist, making it hard to see.

"The ships filling with water!" yelled Tom. "Goban. Go plug the leak."

"With what?"

"Your cloak! Stuff it in the crack and hold it."

"My cloak?"

"Just do it!"

Goban ducked beneath a steam geyser and again through the bulkhead hatch.

After the third collision the ship's autopilot seemed to adjust to the missing fin somewhat, yawing side-to-side like a shark. But then the tunnel turned right. The stern rudder rotated, coaxing the sub to turn, but with only one stabilizer, the ship rolled sideways, sending everyone except Kiran flying across the cabin.

Again, the prop struck the wall, sending more rocks flying. The tunnel angled left, and the hungry prop stopped chewing, but the ship bounced off the right side causing the ship to ring like a gong. Max whined. The others covered their ears.

The sound of muted thunder came from behind.

"Goban!" shouted Tom. "You all right?"

"Everything's good. The tunnel just collapsed behind us is all," Goban's voice sounded strained. "Slowed the leak. Gonna need a new cloak though."

Tom stood over Kiran, white-knuckled from gripping the captain's chair so tight. Tom's face turned an ominous shade of green. "Think I'm gonna be sick."

Kiran jerked on the straps. "Don't you dare!"

Tom was on the verge of erupting when the tunnel ended, and the sub glided out into open water. Tom slowly sighed. "Think I'm OK."

Kiran watched him suspiciously.

An army of gurgling, churning bubbles wriggled their way up past the portholes and the sub rose. Moments later, the ship breached the surface, bobbing like a cork upon a vast body of water, the largest they'd seen by far.

The roar of the engine dropped to a gentle hum as their badly battered ship zig-zagged its way toward shore.

A long dock appeared ahead. The prop reversed its spin, and the engine revved up, water spouting from the stern. They slowed a little, but as if tired and giving up, the sub just thudded head-on into the dock.

The prop spun down. The engine fell silent. A burst of steam echoed throughout the ship as the bow split open and folded back.

Kiran's straps released. He leapt up, his eyes latched on the fiendish bindings as if they might change their mind.

Goban stepped through the hatchway, his soaked and torn cloak in hand. Behind him, the others scrambled ashore.

The four took in the battered remains of their ship: badly dented and floating low in the water. Broken control cables hung limply from jagged tears where the stabilizer fin had been. Water spewed from cracked portholes and steam wafted out from the craft's open hatch.

Tom said, "Ya shoulda seen the other guy." He scanned the distant shore of the lake. "Wow! I can barely see across. It's like the Great Lakes back home."

"Look at that!" Avani said, looking up.

Tom followed her gaze. More so than the previous cavern, this arched ceiling was completely covered in colorful flowering vines, glowing in all their multicolored, phosphorescent splendor. The thick, woody-stemmed vines also covered the gigantic cavern's walls, all the way down to the water. On the vine's rough, gnarled bark, thin veins sparkled with the same brilliant neon blue light as the water, pulsing as it flowed up the stalks.

What's more, light from the vines and flowers glinted off hundreds of floating stones hovering at various heights, ranging in size from tiny pebbles floating just above their heads, to rocks larger than Kiran. The largest hovered halfway to the ceiling.

"That's nothing," said Goban. "Check out what's behind us!" Everyone turned.

"Whoa!" said Kiran.

"Whoa's right," agreed Tom.

They all gazed in silent wonder at the sight before them.

## The king's party

Juanita grabbed hold of yet another madly thrashing vine, her hands bleeding from the rough bark.

She glanced down. King Dakshi hung directly below her and below him, King Abban, a handful of elven guards brought up the rear. Most of the soldiers had already scrambled up to the boulder above. Not exactly mountains,

Juanita leaned out and gazed past the others. They'd climbed about halfway to the top of this chain of floating rocks. Other chains of vine-snared boulders swayed in the breeze nearby.

She called to King Dakshi, "How high should we climb?"

"What?"

With the howling wind, creaking vines and flapping clothes, her words were lost. Carefully releasing one hand, she pointed up yelling, "How—much—higher?"

"We shall rest on the stone up!" he shouted back.

Once they'd reached that level, the King ordered a short break. Juanita sat. King Dakshi plopped down beside her.

"The soldiers are exhausted," she said. "They've been running to and from danger for nearly two days." She rested her hand on his. "They need more than a short break, so could I. Don't you?"

He gazed off across the desert, back the way they'd come. "By now, General Kanak's army troops should have reached the Plains. Goblins are fierce fighters, yet they have short legs and small feet. They will have difficulty traipsing through deep sand, which should provide ample time for the general to catch up."

"So, your army should overtake Naagesh before he arrives here?"

"Exactly. Even if Naagesh arrived first, we are now high enough in the Floating Mountains that the wizard should not be able to spot us."

"And there are hundreds of strands for him to search," she pointed out.

Dakshi twisted, calling to his troops. "We have climbed high enough. We shall wait here for General Kanak. Post lookouts. Take turns resting." Relieved sighs mixed with clinking swords being laid on the boulder's rocky surface.

Juanita rested her head on Dakshi's shoulder and closed her eyes. The king stroked her hair and gazed across the Plains.

# What's lost is found

A loud gurgling behind them cut short their amazement. Wheeling around, a torrent of bubbles burst the lake's surface. Peering over the edge, soft yellow light from the submarine's lamps wavered as the ship sank.

"Made it just in time," said Goban.

Tom felt like he might be sick again.

"What's that?" said Kiran.

A writhing monster rose from the depths. As the beast ascended, its wavering hair glowed neon blue. Everyone stood frozen as the ghostly apparition breached the surface.

"Max!" cried Kiran. "We left you in the ship!"

"Sorry Max," Tom said sheepishly.

Max dog-paddled to the wharf. The two helped him onto the dock, then leapt back before Max had a chance to drench them.

"Got somethin' in his mouth," said Goban.

Kiran knelt and grabbed hold of the object. Max hunkered down. Kiran pulled. Max pulled back, growling playfully.

"No Max," Tom said. "Not tug-a-war." Max's large brown eyes swiveled sideways, looking at Tom.

Tom gave him a stern look. "Max. Let go!"

Max shifted his gaze to Kiran.

Kiran pulled harder. "Let go, Max." The dog reluctantly opened his jaws. Petting Max, Kiran handed the dragonhead key to Tom.

"Good boy, Max!"

Everyone peered over the edge. The last wavering glow from the sub's lights faded, and the craft disappeared into the murky depths and the lake became still.

After the gurgling stopped, they turned and fell silent once more.

A vast wall of buildings stretched for as far as they could see in either direction. Unlike most buildings Tom was familiar with, these had no flat sides or square corners. The fronts of the structures were smooth, flowing waves with glassless oval windows that opened onto large bulbous balconies. The balconies thrust out, with matching curved awnings above, giving the impression of bulging chins, mysterious dark eyes concealed beneath large jutting eyebrows.

Tom felt the eyes gazing down upon him. Oddly though, the feeling wasn't creepy, exactly; it felt more like someone watching with curious amusement.

Matching tiny oval doorways dotted the buildings' ground floors. Off to their left, between two buildings, stood a massive dragonhead archway. The dragon's mouth hung open, exposing the entrance to a dark tunnel.

Kiran and Max set off exploring buildings. While Goban walked into the tunnel.

"The buildings are beautiful," remarked Avani.

"A tad creepy—" Tom added. "—but beautiful."

Avani smiled, took his hand and led him back to the waterfront. Sitting on the dock, her feet dangling over the edge, she flexed her foot, the tip of her sandal just touching the water.

Tom sat beside her and looked over his shoulder.

Leaning back on her elbows, Avani gazed up at the sparkling flowers on the cavern ceiling high above and smiled. "I wish—"

"What? That we didn't hafta save the world? That we could just stay here forever?"

Avani sat up and studied their reflection in the water. Her smile widened. Scissoring her legs back and forth happily, she linked her little finger around Tom's and squeezed.

Tom glanced at her finger, then at her face. He hesitated, squeezed her finger back, then following her gaze, stared at their reflection. *We're an odd pair. A dorky, spiky-haired Earth boy sitting beside a pretty, long-eared elven girl.*

"You're right," she said wistfully.

"What?"

"Wish we could stay here forever."

Tom sighed. "Oh yeah. Me too."

"Hey!" came Goban's distant voice. "Think I found a way out!"

Avani stared at their reflections a moment longer, dipped her toe in the lake and flicked, shattering their reflection.

She grabbed Tom's hand and stood. "Come on. Time to save the world."

# Stranger still

Gazing up, Tom shivered. Gargantuan teeth, larger even than the T-Rex skeleton's he'd seen in the Smithsonian, hung down from above, poised to devour him. Shivering again, he hurried down the stone dragon's cold, dark throat.

Tom flipped on his headlamp. Avani mumbled her light orb incantation, but as before, got nothing, not even a flicker. She glanced sheepishly at Tom. He pretended not to notice.

*Plunking* drips of water and their scraping footsteps echoed throughout the corridor, playing tricks with Tom's mind, the eerie soundscape evoking images of creepy crawlies slithering up behind them.

A moment later, the tunnel opened into a vast dry cavern. At their feet, a deep chasm dropped away. Tom couldn't see any glowing vines or flowers, yet there was enough light to see by. What's more, on the far side of the cavern, a beam of light shone down from above, but from this distance Tom couldn't make out the light's source.

Though only a fraction of the last cavern's width, this one was taller with hundreds of hovering stones, boulders even, some the size of a house. The largest of which pressed against the cavern ceiling, straining to rise farther.

Massive stalactites hung down from the rough, gray ceiling.

A narrow-arched stone footbridge, without sides or rails, spanned the chasm. Tom grabbed Goban's arm and cautiously leaned out. "Hey! There's a platform below. And stairs leading down."

"Stairs?" Goban peered over the edge. "Deeper still, there're more bridges."

"How many?"

"I count four. Beyond that, it's too dark to see."

"The map calls this chasm '*the gateway to the lower levels: uncharted*'," Avani said. "Apparently, Kila only mapped the uppermost level."

"Whoa! Wish I had my drone. I could send her down. View the scene below on my watch."

"What's a drone?" asked Goban.

Kiran kicked a rock over the edge *tick, tap, ting*—, then nothing.

Goban slapped Tom's shoulder, then sauntered across the bridge.

Kiran went next, then Max.

"Kiran!" shouted Avani, hurrying after him. "Be careful!"

Holding his breath, Tom stepped cautiously onto the narrow bridge.

"Hey, check this out," called Goban.

Tom stepped off the bridge at the far side and breathed a sigh of relief. Twenty feet up the path, Goban stood amidst a field of gigantic boulders, all arranged in neat rows and equally spaced apart. Tom walked over.

Each boulder floated a foot off the ground, completely encased by a stout rope mesh. Many of them as large as those pressing against the cavern ceiling.

Goban yanked on a rope. The mess creaked, tipping the boulder slightly, but it didn't drop. "Wants ta rise."

Tom bent down and peered underneath. Six solid metal spikes with holes on top stood firmly anchored into the stone floor. Ropes from the mesh extended through the spikes' holes, with their ends tied in a loop. A single rope ran through the loops, all the way around the base, its end tied securely to a stout metal spike in the ground.

"If you cut that center rope," said Tom, "the rope'll slide through the loops, releasing the stone." He looked up at the ceiling. "Why would someone do this?"

"How'd they hold em down in the first place?" asked Goban.

Max barked. "Look what I found!" shouted Kiran from up ahead.

# The shrine

Following Kiran's voice, Tom and Goban wove their way through the tethered boulder field and onto a vast courtyard surrounded by buildings. But these buildings weren't like the flowing, whimsical structures of the previous cavern. They did have well-rounded corners and roofs, as did the others, but these sat low to the ground. Squat and heavy, these buildings looked more like factories than houses. Where the other buildings looked playful, these looked tough, mean.

A white brick path led to the center of the courtyard. Kiran, Avani and Max waited beside a colossal white statue or something. Kiran waved them over.

When they approached, Tom studied the white stone structure rising above the courtyard. Smooth and dome shaped, the building curved up and out, hanging over them like a giant, fat-stemmed toadstool.

"Look at this!" Kiran ran to the other side.

Hurrying after, they found Kiran standing by a small oval shaped ring attached to the smoothly curving wall. A door? Unlike the rest of the structure, the oval was made of brass with a thick copper ring surrounding it. To the right of the oval were two round raised disks. The left hand disk was engraved with the image of a dragon with rays of light radiating from its eyes and mouth. The right disk had hideous monsters with flaming eyes and wicked grins.

"Weird," Tom remarked. "Is this on the map?"

Avani unfolded it. "It's called *The Vault—or—The Shrine.*" She scrunched up her face. *"The Creche?"* Her eyes flicked back and forth, trying to decipher the inscription. "Below it there's a single word: *Hope.* And a drawing of flames." She scanned the page. "Hope? Rising from the flames?" She rotated the map. "Or else—hope burning.

"Anyway, if we interpreted the symbols correctly, the map says the exit's over there." She sprinted across the square. Tom and Goban couldn't keep up.

\* \* \*

Kiran stared at the oval. He placed his palm on the dragon disk and pushed. The disk slid inward, accompanied by a soft scraping noise. *Click.*

Max pawed Kiran's leg.

Kiran laid his other hand on the other disk and pushed. The disk groaned, then grudgingly slid inward, *clunk.*

Kiran leapt back as a heavy oval door, hinged at the bottom, slammed down onto the courtyard beside him. A cold mist poured from the entranceway. The mist thinned, revealing a narrow passageway leading into darkness.

Kiran peered around the corner. The others were heading toward a round raised platform.

"Come on Max." Mist swirled as Kiran ducked inside.

Whining, Max followed him in.

# A prince claims his crown

Avani tried folding the map various different ways. "I don't understand. The red line ends here, but there's no tunnel, no stairway, no nothing."

Tom nudged her elbow, gesturing to the circular metal platform beside them. The raised platform stood two feet off the ground. Made from a dull gray metal, the platform measured about ten feet across and a foot thick.

Avani cocked her head. "What is it?"

Tom peered underneath. The disk rested on a four-foot-wide metal cylinder which extended up through a metal collar in the ground. He stood. The entire structure seemed to be brighter than the surroundings. He tipped his head back. There was a hole in the cavern ceiling directly overhead. "I think this is it."

"This is what?"

"The way out!"

Avani glanced around uncertainly.

"I think it's a machine. A lift. An elevator." Tom pointed up. "Must rise through the opening above—or—at least, it used to."

"What are those?" she asked. Three large metal hooks, equally spaced around the platform, bolted to the stone courtyard, they hinged up and over, their hooked end resting firmly on top of the platform.

"Clamps."

"What?"

"Clamps. They hold the platform down. Keep it from rising."

"Like the nets over the floating boulders we passed."

*Clink, clunk, boing!* They turned toward the sound. A few feet away, Goban squatted, rummaging through a pile of discarded tools, gears, springs, and other strange objects.

Standing up, he proudly held a brass helmet with leather straps dangling from each side. The headgear sported a set of round brass goggles an inch thick. Delicate brass levers, with lenses attached, stuck out just above the goggles.

Goban plopped the helmet on and pulled the goggles down over his eyes. "Whaddaya think?"

Tom nodded approvingly. "Definitely you." Walking over, Tom tapped his knuckles against the headgear: *thunk, thunk.* "Sorta a dwarf mad scientist look. What do the lenses do?"

Goban flicked a lever, and a lens rotated down in front of his right eye. He wriggled his stubby fingers in front of his face. "This one makes things look bigger." He flicked that lever up and the next down. "Whoa!" He leaned back and viewed the cavern ceiling. This one's a telescope, like the one the Mastersmith built from yer plans."

"And the next?"

*Click, click.* "Odd. This one shows colors—" His eyes looked huge. "—round each of you."

"Maybe it shows our auras," suggested Avani. "What color am I?"

"Purple. With flares of orange, blue and yellow."

"What about Tom?"

"Mostly red."

"Try changing your emotion, Tom," she suggested. "Try feeling scared."

"I am scared."

"So—red means fear, then. Try feeling happy."

He gave a half-hearted smile.

"Hey!" cried Goban. "It worked! Tom's green. Well—greenish."

"What's the last lever do?" said Tom.

Goban flicked it into place and studied his hand. "Wow! I can see my bones!" He looked at his legs. I can see leg bones through my pants!" Raising up, he stared at Avani, flicked up the lever and took off the helmet.

"What did you see?" she asked. "Why's your face red?"

"Nothing."

Tom reached for the helmet. "Can I try?"

"No!" Goban shot Avani a sheepish grin and stashed the helmet in his backpack.

Avani regarded him suspiciously.

"When I used the telescope lens," said Goban, hurriedly changing the subject, "I spotted an opening above us. Maybe it's the way out." He gave Avani another awkward grin.

Her suspicious look intensified. "Ya think?"

Tom hopped onto the platform and walked to the center where a raised control panel, resembling an old-school jukebox, stood waist high above the platform. Mounted on its right side was a large brass lever. "Think I found the control mechanism."

Avani hopped up and walked over. "There are markings beside the lever, pointing up and down."

Too short to hop up, Goban flopped onto his belly, groaning as he struggled up onto the platform. Brushing himself off, he hiked up his pants and strode over. "This is too easy!" Grabbing the lever, Goban strained, but it wouldn't budge.

Tom pointed to a button mounted near the top of the lever. "Try holding in the button."

Goban grasped the lever so that his palm pushed in the button. *Click.* Grinning, Goban tugged on the lever and it swung smoothly all the way to the top. Nothing. His grin faded.

"No power," explained Tom.

"How come the underwater ship worked, and this doesn't?"

"The sub moved. It was self-contained, with its own power source. To power these factories, and the elevator, there's gotta be a power plant nearby."

Goban said, "Ya suppose we could fire up this—ah—power station, if we found it?"

"Not likely. After all these years. Doubt if it'd start."

"But it's possible?" coaxed Avani.

Tom shrugged.

"What would it look like?" asked Goban. "This power station?"

"Probably have a furnace."

"A blast furnace? Like the dwarf forges at Deltar?"

"Could be, but—"

"And tall towers?" said Avani.

Tom nodded. "Smokestacks or cooling towers. Judging from the style of the buildings and this machinery, I'd say everything's steam powered."

"To produce steam—" Avani reasoned, "—there'd have to be water tanks."

"Yeah. So?"

The other two just smiled.


## Sleeping dinosaur


Avani and Goban grabbed Tom by the arms and spun him around. Directly behind him stood a squat building with four smokestacks rising from its slightly arched tile roof. Both sides had massive copper, brass, and iron pipes, of various sizes, rising from the ground and snaking across the building's face.

Twin pipes jutted straight out from the base of the building, growing larger till they abruptly turned down and dove beneath the ground. It gave the unnerving impression of a giant metal monster whose tendon encased arms had clawed their way down under the courtyard.

Tom shuddered, then looked up. Two more large pipes angled up into twin tall cylinders.

Mounted on stout hinges on the face of the structure stood a massive, round cast-iron door with a small glass inspection port at its center.

Tom blinked. "Ahhh—a power plant looks exactly like that."

Sprinting up the power plant's wide steps, the three stopped in front of the blast furnace's thick, heavy door. Attached to the wall, on the left side of the furnace, was a rectangular panel bristling with dials, knobs, and switches. Covered in a thick layer of dust, the dials lay dark and silent.

To either side of the panel dual levers hung down.

Goban grabbed hold of a lever. "Come on."

"It's not gonna work," said Tom. "It's a dinosaur!"

"A what?"

"An antique. A piece a junk from ages past."

Avani grasped the other lever. They stared at Tom expectantly.

He shook his head. "Gotta be hundreds of years old, at least. No way it's gonna start."

"How much time's left?" asked Avani.

Tom glanced at his watch and winced. "Six hours—ah—oorts."

"Only six oorts till the portal opens?" Avani bit her lip.

"Till the creatures gobble up everyone," added Goban.

"They suck life force," Tom corrected. "They don't actually eat people." He paused. "Least—I don't think they do."

"We have to try," urged Avani.

"Even if the machine miraculously fires up, and even if we somehow make it to the surface, no way we can get back to Elfhaven in time." Tom's shoulders sank. "And without Naagesh's remote, it's no use, anyway."

They just stared at him.

Tom shifted his attention to the controls. "Hmmm. The dials background is green on the left side, orange in the middle and red on the right. Bet green means good."

Neither Goban nor Avani blinked.

"Tough crowd." Returning his attention to the panel, Tom said, "Most of the switches point up. Up probably means on."

Goban began flicking switches.

"Wait!" cried Tom.

Goban stopped.

"In the unlikely event it starts—"

"Yes?" they said.

"The lubricant would've dried up long ago."

"What happens if the lubcant dried up?" asked Goban.

"Lubricant," said Tom. "Without lubricant there'd be metal against metal, increasing the friction between parts."

"Lubricant's good?" Goban scratched his head. "Friction's bad?"

Tom grabbed Goban's hands, slapped them together and rubbed them back and forth. "Feel the heat? That's friction. Without lubrication, the friction could cause the machine to heat up beyond its design tolerances."

"And?"

"And explode. Or—"

"Or?"

"Or the metal parts might expand so much they seize together and—"

"And?" shouted Goban and Avani.

"And explode."

Goban nodded to Avani. The pair slammed the levers all the way up.

Tom leapt down a step and closed his eyes. Nothing happened.

Tom's left eye cracked open. The eye scanned the dials. Nothing had changed: the needles all still rested at the bottom.

"What's that?" asked Avani.

Goban bent over the console, then grinned. "Still got that key?" Goban held out his hand. "The dragonhead one?"

Tom pulled the artifact from his belt. "Sure. Why?"

Goban moved aside. At the center of the panel was a small square hole. Tom switched on his headlamp. The hole was a about two inches deep. A thin wavy brass ribbon jutted out from the back side.

"Can't be it," Tom reasoned. "Not the right shape."

Goban kept his hand raised.

Holding the key out for Goban, Tom stepped forward, tripped on the top step and dropped the key. When it struck the stone floor, the key shattered sending pieces clattering down the steps.

"Oh, no!" Avani's face paled. "You broke it."

\* \* \*

Kiran shivered, rubbed his hands together and blew on them. Max whined.

"It's OK, boy. I'll make us some light."

Inching forward, Kiran started reciting the incantation. Before he'd finished, his foot bumped against something hard. *Clink.*

Kiran knelt and patted the icy stone floor till his hand brushed against something. Oblong, it was about the width of his foot and as long as his forearm. He strained to lift the heavy object. Its surface felt rough and cold but warmed quickly to his touch.

Sitting, Kiran placed the object in his lap and finished his incantation. Two bright globes floated up from his raised palms. "Wow! Whadja think Max? Never got two before!" Max turned at a noise from outside.

Max's tail slapped Kiran in the face. Kiran brushed it away. It whapped him again. Kiran frowned. "Don't worry. The others probably just found the way out, is all."

Watching the glow globes rise, Kiran's gaze rose with them. Constructed of the same white stone as the outside, the room's gently arched walls and curved ceiling were ribbed, like bones.

Kiran felt the object in his lap twitch. Clutching it tightly, he raised it once more, watching it critically. It didn't move. *Musta imagined it.* Max's tail brushed his hand. Kiran sighed. *It was just Max.*

Looking up, Kiran gasped, nearly dropping the object.

# Picked a bad time to...

King Abban nudged King Dakshi. "Time to awake, my sleepy friend."

Dakshi removed his arm from Juanita's shoulder. Juanita yawned and stretched.

The king stood. "What is it? Has General Kanak arrived, or Naagesh?"

"We're not sure. Some time back, we spotted a large dust cloud on the northern horizon."

He sighed. "General Kanak!" said Dakshi. "Finally. Why didn't you wake me sooner?"

Abban glanced down at Juanita. She smiled and stood. "We were about to, but the cloud reversed direction. Disappearing back from whence it came."

King Dakshi frowned. "That does not make sense. Any sign of Naagesh?"

Abban shook his head no.

## General Kanak

The general stood on the parapet of Elfhaven castle gazing off to the south. Just then, a messenger ran up.

"News of the king?" Kanak asked hopefully.

"No sir. But the scout you sent to the river returned. He saw no sign of them. But—"

"But the ferry was gone. Shall we send troops to look for King Dakshi?"

"Where would we send them?" replied the general, as if to himself. "And with the ogre army camped outside the north gate." Kanak shook his head. "The king said to wait, so we wait."

## Best leave sleeping dinosaurs lie

Tom picked up the remains of the key. Chunks of stone fell away. All that remained was a small white cube.

Goban took the cube and pushed it into the hole in the panel. Nothing. He pulled it out and rolled it over in his palm. One side of the cube had a wavy line carved deep into its smooth surface.

"That's it!" said Avani.

Goban lined up the wavy lines, and once again inserted the cube.

*Clunk, whir.* The cube withdrew inside the panel.

A shudder passed underfoot, followed by a deep rumble. Through the furnace's soot-covered glass inspection port, they saw flames erupting, and felt heat radiating from the massive metal door.

"We did it!" cried Avani. "It's working," shouted Goban.

Tom scanned the panel. Now faintly lit, the dials began to rise.

A mechanical groan came from the building to their left. Through large arched windows, they could see massive rods and pistons rising from below, slowing as they neared their peak twenty feet above ground-level, then circled back down. The cycle continued, picking up speed with each revolution.

Goban grabbed Tom's sleeve. "There's another one." In the next building over, more wheels sprang to life

Tom pivoted slowly. In factory after factory, lights lit up, wheels turned, pistons rose and fell. "I don't believe it. They're all firing up!" He glanced at the panel. The gauge's needles were rising, some already in the orange, a couple in the red. "Yikes!"

"Where's Kiran?" Avani scanned the courtyard. "Kiran? Kiran!"

They heard a distant muted bark.

Avani dashed down the steps. "Kiran? Max? Where are you?"

"Avani!" shouted Tom. "It's starting. We have to go!"

"Kiran!" She picked up speed.

*Blam! Blam!* Goban spun around. "Uh oh!" Nudging Tom, Goban pointed at the lift. Two of the massive clamps released as Avani ran past. *Blam!* The third clamp flew back. The platform started rising.

"Avani! The lift!" shouted Tom. She glanced back. "Stop the platform. Pull down the lever!"

She stopped and started back for the platform. In the distance came Max's muted bark. Five feet from the lift, Avani slowed. Max barked again. Avani hesitated, then again reversed direction, running full out across the courtyard.

"NO!" Tom charged down the steps, Goban hopping awkwardly after him.

When they got there, the lift was already over Tom's head. He jumped. His fingertips grasped the lip, but he couldn't hold on.
Goban dropped to his knees and bent over. "Climb on!" Tom scrambled up his back, Goban groaned and stood. Tom climbed to Goban's shoulders and stood up, wobbling. He stretched, but the lift was out of reach.

# Chloe and Larraj

As the pair crested yet another dune, Larraj pulled his hood lower and headed down the other side. In the trough, the wind lessened somewhat, and the wizard stopped to catch his breath. Chloe rolled up beside him.

"We're running out of time," he said absently. "As the wind builds, the drifts get deeper, slowing us down. How much time till the portal opens?"

"6.735 oorts," Chloe replied.

"We must find a way to speed up."

"Do they have wake boards on your planet?" asked the robot.

"What?"

# Kiran

His magical light globes brightened from the dim glow of a candle to that of an oil lamp. Kiran glanced from the object in his hands to the towering stack at his feet. "They're Eggs. A giant pile of eggs!"

He sat down, groaning, resting the heavy egg in his lap.

"Kiran? Kiran!" came his sister's muted voice. He ignored her.

"Whaddya think Max? Zhanderbeast eggs?"

Max barked.

Kiran nodded. "Good point. Who'd keep zhanderbeast eggs?" He bit his lip, considering. "Besides, they're too big." He made a fist and held it in front of Max's nose. "Zhanderbeast eggs are about this size." Max licked his fist. Kiran flicked dog slobber from this hand. "Plus, zhanderbeast eggs are smooth as flash-worm silk, shiny and black as night, these are bumpy and they're not black they're—"

Kiran leaned forward and waved his hand absently. At his command, the light orbs floated closer. The brighter light revealed the eggs were a dull, faded blue.

"Hey! Maybe the people who built this place were birds. Very smart birds."

Max shook his head.

"No?" Kiran waved again, and the orbs made a low pass over the pile.

Kiran squinted at a sudden flash. He studied the egg in his lap. Delicate lines of gold, finer than an elven hair, sparkled in the soft light. When the orbs passed over the stack, flashes of gold, reflecting from the eggs, danced across the walls and ceiling. "Whoa!"

"Kiran? Max? Where are you?" came his sister's urgent voice.

Max barked again and pawed Kiran's leg.

"I know what these are!" Kiran said reverently. He stared at the egg in his lap. "Think I'll name you Sparky, no Puff, no—" He grinned. "Frost!"

The egg shuddered. "It moved!" Kiran nudged Max. "Did you see that?"

Max barked urgently.

"OK! OK." Kiran gently laid the egg back on the pile.

"Kiran!" screamed his sister.

Max bit down on Kiran's pant leg and began dragging him away.

"I'm going already!"

# Time to go

"Kiran!" Avani screamed again.

Kiran dashed from the building and ran smack into his sister. They both fell over. Max bounded out.

Tom sprinted up, followed by Goban, both panting hard.

Avani stood.

Kiran leapt up, grabbed his sister by the hand and tried to pull her toward the building. "Avani! You gotta see what's inside."

A grinding noise caused them to turn. The lift platform had risen three hundred feet above the courtyard, about a third of the way to the hole in the cavern ceiling. The lift shuddered, screeched, continued to climb.

"Eggs!" cried Kiran. "Hundreds of em. Guess what they are?"

Tom grabbed Avani's arm. "Why didn't you stop the lift?"

"Not my fault! Goban left the lever up!"

"If Kiran hadn't wandered off," argued Goban, "then—"

"That's right!" Avani turned on her brother. "You ruined everything! If it weren't for you, we'd be safely on that platform on our way to the surface!"

A loud scrapping, creaking, grinding sounded.

"No," said Tom. "Look." Behind them, the lift had stopped. It shuddered, jerked up a couple of feet and froze. The grinding, screeching grew louder. "Kiran saved our lives."

"What's happening?" said Avani.

"It's ceasing up."

The ground shook. Shook again. Tom glanced at the power plant. The wheels, pistons and gears chugged along at incredible speed. The column supporting the platform began to vibrate. Cracks formed.

"It's gonna blow!" shouted Tom. The platform flexed sideways. A loud *boom* rocked the courtyard. The platform tipped, and its supporting column burst apart. The whole thing plummeted downward.

Tom's eyes bulged. "Oh, no."

"It's gonna hit the power plant!" shouted Goban.

A massive explosion shook the area as the platform crashed into the plant. Fire erupted, engulfing the buildings to either side.

Max barked, bounded off the way they'd come in.

"The tunnel to the lake!" Kiran ran after Max, Avani chasing them.

"Without the sub," said Tom, "we're trapped."

"Might be another way out," shouted Goban, barely above the noise of the explosions.

Tom just stared at the hole in the ceiling, their last hope of escape. Goban grabbed Tom's arm and jerked him along.

Halfway through the boulder field, Kiran screeched to a stop.

"Keep moving!" yelled his sister.

"I forgot to shut the door!"

"What?"

"The eggs! They'll get burned." Kiran turned back.

Avani grabbed his arm. "Are you crazy? This place is going to blow!"

"But Frost! I've gotta protect Frosty!"

"Frosty?"

Another explosion. The tethered boulders wobbled. Small stones began raining down from the ceiling high above.

Avani covered her head. Bigger rocks started falling. One of them struck a large floating stone above, sending it careening off to one side. Across the courtyard, a huge stalactite broke loose and crashed down into a building, causing yet another explosion.

Kiran jerked free and ran back. Max bounded after him.

"Stop him!" cried Avani.

Kiran ducked as first Goban, then Tom tried to grab him. Both missed. Max ran past and leapt.

"Aaaah!" shouted Kiran. *Thump!*

Tom and Goban turned. Kiran lay face down with Max sitting on top of him. Tom and Goban ran back.

"Good boy, Max!" Tom grabbed one arm and Goban the other and they jerked Kiran to his feet, dragging the struggling boy with them.

"No! I've gotta close the door!"

## Juanita and Dakshi

The boulder they stood on, the whole string of boulder pearls in fact, had begun to sway violently, evidence of the approaching storm.

Juanita glanced to the south. A massive wall cloud, the leading edge of the storm was nearly upon them.

Lightning flashed. "The wind is just the leading edge of a bigger storm. The storm'll arrive soon. Hope your general arrives soon," she said. "If the wind gets any stronger, we may get thrown from these bucking stones."

"Juanita," said Dakshi. "We need to talk."

"I thought we were talking."

King Dakshi glanced around nervously. King Abban stood conversing with Tappus and Zhang. His soldiers all peered down, looking for any signs of Naagesh. They were as alone as possible.

The king removed the heavy gold chain from around his neck. As the royal medallion slowly rotated, ribbons of reflected ruby light washed across Juanita's face. Raising her hand, she squinted, half turning away.

Dakshi knelt and awkwardly offered her his medallion.

Juanita's eyes ballooned. "What?"

"Juanita. Will you do me the great honor of becoming my queen?"

"You mean—theoretically, right?"

He just stared at her.

"Seriously? You—you—" Her hands began to shake. "You're—asking me here? Now?"

He tenderly took her hand.

Juanita tried to swallow, but her throat felt suddenly dry. She slid her hand from his, stood and turned away. "This is absurd! We already discussed this. I—I can't. We, Tom and I, have to go home!"

"I love you Juanita. You admitted you had feelings for me too. Do you love me?"

"Goblins!" cried a soldier. Through the blowing sands, they got a glimpse of hundreds of wriggling bodies scampering across the dunes.

"Naagesh has found us!" cried Tappus.

# Naagesh

Naagesh's cape flapped violently in the wind. He stood as if on an ocean floor, amongst a sea of wavering strands of seaweed, reaching for the surface. Only dryer—and with stout vines, stead of seaweed—and massive floating rocks attached.

Hundreds of strands, spread wide apart, swayed in the wind. Here at the base, the stalks were wider than a troll's thigh.

Naagesh tipped his head back, following the vines upward assent. Fifty feet above, a relatively small boulder, completely encased in a stout web of vines, floated only as high as vines would allow. Above that waved more vines, attached to progressively larger boulders, stacked five or six boulders high. The highest strand rising nearly a kiloter into the sky.

The wizard ran his gloved hand across the rough mass of twisted vines beside him.

"Time runs out, Master," the horned goblin reminded him. "This is the one they climbed."

"I know." Naagesh called to his minions, "After them you sniveling fools! Kill the rest, but I want the elf king alive."

# Below

Once past the boulder field they picked up speed, Avani leading the pack. Tom could just make out the arching bridge that spanned the chasm and the tunnel beyond.

Max barked.

Still running, Tom glanced up. High above, cracks formed in the cavern ceiling. Fingers of light shone through the cracks. A massive stalactite broke loose, fell a short distance, then jerked to a stop. The stalactite dangled there directly over the bridge, hanging by a single vine. The vine creaked.

"Avani stop!" cried Tom.

She skidded to a halt, one foot on the bridge.

"Look out!"

She stared above. The vine snapped. The stalactite fell. Avani leapt back as the stone crashed down, smashing the bridge to pieces.

Tom ran to her side.

She squeezed his hand. "Thanks." They leaned over the edge. Jagged chunks of the bridge smashed into the chasm walls, and staircases, taking out the lower bridges as they tumbled downward. Tom looked up. The cracks in the cavern ceiling widened.

"We're trapped!" shouted Kiran.

They turned back. Explosions sent projectiles hurtling across the cavern. A flaming missile landed on a tethered boulder. The rope webbing burst aflame.

"What'll we do now?" asked Avani.

"There's nowhere to go," shouted Goban.

The flaming net groaned, then burst, releasing the boulder and sending embers of burning rope flying. They watched the gigantic stone rise till it struck the ceiling, widening the cracks and raining down more pebbles.

"There is one place we could go," said Tom.

## Wizards

Now at the second level, two floating boulders above the Plains, Naagesh gazed upward. Directly above him the bulk of his goblin forces held tightly to the violently swinging vines, scampering up to the next level, the level directly beneath the king's party.

Naagesh ignored a yank on his sleeve. There was a second, more insistent tug.

"What is it?" snapped the wizard. The horned goblin hobbled over to the edge of their waving stone and pointed.

Naagesh joined him. Muffled explosions sounded below. Thick clouds of black smoke billowed up from nearby sink holes. Here and there, hungry flames licked the edges of the holes as if tasting them.

"Yes, yes!" spat Naagesh. "Smoke. Fire. Something's going on in the underworld, but of what concern is—"

"Not that." The goblin pointed across the dunes. "That!"

Naagesh squinted. In the distance, twin plumes of sand jetted skyward, blasted up through the drifting windblown sand. Something unnatural raced across the dunes at incredible speed.

As the apparition neared, out of a sand cloud, a long, flowing cape appeared, snapping wildly. A tall figure, his legs spread wide, balanced on a sort of glowing board. The figure leaned back, a sparkling rope clutched tightly in his hands. The rope led ahead to an obviously enchanted mechanical monstrosity, sand spewing from its sides as it sped across the dunes.

The metal beast slowed, then stopped below, and the magical board and ropes dissolved.

Naagesh stared down at his archrival.

# Up, up and away!

Tom grabbed hold of the rope net and climbed up the side of the largest of the ensnared floating boulders. When he neared the top, Avani bent down and wrapped her hand around Tom's wrist and tugged, groaning, "You been gaining weight?"

"Can't have," called Goban from below. "Since we haven't eaten in days."

They ducked as another flaming missile hurtled overhead. The projectile crashed down and two more rope nets burst into flames.

"Help me with Max!" shouted Kiran.

Leaning over the edge, Tom grabbed Max's left front leg while Avani grabbed his right. Below, Goban and Kiran shoved Max's rump, while those above pulled. Everyone groaned till Max finally scampered up on top. Kiran climbed up and sat beside him.

"Ok Goban," Tom called. "Cut er loose!"

Goban swung Aileen. *Twang.* He swung again. *Twang. Creak.* Their stone balloon shuddered. *Thwack, zing!* They lifted off.

"Goban?" shouted the three of them. "Goban!" A stubby hand reached up and slapped down. The others grabbed hold and pulled. Goban collapsed beside them.

Tom stared up. They picked up speed.

Three hundred feet from the stone cavern ceiling and climbing.

"Maybe this wasn't such a good idea," muttered Tom. "What if I miscalculated? What if we don't have enough mass to break through?"

"Now ya tell us," replied Goban.

Tom watched in shock as waves of ghostly crimson light, from the flaming buildings below, washed across the cavern walls and ceiling. Explosions sent more flaming missiles whizzing beneath them. Directly below, all the boulder nets were ablaze. One of them broke free, then another.

A hundred feet from the roof, a massive, slowly gyrating stone appeared above and to their left. Even though they were the ones who were actually moving, it looked like the boulder above was falling. As they rose past it, the stone narrowly missed them and appeared to drop below.

The higher they rose, the bigger the stones, though theirs was by far the biggest.

A series of explosions sent more rocks raining upon them. "Ouch!"

"The ceiling's cracking," cried Kiran. "It's gonna collapse!"

"It better," warned Goban. "Or we'll be crushed."

Fifty feet from the top, long cracks spread across the ceiling, sand cascading down through the cracks.

Another explosion. A nearby stalactite broke loose and plummeted down. It struck a floating stone and sent it careening wildly toward them.

"Hold on!" shouted Tom. The stone struck theirs, making their boulder wobble violently.

"The ceiling didn't collapse!" cried Kiran.

"We're gonna hit!" shouted Avani. "Quick! Over the sides, climb down the ropes. Someone grab Max!"

Ten feet.

Several more stones, freed from their burning rope nets below, struck the ceiling nearby. The cracks widened. Sand gushed downward, making it hard to see.

Five feet.

Tom screamed.

Everyone screamed.

# Larraj

Larraj raised his arm, golden sparks crackling around his wrists.

"Consider your actions wisely," warned Naagesh, yanking a bound and gagged figure in front of him. Prince Devraj struggled against his bonds.

The dunes suddenly shook. Massive cracks formed. Chloe's motors screamed as she sped away in reverse.

The sand at Larraj's feet shifted, shuddered, dropped a foot. Shuddered again.

All at once, the dunes beneath him just fell away. Arcing tongues of magic licked out from Larraj's hands, desperately trying to latch onto something.

\* \* \*

As their boulder blasted up past the lip of the plains, Avani gasped at the sight of Larraj plummeting into the inferno below. "NO!"

# Naagesh and Devraj

Naagesh watched Larraj fall through the ever-widening hole, bolts of magical lightning flashing long after Naagesh lost sight of him.

"Well that was strange," said Naagesh.

"NO!" yelled a female voice.

Naagesh followed the voice. A behemoth of a boulder rose past them with several kids dangling beneath it.

Devraj blinked. "Avani?"

"What?" Naagesh shoved the prince aside, a ball of energy forming in the wizard's hand. He drew back. Devraj rammed his head into Naagesh's side just as Naagesh let fly. The lethal, crackling ball missed Avani and struck the boulder an arm's length above her head. The rope net burst into flames.

Naagesh screamed. Goblins tackled the prince and held him down. Another seething ball of energy erupted in his hand. He drew back.

Suddenly, hundreds of screeching, cackling, winged beasts burst from the world below and swarmed around the evil wizard. Naagesh shielded his face with his cloak.

A moment later, the crazed flock rocketed upward, circling the floating mountain chain on their way.

Naagesh looked up. Avani's boulder was out of sight, his view blocked by the stone above.

"Odd day, Master," said the horned goblin. "First the underworld swallows the youngins. Then spits them out midst fire and smoke!" It paused. "Not to mention the dragon hatchlings."


# Kiran


Kiran clung to a rope on the far side, out of sight of the others. He'd also seen Larraj fall.

At that moment, strange squawking cries sounded. Within moments, their stone became completely engulfed by a flock of baby dragons.

"Frosty!" cried Kiran. One of the dragon chicks hovered, staring at Kiran.

"Help us, Frost!" shouted Kiran. "Go find Ninosh. Big papa dragon! Tell him Larraj is in trouble." Kiran pointed. "He fell in that hole." The chick blinked, then flew off after the other hatchlings.

"No, wait!" cried Kiran. "And tell Ninosh *we're* in trouble!"

# Avani

"Help!" cried Avani. The rope she held burned through and dropped away. She grabbed another. Above her, it was on fire too. The fire quickly spread to the ropes beside it.

Three feet away, Tom hung with one hand to a rope that hadn't yet started burning. In his other hand he held Max by his collar. Goban dangled two feet beyond Tom. Kiran was out of sight.

Now fully ablaze, strands of Avani's rope broke. Avani reached for the next rope, but it fell away.

"Help!" she cried again.

Tom stared at Max dangling below him, then back at Avani, her eyes pleading with him.

"Sorry, Max." He turned to Goban. "Goban! Take Max!"

"What?"

Tom let go of Max and stretched out his arm toward Avani.

Max chomped down on the net, holding on with his teeth.

Wide eyed, Goban swung sideways and grabbed Max's leg.

Avani's rope creaked.

Tom edged over onto the next rung of the net and leaned closer. Their little fingers wrapped around each other.

Avani's rope snapped.

All color drained from her face. "The Prophecy…"

"What?" cried Tom. "NO! Avani hold on!"

Tom's finger trembled from the strain. His hand started sweating.

Time altered.

A tear formed. Avani blinked it away. "The Prophecy," she repeated.

Tom's finger slipped. Avani fell.

Suddenly, the prophecy's prediction came back to him:

> "The boy and The Chosen One stands at a precipice;
> The two must decide;
> One shall live;
> One must die;
> Elfhaven hangs in the balance;
> The boy chooses—poorly."

## Apprentice falling

Kiran watched till the dragon chicks disappeared in the distance. After they'd gone, Kiran scrambled up his side of the rock as Tom climbed up the other side.

Kiran ran over and helped Tom pull Max from above, while Goban pushed from below. Once up, Max rubbed against Kiran's leg and whined. Tom plopped down. Goban crawled up and flopped down beside him.

"Where's Avani?" Kiran scanned their faces.

Tom's lip quivered.

"Avani!" Their boulder wobbled as Kiran circled outer the edge. "Avani!" He grabbed Tom by his hoodie.

"Where's my sister?"

Waves of sobs washed over Tom. "I—I tried to save her but—"

"NOOOOO!!!!" screamed Kiran.

\* \* \*

Still pinned down by goblins, Devraj raised his head and spotted Avani plummeting past. He screamed at Naagesh, "You murderer! You monster!"

Naagesh watched calmly till Avani disappeared into the sandstorm below. Then he ordered his goblins to bring the thrashing prince up to the next level.

# Avani

Avani's arms flailed, her hair whipping wildly.

"Think of something!" she screamed, her words swallowed by the rushing wind.

She cast a spell. Nothing. *NO!* She tried another incantation. Still nothing. Reaching into her satchel, she yanked out a handful of crystals. They were dark. Their magic spent. Dropping them, she grabbed the rest. All dark. She tossed them away.

Small floating stones whizzed past as she plummeted downward. Stretching out, she tried to grab one but missed. She tried again. A rock smacked her arm, tumbling as it rocketed upward.

Twisting in mid-fall, she glanced around frantically. There were no more floating stones.

Her necklace slid from beneath her wildly flapping smock. Catching the wind, the pendant whipped around and smacked her face. It smacked her again.

*Stop it!* She raised her hand, trying to block the seemingly possessed pendant.

Below, the ground rushed up fast.

Two hundred metrons.

The pendant slapped her a third time.

One hundred metrons.

The wind's roar got louder, more insistent. Her flapping tunic stung her exposed skin.

Fifty metrons.

A glint of light, reflecting from the pendant, caught her eye.

Time shifted.

In slow motion, she studied the pendant slowly turning in front of her face. The pendant that Mab, the fairy queen, had given her.

Avani grabbed hold of the pendant, halting its incessant attack. Immediately, Mab's last words echoed in her mind:

*Keep this pendant with you always, child.*
*What is it?*
*It's a magical charm, a course. What else would it be?*
*What's it for?*
*When the time comes, you will know.*

Avani glanced down.

Twenty metrons.

Clasping the pendant tightly to her chest, Avani screamed, "Help me Mab! Help me now!"

# Rising Son

When they'd spotted Naagesh. King Dakshi ordered his soldiers to climb upward again, a task made far more difficult in the now raging wind. They finally stood atop the last boulder in their chain, with nowhere else to go.

Abban, Dakshi and Juanita watched in stunned silence as the flock of baby dragons veered off and flew north.

King Abban shook his head. "There's been no sign of the Kanak or the army."

"The scouts must've failed," said Tappus.

King Abban glanced below. Goblins had reached the stone two below, and the fastest were scurrying up the sides of the mountain directly beneath them.

"Ready yourselves, lads," warned the dwarf king. "The goblins are upon us!" He heard a familiar voice.

"Dad! It's me, Goban."

"Goban?" King Abban blinked in shock. His son stood atop a free flying boulder, Thomas Holland at his side. Kiran knelt, hands covering his face, sobbing.

"Goban? What are you—"

"No time, Dad! Naagesh has a device that controls the Citadel."

"Yes," shouted his father. "We saw."

"Tom!" cried Juanita, spotting her son.

Tom turned and stared at her.

"Tom, it's me. Your mother!"

He didn't react.

"Tom? What's wrong?"

A hundred feet above, the kids' boulder stopped rising. Now out of the wind shadow of the Floating Mountains, their boulder caught the breeze and started drifting northward.

Goban cupped his hands and yelled, "We hafta get the device to the Citadel before midnight! Else Pandora's Portal'll open!"

"What did he say?" asked Dakshi.

"Something about a portal opening at midnight." Juanita waved. "Tom!" His boulder just glided away.

"Pandora's Portal," said King Abban. "I'd swear Goban mentioned Pandora's Portal."

"And something about the Citadel." Juanita watched the receding boulder grow smaller in the distance.

"Midnight!" King Dakshi glanced at the darkening sky. "We have but five oorts."

# Avani

A mesh of crisscrossing twine pressed firmly against Avani's face, tufts of her long golden hair poking through the net at odd angles. She struggled to break free, but struggling only managed to tangle her more.

Peeking out between threads, she could see she hung suspended above a small forest glen covered with giant tropical plants, brightly colored flowers, and spotted mushrooms.

The air smelled fresh and moist. Beams of sunshine filtered through the rich green canopy above, warming the clearing below. Chirps of exotic birdsong and buzzing insects filled the air, along with sweet smells of vanilla, honey, and licorice that somehow mixed pleasantly with the faint musty smell of mushrooms.

She grimaced, pushed the net away from her face and studied her predicament: she was tangled in some sort of webbing. A long wooden handle extended out from the back of the net, the entire thing hovering not far above the forest floor.

Hot steamy breath brushed her cheek. She turned her head. Directly beneath her stood a ferocious beast, long razer-sharp spikes jutting from its knuckles, elbows and shoulder blades. Powerful muscles rippled underneath its red skin.

The monster opened its mouth, light reflecting off spiked teeth. Raising its head, it sniffed Avani hungrily.

Avani screamed.

"It's all right, child," Mab assured her. "It's just my pet, Bubbles."

"Bad zhanderbeast!" the sprite queen scolded. "You're scaring Avani. Now shoo!" Mab frowned. The zhanderbeast hunkered down and let out a deep rumbling growl in protest.

"Bubbles?" Mab waggled her finger. "Remember what happened last time you disobeyed Momma?"

The zhanderbeast drew back its lips and roared. When Mab's stern look didn't falter, the zhanderbeast snorted its displeasure and stomped off into the forest, a trail of smashed toadstools in her wake.

"Teenagers," huffed the fairy queen. "Always want everything their way."

Avani watched till the zhanderbeast disappeared, then struggled to free an arm. "Seriously? A giant firebug net?"

Mab flitted over and hovered beside her face. "You asked for my help, deary."

"Yes, but a firebug net? Couldn't you think of something a bit—more— dignified?"

Mab huffed. "Never thought of you as the dignified sort." She touched a tiny finger to her tiny cheek, her equally tiny eyes rolling up in frustration. "Let me see—you didn't exactly give me much time to think did you?" She drummed her fingers on her arm. "What was it? A sectar? Two? A moment later and—" Mab slapped her hands together, *thwack!* "—you'd a been splattered flatter than a giant's ear!"

Avani returned Mab's icy glare.

Another sprite flew up, buzzing excitedly, conversing with her queen in their fast, high-pitched native tongue.

"Indeed!" Mab folded her arms. "She is ungrateful."

Avani glanced from one to the other. "Just get me out of this."

"Done!" Mab blinked, and the net disappeared with a soft *pop.*

Avani crashed to the forest floor. "Ouch!" She stood and rubbed her elbow.

"You're welcome!" said Mab.

The other sprite giggled.

"What?" said Avani. The sprite pointed. Avani twisted around and brushed squashed orange and pink toadstool from her bottom. The sprite giggled again. Avani leaned forward and bared her teeth. The sprite's eyes ballooned. She rocketed off.

Avani faced the fairy queen. "Mab. I need your help."

"What? Savin' yer life wasn't enough?" Mab shook her head sadly. "My, but elven girls have gotten pushy in the last thousand yaras."

# A wizard, a monk, and a prince

"They're here!" screamed Tappus. As the first two goblins scurried up the side of their rock, Tappus swung his sword and the goblins tumbled off the edge. "Naagesh's right below us!"

Juanita and the elven king peered over the edge.

Naagesh tipped his head back. "King Dakshi," he shouted. "I've something to show you." When their eyes met, the wizard snapped his fingers, and goblins shoved a bound prisoner into view. The young elf looked up.

Juanita gasped. "Is that—"

"Yes. Naagesh has my son."

Oblivious to the sounds of slashing swords, whizzing arrows, and the cries of falling goblins, King Dakshi stared down at Devraj in shock.

"We must save my son," said King Dakshi.

"Sire," began Tappus. "We have too few soldiers left. If we split our forces—" Tappus ducked, avoiding a goblin's swiping claws. Tappus thrust and the beast fell. "If we split our forces now, we will not survive."

King Dakshi's gaze remained fixed on his son. Juanita and King Abban stood behind him. Juanita parried a goblin's claws with her sword, while the dwarf king swung his axe.

King Dakshi drew his own sword. "Then I shall free him myself."

"No!" screamed Juanita.

King Abban stepped beside his friend, then came Tappus. Juanita took a deep breath and joined them.

"We'll all go," said King Abban.

Zhang suddenly appeared beside them. He pulled a magic infused throwing star from his belt and tossed it below. "I'll retrieve your son." Zhang grabbed hold of a vine. The moment the star exploded, Zhang leapt over the edge.

Juanita blinked. "Didn't think Zhang liked Devraj."

"Zhang means to kill Naagesh," explained Abban. "Saving the prince comes second."

# Zhang

Zhang landed in the chaos his magic throwing star had wrought. Goblins scurried away in panic as the monk strode toward the wizard.

"Stop him!" Naagesh commanded. Baring their crooked teeth and extending their claws, goblins crept up behind the monk.

Zhang pulled out another throwing star and tossed it over his shoulder. The blast sent goblin's flying through the air.

The monk kept walking; the wizard locked in his sights.

Magical energy crackled between Naagesh's fingers. He raised his arms. The wind blew back his cape, and a smooth black object fell from his cloak. The remote struck the rock, bounced, bounced again, finally coming to rest a few paces away.

"Zhang!" cried Devraj. "That device is our only hope!"

Zhang stopped.

Naagesh, Devraj, Zhang, and the horned goblin all stared at the remote.

Zhang aimed his sword at Devraj and lunged. Devraj's eyes popped. "Zhang! What are you doing?" The prince raised his bound hands and turned away. "Zhang, no!" The monk's sword flashed.

Turning back, Zhang drew his second sword and headed for Naagesh. "Well prince? What are you waiting for?"

Devraj glanced at his hands. The monk had cut his bonds.

The prince and the horned goblin locked eyes. They both dove for the remote.

# Juanita

Hissing and snarling goblins pressed their attack. Elven guards tried preventing them from reaching the top, but there were too many.

As in the Bog, the elven guards formed a tight ring around Dakshi, Abban, and Juanita.

Juanita sheathed her sword and stared across the Plains at the distant speck of the kids' stone airship as it receded into the distance. "Oh!" She blinked, tapped her bracelet's screen. Numbers appeared. She bit her lip, calculating.

King Dakshi leaned over the edge. "I cannot see Devraj. Nor Zhang."

"If the howls be any measure," the dwarf king assured, "the monk's winning."

From everywhere, claw-tipped fingers reached up from below.

"Is there no end to these foul beasts?" shouted Dakshi.

"For each goblin a soldier dispatches," agreed King Abban. "Three more take its place."

King Dakshi drew his sword. "I fear this may be our last battle, my friend."

King Abban's snorted. "Ye said that in the Bog." He slapped his hand onto his best friend's shoulder. "Still, if it be true, let 'er be a fight to live on in legend!"

The pair raised their weapons.

Juanita said, "Estimating the mass of the kid's boulder at four and a half tons, and wind speed at twenty meters-per-second—" She tapped her bracelet again. "They should reach maximum velocity in four and a half minutes."

"Juanita. We have more pressing matters to—"

"I don't have a compass," she said. "Which way would you say they're headed?"

Dakshi sighed. "North."

King Abban added, "Toward the Icebain River."

The pair tightened their grips on their weapons.

"And beyond the river?" Juanita grinned. "What else lies in that direction?"

"Elfhaven!" they cried.

"Cut the vines beneath us!" ordered King Dakshi. "Cut us loose!"

The dwarf king leaned over the side. "Zhang! Cease yer one monk vendetta! Free the prince and get up here. It's time to leave!"

\* \* \*

Ignoring the dwarf king's cry, Zhang continued on. Now fearful of the monk's slashing blades, the goblins scrambled out of his way, opening a wide path to Naagesh.

"You fools!" cried the wizard. "There're hundreds of you and just one of him. Kill him!" The goblins hesitated.

Zhang reached for another throwing star, but he'd used the last.

As the monk drew near, a ball of crackling energy spiraled above Naagesh's hands. Flicking his wrists, the deadly ball hurtled straight for Zhang.

Zhang snapped up his swords, forming an 'X' in front of his body. When the magic neared, the arcing ball mysteriously slowed, as if some powerful unseen force inside the swords themselves resisted the evil wizard's magic. The fireball reversed course, blasting backwards.

Naagesh leapt aside, but the deadly swirling magic grazed his left shoulder. A boulder in the next chain over exploded in flames.

Falling onto his back, Naagesh grasped his smoking shoulder. His arms, below the shoulders, had turned to swirling black smoke. Naagesh stared at Zhang's swords in shock.

Zhang too, stared at them. "What the?"

\* \* \*

Devraj grabbed hold of the remote. The horned goblin leapt onto his back. The prince rolled over, pinning the squirming goblin beneath him. The goblin hissed, slashing out with its claws, Devraj jerked his head to the side, but too late, a single claw raked the prince's face. Losing his grip on the device, it clattered away. The two scrambled for it.

\* \* \*

The twang of breaking vines mixed with shouts from above. Zhang glanced back. The elven guards had managed to sever most of the strands that anchored the floating mountain above to the one Zhang stood upon. Goblins howled as vines they'd been climbing, suddenly fell away.

Only three strands remained.

Zhang returned his focus to the wizard. Naagesh watched him cautiously. The black smoke withdrew inward and the wizard's arms returned to normal. Zhang raised his swords.

\* \* \*

Devraj reached the device first. "Zhang!" he cried. "Catch!" Tossing the remote, the goblin leapt. Its fingers just grazed the device, sending it careening to one side. The horned goblin tried to scurry after it, but the prince grabbed its leg.

The goblin hissed, turned back, and pounced on the prince. Devraj struggled, trying to keep away from its deadly claws. "Zhang! Help me!"

The remote landed beside Naagesh.

*Twang, twang.* The single remaining vine snapped taught beside the monk, the only thing left holding the two boulders together.

"Zhang!" called King Abban from above. "Cut us loose!"

Zhang's eyes met Naagesh's. His sword slashed sideways, cutting the vine. The boulder above began to rise. The monk ran and leapt. Sheathing his swords in midair, he landed on the horned goblin, grabbed Devraj and sprang off the boulder into open air, the prince dangling beneath him.

The monk reached for the vine.


# Naagesh

Naagesh picked up the remote, stood and dusted himself off, all the while watching the king's now free-flying boulder drift away.

Atop the king's rock, elven soldiers leapt, parried and thrust, battling the few remaining goblins who'd waited too long to make good their escape. Below, the monk held tightly to the severed end of a vine with one hand, while grasping the prince with his other.

*Even as the crazed monk dangles precariously, he watches me.*

Naagesh's gaze dropped to the horned goblin, standing nearby, its beady eyes fixed on the remote. Slipping the device into his cloak, Naagesh screamed at his remaining goblin horde. "Well? What are you waiting for, you fools? Follow them!" The goblins looked around in confusion.

"Aaaah! Must I do everything?" Thrusting out his arms, twin writhing, jade serpents shot skyward then dove, slicing through the stiff, woody vines below like a razor through butter.


# The king

The kings' stone airship gained speed. The elven soldiers had dispatched the last few goblins, and their stone's surface was littered with their bodies. A guard nudged a fallen beast with his foot. The goblin didn't move. He tested another.

A crack of thunder brought Juanita around. Behind them, massive churning, black clouds filled the sky and bolts of lightning flashed across the leading edge of the storm. The storm had already swallowed the southernmost strands of the Floating Mountains.

Just ahead of the writhing wall of clouds raced another free-flying mountain. This boulder, however, emitted crackling magical black lightning, heralding the angry wizard's pursuit.

Juanita monitored their progress, her son's boulder now just a spec on the northern horizon.

At that moment, a well calloused hand slapped down on top of her shoulder. Juanita gave King Dakshi a weak smile.

Brushing a lock of hair from her face, he asked, "What's wrong, my love? We escaped. You should be happy."

Juanita managed a weak smile. "I'm worried about Tom. He didn't seem to recognize me."

"You should be proud of your son. He and Goban saved our lives, giving you the idea to cut us loose."

Juanita nodded.

"Have you reconsidered my proposal?"

Juanita smiled at him, her eyes glistening from tears. "I have."

There was a commotion across the way. Tappus helped Devraj climb up, then offered Zhang his hand.

"Father!" cried the prince.

King Dakshi and Juanita turned. Behind the king, a fallen goblin picked up a dagger and stood.

"Father look out!" shouted Devraj, running forward.

An odd look washed across the king's face.

"What is it, darling?" asked Juanita.

The king touched his finger to her lips, then sagged into her arms, a dagger in his back.

"NO!!!" she screamed.

King Abban and Devraj's fists connected with the goblin at the same instant, sending the howling beast flailing over the edge.

"Check all the goblins!" ordered Tappus, running to his fallen king. "Make sure they're all dead!"

Juanita covered her mouth, tears cascading down her cheeks. King Abban stood in silence.

Devraj pushed his way through the crowd and knelt. "Father!" He held his father's hand. "You will be alright."

"Healer!" shouted Tappus. "Where's the healer?"

King Dakshi coughed and opened his eyelids. "Devraj my son. You're hurt." With trembling hand, he touched the bleeding claw marks on his son's face.

"It is nothing, Father."

King Abban knelt beside Devraj. "Dakshi. Ye bloody fool! Together, we've fought trolls 'n ogres with nary a scratch. Even a zhanderbeast, fer the love a Turin." King Abban spat. "I'll not have ye bested by a measly goblin!"

King Dakshi grabbed hold of his best friend's arm. "We have had our share of adventures, old friend." He managed a weak grin. "But for the record, the zhanderbeast had only three legs and was nearly blind."

King Abban frowned so deeply his eyes disappeared beneath his bushy brow. "Where's that healer?!"

"Dead," came a sober voice. "We lost the healer in the Bog."

King Dakshi let out a deep rasping cough. "Too late for a healer, my friend. Wipe that ridiculous tear from your beard and move aside so I can say my goodbyes."

King Abban rose, stepped back and dabbed his eye with his stubby finger.

Tears moistened the prince's cheeks. "Father, I failed you. Just as I failed mother. And failed Avani."

"Avani?" Dakshi frowned in confusion. "You did not fail us, son. I am sorry I did not prepare you better, trust you sooner. Lead well and be kind, my son."

The king turned to Juanita, took her hand and squeezed it. His smile faded. His grip relaxed.

"No!" She laid her head on his chest and sobbed.


# What goes up . . .

Goban watched as plumes of smoke and flames rose from sinkholes behind in the distance. Just beyond, the approaching storm, the biggest he'd ever seen, had already devoured the Floating Mountains.

Beneath them, the last of the dunes drifted by. Ahead, the narrow strip of sparse trees of the whispering forest marked the end of the Plains. Within moments, the snaking blue ribbon of the Icebain River came into view.

"Hey!" Goban tapped Tom's shoulder. "We're almost to the river. And look!" He gestured off to their left. "That huge swirling fog bank. That's the Deathly Bog."

Goban squinted ahead. "Smoke. Oh, no! Elfhaven..." Goban spun Tom around to face him. "Elfhaven! We're too late! The creatures—"

"No," said Tom, speaking for the first time since Avani... *Since I dropped her. If I hadn't hesitated. If I wasn't forced to choose between Max and Avani.*

"No?" said Goban.

Tom blinked. "The portal won't open till midnight."

Goban sighed.

"Probably just the ogre army's watch fires, preparing to attack Elfhaven."

"That's all? Oh, good." Goban scanned the eastern horizon. The rugged peaks of the Tontiel Mountains stood outlined in pink. "The sun's goin' down. Four oorts till the portal opens."

A rasping squawk preceded a loud flapping of wings.

"What's that?" said Kiran.

Goban's eyes lit up. "It's Kiki! And Mr. Squinkles!" Goban held his arm out to the side. His pet extended its sharp talons and clamped down onto Goban's arm. Goban winced. The raptor's left head nuzzled Goban's shoulder, while the right head hissed at Tom.

"Yikes!" Tom stepped back, tripped over the rope net and nearly fell off the rock.

"There, there," soothed Goban. "Be nice ta Tom." The right head snapped at the left instead.

"You named each head?" said Tom.

"Course!"

"But—" Tom frowned. "Mr. Squinkles is obviously male, while Kiki—"

"Short for Kikiboo," Goban confided. "But she doesn't like it, so I just call her Kiki."

Tom paused. "Kiki sounds like a girl's name."

"Course it does. Can't ya tell the difference?"

Tom stared at the two heads oddly.

"There's a note!" Goban reached down and untied a tiny scroll attached to the bird's leg. Bending forward at the neck, Kiki thrust her head firmly against Goban's chest.

Goban unrolled the note with one hand, while scratching Kikiboo with his other. Mr. Squinkles squawked.

"Tom. Ya mind?" Goban motioned. Mr. Squinkles regarded Tom skeptically.

"What? No way!"

"Just rub its neck, like me."

Tom reached out and hesitantly scratched the bird's neck. It squawked. Tom jerked his hand away.

"Firmer," coached Goban. Tom tried again at arm's length. This time the bird cooed happily. Tom watched the bird like it might explode.

"The note's from the Mastersmith!" shouted Goban. He rolled the note over with his thumb. A shudder passed through their boulder. Goban stumbled. A sudden gust tore the note from his hands. "Aaaah!" They grabbed for the note, but it fluttered away.

"What was that?" asked Kiran.

"Gust a wind," hissed Goban. "Lost the note." Both heads squawked! Goban and Tom resumed their grooming tasks.

"No," said Kiran. "Before that! The boulder shook."

"If Avani was right," Tom winced and glanced at her brother. Kiran's eyes watered. He turned away.

"Sorry," said Tom. "If she was right—then it's just air turbulence."

"Whaddaya mean?" asked Goban.

"Avani thought magic kept these rocks aloft. But if she was wrong and I'm right—"

"Yeah?"

"I think there's a huge deposit, buried beneath the Plains of Illusion, made of the same mineral as this boulder."

"So?"

"So, when we pass over the Icebain River and leave the Plains behind, we'll lose the repulsion force that holds us up."

Goban leaned over the edge. The Icebain River lay directly below. Another shudder. They started losing altitude.

"We're gonna crash!" cried Kiran.

"Yup," agreed Tom. "But the stone's heavy, so inertia's in our favor."

"That helps us how?" shouted Goban.

"We'll be closer to Elfhaven when we crash. Won't hafta walk so far."

"If—we kin still walk!"

Careful not to stop petting Mr. Squinkles, Tom tapped his watch. I calculate we'll crash in the forest before we reach the Pillars. The trees should cushion our fall."

"That's nice."

"Unless we've got more inertia than I think, in which case we'll smash into the cliff at the Pillars."

# King rising

Standing, Devraj watched the tragic scene before him. Kneeling beside his father, Juanita's hands rested tenderly upon his shoulder. King Abban and Tappus stared in silence at the fallen king.

Devraj wiped the last tear from his face and glanced at his moist hand. If truth be told, he no longer felt anything. Not sorrow nor grief. Nothing.

Devraj gazed back the way they'd come. At least they had a head start. He'd seen Naagesh cut his boulder free, but he could no longer spot the wizard's stone against the black wall of clouds.

Lightning flashed as the storm bore down upon them. *Perhaps the storm will destroy Naagesh and his goblins.* He sighed. *The wizard still has the device. Without it, we are lost.*

He faced the others. The guards stared at him. A soldier balanced a sword across his open palms and knelt. Then another. They all did.

"Long live King Devraj!" they shouted.

\* \* \*

"Good news," said Tom. "We're gonna crash in the trees, 'stead of the cliff, in about—" He tapped his watch. "—twelve seconds."

Max whined. Kiran and Goban stared ahead, their faces masked in panic.

"Hey look!" shouted Kiran. "Horses!" Below, half a dozen horses grazed on tufts of grass.

"They're wet," said Goban. "Musta swum the river."

Tom watched trees speeding by just beneath them. "Six, five, four." Treetops slapped the belly of their airship turned hunk of falling rock. 'Whap, whap, whap!'

Goban's pet squawked and took off.

"Make sure your seats and tray tables are in their upright and locked positions," said Tom. "Prepare to crash."


## Dumerre

Dumerre had walked all day yesterday, through the night, and most of the next day. Traipsing up the steep and rocky southern river trail, across the rickety bridge, over the upper falls, and all the way back down the river's north side trail. The sun's rays had just dipped below the jagged peaks to the east. It would be dark soon.

The ogre flopped down onto his back in a small clearing not far from the entrance to the Pillars, taking a well-deserved rest.

Crossing his arms behind his head, the ogre gazed up at the slowly darkening sky. A chill breeze rustled the trees. He glanced back toward the Plains. Lightning flashed in the distance. A massive storm was headed this way.

"Dumerre no afraid a storm." He grinned. "Dumerre not afraid a nuttin'! Not trolls. Not storm. Not—" He sat up, leaned forward and squinted. "What da?" A dark spot appeared in the southern sky. The spot grew larger.

Leaping to his feet, the ogre charged off through the forest.

*Whap, whap, whap!* Dumerre's eyes popped. Directly behind him, a giant boulder plummeted from the sky, snapping down trees like twigs. Zigging and zagging, he stumbled through the woods screaming!

\* \* \*

Creaking, cracking sounds filled the newly formed clearing where Tom and Max surveyed the damage. The pair stood at the tail of a long swath of flattened trees, stacked side-by-side, pointing in the same direction. At the far end of the swath, a steaming boulder rested against the cliff face just outside the Pillars of the Giants.

A series of moans and groans sent Tom and Max bounding around stumps and over broken tree limbs till they found the others.

"You guys OK?" asked Tom.

Goban and Kiran lay on their stomachs covered in twigs and shredded leaves. They rolled over, their clothes torn, and their faces smudged with dirt.

Kiran rose shakily to his feet and dusted himself off.

Goban rolled onto his back and stared up at Tom. Tom's face was clean and his clothes weren't torn, not even dirty. "How come you're not—"

"Max and I jumped off just before we crashed."

"So?"

"So we lucked out. Landed in a soft bush." Tom bend down and offered Goban his hand. "Come on. We gotta warn the townsfolk, remember? Only three and a half hours left till midnight."

Goban gestured to the horses. "Fastest way is on horseback."

Tom stared up into the four enormous eyes of the nearest steed with dread. The horse shook its head.

\* \* \*

Dumerre groaned. He'd dove to one side just in time to avoid being squished by the falling boulder. Grabbing hold of a tree limb, he moaned and pulled himself up to his feet, swaying dizzily.

It seemed darker. He glanced up. The storm was nearly upon him. "Musta passed out." Holding his head, he hobbled toward the entrance of the Pillars. A familiar sound stopped him. *Thwap, thwap, snap.* He turned back as yet a second boulder dropped from the sky.

Grunting and groaning and swearing every ogre curse he knew, Dumerre raced into the canyon.

\* \* \*

Zhang and Tappus stood atop their plummeting rock while everyone else hung below, dangling from vines. When the vines began to drag on the ground, the soldiers leapt off. Juanita did the same, managing a perfectly timed roll and popped up running.

After the cracking trees and stone-on-stone grinding fell silent, Tappus picked himself up and winced, having landed on his bad shoulder. Zhang had somehow managed to remain standing atop the boulder. Soldiers climbed up and helped the monk lower King Dakshi's body over the side.

The troops laid the body gingerly on the ground and wrapped it in a cloak.

Juanita, King Abban, and Tappus watched the grim spectacle from the side.

Devraj stood motionless, apart from the others.

Once the soldiers finished, they faced Devraj.

Devraj stared at the limp bundle before him.

"The guards await their king's command," whispered Tappus.

The brush rustled. Soldiers drew their weapons. Zhang raised his hand, stopping them. Out of the trees came Devraj's horse, followed by two more. His steed clopped up to him and nudged the boy king with its head.

Devraj didn't seem to notice.

# The Pillars revisited

A soft *clip, clop,* echoed off the canyon walls and the stone carvings as Tom,

Goban, and Kiran hurriedly led their horses through the Pillars.

Tom slid his hand across the smooth, chill ankle of a stone giant.

"Still feel sorry for em?" asked Goban.

Tom nodded. "Still think they're monsters?"

Goban gazed up at the towering figure above him. Its enormous muscles bulging with power and its jutting jaw stood frozen in a determined look, yet its eyes appeared soft, almost thoughtful. Goban looked away.

Once they'd exited the canyon, and with some effort, Tom got his foot into the stirrup, grabbed hold of the saddle-horn and wriggled up into the saddle, groaning all the while. Goban, though shorter, had no problem vaulting up onto his saddle. Kiran even less so.

Knowing the way home well from here, the horses started ambling down the main trail toward Elfhaven, Max at their heels.

"Goban! There you are," came a voice. "What took you so long?"

The three stopped. A rotund dwarf stepped from the shadows.

"Bodhi?" said Goban. "What are you doing here?"

"The Mastersmith is waiting for you." The dwarf motioned to a steep, rocky trail heading up the mountain beside the canyon.

"Uncle Zanda? Here?"

"Hurry. Mustn't keep the Mastersmith waiting. You know how he gets."

"But we hafta warn Elfhaven," blurted Tom.

"Master Zanda'll explain everything."

"I'll go," shouted Kiran. He dug in his heels and his horse galloped off, Max bounding along beside him.

Tom watched him go.

"The trails too steep." Zanda offered them a hand down. "Best leave the horses here." The dwarf led their steeds into the woods and tied them up.

When he'd finished, Bodhi started up the trail. "This way, lads!"

\* \* \*

Once the sound of hooves faded away, Dumerre poked his head out. The coast clear, the ogre strained to squeeze his fat body through the narrow slit in the canyon wall, then loped off toward Elfhaven.

## The Mastersmith

Halfway up the trail, they met Goban's uncle Zanda. As promised, The Mastersmith had been waiting for them. Bodhi tipped his head to Zanda then made his way back down, while The Mastersmith led Tom and Goban uphill.

Walking along, Zanda bit into a large round of smelly, well-aged cheese and spit out the tough rind. He grinned at this nephew. "You received my missive!"

"Yes—but—" Goban stammered, the cheese fixed in his sights.

His uncle pulled a long knife from his belt, cut off a couple of hunks, offering one to Tom and one to Goban. Goban's eyes lit up. He chomped his down in a single bite. Zanda handed him the rest.

The Mastersmith's grin dissolved. "But what? Did you receive my message or not?"

Goban fidgeted. "I—I dropped it," he admitted. "Before I could read it."

This uncle's face paled. "So, you didn't leave word for your father, as I instructed, appraising him of my plans?"

Goban glanced at Tom.

"We were about to crash," Tom explained. "The wind was really howling."

Master Zanda looked Tom up and down. "And who might ye be? Is it Thomas, the great inventor?"

"Well, I—"

The Mastersmith grabbed Tom's hand and heartily shook it. "Goban's gone on and on about you. Says yer almost as smart as he!" He winked at his nephew.

"Ah—thanks, but we need to get to Elfhaven. The portal's gonna open and—"

"Portal?"

Goban hurriedly brought his uncle up to speed. Zanda looked grim.

"In any case," Goban continued. "Father's trapped in the Floating Mountains battling Naagesh and his goblins. We need ta send help."

"No, he's not."

"He's not?"

"No. King Abban's stone fell from the sky not long after yers."

"How did you know that we were on a—"

Goban's uncle held up a metal and wood tube and handed it to Tom. "Great view, from up top."

Tom gazed through the tube. "It's a telescope!"

"Based on yer design, actually," explained the Mastersmith. "Made some improvements of my own, a course."

Tom handed the telescope to Goban. "So mom, Goban's dad, and King Dakshi escaped!"

"King Abban rode the flying stone, along with an odd-looking woman: short flat ears, hairless face, oddly dressed. Didn't see King Dakshi though, but yer half-right."

"Half-right?"

"A third stone cometh."

"Naagesh," said Goban and Tom.

Zanda grumbled, "The foul wizard's almost here."

"We still need the remote," Tom reminded them.

The Mastersmith glanced from one to the other. "Remote? Ah. The device you spoke of earlier."

"You didn't read my note, so your father doesn't know the plan."

"Neither do we."

"Alas," the Mastersmith said mournfully. "King Abban'll know soon enough."

"Hope yer plan involves the dwarf army," said Goban. "Where are they?"

"As usual, the high council's dragging their furry feet." He spat. "My fault. Wasn't convincing enough. Don't have yer father's gift fer winning lengthy squabbles with the sniveling twits on the council."

"Why those pompous, inflated blow-toads!" shouted Goban. "Just wait till I get hold of em."

Both Tom and Zanda stared at Goban, oddly.

"What?"

"Thought you didn't care for politics?" said Tom.

Zanda nodded agreement. "The council'll make up their minds in a day er two."

"We don't have a day or two!" snapped Goban. "The portal opens at midnight, remember?"

The Mastersmith glanced at Tom.

Tom stopped. "Ah Goban. Why don't ya show your uncle your new helmet?"

Goban's frown evaporated. Yanking off his knapsack, he sat down and began rummaging through it, tossing out a coil of rope, a dagger, a whetstone. Raising his hand, his stubby fingers held a dead rodent dangling by its tail.

Tom moved away.

"Wasn't fer me," replied Goban. "Ya think I'd eat this?"

Tom tipped his head, considering.

"Was fer Kiki and Mr. Squinkles. Forgot to give it to em." Tossing the rodent aside, he pulled out his leather and brass helmet, slipped it on, pulled down the goggles and faced his uncle. "Whaddaya think?"

His uncle nodded approvingly. "Where d'ya get it?"

"In the lost city."

"Lost city?"

"Beneath the Plains of Illusion," added Tom.

Goban's uncle blinked.

"We'll explain later." Goban stuffed things back into his backpack, minus the rodent, stood, and continued on.

Soon they arrived on top of the mountain. Up here, the chill, turbulent wind whipped their hair violently. The massive black wall of the storm loomed less than a mile away. Lightning cracked, splitting the sky. Almost instantly, thunder shook the mountain, sending small stones clattering over the cliff.

Tom inched his way to the edge and peered cautiously downward. Five hundred feet below, the Pillars of the Giants lay cloaked in darkness. Even over the wind, the sound of running feet and frantic voices echoed off the cavern walls. He stepped back.

"I do hope the prototypes meet with your approval, master Tom."

"The what?"

"I oversaw the project," added Goban proudly.

His uncle snorted, then drew back a bush so Tom could see what lay beyond.

Tom gasped. "Oh!"

"Quickly now into your harnesses," urged Zanda, turning to leave. "It's nearly dark, and you've only myntars afore the storm strikes. Good luck!"

"Wait!" cried Goban. "Aren't you comin' with us?"

"Think I'm crazy?" The Mastersmith shivered. "Just standin' near one of them flimsy contraptions gives me the willies! Dwarves're meant to be underground." He winked at Tom. "Besides—I've another of Tom's designs to *battle test* in Elfhaven, if I'm not already too late."

A pair of broad hands slapped down upon the boys' shoulders. "Oh, and Goban. I expect a complete report on *our* lil' experiment." Humming a light-hearted dwarf shanty, Goban's uncle sauntered off down the trail. "Assumin' you don't break yer darn fool necks!" His chuckling was quickly drowned out by the wind.

# Devraj

"We've gotta come up with a plan," said King Abban. He glanced across the clearing at Devraj, standing motionless, staring down at his father's body. "The prince is worthless."

"The king's worthless," Zhang corrected.

Tappus winced.

Zhang scanned the southern horizon. Another rock began its downward decent. "Naagesh'll be any sectar."

"We should warn Elfhaven," said Tappus. "That should be our first priority."

"Agreed," said King Abban.

"No!" snapped Devraj, walking over.

"Your highness." Tappus bowed.

"I am the king! I decide strategy."

"Warning Elfhaven isn't strategy," Juanita corrected. "It's not even a tactic. Warning Elfhaven is more of a—"

"Of course, my liege," Tappus broke in. "We thought to leave you to your grief."

"There is no time for grief. We shall set a trap for Naagesh, ambush him when he enters the Pillars."

"But my lord—"

"If we do not retrieve the wizard's device, all is lost!"

"Yes, but—"

"My decision stands!" Devraj slammed his fist against his palm.

King Abban spoke, "Tappus was only—"

"SILENCE!" shouted Devraj.

King Abban faced him. "You may be Dakshi's son, but that does not give you the right to—"

Zhang stepped between them. "I'll go. I'll ride to Elfhaven and bring back the elven army, I can drop off King Dakshi's body while I'm at it."

"NO!" snapped Devraj. "I will not have you, a lowly monk who *despised* my father, *drop off* his royal body like a sack of meat!"

The others stared at him.

Devraj signaled two troops to lash his father's body onto his horse. When they'd finished, Devraj ordered his soldiers to stay and fight. "I will be back with the army within the oort."

Devraj faced King Abban. "You may accompany me or stay."

The king tapped his axe handle. "Think I'll stay."

Devraj glanced at the others. Juanita spoke first, "I'll stay and fight."

Zhang nodded. "I intend to kill Naagesh. Might as well be here."

Devraj grabbed the reins and vaulted up into his saddle. "Retrieve that device. Nothing else matters."

# Naagesh

The forest crackled and hissed. Steam rose from splintered trees and the deep scorched trench their boulder made till it slammed into the stone ahead and stopped.

"Where's Lardas and the ogre army?" snapped Naagesh. "I gave that fool Dumerre strict instructions. The ogres should've been here by now! First the trolls. Now the ogres!"

Naagesh strode briskly to the Pillar's entrance.

"Master?"

Naagesh snap turned and glared at his servant. "I am *not* losing control!" The wizard's arms faded, replaced by dark tendrils of oily smoke. "Choose your words carefully, you *weak* and *worthless* beast!"

The horned goblin watched as smoke slowly solidified back into arms.

"Get on with it!"

"It saddens me, Master, that you think me worthless." The goblin pointed at the canyon's entrance. "I only meant to warn you. I smell elves and dwarves and something more. Something not of this world." The goblin paused. "But mostly I smell a trap."

"Of course it's a trap!"

The goblin tipped its head respectfully. "Wouldn't want Master to get killed. Not when we're so close to achieving *our*—"

"Kill me? You think a handful of scrawny elves could kill the most powerful wizard that ever lived?"

Through clenched teeth, Naagesh hissed, "That'll happen when—when—"

"When dwarves fly?" suggested the goblin.

Naagesh stormed into the canyon. "Exactly!"

The wizard stopped just inside the Pillars. A host of goblins scurried in beside him. A handful of elven soldiers blocked their way.

"Only this few?" Naagesh said ruefully. "I suppose the rest must've gotten crushed when you plummeted from the sky. A pity." To his goblins, he said, "Kill them quickly! I have to reach Elfhaven and make sure Lardas doesn't start the attack until just before the portal opens."

The elves charged. The goblins sprang.

"You know it's a trick, Master?" said the horned goblin. "Most of the elves're hiding."

"Obviously."

The goblin gestured to its brethren. "Many goblins'll die needlessly."

"So? I've plenty." Naagesh shrugged. "Let the elves believe their pathetic tactic worked. Besides, once the portal opens, I'll have no need for goblins—or trolls, or ogres for that matter. The creatures can have em."

The goblin raised its crooked brow.

"'Cept for you, of course."

The goblin grinned. "'Cept for me!"

# Last stand

Juanita bit her lip. "Why aren't they retreating? I told them to retreat."

"They will," King Abban assured her.

"Your tactic might've worked," Zhang told Juanita.

"If we'd enough soldiers to win," agreed King Abban.

"We don't need to win," she said. "We just need to separate Naagesh from his goblins."

Abban nodded. "And get that device."

"There they go!" she said. "The guards are running down the middle and the goblins are chasing em."

"King Abban drew his axe.

"Distract the goblins," ordered Zhang. "I'll retrieve the device."

"Ready?" she said.

"Ready," they replied.

"Now!" she shouted.

From both sides, elves sprang from the long, dark shadows cast by the pillars and attacked. When the goblins turned to face their new threat, the elves they'd been chasing, reversed course, trapping the goblins. Swishing swords and whizzing arrows overlaid the hissing, cursing goblins.

Naagesh gazed calmly at the battle. Then, facing the riverside entrance to the Pillars. "Come, my pets." He snapped his fingers and hundreds more goblins pushed and shoved their way inside to join the fray.

* * *

"Retreat!" shouted Juanita.

The dwarf king led the retreat, charged off toward the exit on the far side of the Pillars.

As King Abban, Juanita and the elven guard approached the canyon's exit, the whole cliff face began to glow. When the magic faded, the exit was gone. Naagesh had sealed their escape route, and their fate. They turned back as hundreds of hissing goblins charged.

\* \* \*

"There's someone up ahead," shouted Tappus, galloping alongside Devraj. "It's Kiran, and Tom's shaggy pet. It's not safe here. We should pick Kiran up."

"He will only slow us down."

Tappus drew back hard on the reins and his horse skidded to a stop. Devraj kept going. Tappus twisted in his saddle. From the direction of the Pillars, sounds of desperate fighting drifted in the air.

He leaned over and offered Kiran his hand. "Come on! Gotta hurry."

"What about Max?"

"He'll hafta keep up."

## Tom and Goban

"You OK?" asked Tom. "Ya look kinda pale."

Goban leaned cautiously over the cliff. A blast of wind swept his hair straight up. He stepped back. "Uncle Zanda tried to spook me, that's all."

"Looks like it worked."

"I'm good." Goban picked up a rock-filled canvas sack and tied it to his belt. Meanwhile, Tom buckled the last few straps of their harness.

Faint clicks sounded as a dozen dwarf smiths, to either side, donned their own gear.

"They aren't soldiers," observed Tom.

"Nah," Goban replied. "But smiths are smarter 'n soldiers, anyway."

Tom groaned. "Help me lift her." With Goban's help, the two lifted the awkward contraption off the ground. The wind kept twisting it, threatening to rip the thing from their grasp.

"What next?" asked Goban.

"Can't do it alone. Member what I told you?"

"Pull in. Push out." Goban managed a brave grin. "Slice of stink-slug pie!"

Balancing the rickety structure above them, Tom inched toward the cliff, forcing Goban to do the same.

At this height and with the approaching storm, the howling wind struck the cliff face below and angled up, creating turbulent eddies at the top of the cliff, making it tough to keep their primitive contraption steady while they peered over the edge.

Below, the canyon lay hidden in shadow, but they heard the sounds of a desperate battle. Tom's palms began to sweat.

"The goblins are attacking full force," cried a dwarf beside them.

"Naagesh used magic to seal the exit," called another. "King Abban's trapped!"

Tom scanned the expectant faces of the surrounding dwarves. Ringing the cliff edge, a dozen dwarf smiths awaited Tom and Goban's signal.

"What's wrong?" asked Goban. "Yer fear of heights?" He winced. "Sorry! Shouldn't a mentioned it."

"No. It's not that."

"Then what? You've done this hundreds of times—right?"

Tom shifted his weight awkwardly. "Not quite that many."

"Sooooo—how many times?"

"Uncle Carlos spent a week with me at the coast. So—fifty, maybe seventy-five times."

Goban grinned. "You're a pro!"

"Never actually did it by myself, though."

"What?"

"We used a tandem harness, like this one. Uncle Carlos was always with me. And never with this much wind."

Goban's face blanched.

"Plus, we were only ten feet off the ground."

"What?" cried Goban. "You're telling me this now!"

"Back up," instructed Tom. They took a few steps back. Goban's eyes bulged. Tom gripped the bar so hard his knuckles turned white.

This time *Goban* looked like he might be sick.

"Mind the gap!" Tom pulled in hard on the control bar and the pair sprinted off the cliff, screaming.

# That'll happen when . . .

A goblin fell, a host of arrows in its back. Another fell, then another. Naagesh watched as the archer notched a fourth arrow and drew back. The bow twanged. Yet another goblin fell. Naagesh aimed his finger at the archer. Dark magic swirled around him. Naagesh clenched his fist. The elf cried out and collapsed.

Suddenly, dark hideous shadows crisscrossed the floor of the Pillars. Naagesh glanced up. A flock of huge winged monsters circled the canyon, high above.

*Thump. Thump, thump.* A goblin to Naagesh's left toppled over. Then another. One of the projectiles, burst into smoke when it hit the ground.

"Dragons!" shouted a goblin. Instantly, the whole of Naagesh's goblin horde stopped fighting and ran panicked into pillars, into the cliff walls and out of the canyon's exit behind.

Naagesh stared upward. Indeed, huge winged beasts flew overhead, holding what appeared to be dwarves in their talons.

"Odd?" mused the horned goblin. "Unusual behavior for dragons;

throwing stones."

"Stop running, you fools!" Naagesh shouted. "Those aren't dragons, their dwarves!" He shot his servant a *warning* look. "Flying dwarves."

# Goban and Tom

Tom and Goban lay flat beside each other in their primitive leather and rope tandem hang glider harness. The glider's leather wing flapped here and there, but otherwise, all they heard was the hum of the rigging, vibrating as the wind passed through it.

Three hundred feet below, Goban's father, King Abban, along with Tom's mom, Zhang and the elven soldiers, fought ferociously, but were hopelessly outnumbered and trapped against the canyon wall. The goblins tightened the noose.

Goban drew two rocks from his sack, one in each hand, took aim and let go. A second later, two goblins collapsed face down in the dirt.

Tom grinned and raised his palm. Grinning back, Goban smacked Tom's hand.

Directly below, a goblin cried, "dragons!" And the beasts scattered in panic.

"They think we're dragons." Tom yelled, "Roar!"

Goban grimaced. "Was that sposta be a dragon call?"

"Can you do better?"

"AAAGGRRumpth!"

Tom plugged his ear.

Goban shrugged, hefted his last stone, hesitated, then offered it to Tom. "Care to try?"

Accepting the stone, Tom took aim and released. "Bombs away!" He made a whistling sound as the stone fell. Missing his target's head, the stone landed on the goblin's foot. The beast howled, grabbed its toe, hopped around, slammed into a pillar and toppled over.

"That works," said Goban.

"That was your last rock, right?"

"Yup."

Entering a patch of strong turbulence, Tom jerked the control bar, fighting to keep the bucking glider right-side-up. "The wind's funneling through the riverside entrance. I'm gonna head to the other side. The breeze should hit the cliff-face and angle up, generating lift."

Tom pulled in on his control bar and shifted his weight to the right. Surprisingly, their primitive aircraft smoothly banked right. Straining, Tom pushed out slightly, stabilizing the glider's turn.

"Without the rocks, we're lighter. The glider's performance is better. Not that we'll need it. There'll be plenty of lift."

The wind lashed Tom's hair, pants and hoodie. "Woo hoo!" he shouted. Goban glanced sidelong at him.

Reversing the maneuver, Tom pulled out of the turn and headed straight for the cliff.

Goban swallowed hard. "You sure 'bout this?"

"Trust me!"

As the cliff face loomed ahead, sure enough, the updraft caught the glider, lifting them up and making them heavy from the g-forces. Tom banked hard left then rolled out facing into the wind, crabbing sideways along the cliff-face. Within moments, they vaulted up over the canyon's lip and kept rising.

Below, several gliders still strafed the panicked goblins, making feeble attempts at their own dragon calls. The rocks and smoke bombs worked perfectly, spreading chaos through the goblin ranks, allowing his mom, Goban's father and the elves, to reverse the tide. They were actually winning!

"Nothing more for us to do here," said Tom.

"What?" called back Goban. This high up the battle noise lessened, yet the wind's howl increased. Churning black anvil clouds arched over the southern end of the canyon. Lightning flashed. Flashed again.

Tom leaned over and shouted, "I'll turn downwind! Head for Elfhaven! At this altitude, if our glide ratio's good enough, we might actually make it there!"

Goban nodded.

Tom pulled in and shifted his weight once more. One wing dropped, putting the glider into a steep bank. Tom leveled her out and aimed for the distant flickering torches atop Elfhaven's shield wall.

## Dumerre

Trudging down the narrow trail, Dumerre glanced skyward. Twilight had long given way to night. Though dark, it would be darker still once the storm hit. As if to agree, thunder punctuated the fact.

Dumerre groaned and brushed the first raindrops from his nearly bald head.

*Wizard sent me on important mission! Find Lardas. Pass on wizard's orders.* Dumerre puffed out his broad chest proudly.

Dumerre knew the ogre forces were camped somewhere nearby. As he approached the shield wall, thundering hooves sounded behind him. Dumerre crouched behind a dense thicket and waited.

He didn't have long to wait before three riders, two on one horse and one on the other, skidded to a stop just outside the east gate in the shield wall.

Dumerre sunk lower.

"Open the gate!" shouted a rider.

Brandishing a wind-whipped torch, an elven guard leaned over the parapet and called down, "In who's name?"

"King Devraj's name. And *that* is a royal order!"

"Bring General Kanak at once!" demanded Devraj. Leaping from his horse, he thrust his reins into a startled soldier's hands. Kiran slid off Tappus's horse and ran through the now open east gate, a shaggy-haired beast loping behind.

The soldier looked from Tappus to the tightly wrapped bundle lashed to his horse's rump.

"Devraj is now your king," said Tappus.

The soldier continued to stare.

Tappus laid his hand on the stricken guard's shoulder. "Do as your king orders."

A crowd of soldiers holding torches gathered at the entrance to the east gate. Everyone shot quick glances at the wrapped body lying at Devraj's feet. Hushed murmurs passed through the crowd. Heavy boot-steps silenced them. They stepped aside and let General Kanak pass.

The general listened gravely as Devraj and Tappus explained the dire situation.

"The ogres are camped by the north gate," Kanak reported. "They've lit their siege fires."

"How many?" asked Tappus.

"Thousands. The entire ogre army."

"As I feared. Why haven't they attacked?"

"Not like ogres," agreed Kanak. "They appear to be waiting for something. A signal from Naagesh, most likely."

Devraj nodded. "The wizard would wish to signal the attack."

"Yet they're ogres, sire," Kanak pointed out. "They grow restless."

"The ogres are but Naagesh's pawns," Devraj said. "They dare not disobey their dark lord's command." He faced Kanak. "Ready my troops, general. We leave for the Pillars in five myntars."

"Even if the ogres hold off," reasoned Tappus, "the elven troops are on foot. There's barely time for them to reach the Pillars, let alone make it back here before the portal opens."

"All that matters!" snapped Devraj, "is that we retrieve the device! Once we have it, I shall gallop back and deliver it to the Guardian myself."

"And if you don't make it back in time?" began Tappus. "Without the elven army, the creatures will slaughter the townsfolk."

Devraj leaned toward Tappus. "If the portal opens, the townsfolk are dead, anyway!"

Tappus glanced at Kanak.

"Your highness," General Kanak said hesitantly. "I must agree with Tappus. We should have a contingency plan in case the ogres grow weary of waiting and attack."

Tappus added, "We don't need all the troops to overcome one wizard."

Kanak suggested, "Why doesn't Tappus take half the troops and retrieve the device from Naagesh, while I command the other half here to—"

Devraj stamped his foot. "No! I will lead the *entire* army to confront Naagesh, and that is final!"

Tappus ventured, "But—"

"But—your—highness!"

Tappus bowed. "But—your highness—"

"Who is your king?!"

Tappus stopped. "You are, my liege, but as the Right Hand of the King—"

"What?"

Tappus squared his shoulders. "In the Deathly Bog, after we lost Sanuu, your father promoted me to—"

"Enough!" Devraj face flushed with anger. "I am the king! King of *all* Elfhaven!"

Tappus and General Kanak stood silent.

Devraj's glare remained fixed. "It is my decision and mine alone. The matter is closed."

In a respectful tone, Tappus responded, "Agreed your highness, but your father always considered the suggestions of his—"

"Silence!" demanded Devraj. "My father is dead!" He glanced at the shocked faces around him, seeming to flicker in the torchlight. "I am king now. And I will not tolerate being challenged." His face flushed scarlet. "If the old fool made *you* his Right Hand, my father was an idiot!" Gasps sounded.

"You are not *my* Right Hand. In fact—I am stripping you of your rank and titles! You are no longer head of my palace guard, nor even a soldier in my service!"

Tappus stood in stunned silence.

"Why are you still here?" the king demanded.

Tappus glanced at General Kanak. The general said nothing.

"As you wish, my lord." Tappus gave a slight bow and staggered away.

Devraj addressed General Kanak, "And do *you* also question my judgment?"

"No my lord, but—"

"But what?"

General Kanak lowered his head and sank to one knee. "Your highness, please. At least leave me a few troops."

Devraj stared down at the General. "Fine. Keep two hundred. Assemble the rest."

\* \* \*

A light drizzle began to fall.

Dumerre watched from the dark forest as the boy king, leading thousands of elven troops, ran through the east gate heading toward the Pillars.

After they'd gone, Dumerre ran off in the opposite direction, heading for the ogre encampment.

# Naagesh and Zhang

Naagesh watched in shock as the battle's scales tipped. Moments ago, his goblins were about to finish off the paltry few remaining elven guard. Now, from out of nowhere, the tides had turned.

*The idiot goblins panicked when the flying dwarves arrived, thinking them dragons. The fools!* He'd tried to calm them, but the beasts were too stupid. Now the unthinkable had happened. The elves were actually winning!

Naagesh slammed his fist into the pillar beside him, causing the massive stone to vibrate like a gong. He glanced at the pillar, then scanned the hopeless scene before him. By now, most of the dwarves had landed and now fought on foot. At that moment, the last dwarf left aloft flew by.

Cursing, Naagesh fired a bolt of crackling dark energy. The magic struck the left wing, lighting it on fire. The craft crashed into a pillar, crumpled, and slid down the pillar. Out of the tangled mess of wood and rope, the dwarf pilot wriggled herself free, pulled out a dagger and joined the fray.

Naagesh cursed again but froze when he spotted the accursed monk, coattails flapping, striding calmly through the panicked goblins, heading his way.

Muttering an incantation, swirling emerald and black magic engulfed his arms. Compressing the crackling energy between his hands like a snowball, Naagesh drew back his arm and took aim.

Zhang raised his swords, forming an 'X' in front of him. "Have you forgotten our battle in the Floating Mountains so soon? Larraj obviously *enhanced* my swords. Whatever you throw at me returns full force. Your magic is useless."

Zhang Wu kept advancing.

Naagesh flicked his wrists, and the magic snuffed out. He glanced around frantically. All the goblins nearby backed away from Zhang, all save one. The horned goblin stood off to one side, calmly watching the advancing monk.

"Kill him!" Naagesh ordered. "Kill the monk!"

"Like father, like son," hissed the goblin.

"What?"

"I'm but a weak and worthless beast. Isn't that what you said?"

The wizard turned. Zhang kept coming.

"Give me the device!" shouted the monk. "Save me the trouble of prying it from your dead hands!"

Naagesh stepped back and bumped into a pillar. Reaching behind, he patted the massive, muscular stone calf. He hurriedly recited an incantation. Jade lightning lanced from his hands to a pillar beside Zhang. Cracks formed on the statue. The sound of shattering pottery echoed throughout the canyon. The magic arced from pillar to pillar. Goblins, elves, and dwarves all froze in their tracks.

Curved chunks of stone blasted out, crashing down beside Zhang. He didn't flinch.

Finally, a loud groan brought the monk to a halt. Zhang glanced back over his shoulder. A giant, a real one, shook its massive head, shards of its stone cocoon flying. Cracks formed on the other pillars. Slowly pivoting, Zhang watched in disbelief as all across the canyon, giants burst free from their stone prisons.

A lone giant howled, then took off running, *thud, thud,* bouncing startled elves, dwarves and goblins up into the air with each footfall. Everyone dove out of the way of the crazed giants, charging around in confusion and panic.

Another giant slammed into the canyon wall near where Naagesh had sealed the exit. *Boom!* Sending rocks cascading down from above. Another giant smashed into the wall beside the first. Cracks formed in the cliff face. More giants joined in. Within moments, cracks spread across the entire northern wall of the canyon.

Zhang whipped back around.

Naagesh was gone.


## Tappus and Kanak


"Tappus. There you are," began General Kanak. "As soon as Devraj left, I sent runners to find you."

"I'm no longer in charge. I'm not even a soldier."

"I still need your help. Elfhaven needs your help."

Tappus paused.

"We need a plan," said Kanak.

"What preparations have you made?"

Kanak pointed across the vast field to the north gate in the shield wall. "When the ogres first arrived, I had troops dig trenches."

"How many?"

"Three trenches spanning the breadth of the field, covered with cloth and dirt. They are nearly invisible."

"After the first trench," said Tappus, "the ogres will be wary. They'll expect more."

"Which will slow em down. The trench closest to the north gate has nothing in it—" General Kanak grinned. "–but the next two have surprises."

"Good," said Tappus. "Have the soldiers set up a wall of pikes, aiming outward, just past the third trench. When the ogres make it past your last *surprise*, they'll have spears to contend with."

"My thoughts as well. They're already constructing it."

"I suggest we arm the troops with cross bows first," reasoned Tappus, "next regular bows, and finally swords and spears when in close quarters."

"Even with all these preparations, should the ogres attack before Devraj returns with the army…"

Tappus stared off across the vast expanse of the outer field toward the north gate in the shield wall. "We must get the townsfolk inside the castle. We need to sound the alarm."

"I sent a messenger. Any moment now we should hear—"

From the castle's main tower, came the haunting moan of the giant blandaloo horn. Panicked shouts rang out as townsfolk burst from their homes.

"If the portal opens," Tappus mused, "the castle won't protect them from the creatures."

Kanak didn't respond.

"Let's split what troops we have in half," Tappus suggested. "I'll lead the left squad. You take the right."

"I cannot allow that." General Kanak sighed. "Devraj relieved you of command. As foolish as the boy is, he is still the king. My king."

Tappus scanned the general's face, then clasped Kanak's forearm. "I understand. Good luck!" Tappus ran off.

"Where are you going?"

"To raise my own army!"

## A view to remember

Tom and Goban had gained nearly six hundred feet in the ridge lift before Tom finally banked their glider and left the Pillars behind. The wind at this altitude was stronger yet smoother, having risen above the swirling turbulence caused by the canyon.

In the distance, they could see faint flickering torchlight atop the shield wall and the castle proper, sparkling like gems. "Kinda beautiful, huh?" said Tom.

"'Cept for the storm, the battle, and the fact that the world's 'bout to end," replied Goban.

"Uncle Carlos told me about a hang-gliding trip he once took in the

Oregon desert. A place called Doherty's Slide. He and his friends were the first ever to fly there. They caught a thermal and gained a thousand feet over the top of the ridge. Carlos realized he was the first human to ever see that exact view."

"Thought there were airships on your world."

"Yeah. But there weren't any airports nearby, so planes would've flown much higher, and the pilots would've seen a completely different view."

"So?"

"So this exact view—the one we're seeing right now—we're the only ones who've ever seen it!"

For a time, the two just glided along in silence.

"Less someone was riding a dragon," Goban said.

"Good point."

Tom checked out the dwarves' handiwork on their primitive glider. He'd done a quick pre-flight before they launched. Now he had time to study it more critically: the neatly sewn animal skin sail, the long wooden poles that comprised the wings' leading edges, crossbar and keel. The triangular control bar, made from three short poles, was suspended from a point directly above them where the keel and the crossbar met. The spars were lashed together tightly with animal gut twine. And the rigging, comprised long thin ropes, connected all the pieces and kept their flimsy craft from falling apart.

"Nice job!" said Tom.

"What?"

"Nice job building this."

"Wasn't all me," Goban confessed. "Uncle Zanda helped a little."

Tom let go of the control bar.

"What are you doing?"

"Checking to see if the CG's right," explained Tom. "Let go!"

"Are ya crazy?" Goban shouted.

"Just for a sec."

With a look of horror, Goban slowly let go, his stubby hands hovering just above the control bar.

The glider drifted slightly to the right. Tom took hold and shifted his weight left, bringing their craft back on course.

"CG's almost perfect. Didn't wanna dive or stall. Wants to turn right a tad. Could be the harness attachment point is—"

A deep *boom* came from behind.

They craned their necks.

"What was that?" asked Goban. "Thunder?"

Tom squinted. "Not sure. Here, take the wheel."

"What?"

Tom let go of the control bar and rummaged through the contents of his adventurers' belt. Goban grabbed the bar, all color draining from his face.

"Nice job," remarked Tom without looking. "Just keep her level." He yanked out his infra-red night goggles, strapped them on and flicked the switch. As usual, the scene burst into various intensities of green, showing the world around him in vivid detail. He looked back.

"Whaddaya see?"

"The whole north face of the canyon. It's—it's gone."

"Gone?"

"Destroyed! Wait a minute." Tom fiddled with the controls, increasing the magnification. "Someone's running from the Pillars." He tweaked the focus. "Two of em. One's Naagesh."

"And the other?"

"The question isn't who, it's what."

"Huh?"

"Some—*thing*—is walking beside the wizard. Whatever it is, it's huge and covered in flames." Tom slid the goggles up onto his forehead and blinked.

"Ya sure?"

He flipped them back down. "Yeah. Tall, long muscular arms, flames. Kinda hard ta miss." He pressed a button. "Wait a sec."

"What?"

"When I switch to regular binoculars, 'stead of infrared, it's hard to see, but—"

"But what?" shouted Goban.

"It's nothing but a scrawny—"

"Birds!" cried Goban. "Look out!" Suddenly, they flew into the midst of a flock of loudly squawking, madly flapping birds. Tom flipped up his goggles, grabbed the control bar and threw his weight around wildly, sending the glider gyrating through a crazed set of maneuvers.

One of the birds landed on the crossbar above Goban. "Ahhh, Tom?" The bird cocked its scaled head and studied the dwarf curiously, then burped smoke right in Goban's face.

Goban coughed. "They ain't birds!" The thing raised its head and let out a strange warbling call.

"They're dragons!" said Tom. "Baby dragons."

"The ones from beneath the Plains."

"Musta hatched in the fire."

The hatchling burped again, this time spitting a tiny flame. The flame touched the sail. The sail began to smoke.

"Shoo it away!" shouted Tom. "Before it sets the glider on fire!"

"Me?" cried Goban.

"Yes you! Unless you wanna fly this thing?"

Goban waved his hand. "Shoo!" The chick stared down at him contentedly from its dry perch.

"Climb up and shoo it away!"

"Climb up? You crazy? How?"

"Grab the control bar uprights, swivel from prone to seated. Put your feet on the control bar and stand up."

Fanned by the wind, the smoke increased, a spot on the sail burst into flame.

"Before there's no sail left!" shouted Tom.

Goban stood shakily. The glider bucked. Goban's foot slipped, sending him dangling by his harness straps till he regained his footing.

"Easy!" cried Tom. "It's hard enough keeping her level without you flailing about."

Goban gritted his teeth and tried again. Standing precariously inside the control bar's triangular frame, his arms wrapped tightly around the uprights, he inched his way toward the baby dragon. The hatchling squawked, spread its wings and dove. Goban ducked. The rest of the flock dove, following their squawking friend.

Goban patted out the flames, leaving a smoldering hole in the sail the size of his fist.

"Good job!" said Tom. "Now get back down here. There's too much drag with you standing. We're losing altitude."

Goban climbed down.

"We're still losing altitude." Tom glanced up at the hole. The sail started to rip.

Goban nudged Tom.

"What is it? Naagesh again?"

"No." Goban pointed ahead. "It's the elven army. And Devraj is leading em!"

"Devraj? Where's his father?"

Goban pulled Tom's sleeve. "Something's happening. Look! The elves r' goin' crazy."

Tom nodded. "They're scattering like deer."

"What's a deer?"

Tom swiveled in his harness. Behind and below, jagged lines crisscrossed the forest. As the lines approached, they heard trees snapping, saw trees smash down at the head of each line. One line passed directly underneath them.

Staring downward, they watched as an immense head, attached to enormous shoulders, stomped by, leaving a trail of flattened trees in its wake.

"What the heck?" gasped Tom.

"Giants," Goban said in shock. "Real ones. Live ones!" He stared at Tom. Tom stared back.

"That's why the elven army scattered," Goban realized. "The giants are attacking the elves!"

Tom pulled down his night goggles once more. "No. The giants are scattering. Three are running toward Elfhaven. Some turned back. The rest are heading into the hills. If they were attacking, they'd be—"

"Yer wrong!" snapped Goban. "Giants're mean and angry! Why, giants'd sooner squash ya than look at ya!"

Tom stared at Goban, then down at the giant. "They don't look mean to me. They look scared." Tom studied his friend's face, flushed with anger. He still had on the leather helmet with the brass goggles. *Kinda looks out a place, the silly helmet with the angry face.* Tom grinned.

"What's so funny?"

"Hey!" Tom's eyes lit up. "Try the lenses! On your helmet! Whaddaya see?"

Goban flipped a lens down over his eye, *click.* "Bones. Huge bones."

"No. Not the x-ray lens. The one that shows feelings."

Goban flicked down another lens.

"What's it say? Are they angry?"

"No. Shows red." He blinked. "The same color as when you was afraid." Goban raised the lens. "Giants are afraid? I don't get it."

"Not important right now." Tom glanced at his watch. "Less than an oort till midnight." He pulled in hard. Their clothing flapped, the glider humming and creaking as they picked up speed. Tom tightened his grip.


## Dumerre

The blustery wind thrashed tree limbs about, providing glimpses of thousands of ogre campfires stretching far down the shield wall in both directions.

Lardas, the ogre commander and his lieutenants, sat beside one such fire just outside the north gate.

The clicking of bone armor and the rasping of metal daggers and obsidian tipped spears being sharpened, mixed with grumbling ogres impatiently awaiting the order to attack. Worse, it had started to rain, making the ogres mood even fouler than usual.

Angry curses gave way to a lone ogre who stomped through their midst and stopped beside their commander.

"Dumerre." Lardas stabbed a long, crooked dagger into the fire, sending red sparks rising. "I hoped you dead by now."

"Hoped me dead?"

"Did I say hoped?" Lardas grinned at those sitting beside him, firelight dancing across their plump faces. "Meant ta say—*thought* you'd be dead." The others chuckled.

Lardas craned his neck and peered behind Dumerre. "Where your friend?" Lardas spat. "Dat troll?"

"Bellchar no friend!" said Dumerre.

"So why you here? You here ta fight?" Lardas leaned over and grabbed a spear from a stack and thrust the weapon toward Dumerre.

Dumerre's face paled. Yet more ogres erupted with laughter.

Pretending not to hear, Dumerre straighten himself up. "Wizard gave me important message fer you—"

"Oh?" the commander yawned. "So get on wid it!"

"Wizard say," Dumerre paused, trying to remember Naagesh's exact words. "Tell Lardas ta bring ogre army to river crossing. Dat an order!"

Lardas gritted his teeth. "Naagesh order me?!" He leaned forward till his snot-covered nose bumped into Dumerre's. "Thought wizard want us ta wait here? Phawta and the *trolls* supposed to meet wizard at river."

Dumerre leaned back. "Trolls go home."

Lardas snorted. "Trolls." He spat. "Dey all cowards."

Lardas stared at the fire. When Dumerre didn't move Lardas asked, "Sometin' more?"

"Oh yeah! Almost forgot." Dumerre rushed to tell what he'd seen and heard at the east gate.

Lardas scratched his head with the tip of his dagger, considering. "Dakshi dead? Boy now king? 'N take elven army to da Pillars. All da troops?"

"All but a couple hundred."

A wide grin slowly spread across Lardas' face. "Elven army gone? Dat boy an idiot!" Lardas leapt to his feet. "Attack!"

Ogre battle cries rang out. Moments later, a massive battering ram slammed into the north gate. *Thump.* Nearby trees shuddered. Another *thump*, this time accompanied by the sound of splintering timbers.

"What I tell wizard?" asked Dumerre.

"Tell Naagesh, ogres no need wizard anymore." Lardas hoisted his spear and stomped off. "Ogres destroy elven city by ourselves."

"But—if I tell wizard dat, he kill me!"

Lardas just kept walking.

## General Kanak

*Boom! Boom! Boom!*

General Kanak stared across the field. Torchlight from the shield wall dimly illuminated the north gate. Even at this distance, he could see the massive wooden gate shudder with each strike of the battering ram.

"The gate won't hold much longer," shouted a soldier.

Behind them came the panicked cries of townsfolk, desperately trying to reach the castle.

General Kanak scanned the faces of his vastly outnumbered soldiers. Young faces, both men and women. Faces filled with courage as well as fear.

The general inhaled deeply. "Tonight, is the most important night of our lives. Tonight, we fight to save our children, our parents, our grandparents. To that end, we must hold back the ogre onslaught till the townsfolk are safely inside the castle."

His soldiers nodded grimly.

"But tonight, we fight for more than just Elfhaven. Tonight, we fight for the survival of the elven race. No! For the survival of our entire world!"

Soldiers raised their weapons and shouted.

Kanak met the eyes of soldier after soldier. "Many of us, perhaps all, will not survive this night." He drew his sword. "But if we must die, let the ogres cower in fear at the sight of elven courage. And fall to elven steel!"

Deafening cheers rang out as elves thrust their weapons skyward.

As if in answer to their challenge, the north gate splintered apart, and hundreds of roaring ogres stormed through.


# Elfhaven or bust

Tom checked his watch. They'd made good time. But by picking up speed, it also increased the drag on the glider, which unfortunately decreased their glide ratio. As a result, they'd lost so much altitude they were now only a couple hundred feet above the treetops.

A flash of lightning gave a brief glimpse of the shield wall in the distance.

"Surprised we beat the giants here," said Goban.

Tom looked back. Cracks, snaps, and thuds came from newly formed zig-zag swaths of forest being smashed down as he watched. "They're running all over the place. We're going straight. Well, mostly."

"How much time we got?"

"Five myntars, I'd guess."

"Till the portal opens?!"

"No. Till we're forced to land." Tom checked his watch again. "Forty-five myntars, till the world is swarming with ravenous creatures."

"Nice way to put it. Ya coulda just said 'till the portal opens'."

"Thought '*ravenous creatures*' had a nice ring to it."

Tom changed the subject, "Even at this speed, and with the added drag." He gestured to the scorched flapping hole the baby dragon caused. "At our present glide ratio, we still clear the shield wall. As long as—"

"As what?"

"As long as it doesn't start to rain."

"Rain?"

"Rain'd soak the sail, adding weight and decreasing our performance."

Thunder boomed. Droplets began peppering their glider.

"Why do ya always hafta say things like that?"

Descending lower, trees whizzed by beneath them, yet Elfhaven seemed no closer. Soon, they lost sight of the shield wall, altogether.

Turbulence increased as they neared the trees. Tom struggled to keep the glider level. "We're not gonna make it."

Tom scanned the forest. "Gotta find a place to land." The main path was too narrow, their wingspan at least twice as wide. A small clearing appeared off to their left. "There!" Tom banked hard left. "I'll try an set 'er down there."

One of the taller treetops brushed the left wingtip. Then another. Tom leveled the glider.

"Come on!" Tom bit his lip. "Just fifty feet more." He eased the control bar forward slightly, trying to coax a little more distance. The clearing lay to their left. Setting up for landing, Tom banked the glider one last time, then leveled out, heading straight into the wind. Only a small thicket of saplings separated them from the landing area.

"Yes!" shouted Tom.

Out of the darkness, a tall snag appeared.

"No!" cried Goban.

*Thuwak!* The right wingtip struck the tree. The glider yawed. Tom jammed the control bar, throwing his weight to the left. The glider responded sluggishly but leveled out.

"You did it!" cried Goban.

*Crack.*

"Hope that was the tree—" Tom glanced at Goban.

"And not the glider."

Another *crack.*

The two watched in horror as the starboard leading edge, just behind the crossbar, buckled and the wingtip collapsed, sending the glider into a spin.

They screamed!

# Goban

"Tom," said Goban. "Tom. Wake up!" The pair hung upside down in a tree, thirty feet above the forest floor, their glider twisted and broken, its rigging hopelessly tangled in the branches.

Goban shook Tom. "Wake up!"

Tom's eyes opened. "Where are we?"

"We crashed, remember?"

"Crashed?"

"Yeah. Hit a tree. *Crack.* Wing broke." Goban made a whirring sound, circling his hand in a downward spiral. "*Boom!*" Remember?"

Tom held his head and moaned, "Yeah. I remember."

"Good. Come on. We gotta cut ourselves loose." Goban yanked Aileen off his back and, using the blade like a saw, began cutting through their rope harness.

"Careful," warned Tom. "Else we might—"

*Twang.* The harness let loose. Branches snapped beneath them as they fell. *Thud.*

Tom lay on his back and moaned again.

The ground shook.

The trees shook.

Goban tugged frantically on Tom's arm. "Giants! Get up!"

Suddenly, a giant with two missing fingers on its left-hand burst from the forest. His foot stomped down, splintering a tree behind them. The giant raised his other leg, his enormous foot poised directly above them.

## Goban vs Goliath

"Stop!" cried Goban.

The giant froze in mid-step and gazed down. "Huh?"

"Please don't kill us," pleaded Goban.

The giant blinked. Teetering forward, his foot began to drop.

Goban closed his eyes. *Thud.* He opened them. Goban reached out and patted the huge, hairy ankle beside them.

Goban yelled up, "Thanks!"

All around, trees blasted apart, launching splinters everywhere as two more stampeding giants thundered past.

The giant stared down dully at them a moment longer, then stomped off after his kind.

"See," groaned Tom, struggling to sit up. "Like Uncle Carlos says: don't judge someone by their looks, judge em by what they do."

"Ya mean that monstrous giant?"

"I mean that *nice* giant who didn't squish us."

"We gotta go." Tom tried to stand and winced.

"Yer leg?"

Tom nodded. Goban offered him his hand. Grabbing hold, Tom winced again as he stood.

Goban wrapped Tom's arm around his shoulder. "Can ya walk?"

"Think so."

"Good. Cause we gotta run."

# Devraj

After the trees stopped shaking, Devraj stepped from the forest onto the trail now slick with rain.

Little by little, the elven army crept out and stared at all the splintered trees around them. Most of the giants had charged off into the hills. Three continued toward Elfhaven.

Devraj turned at the sound of galloping hooves. King Abban, Zhang Wu, and Juanita drew their horses to a stop, steam jetting from the steed's nostrils.

"Where is Naagesh?" Devraj asked.

Zhang stared at him.

"Naagesh released the giants," explained Juanita.

"But where is he?"

King Abban replied, "We lost sight of him, in all the confusion."

"And the device?" Devraj scanned their blank faces.

"Look!" cried a soldier, pointing toward Elfhaven. Even at this distance, they could see an orange glow of fires, and hear the faint cries of battle.

"Oh, no!" said Juanita.

"Elfhaven's under attack," agreed Zhang.

"But that—that's impossible!" Devraj stammered. "The ogres would not dare attack without Naagesh's order."

Zhang twisted in his saddle to face Devraj. "Lardas attacked the moment you left Elfhaven unprotected." Grumbling soldiers leapt out of the monk's way as he galloped through their midst.

Devraj kept staring long after the monk disappeared.

"Devraj!" shouted King Abban. "Snap out of it, boy! Elfhaven needs their army *and* their king!"

## Dumerre

"Gotta tell wizard," Dumerre mumbled, wiping rain from his eyes as he sloshed down the trail to the Pillars. "Wizard trust Dumerre. Count on Dumerre. Gotta tell em Lardas not coming. Ogres not coming." Dumerre stepped into a deep puddle. "Wizard be angry. Angry wid Lardas doe, not me, right?" He bit his lip.

By now, he'd walked nearly halfway to the Pillars. He stopped to catch his breath. Dumerre bent over, staring at his reflection in a puddle. Ripples formed in the puddle. The ground shuddered. Trees, to either side of the path cracked, snapped, crashed down.

Dumerre stood. "Giants!" He dove into the forest.

A giant's foot smashed down. The tree to his left exploded. Dumerre leapt right. Another giant stormed by. Dumerre crouched behind a boulder, covered his head. Moments later, the thudding and crashing grew distant.

Dumerre crept cautiously from the trees to the trail and peered out. The giants were gone.

Cinching up his loincloth, Dumerre stepped onto the trail and was nearly trampled under hoof as the crazed monk galloped by. Dumerre watched the monk's back, his long coattails flapping till he disappeared round the bend. Turning back again he dove into the trees, as three more riders galloped past. Dumerre recognized King Dakshi's son and the dwarf king, but not the third.

Standing, Dumerre wiped mud from his face and stepped back onto the trail yet again. The thudding of running feet brought him around once more. His eyes bulged at the sight of thousands of elven troops rounding the bend, storming down the trail straight toward him.

Dumerre ran off into the forest, away from the battle, and never looked back.

# General Kanak

General Kanak watched agape as three giants charged across the battlefield. He glanced toward the east gate, or rather, what had been the east gate until the giants plowed through it as if it was made of straw, littering the field with splintered beams and massive stone slabs.

The beasts, however, didn't seem to be aiding the ogres, nor attacking the elves. In fact, they seemed confused, running this way and that for no apparent reason.

"General!" A soldier pointed.

Kanak watched the advancing ogres. The leading wave had fallen into the first trench and were just now climbing out.

"The ogres'll reach our position in five myntars," calculated the general. "Maybe less. Archers at the ready! Wait till they pass the second trench. I'll give the signal." Faint clicks sounded as archers notched arrow to bow.

A flash of lightning lit up what remained of the shield wall, thunder close behind. Rain pelted the ground. He gazed up at a towering wall of black, roiling clouds approaching from the south.

"The storm!" cried a soldier. "It'll make it hard to see."

"Keep focused!" ordered the general. "It'll make it hard for the ogres, as well." The leading edge of ogres dropped from sight into the second trench. Deep rasping cries rang out.

"Sounds like the ogres found our little gifts," shouted someone.

"Stay focused!" repeated Kanak. Ogres scrambled, screaming from the trench with huge acid spitting toads latched firmly to their ankles.

The general raised his arm. Archers raised their bows and drew back.

"Hold," shouted the general.

A wall of angry ogres pulled toads from their hides, tossed them aside, and charged.

"Hold!"

The beasts hefted clubs and roared their battle cry.

Kanak dropped his arm. "Fire!"

## Avani and Mab

Far across the outer field, the frightened elven townsfolk desperately tried to squeeze through the castle gate. As such, no one seemed to notice the brilliant flash of violet light behind them, nor the sudden appearance of an elven girl and the fairy queen.

Avani covered her mouth. "Oh, no!"

"The battle's begun," said Mab.

Avani looked around. "Don't see the portal."

"Thought you said the portal wouldn't open till midnight." Mab blinked, and a massive wooden clock appeared, floating beside them. "Still got forty myntars." She blinked, and the clock disappeared.

"Where are the others?" asked Avani.

Mab snapped her tiny fingers, and flashes of multi-colored light sparkled around them. When the light faded, a host of fairies flittered about. At this, the townsfolk finally took notice, momentarily forgetting their dire situation.

Whizzing through the crowd huddled outside the castle gate, the fairies giggled with high-pitched delight at the shocked elven faces, then rocketed back to hover beside their queen.

Mab leaned her tiny head toward Avani. "The girls do so love ta make an entrance!"

Avani squinted, scanning the battle.

"Where's the elven army? I see General Kanak, leading a few troops, but where's King Dakshi and Tappus?" She wheeled round. "There's Tappus! Over by the castle gate." She waved. "What's he doing there? Why isn't he helping General Kanak?" Avani ran off, calling over her shoulder, "Mab. Wait here. I'll be right back."

Mab watched Avani run off. "Fine! The queen of the faeries'll just wait right here then." Mab crossed her tiny arms impatiently. "The war's begun. The portal's about to open. The world's about to end. But hey! Guess she thinks I've nothin' better ta do."

"Tappus!" said Avani, stopping beside him. "Where's King Dakshi? Why aren't you leading the troops?"

Tappus glanced over at the advancing line of ogres and winced. He handed an elderly woman a yellow ribbon. "Thank you. You're now officially a member of the Elfhaven Irregulars." He gestured to his right. "Please wait with the rest."

Avani asked, "What's going on?"

Tappus sighed. "Devraj stripped me of my rank. I'm no longer a soldier."

"What? Devraj? Where's King Dakshi?"

Tappus just stared at her.

"Oh no!" she gasped, her face turning pale. "Then that means—"

"Devraj is king." Tappus paused for emphases. "And tomorrow you'll be queen." He gave her a slight bow. "Assuming there is a tomorrow."

She staggered.

Tappus grabbed her arm. "Devraj took the bulk of the army to the Pillars to retrieve the device. He left General Kanak only those few. There's one more trench and then the spear fence, but that won't hold for long.

"And if the portal opens before Devraj returns…" He changed the subject. "I'm trying to raise a volunteer army, such as it is."

Shouts caused her to turn. A huge towering figure stomped past. "Was that a—"

"A giant," confirmed Tappus. "Haven't the slightest idea where they came from." The giant thudded past again, this time going in the opposite direction.

Avani watched it go by.

Tappus handed the next in line a ribbon. "Please wait over there."

Still in a daze, Avani walked down the line of *volunteers*. She could see the fear in their eyes, almost taste their distress. A scant few elderly men, women and even some teenagers, nervously awaited orders. Several had bandaged arms and legs. A few walked with a cane. Avani's eyes began to water.

She heard running feet. "Avani!" came an excited voice from behind. Kiran screeched to a stop beside her, Max at his heels. Kiran hugged her tight. "Your alive!"

"I'm fine. Do you know where Nanni and Nadda are?"

Kiran sniffled. Wiped his tears. Grabbing her hand, he led her toward the castle.

As they neared the castle gate, Avani spotted a familiar face shuffling along in the frantic group trying to enter the castle. "Nadda!" Leaping up, she wrapped her arms tightly around his neck.

"Avani!"

"Where's Nanni?"

Her grandfather's shoulders sank. "When the alarm sounded, we ran from our home. The streets were crowded, everyone shouting and shoving and—"

Avani grabbed her grandfather by the arms. "Where's Nanni?"

He sighed. "We got separated. I called and called, but if she answered, I couldn't hear her over the commotion." Nadda met Avani's hard stare. "I looked everywhere for her, child. I did!"

"I know you did." Avani motioned to the castle. "She's probably already inside."

He nodded.

"Kiran. Take Nadda inside and see if Nanni's there. I'll retrace her steps."

Nadda gave her a weak smile.

"I'll find her," Avani assured him. "I promised dad I'd never let anything happen to any of you." She locked eyes with him. "You believe me?"

Nadda's eyes misted over. He sniffled. "I know you will, child. Nanni and I trust you with our lives."

Avani watched Kiran led her grandfather into the swelling line of terrified elves trying to enter the castle. Avani raced off into the city, against the flow of frightened townsfolk going the other way.


# Mab


Mab tapped her fingers on her folded arms, watching Avani run off yet again. "Fine! Guess I'll just hafta improvise."

The fairy queen's face steeled into the look of a determined general, a very tiny general. Her arm shot out. "Sprites attack!"

Immediately the fairies came together, hovering in a line, then blasted forth straight at the first few ogres who'd freed themselves of snapping toads and were charging the meager elven forces.

The fairy brigade flew over the heads of startled elves and attacked, unleashing the full force of their magic on the hapless beasts! Explosions sent flower petals, colorful mushrooms, and fragrant smells raining down upon the ogres.

The ogres sneezed and ran on.

Mab shook her head. "The girls are a bit out a practice in the ways of war."

*Thud!* Ogres cursed, pointing at the sky. Mab followed the beasts' gaze. An enormous stone hurtled through the air and crashed down, flattening an ogre and bowling down three more. Ogres howled with rage! Two more projectiles whizzed overhead, coming from the other side of the shield wall.

"Hmmm." Mab blinked and a monstrous beast appeared. Spikes jutted out from the joints on its low muscular body. Opening its mouth, exposing long, sharp teeth, the monster roared, then plopped down on its haunches, staring up expectantly at the hovering fairy.

"Go get em, Fluffy!" shouted Mab. The zhanderbeast wagged its long tail. "Just the ogres, mind you. Don't bite the nice elves."

The zhanderbeast sprang up, whipped its long powerful body around and raced across the field. Scampering between the startled elves, it leapt over the spear fence and the third trench and landed in the ogres' midst.

The zhanderbeast roared. The ogres scrabbled back.

Mab smiled. She watched another stone's flight till it crashed down amongst the ogres. Like the others, the projectile had come from beyond the shield wall.

Mab blinked and disappeared.

## The Mastersmith and Mab

The Mastersmith sat on a massive slab of what had until recently been the shield wall. Watching each boulder's trajectory, and the resulting ogre turmoil they caused, his stubby hand hovered above a notepad.

*Whoomp!* A massive stone whizzed overhead. Zanda watched the stones arc and the resulting ogre turmoil it caused, then dipped his feather quill into a crock of ink and put quill to parchment.

A flash of violet light caused him to leap up in surprise, spilling his ink well.

"What?" said Mab. "Never seen a fairy before?"

"Not since I was a wee lad," Zanda admitted. He frowned in frustration at his ink smeared notes. "Look what ye made me do!"

Mab flitted over and studied the papers.

"Takin' notes," explained Master Zanda, still frowning. "Fer future reference. To improve the design, ya see." He gestured to the nearest catapult. A loud clacking, creaking noise emanated from the contraption as two dwarves struggled with a wooden cross, ratcheting back a huge wooden pole.

Three others rolled a boulder down a narrow chute where it dropped into a cup attached at the end of the catapult's long pole. A dwarf shoved a lever forward. *Whoosh!* The pole shot up and out, launching the boulder. A *thump* preceded a host of satisfying ogres' curses.

It started to rain. Zanda leaned over, shielding his notes the best he could.

Mab blinked, and it stopped raining on Zanda. The Mastersmith glanced around. It was raining everywhere except on him. "Thanks!" He resumed taking notes.

"Mind if I help?" asked Mab.

Still scribbling, Zanda shrugged absently.

Rocketing up, Mab hovered beside the catapult's cup till the next boulder thudded into place. Snapping her fingers, the stone began to sparkle. "Try that!"

The Mastersmith nodded to the dwarves manning the device. The stone whizzed through the air. This time when it landed, however, there was a softer *whoomp,* and a wobbling bubble expanded. Rolling slowly, the bubble enveloped the nearest ogres… who began moving in slow motion.

Mab darted back down and hovered beside the Mastersmith. "Slows em down," she explained. "Makes em easier to catch."

The pair watched ogres moving as if wallowing through goomelon jelly.

"I call it a time bomb—" Mab grinned. "—cause—"

"Cause it slows down time." Zanda grinned back.

## Tom and Goban

Tom, his arm still around Goban's shoulder, hobbled along as fast as he could. Broken branches, leaves, and even entire trees littered the trail. The rain now came in sheets, and the wind whipped their soaked clothing wildly.

They heard desperate shouts and clanging swords from up ahead. "Oh no! The war's begun," cried Tom. "The gates'll be locked."

Stumbling through the last stand of trees, the pair stopped short.

"Don't think that'll be a problem," said Goban.

Directly ahead, a massive pile of rubble lay across their path. To their right, an entire section of the shield wall suddenly just fell over.

"Looks like the giants took care of that," Goban replied.

"There's not much time left." Tom slumped against Goban. "We still hafta find Naagesh and get the remote."

"We don't know where the wizard is," said Goban.

Lightning flashed, highlighting two figures. A goblin scampered over the stone slabs ahead. Beside him a tall figure wearing a long cloak just seemed to float over the rubble.

"Well. Guess finding him was easy," whispered Goban.

"Now for the hard part."

## Naagesh

Rain ran down Naagesh's skeletal face as he studied the raging battle. The elves' pathetic tactic of using trenches barely slowed the ogres down. True, some ogres with acid spitting toads attached hopped around howling in pain. And giants stomped through the midst, adding to the chaos.

"Thought Lardas was supposed to wait for your signal, Master," said the goblin.

Naagesh clenched his fists. His arms, all the way up to his shoulders, dissolved into swirling black smoke.

## Kiran

An unmistakable roar caused Kiran to look up. Five flames lit the sky. "The dragons are here!" The largest of them dove. Dashing off, Kiran shouted, "Nadda! Go see if Nanni's inside the castle."

## Naagesh

Naagesh and his servant watched the dragon and its lone rider approach.

"That wizard's hard to kill, Master."

## Ninosh

Ninosh flared his wings, pumping air forward and down, while extending his powerful legs. His talons ripped deep furrows in the muddy soil till the dragon finally jerked to a stop.

Water drained from his wings as the dragon folded them by his sides. Craning his neck, Ninosh studied his rider, and the strange metal contraption held tightly in his grasp.

Raising his arm, the object obediently floated up and over and settled softly to the ground. The rider then slid off the dragon's back.

"Chloe," began Larraj. "I don't know if Tom's in Elfhaven, but—"

"Tom is 52.374 meters due southeast of our current location."

"How could you possibly know—"

"I assume he's the one carrying the Guardian's nano-droid."

"Good. We've scant myntars left. Tell Tom I'll retrieve the remote. It'll be Tom's job to get it to the Guardian before the portal opens."

"I'm on it!" Motors whined. Wheels spun. Plumes of mud shot skyward and the robot raced off.

"Odd contraption," remarked Ninosh.

Kiran ran up with Max at his side. "Ninosh! Larraj? But I thought—"

Larraj rested his hand on Kiran's shoulder. By way of answer, Larraj said, "Thanks for rescuing me, Ninosh. My magical reserves were almost depleted. Couldn't protect myself from the heat and flames much longer. How did you know I was in trouble?"

As if on cue, a flock of baby dragons circled overhead.

"Adult dragons can sense a hatchling's cries of distress from hundreds of kiloters away. When we arrived, the hatchlings made quite a ruckus."

One of the chicks swooped over and landed on Kiran's shoulder.

"That one in particular. Wouldn't stop squawking till I followed it down into the flaming abyss and found you."

"Good boy, Frost!" cried Kiran. The chick raised its wings and chirped.

"Frost?" said Ninosh. "She's a girl, actually."

Kiran blinked. "Frosty? Frostette?"

"Ninosh," began Larraj. "I've gotta device to retrieve and little time. Can you help the elves?" Larraj sprinted off without waiting for a reply.

Ninosh swiveled his long neck to regard Kiran. "Well boy? What are you waiting for? With the darkness and the storm, seems I'm in need of an elven lad's keen eyesight."

Kiran's face blossomed into a wide grin.

# Naagesh

Naagesh pulled out the remote, water droplets beading on it.

"Master! Larraj! He's on his way here!"

Naagesh ran his fingers across the remote's smooth, wet surface. "Doesn't matter. Soon, nothing will matter."

The goblin's eyes latched onto the remote. "Destroy that cursed device, Master! If Larraj takes it from you..."

Naagesh stared at the remote.

The goblin's gaze flicked from the device to Larraj, now halfway there. "Give it to me, Master! I'll destroy it!" The goblin reached up.

Naagesh yanked his hand away. "You useless, sniveling, malformed beast! I've had enough of your insolence!" Naagesh spread his arm wide, silver tinged dark energy swirled between his palms. "You fool! Have you forgotten who's the master?"

The goblin bared its teeth, hissed, and leapt for the remote.

Naagesh slapped his hands together. There was a blinding flash. The goblin began inflating like a balloon. Cracks spread across its spindly body. The goblin's eyes grew impossibly large. The beast exploded, sending hundreds of flaming bits skyward.

Remote still in hand, Naagesh walked off to meet his enemy.


# Kiran and Ninosh

**Thirty myntars till the portal opens.**

The dragon sank lower, and Kiran felt Ninosh's powerful shoulder muscles flex under him. Laying his head on Ninosh's neck, Kiran tightened his grip on the dragon's scales. Even so, when Ninosh sprang skyward, the force nearly tore him off the dragon's back. Below, Max started barking.

Kiran leaned over the side. Max barked again, bounding off after him. Kiran smiled, then shifted his gaze ahead just as they vaulted over the castle parapet, sending startled guards diving out of their way.

Ninosh circled, gaining altitude, then banked hard and headed for the battlefield.

## General Kanak

"The ogres are almost to the last trench!" cried a soldier. "The one filled with Ironoak tar."

"Hold," shouted General Kanak.

"But sir—the flaming arrows won't stay lit!"

"Hold!" cried the general.

## Kiran and Ninosh

From their aerial vantage point, Kiran saw the ogres climb from the third trench, their bodies covered in a thick black goo. They were approaching the spear defense.

"That won't hold em long," muttered Kiran. Ninosh didn't reply.

Below and to their right, three giants stomped around in panic. Two of the three crashed through a hitherto unbroken section of the shield wall and bounded off into the woods. The only remaining giant just kept charging around, ogres and elves leaping out of its way.

"At least the giants are distracting the ogres."

Again, Ninosh remained silent.

Behind them, the massive wall of churning black clouds grew ever nearer. The rain increased, pelting the battlefield and the warriors below.

Finally Ninosh said, "Time we entered this fight." He let out a long piercing cry. Four dragons swooped down from above and flew beside them.

The five drew in their wings and dove, picking up speed, their exposed wingtips vibrating from the strain. Just before it appeared they'd plow full speed into the ground, the dragons thrust out their wings and pulled up hard.

Elven soldiers ducked as dragons, not far above their heads, spewed flames through the ogre ranks. The cloth covering the third trench caught fire and fell. Flames erupted from the oil-filled trench, driving the ogres back.

"Wow!" said Kiran.

## Kibbles 'n Goblin bits

The last smoldering fragments of the goblin slowly settled to the soggy soil. For a time, the crackling embers just lay there steaming. Then the bits began to twitch, then move, all skittering across the field toward the exact same spot.

## Wizards

"You somehow managed to escape my prison of tortured souls," began Naagesh. "And then the flaming underworld. My, but you're a resourceful type."

Larraj stopped in front of him. "Give me the device."

Naagesh shot him a thin, hard smile.

"The trolls have abandoned you," said Larraj. "Ogres too, by the look of it. And I don't see any goblins. Save the one you just blasted to bits."

Larraj raised his hand. "It's over. Give me the device. We may yet save us all."

Naagesh gazed at the remote, then placed it inside his cloak.

Larraj whispered an incantation. All across the battlefield mist began to form. The mist swirled. Vague forms took shape within the mist.

Naagesh opened his hands, palms facing downward. His hands glowed white hot. A blast of heat slammed to the ground, sending a wave of super-heated air flooding across the battlefield, evaporating the fog.

"Mist wraiths?" scoffed Naagesh, blowing on his hands. "Think I'd fall for the same trick twice?"

Larraj thrust out his arm. A lance of golden magic struck Naagesh's shoulder, spinning him around.

Naagesh straightened himself, patting out the small flame on his shoulder. "Pathetic! White magic is no match for the dark."

"White magic is darks equal."

Naagesh shrugged. "In any case, I command both. I've spared your life this long because I wanted you to witness the end of the Age of Light. But I grow weary of these constant interruptions. Goodbye—old—friend." Energy erupted from his hands, unleashing a swirling tornado of both light and dark magic.

The blast sent Larraj spinning through the air. Thirty paces away, he crashed to the ground, tumbling till he thudded against a large slab of the collapsed shield wall.

Naagesh walked over and gazed down at his longtime foe, lying face down in the mud. Slipping his boot under the fallen wizard, Naagesh rolled him over.

Larraj's eyes remained shut.

## Zhang

Horse and rider vaulted over the rubble and skidded to a stop in the mud.

Lightning struck the shield wall. Fifty paces away, a dark figure, highlighted by the flash, stared down at something hidden from view behind a stone slab.

"Naagesh!" Leaping from his horse, Zhang drew a sword even before his feet hit the ground.


## Reunited it stands!

Flecks of ash floated while larger chunks tumbled, drawn to one another by some unseen force.

When the smoldering bits met, they fused together. An amorphous, wobbling blob formed, swelled larger. Within the blob, hideous shapes took form, morphed into even more hideous shapes, then dissolved once more.

The pattern repeated until finally, a familiar figure began to solidify.

As the last bits drifted into place, the horned goblin scratched its left horn absently, watching Naagesh standing over Larraj's unmoving body.

"Wizards. Fools! Dabbling with forces they'll never comprehend."


## Reunion—of sorts

Naagesh gazed down at Larraj, a thin smile crossing his rain-splattered face.

"Dead at last."

"As soon will you be," came a voice from above.

Naagesh's head snapped up. Zhang vaulted through the air, his coattails flapping, a sword aimed at the evil wizard's chest.

Larraj's eyes popped open. The scene slowed, almost frozen in time:

Naagesh focused on Zhang's sword, magic crackling around the wizard's hand.

Zhang's gaze locked onto Naagesh. As he dropped, the monk's left hand swiveled from behind his back, exposing the dagger.

Larraj thrust out his arm and touched Naagesh's leg.

Magic flashed.

The dagger flashed.

The monk landed hard, stumbled and fell. Leaping to his feet, he spun to face—no one… The area lay deserted.

## Schooled again

*"Professor Septus,"* said the student. *"Headmaster, sir. I need your help!"*

*The headmaster tapped his magic wrist sundial and frowned. "What is it, Larraj? I have only half an oort before my next lecture, Magical Insects-Proper Care and Usage. I really must prepare."*

*"Sir, it's important. Beety's sister is in danger!"*

"Why have you brought me here?" snapped Naagesh, hovering in the same hallway as before. "I already showed you this in the Deathly Bog."

"You need to see what happened in the moments leading up to this." Larraj flicked his wrist and the scene rewound. The boy, student Larraj, sped backwards down another hallway, through a doorway where the speed increased so fast it became impossible to focus on what was going on. The scene froze with young Larraj back out in the hall, his hand poised above a doorknob.

Larraj flicked his wrist, and the scene resumed at normal speed. Student Larraj opened the door and slipped inside.

Naagesh yawned. "So where are we now?"

"You don't recognize your father's lab?"

"What were you doing in Father's—"

"Retrieving my notes."

"Stealing em you mean."

"Just watch."

*The open doorway cast a narrow swath of light across the floor. Young Larraj closed the door. Though mostly in shadow, a few candles floated magically overhead, casting dim, flickering light, providing faint glimpses of the room's contents.*

*At the far end sat a small wooden desk. To the left stood a waist high raised stone slab with five stout leather straps bolted to it.*

*Heading to the desk, the boy passed a long lab bench, its top brimming with test tubes and beakers filled with various colored liquids. At the end of the bench, a hooded brass cauldron bubbled softly over a low flame. Steam from the cauldron, captured by a wide metal hood, rose through coiled tubing, passed through a fibrous filter, and finally emptied into a small ceramic jug. Hissing each time a drop dripped into the container.*

*Young Larraj sniffed the jug. Grimacing, his head recoiled from the stench.*

*Hurrying on, he made his way to the desk. Parchment pages, containing sketches of ferocious beasts, potion formulas and scribbled spells, lay strewn across the desktop. On the left sat a crystal ball, a skull paperweight and a long feather quill resting in a bottle marked 'disappearing ink.'*

*On the other side of the desk, sat a tall stack of student papers. Rifling through the stack, he pulled one out.*

*"My notes." Stuffing the paper into his tunic, as he turned toward the door, something caught his attention. An odd diagram peeked out from below a*

lecture book. Larraj slid the book aside and lifted a wrinkled sheet of paper. He grabbed a floating candle from the air and held it over the page. The flickering candlelight revealed a sketch of a pentacle beside that of a monster. Leaning closer, he read the inscription, "Drekton. Demon — seventh order. Master of 'plague, sickness and death'."

Young Larraj gasped, letting go of the page as if it had burned him. He released the candle, and it floated back up.

Racing across the room, he reached for the doorknob and froze. Footsteps and whispers came from the hallway. The footsteps stopped. The doorknob turned.

Glancing around frantically, the boy leapt behind the lab bench just as the door opened.

Two sets of footsteps, one soft, the other strong, continued across the room.

"Remove your gloves," said a commanding male voice.

"Father?" came a girl's voice. "You know what you'll see."

Larraj raised his head and peered between two darkly stained beakers.

Naagesh's sister, Dendra, stood facing her father, Professor Valdor.

The girl removed her gloves. Her hands were cracked and gray as stone.

Her father pulled up her sleeve. Her arm too was gray and cracked well past her elbow.

The girl's eyes teared up. "Did you do this to me, Father?"

"There, there," he soothed. "No. I did not do this to you." He looked away. "Not intentionally anyway." He paused. "I promised I'd find a cure and I have."

"What do you mean 'not intentionally'?"

He sighed. "Doesn't matter. What matters is I've found a cure."

A lone tear trickled down her cheek. "You said there was no cure."

"I said wizards and healers know of no such cure."

"Then—"

"Shush. I found a cure—from an unconventional source. You'll see."

"Unconventional?"

"Lie down on the slab, please."

"What?"

"*Please. Trust me.*"

*She lay down, her hands trembling.*

*Kneeling beside her, her father fastened the straps around her arms and legs.*

"*What are you doing, Father?*"

"*It's for your own protection, Dendra.*" *The professor's hands shook as he tightened the last strap.*

*Striding briskly to his desk, he scanned a document, pulled his wand from his cloak, faced his daughter and flicked the wand. A glowing pentacle appeared, surrounding her. He flicked his wand again. Another pentacle appeared directly in front of him. He stepped inside, careful not to touch on any of the pentacle's lines. With a third flick, candles appeared, surrounding both pentacles.*

"*What's happening Father?*"

"*I am summoning a healer. One far more powerful than I.*"

Scanning the room, her gaze froze on the pentacles. She gasped. "*Father no! It'll kill you!*"

*In a voice barely above a whisper he said,* "*There's no other way.*" *He began to chant.*

*The room wavered, shifting slightly as if the world itself had lost its grip on reality. The candles flickered and dimmed. Ice formed on the walls and ceiling.*

*A dark crack split the room from floor to ceiling, blacker than night. From the crack oozed a thick cloud of putrid smoke, tendrils of which licked the walls, the ceiling, then spread across the floor. Next, a towering monster, with long muscular arms and legs, horns on its grotesque knobbed head and crimson flaming orbs for eyes, climbed through the rift.*

*The demon glanced around the room, scratching its left horn absently with a long, hooked claw.*

## Tom and Goban

**Twenty myntars till the portal opens.**

"How's it doing?" Goban asked.

Tom rubbed his leg. "Better."

The two turned at the sound of whining motors. "Chloe! How'd you get out of the desert? How'd you find me?"

"Rode a dragon. The nano-droid."

Tom yanked the miniature robot from his pocket. "Wow! I forgot!" He blinked in surprise. "What about a dragon?"

"Large winged beast. Similar to the extinct genus of pterosaurs, commonly known as pterodactyls. Unlike pterodactyls, however, dragons can talk and belch fire."

"I know what a dragon is! But how did you—"

"Larraj. He instructed me to tell you—"

"Larraj is here?"

"Yes. He instructed me to—"

"Where is he?"

"By the shield wall. He instructed me—"

Tom half-hobbled, half-ran, with Goban at his heels.

## The irregulars

Unable to locate Nanni inside the castle, Nadda went back outside. No small feat with the throngs of desperate folks trying to push their way inside.

Seeing no sign of Nanni or Avani outside either, Nadda joined the
irregulars. Under Tappus' leadership, the irregulars had somehow managed
to drive back the few ogres that had made it past the crazed zhanderbeast,
broken through the spear fence, and fought their way through a break in
General Kanaks line.

So far, only three ogres had made it this far. The irregulars had bested
the beasts with the meager weapons they had. A few of the irregulars held
swords, but most faced off against the ogres with only kitchen utensils and
cutlery. Having arrived late, Nadda held a wooden rolling pin, all that was
left.

Another ogre broke through the elven defenses and charged.

Nadda spotted a woman, wearing a tin bowl for a helmet, trip an ogre
with a mop. Instantly, a host of irregulars pummeled the fallen beast with
stones.

The ogre stood up, stumbled off in a daze.

For the hundredth time, Nadda glanced down the street toward their
home. The street lay deserted. Avani and Nanni were nowhere in sight.

Behind Nadda, the last of the townsfolk finally crowded through the
castle gate. Chains rattled, accompanied by a deep wooden groan, as the
sharp wooden spikes of the portcullis began to lower.

"Retreat!" shouted Tappus to his irregulars.

"But the soldiers still need our help," protested one.

"The ogres are too many!" shouted Tappus.

"But—"

"The irregulars must protect the castle gate from the inside!" shouted
Tappus. "Go!"

At that moment, a group of ogres, carrying a massive tree trunk, broke
through the elven lines and stormed the castle.

Tappus drew his sword with his right hand, winced, and shifted his
blade to his left hand and faced the onrushing ogres. "Go now!" he
screamed. But these weren't trained soldiers, accustomed to following
orders. Instead, the irregulars raised their feeble weapons and stepped

beside him.

With trembling hands, Nadda took his place in line.

A flash of light caused Nadda to blink. When his eyes cleared, a fairy hovered before him. Sticking two tiny fingers in her tiny mouth, Mab let loose a deafening whistle. Nadda winced.

A ferocious zhanderbeast bounded across the field, leapt in front of the frightened irregulars, spun around, hunkered down and roared its challenge at the advancing ogres.

The ogres screeched to a halt.

Raising its hackles, the zhanderbeast flared its neck ridge spikes and roared again. The ogres crowded back, struggling to get away from the monster.

"Go!" cried Tappus. This time the irregulars heeded his command, ducking underneath the rapidly lowering gate. All but one, that is.

In the darkness, no one noticed the elderly elven gentleman as he hurried off into the city.

The zhanderbeast grabbed an ogre by his foot, whapped him side-to-side, then tossed him into the air.

"Thanks," said Tappus.

Mab grinned, motioning to her pet. "Don't thank me, thank Bubbles!"

Tappus raised his brow. Mab flitted close to his ear. "Makes a bubbling sound when he farts."

Tappus blinked, then dove, rolling under the spikes a sectar before the gate slammed shut.


## Kiran and Ninosh


Kiran wiped his eyes. "The spear fence has fallen. We gotta keep the ogres away from the soldiers."

"If we spew dragon fire any closer," argued Ninosh, "we risk hitting the elves."

"We could attack from the side, at the line between the two. That might force the ogres back."

"We can try." Ninosh tipped its head up and gave a deep warbling call.

Ninosh dove and banked hard left. The other dragons followed. Pulling up, they sprayed an immense wall of flames just ahead of the elven forces, sending the howling ogres thudding away in all directions.

"We did it!" cried Kiran. "My plan worked!"

"But we also scattered the beasts. Some went round the elven forces and are heading into the city."

"Who cares?" said Kiran. "Everyone's inside the castle."

# Avani and Nanni

Avani peered around a corner. Nadda and Nanni's cottage was just three blocks away. She started forward but stopped at the sound of thudding feet. Avani jerked back and hid behind a stack of crates the instant before a dozen ogres charged past.

*This is the quickest way to the castle.* She bit her lip. *It's the route Nanni would take.*

Avani heard smashing windows and crushing barrels down the block. Soon the sounds of the beasts' passing faded.

She stepped out and started for her grandparent's cottage, but a faint noise stopped her. Scanning the area, she took in the debris-littered street: pots and pans, foodstuffs, even prized possessions dropped in the mad rush to safety, lay scattered amongst broken glass, broken barrels and fallen shop signs.

Avani spotted something shiny poking out from beneath a roasting pan. Bending over, she lifted a small necklace, made from seadragon oyster shells crafted by lake elves. It was Nanni's necklace. The one Nadda had given her on their hundredth anniversary. *Avani's eyes started watering.*

She clutched the necklace tightly, slipped it into her pocket and glanced around one last time. She heard a faint rasping.

"Is someone there?"

"Help," came a feeble voice.

"Where are you?" called Avani. A pile of wooden slats, the remains of a broken barrel shifted. A shaking hand poked up, sending slats clattering to the boardwalk. Avani dashed over and tossed broken boards aside.

"Nanni!" Tears welled in Avani's eyes as she gently stroked her grandmother's age-wrinkled cheek. "Oh, Nanni."

"It's alright, dearie." Nanni coughed. "Nadda and I got separated, is all. Some dang fool bumped me and I fell head over teapot into these blasted barrels." Her faced reddened. "Made quite a mess of em, I'm afraid."

A tear trickled down Avani's cheek. "Here, let me help you up."

"Ouch!" cried Nanni. Avani quickly laid her back down.

"Musta twisted my arm." Nanni shot her granddaughter an apologetic look.

Avani's eyes glistened again. "Not your fault."

The slats covering Nanni started bouncing and clacking. Deep grunts and thudding feet sounded from nearby.

"Ogres!" whispered Avani. "Quick. Hide!"

"Hide?"

Avani started piling slats on top of Nanni.

Nanni helped.

"Proly won't see me," Nanni assured her.

Avani hesitated.

"Go!" urged Nanni.

Avani glanced around. Beside her, a shop's door stood ajar, dangling on twisted hinges. Avani squeezed her grandmother's hand, covered the hand with wood and raced through the doorway.

Deep voices grew louder, then quieter as the ogres passed by.

"Halt!" shouted a grumbling voice.

Avani held her breath.

"What dat stench?"

"Stench?"

"Smell like elf."

"Course it stink of elves! We in elven city."

There was a faint sneeze and the clacking of slats.

Avani peered through the doorframe.

An ogre stared suspiciously at the pile Nanni hid under.

# Devraj

Dragons strafed the ogres, but even so, General Kanak's beleaguered troops were nearly surrounded. What's more, though the castle gate was closed, ogres, wielding a massive battering ram, stood ready to strike, but were being held off by an enraged zhanderbeast.

Three riders galloped up, sprang from their horses and climbed over the slick, wet slabs and took in the chaos before them.

General Kanak spotted the new arrivals, spoke to a soldier, and the soldier sprinted their way.

"Why aren't the ogres breaking down the castle gate?" asked Juanita.

"Not sure, my lady," replied the dwarf king.

The elven guard ran up and bowed. "King Devraj! Thank Turin you're back. General Kanak requests you have the elven army attack the ogres' flank."

Devraj just stared blankly at the disaster before him.

"Devraj?" said the messenger. "Your Highness?"

He didn't respond.

"We came on horseback," said Juanita.

"The elven army is on foot," added King Abban.

"How soon will the troops be here?"

"An oort," said Abban. "Perhaps two."

All color drained from the messenger's face. "We can't last an oort. We'll be overrun in myntars."

A group of ogres spotted them and charged. "Make ready!" Abban drew his battle axe. "We've guests."

## Mab

### Fifteen myntars till the portal opens.

Thick globs of saliva dripped from the zhanderbeast's razer-sharp teeth as it paced back and forth, keeping the ogres back.

With the townsfolk safely inside the castle, Mab spotted King Abban, King Devraj and Juanita standing near the shield wall surrounded by ogres. A beast leapt back as King Abban swung his axe. Juanita parried a spear thrust and counterattacked. The boy king just stood there.

"Come on, Bubbles. Looks like the late arrivals could use our help." Mab blinked, and the pair disappeared.

At the sudden disappearance of the zhanderbeast, the ogres looked around warily. Once convinced it was gone, they hefted their battering ram and charged the castle gate.

## Tappus

*Boom! Boom! Boom!*

Just inside the castle gate, Tappus studied the grim faces of the irregulars huddled beside him. "Where's Nadda?" he asked.

*Boom. Boom.* Cracks formed on the castle gate. *Boom.* The cracks widened.

## Nadda

Still staring at the pile of broken slats, the ogre said, "You hear sometin'?"

"Thunder?" suggested one.

The leader sniffed the air, then walked away. "Come."

"Nanni?" called a voice. "Nanni, it's Nadda. Where are you?"

The ogres stopped.

"Oh, no!" Avani peeked through the doorway just as Nadda rounded the corner.

## The wayward boys return

Tom rubbed his eyes. "Where are they?"

"Larraj and Naagesh were right over there." Goban pointed.

"I see Zhang, but where's the other two?"

"Oh no," gasped Goban. "The ogres have broken through the elven line. They're heading for the castle."

Tom stood, horror-struck. The dragons still flew strafing runs, but ogres ran around the sides of the elven guard, penning them in. The rest of the ogre army raced for the castle. Even at this distance, he felt the delayed boom of the battering ram underfoot.

A loud, shrill horn blast sounded. All fighting stopped. Ogres and elves alike stopped fighting and stared across the soggy battlefield at the north gate.

Tom scrambled up a slab of the shattered shield wall and strained to see.

He could just make out, in the distance, the faint outline of two short figures stepping through the north gate. One carried a large horn and the other a tall pole with a forked banner that snapped and cracked in the wind.

Lightning flashed, illuminating the battlefield.

"Malak and Chatur?" gasped Tom. "No way!"

Ogres chuckled but stopped laughing when row upon row of elven soldiers, dressed in full-leather body armor, marched through the gate to stand beside Malak and Chatur. Still more rushed past, fanning out across the whole northern end of the field.

Two-thousand elven soldiers gripped their swords, awaiting their king's signal.

General Kanak's troops cheered.

King Bharat of the lake elves took his battle standard from Chatur and thrust it skyward.


# Et Tu, Bellchar?


Tom watched King Bharat raise his hand, poised to signal the attack. But his hand faltered.

"What's he waiting for?" asked Goban.

Drums sounded to the east. Louder than the thunder. Deep, powerful drums. The drumbeats sped up. Grew louder.

The drums stopped.

A single troll stepped through the east gate. An instant later, a tall dark wave flooded through the gate as the troll army covered the east side of the battlefield.

The ogres cheered.

The lake elves stood frozen in shock.

"Oh no," said Tom. "Bellchar? Not you too."

Bellchar raised an ornate dagger, blazing with ruby light. The trolls charged.

"The Prophecy was right," Tom said. "First, I killed Avani. Now I've destroyed their world." He started to shake.

# The sleeper awakens!

"Nanni?" Nadda called again.

Avani winced. She leaned forward, trying to see what was happening outside.

Slats clattered to the boardwalk as Nanni raised her head. "Over here Nadda!"

Avani's shoulders sank. She closed her eyes. *Nanni and Nadda are going to die.* More than ever, she needed her magic, but it had abandoned her. Her hands started trembling.

An ogre grabbed Nanni's hand and jerked her up from the pile. "What we have here?"

Nanni screamed.

Nadda started for her, but ogres grabbed him.

The door slapped against the building, and Avani stepped out into the rain-drenched street. "Let them go! Or you'll regret it."

The ogres turned.

Avani stood up tall. "I am the chosen one by the magic crystals. I'm warning you. Let them go or I'll unleash my magic!"

The head ogre tossed Nanni to the ground and headed for Avani. Nadda struggled, trying to break free.

"Go ahead li'l girl, Show us yer magic."

Avani chanted an incantation. Sparks of golden magic danced across her hands. The ogre's grin dissolved.

Avani's magic winked out. "Oh, no." She flipped open her satchel. It was empty.

The ogre's grin returned. "Kill da old ones first. Den da young one wid her *powerful* magic." His brethren laughed.

Avani's vision blurred through tear-filled eyes. In slow motion, she saw the ogres raise their clubs above her grandparents' heads.

*Tom said fear is holding me back. Fear of failure. Fear of failing my father. Tom was right!* Tom's exact words, spoken to her just yesterday in the Deathly Bog, sprang to mind, *'You're the chosen one. Let go of fear. Unleash your power! Unleash your magic!'*

Time sped back up. Avani's eyes cleared. "Stop!" she screamed.

The beasts' clubs froze, suspended in midair.

"I warned you." Avani's arms sprang out. Golden magic engulfed her hands, her arms, and this time, the magic didn't fail. This time the magic sparkled with barely contained energy. Thousands of clear, distinct voices sang in her head, as the crystal spirits answered her call.

Rotating her palms skyward, her fingers grew ridged. Her hands shook. The ground shook.

The ogres glanced at each other nervously.

All down the street, hundreds of magic crystals suddenly sprouted from the ground. The crystals lit their surroundings brighter than the noonday sun. Nanni and Nadda squinted.

The ogres stepped back.

Avani whirled her arms in front of her, and the magic crystals heeded their chosen one's call. Multi-colored magic burst from the crystals, swirled around Avani's body, growing so bright, Nanni and Nadda had to turn away. Avani thrust her arms out, sending a tidal wave of blinding magic straight for the now fearful ogres. When the wave struck, it blasted the beasts backwards with tremendous force.

When the magic finally faded, shattered chunks of wood rained from the sky. As the debris settled, ogre shaped holes stood in the shop across the street and matching holes in the building beyond. There were no ogres in sight.

"Oh my," gasped Nanni, covering her mouth. "What have you done, child?" She gaped wide-eyed, first at Avani, then at Nadda, and finally at the destruction Avani had wrought. "And I thought I made a mess!"

Nadda hurried over and knelt beside his wife.

At that moment, a lone ogre stumbled from the building directly behind them, swaying drunkenly. Avani raised her hands once more. Nanni grabbed a chunk of wood and whacked the ogre behind its knee. Losing its balance, the beast flailed its arms. Nanni whacked it again, and the ogre fell backwards, crashing through the storefront wall, followed by a symphony of pots and pans clattering to the floor. They heard no more from the ogre.

Avani stared at her grandmother in shock.

"What?" said Nanni. She glanced at the motionless ogre, half covered in pots and pans. "Never mess with granny, I always say." Nanni flashed Avani a toothless grin.

"Ummm," said Avani, pointing at Nanni's mouth. "Yer—ah—teeth. They seem to be missing."

Nanni's wrinkled hand covered her mouth, an embarrassed look on her face.

Nadda bent over and fished her dentures from a mud puddle. "Here they go, dear." He shook them off and handed them to his wife. Nanni wiped them on her dress, then plopped them in her mouth.

Avani frowned.

Nanni ground her jaw back and forth. "Kinda gritty."

"We gotta hurry," said Avani. "Can you walk?"

## King Bharat

King Bharat dropped his arm, signaling the attack. Swords drawn, the lake elven army charged across the mud-soaked field then split in two, half preparing to engage the onrushing trolls while the other half faced the rapidly advancing ogres.

## Strange allies

King Abban and Juanita, having been rescued by the fairy queen and her pet zhanderbeast, sprinted over to General Kanak. The pair held their breath as the trolls neared King Bharat's forces.

A moment before the two armies collided, Bellchar barked a command and the entire troll army veered off, charged past the startled elves and attacked the equally startled ogres.

"Come on, General!" cried King Abban. "What're yee waitin' for? Let's help our new allies, shall we?"

General Kanak barked the order and his troops, along with King Bharat's, joined Bellchar and the trolls and attacked the ogres.

## Tom and Goban

### Ten myntars till the portal opens.

"The trolls are helping us?" Goban's jaw fell. "Can't be!"

Tom slapped Goban on the shoulder. "I knew Bellchar'd come through!"

"You were right." Goban blinked in shock. "You trusted Bellchar. A troll! And he's helping us."

"Told ya! Like Uncle Carlos said, never judge someone by—"

"By their looks," Goban finished. "Judge em by their actions. I remember. But Bellchar's not a someone. He's a troll!"

"Isn't he?" Tom said. "Look."

Goban watched Bellchar, at the head of the roaring, club swinging, troll army, slam head on into the ogre ranks.

## Nadda and Nanni

"Where are the ogres?" asked Avani.

"They were there when I left," said Nadda. "About to break down the castle gate."

"Wait here." Avani ran off. Moments later, she ran back.

"The lake elven army's here, but so are the trolls."

"Oh no," said Nadda.

"It's alright. The trolls are helping the elves fight the ogres!"

"Trolls helping elves?" Nanni exclaimed.

"Can we get into the castle?" asked Nadda.

Avani shook her head. "The castle gate's closed. We have to find someplace safe for you to hide." Avani face lit up. "I know. Follow me."

Waiting at the entrance to a garden maze, when her grandparents finally caught up, Avani led them through the maze and stopped in the small courtyard behind the castle. The one with the gurgling fountain and the statue of the unicorn. Her grandparents, hands on knees, stood there wheezing, catching their breath as Avani strained, pushing on the unicorn's raised leg. The leg pivoted back. A deep grinding accompanied a section of the castle wall hinging inward.

"It'll be safe inside," Avani assured them. "No one knows of these secret tunnels except Kiran and I. Oh, and Tom and Goban. Ah—and the blue-haired rats and the spiders."

"Rats?" said Nadda.

"Spiders?" Nanni turned pale. Avani shoved them inside, then followed them in.

"But," complained Nadda. "It's dark in here."

Avani picked up two firebrands from the stone floor and muttered an incantation. Flames engulfed the top half of each torch. She placed them in iron holders on the wall.

"Don't go anywhere," Avani told them.

Her grandparents gazed up at the dark cobweb laden beams. Nanni said, "Where would we go, child?"

## One final lesson

*The demon scanned the room till it spotted the complex symbol drawn on the floor surrounding the wizard. For several sectars the monster carefully studied the lines and squiggles making up the pentacle, searching for any break, any flaw, any weakness it might exploit. But there were none. The pentacle was complete, whole, unbroken, perfect.*

*When the demon finally spoke, glass beakers rattled on the lab bench young Larraj hid behind. "Who dares summon Drekton, king of the demons and master of illness and death?"*

*"I am the wizard Valdor," declared the Professor. "I summoned you following the true and proper rites as outlined in 'Demons: Summons and Control' penned by the dark wizard Nectus himself. Since the proper rites have been observed, you must obey me."*

*The demon rasped out a hollow laugh. "Let me guess, shall I?" It tapped one long claw on its cheek, thoughtfully. "You wish me to shape shift, assuming the guise of a colleague, perhaps. Then masquerading as your colleague, kill someone who stands in your way. Someone who's keeping you from attaining your pathetic goals: riches, power, fame. Am I correct?"*

*The professor took a deep breath. "You are also the master of healing, are you not?"*

*"Healing?" The demon adopted a smug, knowing look. "Ah, you seek immortality. You wish to live forever." The room shuddered from its dry-throaty laughter. "Would've been my second guess." The demon spat, flames erupting where the spittle struck the floor.*

*The professor gestured toward his daughter. "I did not summon you to enrich myself, nor for life eternal."*

*The demon's gaze shifted. Walking over, it peered down at the frightened girl, struggling to break free of her bonds. At a glance, its flaming eyes took in her gray rash, the stone slab, her shackles, and the pentacle surrounding her, protecting her from evil spirits like itself.*

*The demon reached out a long-pointed finger. As the finger neared the invisible line rising directly above the pentacle, a blast of violet magic sent the demon's hand reeling back. The demon shook his hand absently.*

*Careful to remain outside the circle, the demon studied her rash. "Creeping rock plague, quite an advanced case in fact." It remarked sadly. "Painful. And quite deadly. At this stage it's only a matter of oorts till it reaches her heart, poor thing." The demon clucked in mock sympathy.*

*"Rare too. Only one way to contract the disease. Secondhand magic. Dark magic, to be precise. Living in close proximity to a wizard who's been experimenting with the dark." It wagged a crooked finger at the professor, accusingly.*

*"Wizards. Fools! Dabbling with forces they'll never comprehend." The demon shook its head. "Best leave the dark to us demons.*

*"Too much dark magic'll kill you, ya know? Pieces of you'll start drifting out and back, out and back—till one day..."*

*Ignoring the beast's taunts, the professor demanded, "Can you save her?"*

The demon raised its blazing red eyes to the ceiling, considering. "Certainly, but are you willing to pay the price?"

"I summoned you. You must obey my commands."

The demon yawned, pretending to study a particularly interesting wart on its clawed finger.

The professor hesitated. "What are your terms? What do you ask in payment?"

Using his teeth, the demon pulled a wriggling bug from underneath a fingernail and tossed the insect into the air. When the bug stopped rising and fell, the demon's long purple tongue lashed out. 'Gulp.'

"It's been long since last I walked these lands. Breathed air, felt fire's heat, ice's bitter bite." It stared intently at the Professor. "My price? To borrow your body."

"Father no!"

"Twould only be for a short while. You have my word." The thing raised its right hand. "Demons' oath." It pursed its scaley lips. "Oh. But perhaps you don't believe I have the healing powers you seek, yet so pitiably lack." The demon studied the girl once again. "Remove her pentacle. As you know, I can't work my magic through her protective shield."

"I summoned you. By the ancient rules that bind our two realms, you must obey me."

The demon waved its hand dismissively. "Yes, yes. I am well aware of our contract. I've been summoned thousands of times through the millennia."

"If you harm her—"

"I know!" The demon folded its arms. "The contract grants you the solemn right and power to destroy me." It tapped its claw-tipped finger on its arm, impatiently.

The professor's desperate eyes flicked from the demon to his daughter. "Very well." He mumbled an incantation and the pentacle surrounding her faded. "You will not harm her in any—"

The demon held its skeletal hand over her body. Magic erupted from the floor, walls, and ceiling, then lanced into the girl. Dendra screamed.

*"What have you done?" The wizard drew his wand. "I warned you!"*

*"Wait!" commanded the demon. "Watch!"*

*The cracks above his daughter's elbow faded. Her skin changed from stone gray to soft pink. The effect moved down her arm toward her wrist. She smiled at her father, her eyes glistening with tears.*

*The demon twisted its hand. Cracks reformed, her arm turning to stone once more. Again, she screamed.*

*"No!" Her father lunged, reaching for his daughter. "Don't stop. Save her! I shall pay your price."*

*Dendra started sobbing.*

*The demon flicked its wrist, and the cracks started healing anew.*

*Glancing down at the Professor's foot, the demon's face blossomed into a wicked grin. "I'm afraid my 'price' has just gone up."*

*The professor followed the demon's gaze. The toe of his boot rested just beyond the outer line of his protective pentacle, smearing it. When he'd reached for his daughter, he'd stepped forward. "I release the demon Drekton from its bond of—"*

*A blast of demon fire sent the professor hurtling across the room where he slammed against the wall, slid to his knees and struggled to rise. Drawing his wand from his vest pocket, he cast a spell and the flames surrounding his body snuffed out.*

*"A solar cycle late and a demon short," chuckled the beast, firing another blast.*

*Raising his wand, the professor threw up a protective shield. Deflecting the bolt, it blasted apart a bookcase, scattering flaming spell books across the floor. The next blast deflected to the other side, striking the lab bench and causing the stewing chemicals to explode.*

*Leaping away, Larraj ran to Dendra and began releasing her bonds.*

*"Larraj?"*

*"Shush." The boy glanced around the room. Fire spread from the lab bench to a pile of crates stacked beside it.*

*"That's one," said young Larraj, freeing her left hand and moving to her*

*foot.*

*With her free hand, Dendra struggled with the latch on her other hand. Once free, she leaned forward and began frantically working on her right foot while Larraj released her left.*

*"Larraj! Get out of here!"*

*The demon and her father turned at her cry.*

*"Larraj?" exclaimed the professor.*

*The demon hurled demon fire at the boy. Larraj leapt aside. The floor exploded right where he'd been standing. He started back for the girl.*

*"Run!" she urged.*

*Larraj hesitated. Another, larger blast landed in front of him, sending him flying across the room where he collided hard against the door. By now the fire had engulfed the whole right side of the room. The boy clamored to his feet, preparing to run back.*

*Professor Valdor leapt onto the demon's back, grabbed its twin horns and yanked, yelling, "Larraj! Find the headmaster. Bring help!" The demon spun around. Still hanging on, the professor shouted, "Now boy!"*

*Larraj looked at Dendra, she'd almost freed her last foot.*

*"Go!" she screamed.*

*Larraj bolted from the room and ran down the hall.*

The elder Larraj waved his hand, and the scene froze. He stared at Naagesh.

"Show me what happens next."

"You've already seen what happens next," replied Larraj.

"No. Where we left off in the Deathly Bog. *After* the other professors arrived."

Larraj nodded. Simultaneously twisting his wrist while thrusting his arm forward, the scene raced ahead in fast-forward motion.

"Stop!" cried Naagesh. The scene froze at the point where the door exploded, and the wizards flew back, frozen in mid-air. "There. Now let it play out at normal speed."

*Flames exploded from his father's lab, sending the wizards in the school's hallway flying. The next instant, the flames sucked back inside the room.*

*The wizards raced to the doorway and peered into the charred remains of Professor Valdor's lab. The smoke cleared. Here and there, tongues of flames still licked about the room, but mostly the fire had blown itself out.*

*Smoke billowed from the doorway. Professor Valdor walked out of the smoke, his clothes singed and smoking. He coughed and patted out a lone flame on his sleeve.*

*Several wizards raced past him into the lab, young Larraj at their heels.*

*Headmaster Septus stepped forward, slid Valdor's wand from the professor's vest pocket, and snapped it in half. "Professor Valdor. Where's your demon?"*

*The professor coughed again. "Gone. I released him."*

*"And your daughter?"*

*The professor's shoulders slumped.*

*"I am truly sorry," the Headmaster began. "But I'm afraid you are in serious trouble. I've no choice but to inform the wizard's council of your reckless actions, which resulted in your own daughter's death. Everyone in this school might have been killed! And if the demon had escaped...*

*The headmaster spoke with barely contained rage, "As of this moment, I am relieving you of your title and teaching duties at Dragon Hollow. You shall be held under house arrest till the wizard's council decides your fate."*

*The headmaster gestured to the other professors. "Take him."*

*Two wizards grabbed Valdor by his arms and dragged him away. As he passed young Larraj, Naagesh's father raised his head and met the boy's eyes.*

*Young Larraj watched the wizard's back as they proceeded down the hall.*

"Stop!" cried Naagesh. The scene froze once more. "Go back."

"To where?"

"Just before my father passed you in the hallway."

Larraj rewound.

"There!" Naagesh pointed. Again, the scene froze. "Now run it ahead—slowly."

Larraj flicked his wrist, and the scene crawled forward in slow motion.

The two aged wizards watched as Naagesh's father raised his head toward the boy. The slightest hint of a grin washed across the professor's face."

"Freeze!" Naagesh shouted. "Now run it forward from this point, but even slower. Pay attention to my father's eyes."

*The moment Naagesh's father made eye contact with young Larraj, for an instant, crimson flames flickered deep within the wizard's eyes.*

"That wasn't my father," whispered Naagesh.

The two stared at each other.

Larraj snapped his fingers.

# Wizards

## Five myntars till the portal opens.

To the east, lightning arced across the face of the massive wall of churning black clouds, towering above the forest.

Thunder cracked. Shocked faces stole a quick glance at the largest storm they'd ever seen. Thunder boomed again. Torrential rain dumped down, making it nearly impossible to tell friend from foe.

Zhang just stood there waiting, seemingly oblivious to the battle and the storm raging around him.

*Thud. Thud. Thud.* A crazed giant passed by. The only one left. Zhang ignored it.

He could have joined the fight. Instead, the monk remained still, standing guard over the spot where he'd last seen the evil wizard.

There was a flash. Naagesh materialized directly in front of him, the wizard's back to the monk. Zhang drew his sword. A hand grabbed his arm. Zhang spun around, preparing to strike. "Larraj? You're alive!"

Larraj strode past Zhang as if he didn't even exist.

"Naagesh. You know now what really happened," Larraj began. "We have but sectars till the portal opens, and the world is destroyed." Larraj raised his open palm. "Unlock the device. End this madness." When Naagesh didn't respond immediately, Larraj lowered his arms to his sides. "Or kill me. Decide. But do it quickly."

"No!" cried Zhang. Larraj raised his hand, stopping the monk.

*Thud. Thud.* Chunks of the shield wall bounced up in the air as the giant made another pass.

Naagesh opened his hand. In the dim light, the space above his palm sparkled faintly, and the remote materialized, hovering, rotating slowly, rain glistening on its dark surface. Naagesh stared at the remote.

"Give me the device!" Larraj demanded.

Naagesh just stood there.

Larraj thrust out his hand. "Give it to me!"

Naagesh handed him the device. Two glowing symbols lit up.

"Which one?" Naagesh paused. "The blue one." Larraj touched it. "Voice authentication required for timer deactivation."

"Naagesh. Wizard—" A goblin leapt from the shadows and slapped the device from Larraj's hand.

Larraj, Naagesh, and Zhang's heads swiveled in sync, following the device's spiraling path till it landed twenty paces away. *Thud. Thud.* The remote spun to a halt directly beneath the giant's raised foot.

"No!" cried Larraj.

*Crunch.* The giant continued on, oblivious to what just happened.

Zhang ran over. Pieces of circuitry littered the ground, arcing and popping. The sparks stopped. The glow faded.

The two wizards stared in shocked silence.

Larraj asked, "How did you know the Library of Nalanda hadn't really been destroyed?"

"What?" Naagesh blinked. "Oh. A goblin told me."

"And did a goblin tell you about the Manual to the Citadel? And where

Avani kept her key?"

Naagesh nodded.

"And who suggested opening Pandora's Portal in the first place? A goblin as well?"

Naagesh opened his mouth to speak and froze.

"The same goblin?"

Naagesh just stared at him.

"That same *helpful* goblin who just destroyed our last hope of saving this world?"

The two wizards gazed off into the raging storm, the raging battle, in the direction they'd last seen the horned goblin.

## Tappus and Avani

Tappus stood atop the parapet, taking in his surroundings. To the east, still no sign of the Elfhaven army, his army, at least until recently. Though, with the unexpected arrival of the lake elves and the unprecedented aid of the trolls, their odds had greatly improved.

Tappus leaned over the parapet and squinted. *Is that Prince Goban and master Tom?*

A disturbance near the center of the battlefield drew his attention. A battalion of lake elf troops formed a wedge and steadily pressed forward, King Bharat at their center.

*What's the king up to?* Tappus scanned the area. *There's General Kanak, talking with the troll commander.* Tappus glanced at the lake elves progress. *King Bharat's headed for General Kanak. They're gonna form a battle strategy.*

"Open the gate!" cried Tappus, taking the castle turret's winding stone steps three at a time. "Open the gate!"

Chains clattered, and gate's portcullis rose. Tappus ducked and stepped out as a young elf sprinted around the corner of the castle and collided with him.

"Tappus?"

"Avani?"

"Where are you going?" she asked.

"To aid King Bharat and General Kanak."

"Thought Devraj fired you?"

Tappus winced. "I—I've got to help."

"Have you seen Tom or Goban or Devraj?"

"Haven't seen the prince—er—his majesty, but I know where the other two are. Follow me."

# Malak and Chatur

## Two myntars till the portal opens.

Malak and Chatur ran full out, right behind King Bharat. The two stood sandwiched between a squad of lake elf warriors who constantly slashed swords, thrust spears at the marauding ogres fiercely trying to attack the king.

An archer drew back, elbowing Malak in the head. "Hey, watch it!"

Another backed into Chatur, smashing him against Malak. "Ouch!" Malak shoved Chatur away.

"Hey," Chatur complained. "Not my fault!"

The pushing and shoving continued, accompanied by shouts and cries and the ever-present battle noise.

"We gotta find Tom and Avani," said Malak. "Tell em that thing."

"Huh?"

"We gotta—find—Tom and Avani!" repeated Malak, louder this time.

"Can't hear you." Chatur tapped his ear. "Too loud."

"Hey!" shouted Malak, to no one in particular. "Could you fight a little quieter? My friend Chatur's hard a hearing."

Nothing changed, of course.

Malak smiled. "There. That better?"

"What?"

"AAAAH!!!" screamed Malak.

Once they'd met up with General Kanak's troops. The soldiers stepped aside, opening a path for King Bharat, his lieutenants, and Malak and Chatur to pass through.

Back the way they'd come, the battle still raged, but ahead the space lay clear—well, mostly clear. A lone giant thudded by.

"Wow!" said Chatur. "Kain't remember the last time I seen a giant."

Malak whacked him. "You've never seen a giant!"

"Have too."

"When?"

"Dreamt a one once."

Malak whacked him again.

King Bharat of the lake elves joined General Kanak, Bellchar, and Tom's mom debating battle strategies.

A moment later, two more people ran up. Tappus joined in the strategy argument.

"Chatur!" Avani hugged him. "I thought you two were dead!" She let go and smiled.

"Avani!" Malak hugged her. "I thought we was dead too!" He continued hugging. "We almost drowned. Then we thought a sea monster ate us and—"

"Lake monster," Chatur corrected.

"Sea monster," continued Malak, still holding Avani tight. "But it was actually a sailboat full of lake elf fisherman."

Avani scowled at Malak and pushed him away.

"Thought we was goners," Malak repeated sheepishly.

Chatur nodded. "You seen Tom?"

"We've got some important information for him," Malak insisted.

"For you both," said Chatur, adding, "From the Librarian."

Avani tugged on Tappus's sleeve. "Where's Tom and Goban?"

Without pausing from his conversation, Tappus gestured over his shoulder. Not far away, by where the shield wall met the castle wall, Tom and Goban stood gazing at something.

At the mention of Tom, Juanita stopped arguing and stared in the direction Tappus pointed. She bit her lip, obviously torn between contributing to the critical battle plans and concern for her son.

"We'll make sure Tom's safe," Avani assured her. Their eyes met.

Juanita smiled at Avani and turned back to the conversation. "If we divide our forces," she began, "encircling the ogres' perimeter, we could…"

Avani faced Chatur and Malak. "Come on."

"Malak!" cried Goban, as the pair sprinted up.

"Chatur!" shouted Tom with a grin. "Good goin'! You two saved the day, bringing the lake elves."

"Not only that," Malak gave Chatur a knowing look. "We gotta big surprise for ya." They moved aside, revealing someone standing behind them.

"Avani!" Tom hugged her. "Thought you were dead. Thought I killed you. But yer alive!"

"Obviously." She grinned. Tom stepped back.

"I see you two made it," she said. "Hurry. We need a plan."

Just then Chloe skidded to a stop beside them.

"You didn't allow me to finish," began Chloe. "Larraj told me to tell you—"

Avani jumped in the air and clapped. "Larraj is alive too!" She grabbed Tom, pulled him to her and kissed him smack on the lips. Then held him at arm's length. "Oh. Sorry! Got excited."

Tom glanced at Goban. "It's OK."

Chloe tried again, "Larraj told me to—"

"Just a minute, Chloe."

"Well if it's OK." Avani pulled Tom close and kissed him once more. Finally releasing him, she raised up onto her toes and gazed across the battlefield. "Where is he? Where's Larraj?"

Tom staggered, wiped his lips and stared at Avani. Goban grinned.

Malak glanced from Tom to Avani. "Thought we was a goner, too. Phew! Was a close one." Nobody responded.

"Has anyone seen Kiran lately?" she asked.

A dragon swooped low. Ogres leaped aside as dragon fire swept through their ranks. Tom pointed. "Kiran's leading the air force."

Avani looked up, opened her mouth, closed it.

Chatur piped up, "We got some important information ta tell ya."

"The Librarian entrusted us with it," Malak said proudly.

"Cause we're reliable," added Chatur.

"And brave and trustworthy."

Ignoring the pair, Tom hurriedly brought Avani up to speed, "Thanks to the dragons and the lake elves and Bellchar. Did you see? Bellchar's helping us!"

The lone giant stomped past.

"Where'd the giants come from?" asked Avani.

"The Pillars. Naagesh released em."

Chatur leaned toward Malak and whispered, "What did the ghost say to tell em?"

Malak slugged Chatur. "You said you remembered!"

"I did? When?"

"In the river!"

"Oh, yeah." Chatur scratched his chin. "Somethin' 'bout the creatures?"

Malak glared at him.

"With all these allies," Tom plowed on, "looks like we might actually win! That is—assuming Larraj can retrieve the remote before—"

Malak and Chatur kept arguing while the rest stared at the gigantic wall of thunderheads towering above them.

The storm had arrived.

Bolts of lightning struck the castle, the shield wall, and several points on the battlefield simultaneously. Thunder *boomed,* and the rain increased to monsoon proportions, making it impossible to see more than a few feet.

In the distance, Elfhaven's clock tower began to toll.

"Oh no," whispered Avani.

"Midnight!" said Tom.

They turned at an ominous crackling sound and an eerie blue-green light.

Strands of neon energy arced across an ever-widening hole in the fabric of space-time.

The unthinkable had happened. Pandora's portal had opened.

"Oh no," Avani repeated.

"We failed," said Tom.

Lightning flashed.

As the thunder died, all fighting stopped. Besides the wind and the rain, the only other sounds came from the portal: distant voices and eerie hisses and moans.

Cloaked in near total darkness, the only light came from the faint blue-green sparks arcing around the rectangular portal. What lay beyond remained hidden.

Thousands of warriors stared at the seething gateway between worlds.

The spooky voices suddenly stopped. As did the hissing and moaning. The collective world held its breath.

Deafening banshee screams filled the air as thousands of creatures burst from the portal.

# Too late!

An ogre leapt up and swung his club, miraculously connecting with a creature, sending the screeching monster tumbling through the air.

Immediately, dozens more flew around him. Smokey strands of life-force rose from his body up to the creatures. The ogre collapsed steaming to the ground, and the creatures rocketed off.

With the rain and the darkness, it was hard to see, but here and there, across the battlefield, orange strands of smoke began flowing from ogres, trolls and elves, disappearing into the darkness above. At the same time blindingly fast spots whizzed by glowing bright orange.

The roiling clouds started glowing as hundreds of tangerine darts whizzed around.

No longer fighting, everyone tried to defend themselves against the creatures.

Tom ducked as screeching dark forms rocketed straight for them. "Look out!" Ten feet away, the creatures suddenly veered off.

"What?" Tom blinked. "It's OK. They're gone."

Another swarm streaked from the clouds and dive-bombed Tom and his friends. Tom dropped to the muddy soil. Goban swung his axe. Avani fired a magical bolt. Chatur stepped back, tripped over a fallen ogre and fell backwards.

But as before, the creatures veered off at the last second.

"Did you see that?" shouted Goban. "They had mangy brown fur and huge pincers!"

"No!" Malak argued. "Tan colored and hairless with ragged torn wings."

"They had three arms," said Goban.

Malak shook his head. "Two arms. No legs."

"But a single gigantic eye, though, right?"

"Five tiny eyes on long stalks that swiveled when—"

"Help!" screamed Chatur. "One's got me!" Everyone peered over the fat body of a fallen ogre. Chatur thrashed around on his back, something large and hairy clinging to his face. "Get it off me!"

"Ya tripped over a dead ogre." Malak bent down and yanked a drenched fur, feather, and tooth covered blob from Chatur's face. "It's just the ogre's war bonnet, ya dufus!" Malak tossed the soggy thing away.

Avani asked, "What did you see, Tom?"

"It was too dark. They move too fast. You're the one with the sharp elven eyesight."

"Too dark," she agreed. "Couldn't see anything." She gestured to Malak and Goban. "Neither could they."

Goban and Malak resumed arguing.

"The creatures seem to be avoiding us," said Tom.

Avani gazed up through the rain at the whizzing orange streaks. "I noticed."

# Wizards, Queen, and monk

All the creatures suddenly swarmed up near the portal's dark, waving, pond-like surface and just hovered there.

Naagesh, Larraj, and Zhang all stood gazing up at the grim spectacle before them.

A lone solitary creature, slightly larger than the rest, flew from the portal. The other creatures fell silent.

"We are *the hive*," boomed the hive queen.

"*The hive*," moaned the rest.

"Where is the wizard who summoned *the hive*?" asked their leader.

"*The hive*."

Naagesh stepped forward. "I did."

Zhang tightened his grip on his sword. Larraj wedged his body between them. As he did, the hive queen swooped down and landed in front of them.

Light flared from Larraj's palm, exposing the creature clearly. It had a single, black oval eye. When it blinked, dual eyelids, one on either side, swiveled inward. When they withdrew, thick gloppy mucus covered its eyeball. Tan colored, its entire body, head included, was encased in a tough outer shell. Hooked protrusions extended back behind each of her six legs, slime oozing from each leg joint. Her tattered wings resembled half-decayed leaves.

She faced Larraj. "You are the wizard who summoned *the hive*?"

"*The hive.*"

"No," began Larraj. "But I am a wizard. Leave now and I promise you, no harm will come to the hive."

"*The hive* takes orders from no one." The queen blinked and creatures rocketed down and surrounded him.

Larraj blasted one, but two more took its place. Zhang's swords flashed out, but the creatures were too fast. Larraj thrust out his arm, a wall of golden magic blasted creatures tumbling through the air.

Strands of orange energy began flowing from Larraj to three of the creatures. Zhang leapt up, swords blazing. Only a single creature fell, and this time, dozens more rocketed in.

Zhang kept swinging. Two more dropped, a third.

Larraj collapsed to his knees. His head drooped.

Suddenly, a crackling lance of silver tinged dark magic sliced through the creature's midst. Six creatures fell. Naagesh swiped again, and twelve more collapsed. Spinning around, he thrust out his palm and creatures blasted away in all directions.

Pressing his attack, Naagesh calmly recited an incantation.

Larraj lifted his head. "What are you doing?"

"Don't recognize the Transferrem Potestates spell?" Naagesh opened his arms and tipped back his head. A blinding beam of magical energy flowed from Naagesh to Larraj.

"Stop! Without your magic, they'll kill you!"

The magic transfer abruptly ended. Naagesh dropped to his knees, his face gray and haggard. Larraj stood, now glowing with barely contained power.

"Take it back!" cried Larraj. Naagesh didn't respond.

Larraj swung his arm in a slashing motion, severing the orange strands flowing from his body. Abandoning Larraj, the creatures swarmed Naagesh. Now defenseless without his magic, orange smoke flowed from Naagesh's body.

Larraj blasted the creatures attacking Naagesh. "Take back your magic!" shouted Larraj.

Naagesh gasped. "Too late for that. Be careful of the dark. Use it sparingly." Naagesh's eyes closed. He fell sideways.

"Naagesh!" screamed Larraj, firing another bolt. "Naagesh!" Naagesh didn't answer.

Zhang sprang into the air, a single sword held in his right hand.

The hive queen's black oval eye swiveled up to regard the diving monk and the deadly, gleaming sword.

Though Zhang was fast, the queen was faster. Zhang's sword lashed out. The queen leaned back, the blade passing by a hair's length from her throat. The monk landed in front of her.

"You missed," hissed the queen.

"Did I?"

The queen's gaze dropped. A dagger's hilt protruded from her abdomen. She let out a high-pitched scream. Across the battlefield: elves, trolls, ogres, even the lone giant covered their ears.

The queen stared at the monk. Her eyes clouded. She crumpled to the wet ground, blinding orange light blasting from her eyes and mouth. Her body steamed for a moment, then crumbled into dust.

"Zhang!" Larraj shouted. "What have you done?"

Suddenly all the creatures, the whole hive, darted about totally out of control, slamming into ogres, trolls, and the one remaining giant. Strands of energy erupted from the creatures, crisscrossing each other. Hissing with rage, the creatures started attacking anything that moved, even each other.

"What do you mean?" Zhang asked.

"The queen controlled the hive," Larraj explained. "Control the queen, we control the hive."

Zhang stepped back. "What's happening to you?"

Larraj's left arm glowed with golden magic. Arcing black and silver magic, however, encircled his right arm.

"Dark magic." Larraj glanced from arm to arm. "As well as light."

"Your hand."

Larraj blinked. On his right arm, amidst the seething dark magic, his fingertips turned to smoke. Larraj whipped his wrists and his magic, both light and dark, withdrew and his fingers returned to normal.


## Divide and conquer


"What happened?" cried Tom. "The creatures are freaking out?" Trying to keep off the pouring rain, Tom flipped up his hood. Water gushed out, drenching him further.

Creatures darted around attacking everyone—except them. Every time a creature flew near, they'd veer off at the last moment. One of the creatures, however, didn't change course. Avani stepped forward, crackling energy surrounding her hands.

Two feet from her, the creature just fell and flopped around at her feet. Standing shakily, the creature skittered away on its six spindly legs.

"Avani, what did you do?" said Tom.

"Nothing," Avani sounded confused. "I was about to use my magic, but before I could, the creature just fell."

Malak punched Chatur. "That's it!"

"Ouch!" Chatur rubbed his shoulder. "Whadja do that fer?"

"Just remembered what the Librarian told us!" blurted Chatur. He tugged on Avani's tunic. "It's the crystals!"

Everyone turned.

"The librarian told us to tell you! That's how the star beings and the wizards defeated the creatures last time!"

"There were hundreds of the star beings," Tom reminded him.

"And thousands of wizards," added Avani. "We've got neither."

"I remember now!" shouted Malak. "The magic crystals sap the creature's strength."

Chatur nodded. "They can't hurt ya! They can't even fly."

"Barely walk," said Malak, grinning. "That's how they rounded em up last time."

"N' sent em back to their home world," Chatur added.

"That's why the creatures are avoiding us!" cried Tom. "It's your crystals!"

Malak tapped Avani's satchel sadly. "Too bad you only got these few."

Malak and Chatur's grins faded. An ear-splitting grin, however, spread across Avani's face.

Avani grabbed Tom's arm. "I know what I gotta do!" She took off running.

"Wait!" Tom shouted.

"Hey!" cried Goban. "There's dad. Beside your mom and—and Bellchar." He sprinted away.

"My mom?" Tom gazed across the soggy field to where his mom stood between Bellchar and King Abban, skillfully wielding her sword to ward off creatures.

Tom watched Avani, striding toward the portal, magic swirling around her hands.

He bit his lip, trying to decide who to follow. Tom ducked as a dragon flapped by low overhead. Ninosh, with Kiran clinging to his neck, flew straight into the writhing swarm of creatures, fire spewing, four more dragons following close behind.

Tom swiveled at the sound of a familiar bark. Far to the right, by the remains of the east gate, stood a lone elf staring at the chaos before him. Max barked and pawed Devraj's leg.

# Devraj and Tom

Tom stopped beside Max and Devraj, rain dripping from the king's drenched head. Tom flipped up Devraj's hood. Devraj didn't seem to notice. The boy king just stared at the chaos, a hopeless look in his eyes.

Tom grabbed him and shook him. "Devraj. Snap out of it!" When he didn't respond, Tom raised his hand preparing to slap his face.

Devraj grabbed Tom's arm. "Tom. I have failed. Every decision I made was wrong."

"Don't give up. Your people need you."

"The wizards suddenly appeared. We were so close. But the goblin—and the giant—"

"What are you talking about?"

"Naagesh gave Larraj the device, but a goblin knocked it away."

"A goblin? Wait. Naagesh was helping Larraj? Yer not making sense." Tom paused. "Where's Naagesh? And the remote?"

"Naagesh is dead. The device was destroyed." Devraj slumped. "It is my fault. Everything I did just made things worse. Father was right. I am not ready to lead."

Devraj faced Tom. "What did I do wrong?"

Tom hesitated. "You're just—going about it a bit wonky."

Devraj blinked. "I failed to save my mother."

"What? That was a long time ago. You were just a kid against a trained assassin. You gotta stop blaming yerself."

"If I had not distracted my father, he would be alive too."

"You couldn't of prevented that."

"I could not save Avani."

"Avani's not dead!"

"I do not know how to lead." Devraj clutched Tom's sleeve. "Help me,

Tom."

Tom opened his mouth, closed it. "OK. First off, stop bullying people. A wise king leads by example. People follow him 'cause a what he does, not what he says." Tom stared at him. "I know ya got it in you. Be the king your father would be proud of."

Devraj wiped rain and tears from his face. "Those were my father's words… Almost exactly." The briefest of pauses then, "He said them better, of course." Devraj stood tall and squared his shoulders. "You are right, Thomas Holland. You were always right."

Devraj drew his sword. "I have been a fool."

Thrusting his blade skyward, Devraj charged straight toward the center of the mass of swarming creatures crying, "For Elfhaven!"

"No!" Tom shouted. "I didn't mean—NOW!"

A murmur rippled across the battlefield. Tom pivoted slowly. At the center of the field, the remaining Elfhaven troops under General Kanak's command, heard Devraj's cry and stared at the boy king—their king—charging single handed into the midst of the creatures… and certain death.

The ground shook from charging feet as elven voices joined, booming their battle cry! Across the way, General Kanak stared in shock as his troops deserted him, racing to their king's aid.

"Huh?" said Tom. "Never saw that comin'."


## The Guardian


Tom and Max leapt sideways as Chloe locked up her wheels and skidded to a stop, drenching them further.

Max shook. Tom flicked mud from his hands. "Thanks."

The Guardian's crackling image appeared above the robot.

"Tom. I have regained control of the Citadel, somewhat."

"Naagesh is dead and the remote's destroyed."

"That explains it."

"You said 'somewhat' regained control?"

"Things aren't responding right. I'm running diagnostics."

Loud shouts caused Tom to turn. Avani strode forward, the ground erupting at her heels. Tom stared agape as magic crystals, hundreds of them, sprouted from the ground.

Tom spotted Larraj and Zhang also watching her.

"I got an idea," said Tom. "Hold on." He dashed off. Mud geysers erupted from Chloe's wheels as she fishtailed along behind him.

# Avani

Avani headed toward the densest part of the swarm. Arms forward, palms facing upward, she flicked her fingers and hundreds of crystals burst from the ground at her sides. Still walking, she flicked her fingers again, harder this time. Thousands more crystals erupted, spreading outward in two directions, curving in a wide arc. Ogres, trolls, and elves leapt from the path of the sharp, crystalline furrow.

Ignoring their shouts, Avani continued on. Strands of magical energy flowed from the crystals, engulfing her entire body in a whirlwind of multicolored light.

She flicked her fingers a third time.

# Goban

Almost to his father, Goban unslung Aileen from his back.

To his right, Avani had nearly finished erecting her crystal fence around the creatures. Those creatures who flew too low over the crystals suddenly fell, tumbling to the muddy field. Leaping up, the creatures scurried away from the crystals toward the ever-shrinking break in the circle where the two ends would soon meet.

As Goban started to turn back, he spotted the lone giant, standing in the center of Avani's ring, towering above the soggy field. The creatures trapped inside the ring skittered up the giant's legs. The giant kicked and roared, batting creatures off him with the back of his huge hands.

*The giant's got two missing fingers. It's that same giant! The one what saved Tom and me.*

The giant stomped. Creatures fell. He stomped again.

Goban glanced at his father, taking out two creatures and with a single swipe of his axe. Most of the ogres seemed more concerned with fighting creatures than elves or trolls, but an ogre broke through the elven line, recognized King Abban and circled behind him. The ogre raised his spear.

"Father look out!" cried Goban, but he was too far away. A club suddenly whacked the ogre's head, and the ogre crumpled.

Goban's father smiled up at Bellchar. "Thanks!"

Bellchar grinned down at the dwarf king. "Bellchar hate ogres."

Goban shifted his attention to the thrashing giant, then at Bellchar and his father fighting side-by-side.

Tightening his grip on his battle axe, Goban leapt over the crystal fence and somersaulted to a stop beside the giant. Creatures instantly swarmed all over him. Goban tried swatting them away, but there were too many. The giant bent down and lifting Goban by his vest, he shook the dwarf lad vigorously, creatures flying, till Goban hung there creature free. Then the giant tossed Goban up onto his shoulder.

"Thanks," said Goban.

The giant grunted, kicking and stomping creatures below, while Goban swatted those who managed to climb all the way up to its shoulders.

## Kiran and Ninosh

Kiran squinted through the rain holding tightly to Ninosh. The pair flew just beneath the clouds amongst whizzing orange streaks. Lightning flashed beside them. "Look!" cried Kiran. "Avani's crystals seem to sap the creatures' strength! Let's force the creatures lower."

## Larraj and Zhang

Larraj looked up at a sudden roar and light from above. Five dragons burst from the clouds, spreading a blanket of fire above the creatures, forcing them downward.

"What are they doing?" asked Zhang.

"What's Avani doing?" responded Larraj, watching as thousands upon thousands of crystals kept sprouting beside her.

"Look!" said Zhang. "The creatures are dropping from the sky."

High-pitched motors and splashing feet brought the pair around. Max barked.

"Larraj!" gasped Tom. "The crystals zap the creature's strength. Avani's fencing them in. We just need ta force em back through the portal!"

"Slow down," urged Larraj. "Tell us what's going on."

Tom hurriedly filled them in.

Larraj stared across the battlefield. Multiple lightning strikes crackled across the field. Yet another magic infused boulder landed near the portal, exploding in a mist of brightly colored faerie magic. The creatures who flew through the faerie magic suddenly slowed.

Again the dragons rained fire, forcing the creatures yet lower. As the creatures neared the crystal corral, they fell from the sky, rolled to a stop, then scurried around searching for a way out.

Some creatures, however, avoided both the ring and the dragons and flew in a wide circle just outside the crystal fence.

"Avani needs help," said Larraj.

Zhang drew his swords.

"Not that kind of help. She needs wizards. Lots more wizards."

"What?"

Larraj eyes went out of focus. He chanted an incantation and his hands began to tremble, then glow. Dark magic erupted from the wizard's chest, circled his torso, then slowly spread down his arms.

Tom leapt back. "What the?"

"Don't ask," replied Zhang.

Larraj's eyes turned completely black.

Max barked.

"Yikes!" said Tom.

Still chanting, Larraj raised his trembling arms.

The area before them glimmered with a churning black fog.

Tom stared in shock at the mist. Something—no, several somethings, began to take shape.

## Lardas

The ogre commander stood near the north gate. Glancing once more at the bizarre spectacle around him: glowing creatures, dragons spewing fire, sparkling stones flying overhead, and the crazed dwarf lad hopping around atop the giant's shoulder.

Lardas snorted, signaled the retreat and the ogre army bolted away: some through the north gate, some through the rubble to the east.

The commander spotted a half-dozen ogres, trapped behind the elven and troll lines, run the other way down Elfhaven's deserted streets.

Lardas turned and ran off through the gate.

# Avani

Still striding forward, her crystal fence nearly complete, a few creatures managed to scurry through the gap. She sent a blast of magical fire across the break, preventing any more creatures from escaping.

Crystals tinkled as the two moving mounds, crystalline molehills, slammed together, closing the ring.

Avani stopped and looked around.

The rain of creatures falling from the sky increased. Avani instinctively ducked as Kiran and Ninosh swooped overhead, spraying dragon fire, forcing the creatures lower till they collapsed to the ground. Some, however, crashed down outside the crystal pen. Those crawled off and once far enough away, took flight again.

Avani bit her lip. *They're staying close by though, circling just outside the crystal's range. Why don't they just fly away?* She paused. *Maybe they need to be near each other.* Her eyes widened in realization. *They can't stray far from the hive!*

A brilliant flash caused her to turn. Twelve hooded figures materialized alongside Larraj.

"What the?"

# Dandrol

The figures solidified and the sparkling mist dissolved.

Larraj's hands and eyes returned to normal.

The twelve wizards glanced around in shock.

Larraj stepped forward and shook hands. "Dandrol! Welcome to Elfhaven. Your imprisonment in the Void is at an end. Though the occasion warrants, there's no time for celebration. We need your help."

Dandrol began, "But—how did you—"

Jade magic engulfed Larraj's upraised hand. "I recently acquired the missing key needed to free you. Dark magic. I'll explain later. Right now, what we need you to do is…"

# The giant

Tom watched in awe as twelve wizards raced around the perimeter of the ring, blasting creatures, herding them inward till they flew over the magic crystals and flopped to the ground inside the ring.

Avani sprinted over.

"Wow!" Tom said. "Nice job," He grinned at Avani, then faced his robot. "Chloe. Contact the Guardian."

Larraj arrived as the Guardian's image crackled to life.

"Guardian," began Tom. "Can you close the portal and open a new one under the creatures, just inside the crystal ring?"

"That would take some time, but I could reposition the current portal, laying it on its side beneath the creatures."

"Great. Wait for my signal." Tom glanced at the other two. "Ready?"

"No!" Avani said. "Not yet!"

"Why not?"

She pointed. In the center of the crystal ring, a giant fought off creatures swarming up its legs.

Tom sighed. "I'd hate to send the giant through, but—"

"There isn't time," said Larraj. "Look. The crystals are running out of magic." A quarter of the crystals had already gone dark. Here and there more crystals dimmed.

"They used up their magic," Avani said in shock. "Already?"

"We must send the creatures back now," urged Larraj.

"It's not the *giant* I'm worried about," Avani said. "Look who's on its shoulder."

Tom squinted. "Goban?"

More crystals winked out.

"We hafta save Goban!" Avani pleaded. "I could build another ring."

Larraj shook his head. "There isn't time."

With all yer magic," pleaded Tom. "Isn't there something you can do?"

Larraj just stared at Goban, swinging his axe while struggling to keep his balance as the giant thrashed about.

Tom ran to the edge of the crystal fence, waved his arms and shouted, "Goban! Get out of there! We hafta send the creatures through the portal!" Goban didn't respond. "Goban!" Either Goban couldn't hear him, or he was too busy swatting creatures. Tom ran back.

"I'm sorry, Tom," said Larraj. "Only a third of the crystals still have magic left. We must go now, before the creatures escape. Give the order."

Tom glanced at Avani. She shook her head.

"I—I can't," whispered Tom.

Larraj watched the scene gravely. Creatures scurried closer to the fence, testing it. "Guardian?" said the wizard.

"Yes Larraj?"

"Move the portal beneath the creatures. Now!"

The portal tipped and fell sideways. *Whoomp!* The battlefield shuddered as the portal struck the field. The creatures screamed and howled.

The giant flailed his arms. Goban leapt up and grabbed hold of the giant's ear. Falling, the giant slapped his massive hand down on the edge of the portal, scattering crystal everywhere.

Losing his grip, the giant, with Goban dangling from his ear, disappeared.

"NO!" cried Avani, tears streaming down her face.

"Close the portal," whispered Larraj. The portal slammed shut.

Shouts of joy sounded from the castle parapet and all across the battlefield.

Avani buried her head in Tom's shoulder and wept.

The portal re-opened.

People stopped cheering.

The portal closed. Tom glanced at Avani.

The portal opened.

Max raced across the field and leapt over the crystal barrier.

"Max no!" shouted Tom.

Max didn't quite make it. Landing hard, he tumbled amidst the jagged crystals.

Tom winced.

Max whimpered and stood up, hobbled to the portal's edge and barked.

"Guardian," began Larraj. "Close the—"

"No, wait!" cried Tom. A gigantic hand reached through the portal and slammed down beside Max. Then another hand. Next an immense head appeared. The giant struggled to pull himself up.

"Goban!" Avani clapped her hands, smiling through tears.

Clinging tightly to the giant's hair, Goban swung wildly till his feet touched down on the giant's shoulder.

"Goban!" shouted Tom. "Get away from the portal!" Goban spoke something into the giant's ear. The giant bent over and opened his palm. Max scrambled onto his massive hand. Rising to his feet and towering above the field. The sound of shattering crystals marked the giant's passing as he stomped through the fence.

"Close the portal!" shouted Tom. The portal slammed shut. Then reopened. "Ah—Houston, we have a problem."

"I know!" said the Guardian. "Something's wrong. The portal won't stay closed."

"Kinda figured."

"When the remote was destroyed, it must have corrupted the circuitry."

Long, thin, shell-encrusted legs started reaching up through the portal. Most of the crystals now lay dark. Ninosh and the other dragons laid a sheet of fire just above the ground.

Dandrol and his wizards began firing magical blasts at the creatures, preventing them from climbing out. "Larraj!" called Dandrol. "Help us!"

Larraj faced Tom and the others. "Find a solution." He ran off to help the wizards.

Zhang and Juanita, plus trolls and elven soldiers, rushed forward and began stomping and kicking creatures back through the portal.

The giant thudded to a stop beside Tom, leaned over and lowered its hand. Goban and Max hopped off. Max hobbled up to Tom, his fur matted with blood from his crystal cuts.

"Oh Max." Tom knelt and laid his hand gently on Max's back. Max raised a paw. Tears welled in Tom's eyes.

"Whadda we do?" asked Goban.

"Tom, what do we do?" echoed Avani. Tom just kept petting Max. "Tom!"

Tom stared up at Avani. "What do we do?" she repeated.

"Guardian," Tom began. "Can you bypass the damaged circuitry?"

Silence.

"Guardian! Can you fix it?"

"Given enough time," the Guardian said hesitantly.

"How much time?"

"A day. Two worst case."

"There's gotta be another way!" Avani shouted.

A slight pause. "There is one way," said the Guardian.

"How?" said Tom. "How can we close the portal?"

"You're not going to like it."

## One last hope

"By destroying the Citadel." The Guardian's last words still rang in Tom's mind.

Tom, Avani and Goban stood frozen.

"You're the Keeper of the Light," began Tom. "It's your decision."

"You'll be trapped," Avani said. "In Elfhaven. Forever."

"I know."

She studied his face intently and finally nodded.

"Fine," said Tom. "Light 'r up!"

"Unfortunately," replied The Guardian. "I—cannot do that."

"But you said—"

"It violates my creators' rules for an AI being."

"Like the third law of robotics in Asimov novels?"

"I am not familiar with Asimov's work. Suffice it to say, I cannot initiate my own destruction. Someone truly alive must do it."

"But you told Naagesh—"

"I was bluffing."

Tom sighed. "OK. So, what do I hafta do?"

"First, you must come to the Citadel."

"I can't do it from here?"

"No."

Tom glanced at the others. "Fine. I'm on my way."

Avani grabbed his sleeve. "I'm going with you."

"Me too," added Goban.

Turning to leave, Tom spotted his mom stomping on claw-tipped fingers at the portal's edge. "Chloe. I've got a message for you to deliver."

# Juanita

"Beside you!" cried Juanita.

Juanita kicked three creatures back into the portal. But two more got past her. One scurried up her leg, the other up her back. "Zhang!" she cried, but he was busy fighting creatures of his own.

Juanita knocked the one off her leg, but she couldn't reach the one on her back. "Zhang!"

The creature climbed almost to her neck. Juanita leaped up, arched her back and fell backwards. There was a soft crack. She stood. The creature didn't move. Juanita shuddered and kicked it into the portal. She stepped away from the edge.

Equally spaced around the perimeter, she saw wizards blasting creatures before they could climb out. Across the way, Devraj charged in, leading elven troops. Bellchar came over and flicked a creature that was heading for Juanita's foot. "Thanks."

Bellchar grunted, trudged to the portal's edge.

Juanita studied her surroundings. Most of the crystals lay dark. Even with the dragons preventing the creatures from flying out, if the portal didn't close for good soon, creatures would get past them and take to the sky.

She joined Bellchar and resumed stomping.

"Mistress?"

Juanita kicked. A creature screeched and fell.

"Mistress!"

"I'm a tad busy, Chloe."

Juanita swatted another on her left.

"It's just that—"

"Bad time to chat."

"Tom asked me to relay a message."

"Message? Can't it wait?"

"He instructed me to tell you *after* the Citadel no longer exists, but I thought—"

Juanita stepped back.

Bellchar signaled, and trolls took their places. Then he joined Juanita. "What wrong?" asked the troll.

Juanita gazed up at him. "It's Tom. He sent me a weird message."

She frowned. "What are you talking about Chloe?"

"Tom said, he's sorry you'll never know if you won the Nobel Prize."

"The Nobel Prize? Chloe, you're not making sense! The committee won't make their decision until— Wait? What was that about the Citadel?"

"The Guardian said, the only way to prevent the portal from reopening is to destroy the Citadel."

"The Guardian?" Juanita glanced at Bellchar.

"Without the Citadel," explained Chloe, "you won't be able to get back to Earth, thus Tom's Nobel Prize reference."

Juanita's eyes ballooned. "Where's Tom now?"

"On his way to blow up the Citadel."

# Heroes three

Tom and his friends rounded a corner and dashed across an intersection littered with discarded treasures dropped by townsfolk in their panicked dash for the castle. A toddler's dragon pull-toy lay directly in Tom's path. He leapt, but not far enough, his foot landing on the dragon's head, its crude wooden wheels sending him flying. The Velcro strap on his adventurers' belt released, scattering the belt's contents across the wet street.

Tom groaned, got up and reached for the items.

"Get em later!" shouted Avani.

When he arrived at the Citadel, Avani and Goban stood waiting for him in the dry entryway, their clothing dripping. By the time he shook off his hoodie, Avani and Goban had already entered.

In the distance came the sound of heavy, thudding feet.

Goban cried, "Ogres!"

Avani grabbed Tom and jerked him inside.


# Juanita and Bellchar


Whining motors and splashing feet announced Juanita, Bellchar, and Chloe's progress as they raced down the street, Chloe's wheels spewing fountains of water behind.

Navigating the last corner, they screeched to a halt. Five blocks ahead, the Citadel's round dome loomed above the other buildings. Unfortunately, halfway down the block, six ogres turned at the sound of their approach.

Chloe's laser rose, flipped over and locked into place.

The ogres charged.

Raising his club, Bellchar stormed down the street, meeting the ogre's head on.

An ogre lunged with his spear. Bellchar ducked, then thrust his club upward, smacking the ogre under his chin, launching him backwards into a comrade, knocking them both over.

Bellchar swung wide, taking out yet another and causing two more to leap back, opening a path between them.

"Go!" bellowed Bellchar. "Save da boy!"

Juanita and Chloe bolted through the gap. Chloe's laser tracked the ogres as they bolted past. In the street ahead, lay Tom's adventure belt.

"Thanks, Bellchar!" Juanita called over her shoulder.

"A single troll cannot best six ogres," Chloe said gravely.

Juanita looked back. Bellchar stood completely surrounded.

## Heroes choice?

"Guardian? What do I hafta do?" said Tom.

In the Citadel's central chamber, the Guardian's image crackled to life. By way of answer he said, "Initiating Emergency Destruct Protocol 517-914."

Red lights flashed. A warning siren blared. A detached yet cheery voice boomed, "Emergency destruct protocol 517-914 engaged. Confirmation stage one required for initiation."

A hatch in the central console sprang open, and a small panel rose from below with flashing red symbol on top.

"Press the symbol and say the word 'confirmed' when prompted."

"That's it?"

"That is it."

"Ok time to skedaddle," said Tom.

"I'm staying," said Avani.

"Yeah," Goban agreed. "Press the darn button already."

Tom reached out. "How much time do we have to get away?"

"Twenty sectars."

"Twenty? If we run as fast as we can, we'll hardly make it past the blast radius!"

"Oh. There's one small detail I should mention."

Tom's finger hovered over the button. "Yes?"

"Someone has to hold the button down the entire time."

"What?" Tom froze. "But that means—"

All color drained from Tom's face. He turned to his friends. "Go on. Leave." His voice cracked, "I got this."

Avani brushed Tom's hand aside. "No. You said it yourself. I'm the Keeper of the Light. It's my responsibility." She stretched out her finger.

Goban grabbed her wrist. "You're too important. The portal opened at midnight, right? So, today's your joining day. Today, you'll be crowned queen."

Tom slid his finger under Avani's. "That's right. And one day, you'll be the greatest wizard that's ever lived."

Goban elbowed the other two aside. "That's why I should do it. No one's gonna miss a fat, ugly dwarf. The world needs Tom's genius, and Avani's magic. You two're the real heroes. You always save the day. It's my turn."

"Are you guys nuts? We don't all need to die!" Tom sighed. "I'm not a genius or a hero. I couldn't even stand up to those two bullies, back on Earth, without your help.

"Goban's right," agreed Tom. "Avani, today's your wedding day. You'll be queen. And Goban, someday you'll be king of the dwarves. You can still help the Mastersmith bring in a new age of technology."

"Fine." Avani grabbed their hands and held them all over the symbol. "We'll do it together."

# All for one! And one for...

Three fingers dropped. *Click.*

"Initiation phase one accepted. Awaiting phase two-verbal confirmation."

They all stood still.

"On the count of three," whispered Tom. "One—Two—Three."

"Confirmed," they said in unison.

"Phase two accepted. Commencing Emergency Destruct Sequence. This installation will self-destruct in twenty sectars. Have a pleasant day!

Twenty, nineteen, eighteen—"

"Love you guys," said Goban, hugging the other two with his free arm. Avani stared at the dwarf in shock. "We love you too." She faced Tom. Suddenly, her eyes opened wide.

"Well. What the heck," said Tom. He grabbed her in his arms, closed his eyes and kissed her firmly on the lips.

"Seventeen, sixteen, fifteen—"

Avani pushed him away.

Tom opened his eyes. "What? Was I that bad?" Tom blushed. "It was only my first kiss, well second, I guess. You kissed me a year ago, that time when the barrier reboot took too long and Bellchar was about to kill us. No, wait! Fourth, actually. You just kissed me two more times when you found out that Larraj was alive." He paused. "Ahhhh—fifth if you count Zoe, back on Earth."

"You kissed Zoe?" exclaimed Avani. "That self-righteous, self-centered brat?"

"No! Uhhh—she kissed me." Tom's face flushed even redder. "I—I tried to stop her."

"Fourteen, thirteen—"

"Avani kissed me," said Goban.

"We thought you were dead!" shouted Tom and Avani.

"There's an incoming call," announced the Guardian.

"What?" cried everyone.

"From whom?" asked Tom.

"Your mother's on the line."

"Are you kidding me?"

A crackling sounded, and Juanita's image appeared before them. The scene's perspective appeared to be from a racing, giggling camera below and to her right.

"How?"

"Chloe," explained the Guardian.

"Can she hear me?"

"Audio and visual."

"Mom. Kinda busy right now."

"Tom! Stop what you're doing this second!"

"Mom—"

"There must be another way! Do *not* blowup the Citadel! I forbid it!"

Tom winced, whispering to the others, "Told Chloe not to tell her until afterwards.

"Where are you, mom?" The image rotated. The Citadel dome, just a block away.

"Mom, no! Go back!"

Tom glanced at the Guardian. Then at the symbol beneath their fingers.

"Don't!" exclaimed the Guardian. "If you break contact, we must start the entire process over. That'll be too late."

"Mom! Go back. The Citadel's gonna explode!"

The image seemed to speed up.

"Twelve, eleven—"

"Guardian?" shouted Tom. "Can you open another portal?"

"In theory, though, I've never actually opened two portals at once, but—"

"Do it! Open a portal beneath her. Send mom back to Earth!"

"There's no time and as I said, I've never actually—"

"DO IT!"

"No!" screamed Juanita. "Don't send me back!"

"Ten, nine, eight—"

A four-foot-wide portal, lying flat on the ground, materialized directly in front of Juanita. She leapt, flew through the air and landed with only her toes on the far side, the rest hanging over the dark abyss. Chloe's wheels locked up. She skidded over the edge and fell.

"Seven, six—"

Juanita's toes slipped. "Tom, don't do this!" She stretched her arm out, desperately straining to grab the edge as she fell.

Tom's voice cracked, "Winning the Nobel Prize is the most important thing in your life. You said so. You said it's *all* that matters."

"Tom!" she gasped. "I didn't mean you. I love you! More than any stupid prize. I decided to stay and marry King Dakshi before he died. Never got to tell him, or you, how much…" The transmission abruptly ended in static.

"Five, four—"

Tears streamed down Tom's cheeks.

Avani's eyes popped open. She yanked a handful of crystals from her satchel, thrust them toward Tom and whispered in his ear.

"What's that? A spell?"

"It's *that* spell! From the Library of Nalanda. The one that saved me!" She grabbed Tom's hand and held it above the crystals.

"You said it won't work for more than one person!"

"I said it never worked before. Say it!" His eyes popped.

Entwining their fingers, she gripped the crystals tightly. "SAY IT!!!"

The two began to chant.

Careful not to touch the crystals, Goban laid his hand on top of theirs.

"Three, two, one—"

Magic blasted from the crystals, engulfing them all in a swirling tornado of multi-colored light.


## Juanita

"Tom! No!" screamed Juanita. "Tom!" Time slowed to a crawl. Discarded items from the street above drifted around her.

Juanita gazed down. Chloe floated just below her. The robot's camera trained on Juanita. Beyond Chloe, far below, light came from a small square hole in the fabric of spacetime.

*My lab.* She saw people, *her teammates*, but they weren't moving, frozen in time.

Juanita gazed up once more. The vision grew smaller as she descended. Some part of her scientist brain kicked in; *Which way is up, and which is down? There's no frame of reference here. Space is truly relative in this non-place.*

A soundless explosion of yellow, orange and scarlet flames washed over the portal above.

*No sound?* She raised her hand. *And no heat! I hope Chloe's sensors are still working. Hope she's recording this.*

An item floated past her face. It was Tom's night vision goggles.

Waves of uncontrollable sobs washed over her.


# Kiran and Ninosh


High in the clouds, a small elven boy rode atop a huge dragon. Lightning flashed. With each jar from the storm's turbulence, the dragon tensed his powerful wing muscles, drawing in his wings slightly.

Within moments, the clouds parted, and the wind grew warm and smooth.

Kiran felt the dragon's shoulders relax. Ninosh extended his wings fully, stopped flapping, and just glided.

As the storm moved off to the north, the only sound was the soft hiss of the wind flowing over Ninosh's scales.

Above, the Ring of Turin shared its thousands of twinkling diamonds with them, as if celebrating their victory.

Kiran shook his cloak, droplets flying. "The storm's passed!"

"Indeed," came Ninosh's deep throaty reply.

High above Elfhaven, the pair gazed off at the horizon. They could still see lightning flashing in the distance, but dimly and the thunder faint.

The other four adult dragons joined them, gliding wingtip-to-wingtip.

Far below, trolls and elven soldiers patrolled Elfhaven's streets, searching for ogres. Kiran didn't see any. The blandaloo horn blew. The castle's gate opened, and the townsfolk poured out.

Kiran thought he spotted Nadda helping carry a wounded soldier on a stretcher.

"Nadda!" yelled Kiran, waving vigorously.

"He cannot hear you at this altitude," said Ninosh. But to both their surprise, Nadda looked up and waved.

Directly below, a host of squawking hatchlings flew by. The other four dragons tucked in their wings and dove.

"Had someone told me this morning," began Ninosh, "at the sun's awakening, that hundreds of baby dragons would sprout from the Plains like weeds, that long lost wizards would suddenly re-appear, that trolls would come to our aid, and that giants would again walk this world, I would have thought the speaker mad."

"Look!" cried Kiran, pointing directly below. The Elfhaven army finally arrived. The soldiers drew their swords and charged out onto the battlefield and stopped, glancing around in confusion.

The two glided along in silence for a time. On the far side of the city, the storm moved on into the distance, leaving but a single dark, churning cloud.

"What's that?" asked Kiran.

"Hmmmm?"

Kiran leaned over, hanging beside Ninosh's enormous eye, and pointed. "There. That cloud?"

"That's not a cloud," said Ninosh.

"Not a cloud?"

"It's the remnants of the explosion. It will settle soon."

"Explosion?"

"Why do you think the portal closed?"

Kiran leaned forward and squinted. "Where's the Citadel?"

"Gone. Gone forever."

"Avani!" Kiran gripped the dragon's neck tightly. "Ninosh dive!"

Ninosh tucked in wings, only his wingtips exposed. Diving nearly straight down, the wind and the force of acceleration increased tenfold. Kiran fought to maintain his grip. Ninosh's wingtips fluttered violently. Kiran's legs floated up off Ninosh's back. Kiran tightened his grip on the dragon's scales.

"Pull up!" shouted Kiran. "PULL UP!"

At the last moment, Ninosh jerked up his head and extended his wings. The ground sped by, getting closer and closer as the dragon fought to angle up. Kiran lay plastered against Ninosh's neck, held firm by the immense G-forces of Ninosh's radical move.

Startled elves and trolls leapt aside as the dragon shot overhead.

"We're gonna crash!" shouted Kiran.

Ninosh leveled out just below the rooftops, forcing him to bank left and right, darting between buildings, the street whizzing by beneath them.

Finally, Ninosh flared his wings, his talons digging deep trenches in the street, cobblestones and mud flying till he jerked to a stop.

"This is the closest I dare go." As Ninosh folded his wings, a furry critter bounded past, heading for the crater.

"Max!" cried Kiran. "Wait up!" Kiran slid down Ninosh's leg and took off running.

Max slowed, barking urgently.

Kiran caught up to him and they picked up speed.

"Careful!" warned Ninosh. "It may not yet be safe!"


## Kiran and Max


Kiran ran as fast as he could, Max bounding at his heels.

Two blocks away, the shops lining the street lay completely demolished. Splintered wood and broken goods littered the street, forcing Kiran and Max to slow.

The pair stopped at the edge of a deep crater, two blocks wide, right where the Citadel used to be.

Max sniffed something, pawed it. Kiran glanced down. Something shiny caught his eye. He picked it up. It was Tom's flare gun. He dropped it.

Tears welled in Kiran's eyes. *They can't have been in there. They just can't!* Max bounded down the crater's steep slope.

"Avani!" yelled Kiran, clamoring over thick slabs of stone. "Tom? Goban?"

He tossed rocks and shards of wood aside. The farther he went, the deeper the hole. A steaming strip of twisted metal stood in his way. He bent down and grabbed it. "Ouch!" It was still hot. Shaking his hand, he scrambled around it.

By now he was two stories below street level and still he hadn't reached the bottom. Smoke and popping, sizzling sounds came from off to his right.

More careful now, Kiran tapped his fingers on a smoldering piece of machinery, tossed it aside and half climbed, half slid down a steep embankment. Strands of severed wire and jagged, twisted metal blocked his way forward. Max barked over to his left.

Kiran found Max pawing at a pile of stones.

The two worked together, Max digging, Kiran tossing stones. A ray of yellow light streamed from the rubble. They kept digging. Within moments, they uncovered a large bubble of shimmering golden light.

The magic popped and fizzled. Flickered. Flickered again.

Max pawed the glowing sphere and the bubble burst in a shower of yellow sparks. Three bodies lay there, smoke rising from magic crystals on the ground beside them. The crystal's light faded.

"Avani! NO!" Kiran hugged his sister's limp body and began to sob.

"Leggo." Avani coughed. "You're crushing me."

"You're alive!" shouted Kiran, without letting go.

Goban moaned.

"Goban!"

Max licked the dwarf's face.

Goban frowned and pushed Max away. "Ya can't keep a good dwarf down, ya know." He tried to sit up but fell back.

Max leapt over Goban and licked Tom. Tom didn't move. Max whined and raised his paw.

Kiran let go of his sister and rushed to Tom. He pulled his arm. Nothing. He pinched his cheek. Nothing. He slapped his face.

"Ouch." Tom's eyes opened. "Show a little respect. We just saved Elfhaven, ya know."

## Changed lives

"That was amazing what you did!" Tom told Goban, "risking yer life to save that giant. I'd a never had the courage."

Goban kicked a stone as they walked. "Betcha would've." He glanced sidelong at Tom. "If it weren't fer you. I might not a done it."

"What?"

"Thought about what you said." Goban stared off down the street. The Elfhaven library came into view. "Bout trolls, giants, people in general. *'Judge em by what they do,'* ya said, *'not what they say'.*"

"Bet ya knew it all along. Deep inside."

Goban paused. "Dad says you're a good influence on me. Says I'll make a better king cause a you." Goban raised his palms. "Not that I wanna be king anytime soon!"

They continued walking.

"Wasn't just me, ya know," Goban added, "You changed a lot a people."

As they neared the library, they saw Malak and Chatur leading their gremlin friend up the Library steps. At the doorway, the two looked both ways, then cracked the door open a tad. The gremlin went inside first. Chatur and Malak slunk in after him.

"Hey," said Goban. "You even changed those two delinquents. Stead of screwing things up like usual, they brought the lake elves' army!"

Tom nodded. "Plus, they were the ones that told Avani about the creatures' energy being drained by her crystals."

They'd almost reached the library when they heard a loud commotion coming from inside. The door burst open, and the gremlin bounded down the steps and up the street, Chatur and Malak running full out after him. The Librarian glided out the door and raised a see-through fist. "And don't come back!"

Tom waved at the spirit. The Librarian waved back then, seeming to remember his crotchety image, glared at Chatur and Malak's steadily retreating backs, floated back inside and the door slammed shut.

"Guess I was wrong." Goban gestured toward Malak and Chatur. "Ya didn't change those two."

"Can't win em all."


# A final farewell

When they arrived at Bandipur Park, Tom and Goban stopped in the center. In preparation for Avani and Devraj's bonding ceremony and coronation, the elves and even a few trolls worked tirelessly throughout the night, rebuilding the stage the ogres had destroyed. And the giant helped wind a string of garlands round the castle turrets.

The townsfolk had already started taking their seats, waiting for the festivities to begin.

"Guess who else has been hanging at the Library?" asked Goban.

"Talking to the ghost?"

Goban nodded.

"Who?"

"Guess."

"Ah—I give up."

"Bellchar."

"What?"

"Yep. Asking questions 'bout history. 'Bout long ago when the trolls were friends with dwarves, elves, giants, 'n fairies."

"No way!" said Tom.

"Way!"

Tom smiled and gazed across the park. King Abban, a large stein clutched in his rough, stubby hand, leaned against a wooden cask laughing with King Bharat at something Goban's uncle, the Mastersmith, was saying.

Tom elbowed Goban. "I see your dad found the ale."

"Just doing his bit. Makin' sure the swill hasn't gone bad. Wouldn't want sour ale ta sour the party."

Goban grabbed Tom's arm and led him toward them.

"A pity yer high council couldn't make up their minds in time to send aid," said King Bharat. The jovial grins faded from the other two.

"Tried ta convince em," Master Zanda assured. "But the darn stubborn twits just sat on their arses, squabbling over party rhetoric."

King Abban snorted. "When I get back, first thing I'll do is—"

"First thing I'll do," piped up Goban, "is give the council a piece a my mind. I'll not put up with those sniveling, bickering nitwits anymore. They'll hafta answer to me fer this! People died 'cause the dwarf army wasn't here. If uncle Zanda hadn't shown up when he did, with the hand gliders—"

"Hang gliders," Tom corrected.

"Hang gliders and boulder slingers, the whole world would be dead!" Goban was red in the face.

King Abban leaned over to Zanda and whispered, "Pay up. Looks like Goban's got royal blood in him, after all." The adults laughed.

"I heard that!" said Goban. "No need ta get nasty." They laughed all the harder.

King Abban raised his mug, toasting his son's newfound interest in politics. "To Goban! May the High Council shudder at the lad's wrath!" Steins clinked and ale spilled. They chortled with glee.

Tom spotted Devraj and Tappus across the way. Tom wandered over.

"I'm serious!" shouted Goban in the background. "When I get back to Deltar…" Goban's voice trailed off.

As he walked, Tom took in all the sights, sounds and smells. Fresh flowers had been laid out across the newly rebuilt stage and along the aisles. Most townsfolk sat on the long benches, a few stood behind, sampling the food and drink that were being set up for *after* the ceremonies.

Drawing close, Tom noticed Devraj wearing a formal military uniform, complete with epaulets, a ceremonial sword, and highly polished, black leather boots for the occasion. Sparkling gold tassels, hanging from his sword and shoulders, finished off his outfit.

Tom glanced from Devraj to Tappus. "Looks like you two kissed and made up."

Devraj looked at Tappus strangely.

"Sire, I believe he means," Tappus translated, "he's glad we are working together again."

Devraj nodded. "I apologized. Offered Tappus his old position at twice his former salary."

"Twice zero is still zero." Tappus grinned. "How could I refuse?"

"Nice scar," said Tom admiringly.

Devraj touched his cheek. "The goblin's claw mark. From the Floating Mountains."

"A badge of courage. Makes ya look tough."

Devraj patted Tom's shoulder.

Tom scanned the park. "Looks like everything's ready for your wedding and coronation. You ready?"

Devraj inhaled deeply. "I—I believe so."

"Um—" Tom cleared his throat. What about your dad's funeral?"

"We will have the royal wake tomorrow. As with all elven kings, I shall scatter Father's ashes in the artesian spring high atop the king's peak."

"Where's that?"

"Just north of Deltar."

"That's a hike."

"Ninosh offered us aerial transport."

"Who's going?"

"Myself, King Abban, Tappus and my bride, if she so chooses."

"Speaking of Avani. Where is she?"

Devraj glanced up at the sun. "She should arrive any—"

A trumpet blared.

Avani rounded a hedge, heading straight for them. Delighted murmurs passed through the crowd. The trumpet blared again. Avani glared at the trumpeter. He lowered his horn.

Avani stopped in front of Devraj. "We need to talk." Avani glanced at Tom and Tappus. Tappus bowed. "My lady." Tappus spun on his heel and walked away.

Tom grinned. Emulating Tappus, he tipped his head. "My lady." Avani frowned. Tom grinned. She cleared her throat expectantly.

"Oh!" Tom turned to go.

Devraj grabbed his arm. "My friend Tom can stay."

Avani glanced from one to the other.

"You look stunning," said Devraj and Tom simultaneously. Devraj stared at Tom. Tom zipped his mouth shut.

"I do?" Avani sounded confused.

Devraj smiled at her, his eyes sparkling. "Your long lashes, your hair curled and shining of gold." He reached out and touched a sparkling curl. "And your gown's adorned with ribbons and flowers. Absolutely stunning!"

Avani blinked. "What?" She glanced down. "Not again. Mab!"

There was a faint *pop*, and the fairy queen appeared, hovering beside her. "You're welcome," said Mab with a satisfied grin.

"Put—me—back!" Avani demanded.

The smile drained from the fairy queen's face. "But you look stunning." Mab shrugged toward Devraj. "Even the grumpy prince said so."

"Grumpy King," corrected Devraj.

"Whatever."

Avani yelled, "Mab!"

"Fine!" grumbled the fairy. "Just tryin' to pretty you up a bit. Goddess knows you could use it."

Avani's red face seemed on the verge of exploding.

Mab snapped her fingers. A tornado of colored light whirled around Avani. When the light faded, Avani's clothes changed back to her usual drab attire. Likewise, her hair straightened, and her lashes shrunk back to normal.

Avani looked herself over critically. "Thanks."

Mab rolled her eyes and zoomed away.

"What's going on?" asked Devraj.

A hush fell over the crowd as hundreds of townsfolk stared at their king and soon to be queen.

Laying her hand lightly on Devraj's arm, she said, "Come on," she said, leading him toward the castle. Tom started to follow, but she shook her head. "I'll be back," she assured him.

While he waited, Tom spotted Bellchar over by the food, talking with Tappus. Tom waved, but they didn't notice.

Five minutes later, Avani tapped Tom on the shoulder. She glanced at all the people, grasped Tom's hand in hers and pulled him along after her. "Let's find a quiet place to say our goodbyes."

"Goodbyes? What's going on? Your wedding's about to start?"

She jerked his arm. "Come on."

Tom glanced back.

"They're talking about us."

She shrugged. "Let em."

The two strolled past the magical fountain near the end of the park. The fountain erupted, morphing into the face of some long-dead king. The elven king's watery eyes following them as they passed.

"So, what's going on?" asked Tom.

Avani stopped. "I'm not going to marry Devraj."

"What? You told him that?"

She nodded.

"How'd he take it?"

"Not well." She straightened her tunic. "Think I hurt him."

Tom didn't respond. They resumed their leisurely walk.

"You miss your mom?"

"Course I do."

"But you think it's better this way?"

Tom faced her. "Mom woulda died in the explosion!" His shoulders relaxed. "Sorry."

Avani squeezed his hand. "I just meant—her being on Earth, you being here." They continued on.

"She's got what she always wanted," Tom began. "What she loved most. Hopefully winning the Nobel Prize." Tom glanced sidelong at Avani. "Plus, she's got her work, her teammates, Uncle Carlos."

"You know she loves you, right?"

Tom turned away.

Avani stepped in front of him. She wiped a tear from his cheek. "You know she loves you more than some silly prize, right?"

"She told you that?"

"Not in those exact words, but yes."

"When?"

"A yara ago. Before you two went home to Earth."

Tom stared across the park.

"Anyway. This is your home now." Avani ruffled his hair playfully.

Tom frowned and pushed her hand away. "I hated when mom did that."

She grinned. "I know."

At the corner of the castle, Avani turned right and led Tom through the maze into the tiny pocket garden behind the castle. Mist and the sound of gurgling water filled the air.

"I heard you and Goban are leading an expedition to explore the lost world, under the Plains of Illusion."

"We're going to Deltar first. But yeah! Should be fun."

"Wish I was coming."

Tom sat on the edge of the fountain. "It wasn't my kiss, was it?"

"What?"

"When I kissed you in the Citadel, I—I thought we were gonna be blown to bits."

"So?"

"Is that the reason you're not marrying Devraj? Because I kissed you?"

Avani laughed. Tom looked hurt. She straightened herself. "No. I like Devraj. He's nice—once you get to know him."

She hurried on, "But—"

"But?"

"But I never wanted to be queen. I was only going through with it cause dad and King Dakshi came up with their crazy plan to unite the Keepers with the royal family." Avani sighed. "But dad's dead. King Dakshi's dead. The Citadel's destroyed. There's no purpose for the Keepers anymore.

"You said it yourself. What I want most is to become a wizard. So, I'm going to devote myself to becoming the best wizard that ever lived, next to Larraj, of course."

"So, it wasn't my kiss?"

She snickered.

Tom's shoulders slumped.

She quickly added, "Was a good kiss though. In fact, I'd say it was the best kiss you ever gave me!"

"It was the *only* kiss I ever gave you. You kissed *me* the other times."

She laughed and laughed. Tom finally grinned.

Tom dipped his fingers into the fountain and flicked, droplets flying. "What'll you do next?"

"Larraj, Dandrol and the other wizards are going to open the wizard schools again, starting with Dragon Hollow. I'm gonna help em! We're leaving this evening, right after Devraj's coronation."

"Tonight?"

"We're going on horseback."

"In the dark?"

"It's OK. Everyone's eager to get going. It'll be clear tonight. The Ring of Turin's bright. Plus, wizard magic'll light the way."

"Guess yer well stocked with wizards."

Avani half-snorted. Leaning forward, she kissed Tom gently on his cheek. "Come on. I want to say goodbye to Goban." She stood to leave.

A deep booming sounded, followed by faint cries. Avani gasped, "Nanni and Nadda!" Running over, she shoved her shoulder against the unicorn's leg and pushed. A grinding noise sounded and the castle wall swiveling open.

Her grandparents stumbled out, cobwebs clinging to their hair.

Avani gasped. "Nadda! Nanni! I'm so sorry. I forgot you!" She turned to Tom. "Left them here all night!"

Nadda squinted in the unaccustomed sunlight. "Is it morning already?"

"Did you save the world, child?" asked Nanni.

"Yes, she did!" said Tom.


While Avani escorted her grandparents home to clean up, Tom retraced his steps back to the park and found Goban, not surprisingly, standing by the food table. He told Goban the story about Avani's grandparents, trapped inside the castle wall. By the time he finished, Avani showed up.

"How's Nanni and Nadda?" asked Goban. Avani blushed.

At that moment, up walked Larraj, Zhang, and Kiran. A well-bandaged dog hobbling beside Kiran. Then Mab flitted up, hovering beside Max.

Tom knelt and scratched Max behind the ears. Max shook his head, sending the usual copious amount of slobber flying. Mab flitted over behind Kiran, narrowly avoiding being knocked from the air by a large glob of dog goo.

Tom asked Kiran, "How's Max doing?"

"The healers said Max'll be spry as a slithertoad in spring, in no time."

"That's good, right?" Tom glanced from Kiran to Larraj. "Isn't it?"

"Sure. It's just that—" Kiran looked at Larraj.

"What?" said Tom.

"Nothing to worry about," Larraj assured him. "The healers did find something curious, though. Something we thought you should know about."

"What?" Tom glanced anxiously from face to face.

"When the healers were treating Max's crystal wounds, they had to shave Max's fur around each cut."

"Yeah?"

"So, when the healers shaved Max's left leg, they found this." Larraj nodded to Kiran.

Kiran bent down and gently unwound the bandage.

Tom studied his dog's leg. "Max has a tat?"

"It's not a tattoo. It's actually a birthmark."

Tom leaned closer. A single straight line angled up and to the right. At the top, several short squiggly lines jutted off around the main line, looking like sparks. To the left was a pointy triangle. Tom stared at Larraj. "Is that?"

Larraj pulled up his sleeve. "The Mark of the Wizard." An identical tattoo adorned Larraj's arm.

Tom blinked. "What did you tell me last year? You quoted something from the Prophecy of Elfhaven. Something about Max and me."

"In the yara of the serpent," began Larraj, "space folds;
Creature and boy, odd companions;
Magic and tools, long thought lost;
A Wizard's Mark shall confirm;

The tapestry of destiny—frays;

A heavy burden for one so young;

The future, cast adrift in violent times;

Pity the creature, and his pet—Thomas Holland."

"A Wizard's Mark shall confirm." Tom froze. "Pity the creature and his pet—Thomas Holland."

Tom leapt up. "That's it! Max is the creature, and I'm his pet. Max is the one, not me! The Prophecy is about Max!"

Tom wrapped his arms tightly round Max's head and squeezed, then broke into an uncontrolled fit of laughing. Within moments, everyone joined in.

"Humans!" Mab shook her head. "Thought the boy would never figure it out!"

# Tom's bedtime story

That evening, after Devraj had been crowned king, after Avani had *not* been crowned queen, after all the speeches and the awards, the dancing and partying, which Goban enjoyed a bit too much. After all the exhausted, happy people and beasts settled down for the night, Tom decided to go for a late-night stroll.

He was surprised that Avani, Larraj, Dandrol and the other wizards had made good their plans and left on their journey to reopen the wizard's schools.

Earlier, Avani said they were leaving on horseback, but Mab would not hear of it. Instead, the fairy queen just snapped her fingers and Avani and the wizards left in a flash of fairy magic, presumably to appear at Dragon Hollow school. At least, Tom hoped that's where the fairy queen sent em. She was a bit of a trickster.

Tomorrow, Tom would tag along with Goban and his father and uncle on their longer, slower trip back to Deltar.

Devraj offered Tom a room at the castle. Tom thanked him politely but told him he'd already agreed to stay with Nadda and Nanni.

Rounding the last corner, Avani and Kiran's grandparent's cottage came into view. Walking the last block, Tom glanced up. The Ring of Turin sparkled brighter than he'd ever seen it.

Sprinting up the front steps, Tom knocked. The door creaked open, spilling flickering candlelight onto the stoop.

"Thomas!" cried Nanni. "Come in! Come in, boy. No need to knock. Nadda!" she called over her shoulder, "Thomas has arrived."

"Sorry I'm so late."

"No, no child." She urged him into the living room.

Nadda entered from the kitchen, drying his hands on a dish towel. "Would you like a slice of slithertoad pie? I know it's your favorite."

Tom grabbed his stomach. "No thanks. I'm stuffed. Ate too much at the party. Where's Kiran and Max?"

Nadda glanced upstairs and whispered, "Asleep. Once his head hit the pillow, he was out like a snuffed tarbeast candle. And Max's curled up beside him."

Tom stretched and yawned. "Speaking of sleep."

"We put fresh sheets on Avani's bed," said Nadda.

Nanni nodded. "Her room's yours."

"She won't mind?"

"She'd be delighted!" Nadda assured him.

"Thanks!" Careful not to wake Kiran and Max, Tom tiptoed up the stairs and quietly slipped inside Avani's bedroom.

A large, old-fashioned brass key extended out from the door's lock. He didn't bother to lock it.

Scanning the room, on top of the dresser sat a ceramic wash basin with a water pitcher beside it. On the nightstand by Avani's bed was a stout brass candlestick with a lit candle and a tinderbox for re-lighting it. At the foot of the bed lay a set of clean, neatly folded night clothes.

Tom undressed and put them on. The sleeves of his nightshirt hung down past his arms and the pants were equally long. He cinched up the cord around the wide waist. *Must be Nadda's.*

After washing his hands and face in the washbasin, Tom climbed under the covers and yawned. Leaning over to blow out the candle, he spotted a roll of parchment beside the candlestick. Sliding the nightshirt's long sleeves to his elbows, he lifted the paper. Something fell, clinking to the hardwood floor. Tom leaned over, feeling around till his hand brushed against a cold, hard object. Grabbing hold, he lifted it up into the light. The magic crystal began to glow.

Gasping, Tom dropped the gem and jumped up onto the bed. The crystal clattered on the nightstand, its light slowly fading.

Tom held his breath for what seemed like hours. His hand shook when he finally reached for the page, its corner resting beneath the crystal. He paused, then jerked the paper out from under the gemstone and stared at the crystal as if it might bite him.

The crystal didn't move.

His gaze rose to the note in his hands. He recognized Avani's handwriting, but it was written in Elvish. The sheet suddenly shimmered, and the letters morphed into English. *Wow! Didn't know she could do that.* He scanned the note.

*'Tom. Thanks for everything. If it wasn't for what you told me in the Deathly Bog—'* Tom scratched his head. *What did I say?* Tom read on, *'—I would have, that's to say, I might not have been able to… Well, just thanks! Oh, and since I'll be busy, we both will I guess, we may not get to see each other for a while, so I left you something to remember me by. One of my magic crystals. I know! You're afraid of them. I'm smiling. Can you see me? Now I'm chuckling. My best friend once told me to "Let go of fear. Unleash your power! Unleash your magic!" Wink, wink. 'Hugs, Avani.'*

Tom wiped a tear from his cheek, blew out the candle, flopped his head down on the firm, feather pillow and closed his eyes.

His eyes sprang open.

He stared at the dark ceiling.

He stared out the dark window.

He heard the floorboards creak as Nadda and Nanni shuffled down the hall and the squeak of their bedroom door closing.

Relighting the candle, Tom scooched up, leaned against the wall and just sat there, the events of the last few days playing through his mind.

*Three days ago, I was lying in my own bed in my own room in Chicago. On another world. In another universe.*

He smiled. *In fact, a year ago I was lying in that same bed. At that point, I hadn't met Goban or Avani. Never even heard of Elfhaven. I didn't even believe in magic!*

Finally, he yawned and leaned over, about to blow out the candle. The door creaked open and someone stepped inside.

Tom heard the key turn in the lock.

"Who's there?"

The person stepped into the candlelight.

"Avani?"

"Sorry it's so late," she whispered.

"No! Sorry I'm in your bed." He tossed off the covers and leapt out of bed, tripped over his long pajama bottoms, and did a face plant on the cold wood floor. He sprang back up. "I'll sleep downstairs." He made a move toward the door.

"No. No. Nanni just made up the sofa for me."

"She did?" Tom blinked. "What're you doing here? I thought you'd gone?"

"I did. Then I remembered I'd left something here."

"Where's Larraj?"

"He continued on horseback with the others."

"On—horseback? But I thought—"

"We weren't far. I told them I'd ride back and catch up with them tomorrow."

"On—horseback?"

"Yes. Devraj gave us fresh horses and supplies. That was nice of him, don't you think?" She took a step forward.

Tom stepped back, nearly tripped again, and bumped into the nightstand.

"Why are you still awake?"

"Couldn't sleep." He reached behind and patted the nightstand. "Keep thinking about everything we've been doing the past few days." His fingers brushed the heavy brass candlestick. His fingers tightened on its cold hard surface.

Avani smiled. "Our adventures."

"Like that giant magic spider," quizzed Tom. "Remember?"

"Near the Pillars?" she asked. "Or the one in the Deathly Bog?"

Tom sighed and let go of the candlestick. "The Deathly Bog."

Avani shivered. "Very scary."

"And the time we fell in the sinkhole." Tom smiled.

"Where Naagesh tossed in that thingy."

"The nano-droid!"

"Right."

"And the lost world beneath the Plains—" Tom blurted. "Oh! And the dragon eggs!"

"The eggs! Amazing! And to think. All they needed to hatch was fire."

Tom took a step forward, stopped. "Oh!" He twisted around and picked up the paper. "I read your note. It was nice."

"Note?" Avani glanced at the page, uncertainly. "Oh. Almost forgot."

Tom studied her strangely. "Say. I never thanked you for saving me from those bullies."

Avani hesitated. "Bullies?"

"Back on Earth, remember?"

She stared at him.

Tom held up the note. "You mentioned the bullies in here."

"I did?" She fidgeted, then quickly smiled. "You don't have to thank me."

Tom continued to watch her closely. "I'll never forget the looks on their faces when you changed the three bullies into... What was it you changed them into?"

Avani didn't answer.

"Gremlins!" Tom smacked his forehead. "That's it!"

She smiled. "I particularly enjoyed that part. Their bright eyes, their mischievous grins."

Tom stepped back. "And you and Zoe, you two really hit it off."

"She was nice."

*My flare gun!* Tom glanced around the room, searching for his adventure's belt. Then he remembered he'd lost his belt on his way to the Citadel.

Avani stepped closer.

Tom stepped back, bumping into the nightstand again.

"Zoe was scared, is all," Avani assured him. "Don't blame her." She took another step.

Tom reached back. "Wish you could've convinced her to come to Elfhaven with us." His hand brushed the crystal. He jerked his hand away. Then tried again.

Tom whipped the candlestick in front of him, its burning candle aimed at Avani.

"Tom? What's wrong?"

Keeping the flame trained on her, he replied, "Avani didn't write about Earth in her note. There were *two* bullies, not three, and she turned them into spikey, blue-haired rats, not gremlins. Plus, Avani and Zoe hated each other.

"You're not Avani."

A swirl of smoke and Avani changed into Naagesh.

"Nice try. But Naagesh is dead."

Naagesh's image wavered, and suddenly, Tom stood there staring at himself. The fake Tom grinned.

"Very funny," said the real Tom. "But you can stop shape-shifting. I know who you are."

"You do?" came his own voice.

Tom stepped forward and waved the candle menacingly at himself. "You're Naagesh's servant. The goblin."

Smoke curled around the other Tom, then he morphed into a hideously gnarled beast.

"Ah, but you're a clever one," hissed the horned goblin. "Go on. Finish your tale."

With trembling hands, Tom raised the candlestick threateningly. "You poisoned Naagesh's mind, bent him to your will. He was the puppet. You the puppet master, pulling his strings."

"Naagesh was wise to be wary of you." The goblin stepped closer.

"Stop!" shouted Tom. "But there's more, isn't there?"

The beast stared at him expectantly through dark, beady eyes.

"Naagesh's father conducted forbidden experiments in dark magic in his lab at Dragon Hollow school, correct?"

"Yes. So?"

"Ah hah!" shouted Tom. "How could you know that?" Tom stepped forward, brandishing the candlestick like a sword.

The goblin stepped back. "Naagesh told me."

"That's strange?" Gaining confidence, Tom stepped forward once more. "Larraj said Naagesh didn't know about the demon till last night when they traveled back in time. Naagesh died right afterwards. So Naagesh couldn't have told you."

The goblin remained silent.

"Larraj also said, headmaster Septus made him swear an oath of silence, for fear that if word got out that professors were practicing dark magic, angry citizens would demand the school be closed."

Tom kept advancing. "Neither Larraj nor the headmaster ever told anyone. So you couldn't of known." Tom stopped. "There's no one left who knew." Tom shook his head, frowning.

"No. Wait! There was another." Tom paused. "The demon itself." Tom's eyes widened. "You're Drekton. The demon!"

A flash, and now a tall, muscular monster towered above Tom. The beast had long hooked claws on each of its three fingers and two horns, surrounded by green flames, rose above its skull-like head. The room quickly filled with the stench of smoldering sulfur.

Crimson flames flickered deep within its eyes as it towered over Tom. Raising its skeletal head, its flaming horns punctured the low ceiling, sending chunks of smoldering plaster falling.

"My, my," came the demon's deep throaty laugh. "You're even brighter than I thought. Surely you didn't figure that all out from those few clues?" Drekton pointed at Tom, its arm bursting into flames.

Tom glanced from his tiny candle flame to the demon's flaming arm.

Drekton grinned, extending its flaming claw-tipped fingers, reaching for the boy.

Tom leapt back and collided with the wall. "Avani told me goblins aren't magical beings, so they can't shape shift!" Tom swallowed hard. "But a demon can."

Demon fire launched from the beast's wrists. Tom leapt sideways. The nightstand exploded, lighting Avani's note on fire, and sending the magic crystal skidding across the floor.

Tom raced for the door, but the demon blasted the floor in front of him, leaving a steaming, gaping hole. "Help!" cried Tom. "Nadda! Nanni! Max!"

The demon flashed a wicked grin. "I magically sealed the room. No one can hear you." Stepping forward, its entire body burst into flames. Tom threw the candlestick. It bounced harmlessly off the beast's chest and clattered to the floor.

Drekton took another step.

"Don't you wanna hear the rest of the story?" Tom shouted.

The demon stopped. "Go on."

"You killed Naagesh's sister, made it look like she died in the fire." Watching the demon's reaction, Tom continued, "You killed Naagesh's father, got rid of his body, then shape-shifted, pretending to be him."

The demon grinned. "And then?"

"For years you schemed and plotted. When you heard a rumor that the Library of Nalanda still existed, you realized the Citadel manual was the key. Only, you couldn't get past the library's white magic defenses without a wizard's help."

When the demon didn't respond, Tom rushed on, "So you posed as a particularly bright and helpful goblin, assisting Naagesh every way you could, all the while nudging him in the direction you wanted, having him implement your plan to plunge the Age of Light into the Age of Darkness. The age where demons would once again rule this world, right?"

The demon seemed to swell.

"What I don't understand—" shouted Tom, "—is why you didn't just kill Naagesh once he'd set the timer?"

Drekton gave a thin smile. "For the same reason I haven't yet killed you. I enjoyed watching those two pitiful wizards squabbling and fighting. Besides, by staying with Naagesh, I knew I could destroy the device at the moment of my choosing, as in fact I did."

"So why are you here?"

"Isn't it obvious? Revenge." The demon bared its teeth. "My plan worked perfectly! if you and your meddling friends hadn't destroyed the Citadel, the Age of Darkness would be upon us. And I, Drekton, would lead the demon army into the Age of Darkness!"

The room shook from the force of his anger. The demon leaned forward. "As their leader, you shall die first, Thomas Holland. Then Goban, and lastly Avani."

Tom ducked, and the wall behind him erupted in green flames. Another flaming volley launched from the demon's arms. Tom tried to run, tripped over his long pajama bottoms, landed on his belly and slid across the floor, narrowly escaping.

As he skidded to a stop, Tom's hand rested beside the magic crystal. He jerked his hand away.

Observing the boy's odd reaction, the demon glanced from the crystal to Tom.

Tom thrust out his arm, his open palm hovering above the crystal. "Careful! Avani gave me one of her magic crystals."

The demon gazed at the gem casually.

"They're beings of pure white magic," warned Tom. "Not even a demon can stand against em!"

"Why's your hand shaking, boy?" The demon grinned anew and stepped closer.

"I'm warning you!" shouted Tom, lowing his hand a tad. "It'll destroy you!"

The demon stopped and stared at the crystal. "I know what it is, boy. Far better than you." The demon scratched its left horn, considering. "But legend states that only one person, born of this world and chosen by the magic crystals themselves, can touch, let alone wield a magic crystal's power, without it turning to dust. Naagesh tried once and failed, proving the fact.

"What's more, there can only be one living 'chosen one' at any given time. And Avani, the real Avani, yet lives, so you—are not—the chosen one.

The demon leaned close, crimson flames dancing in its eyes. "You're terrified of the crystal, aren't you?" The beast sniffed. "I can smell your fear." It paused. "You're more afraid of touching the crystal than of dying in my claws. Curious."

Tom pulled his shaking hand away from the crystal, acknowledging defeat. "Blowing up the Citadel was the Guardian's idea. But I pressed the button. You can kill me, just let Avani and Goban live."

Suddenly, there came a loud knock on the door. "Tom?" called Nadda. Max scratched at the door and barked. "Tom! The door's locked. Are you alright?"

Tom stared at the demon. "You said no one could hear!"

"Never trust a demon." It advised. "Demons lie."

Max barked again. There was another frantic knock. "Tom!" cried Kiran. "Let us it!"

Drekton rose, flames engulfing its body. "See what you've done?" It clucked in mock disapproval. "Now I must kill them all."

"Nadda! Kiran! NO!" screamed Tom. "Stay out! Run! There's a demon in here!"

The demon laughed its throaty laugh again and the entire wall, including the closed door, erupted in flames.

"Get away from the door!" cried Tom. "It's on fire!" His gaze dropped to the magic gemstone. With shaking hands, he scooped up the crystal and leapt to his feet, white light blazing from between his fingers.

The demon turned and stared.

The crystal flared. As in the Deathly Bog, hundreds of voices, the crystal spirits, half spoke, half sang: *Who summons the power of the crystals?* murmured one. *It's not the chosen one, whispered another. No. It's the other!*

The voices grew louder. Tom grimaced, holding his head with his free hand. The voices continued: *he is not even of this world. The Prophecy? Could it be? Yes. It's him. Our time has come!*

Tom felt his body shudder. Glistening waves of magic washed over his body and coursed through his veins. "What's happening to me?" he screamed.

*What do you wish of us?* asked a thousand united voices.

Tom's eyes latched onto the demon.

The demon fired a bolt of demon magic; it deflected off Tom and blasted half the side wall away. The demon fired again. This time a wave of golden magic flashed and the demon magic just disappeared.

Max barked again. Kiran yelled, pounding on the door.

Tom's voice cracked when he said, "It's true. No one born of this world, except a chosen one, has ever wielded the crystal's power."

The demon stood frozen.

"Except me." Tom raised his arm. "But technically, I'm not from this world."

Tom's eyes turned white. When he opened his mouth, his voice sounded strange like a thousand voices chanting in unison, "Put out this fire." The flames engulfing the room snuffed out.

"Send the demon back to its dark realm. Make it so Naagesh's father never practiced dark magic. Naagesh's sister never got sick. And the father never summoned the demon in the first place.

"Make it so none of this ever happened." Tom opened his hand. Suddenly, the walls, floor and ceiling flexed inward and outward and a dark circular hole opened behind the demon and began to spin.

The room seemed to stretch, bending into the vortex.

The water basin on the dresser drifted up and floated through the vortex. Other items followed. Tom grabbed hold of a bedpost so as not to be sucked in.

The demon roared, extended its claws and lunged for Tom. Tom raised the crystal. Eyes wide, the demon couldn't stop. When the demon touched the crystal, an explosion sent the demon hurtling through the vortex. And sent Tom blasting back the other way, where he crashed against the wall and crumpled to the floor, half unconscious.

Tom's eyes cleared. He shook his head and glanced around. He was sliding across the floor toward the vortex. There was nothing to grab hold of. His eyelids grew heavy. Tom started to fade.

"No!" Tom forced his eyes open. Still clutching the crystal tightly in his hand, the crystal flashed. The room shuddered. The vortex winked and its spin reversed directions.

The last thing Tom heard before he passed out was Max barking, and someone pounding at the door.

# Epilogue

Max barked. The knocking wouldn't stop.

"It's Ok! I'm alive! The demon's gone. Made a mess of Avani's room, though." Tom opened his eyes. The room was dark.

"Tom!" called his mom from the hallway. "Happy birthday, darling! Your breakfast's ready. I know it's early but, we got a big day planned."

"Mom? But I sent you back to Earth?"

Tom sat bolt upright in bed, his eyes open wide, sweat dripping off his forehead. It was dark out, but faint strands of moonlight filtered through his bedroom window—in Chicago.

*What? Couldn't a been a dream. No way!*

Jumping out of bed, Tom grabbed his covers, preparing to toss them up in his usual feeble attempt at making the bed. He Froze. "Wait! What did you say?" He glanced at his wall clock calendar. "My birthday?"

He heard his mom chuckle from the hallway.

"Which birthday?"

"What?"

"How old am I, mom?"

"Musta been a rough night!" Juanita laughed. "You were eleven yesterday. Do the math."

*My twelfth birthday?* He frowned. *That was almost two years ago.*

"Stop playing around Tom, your breakfast's getting cold."

Tom flipped up his bed covers and turned at a tinkling sound beside him. A long shiny object bounced off his nightstand then fell, coming to rest half buried in the thick carpet.

Tom picked it up. The magic crystal lit up but suddenly cracked. The gem flickered, fizzled, and popped. The light faded… its magic spent.

Tom's eyes widened. *It's my twelfth birthday!*

His door sprang open. Max bounded in, followed by his mother.

"Mom! It's my twelfth birthday! We hafta go to the lab! A portal's gonna open!"

She chuckled again. "You did have a wild dream!"

"No mom, it's true!" He held up the broken crystal. She just stared at it.

Tossing the crystal aside, Tom grabbed her hand and yanked her toward the door.

"Tom stop! It was just a dream."

"A portal opened last week, right?"

"You were there. You know it did."

"And Chloe went through and the portal closed before we could bring her back, right?"

"Yeesss."

Tom tugged her harder. "Another portal's gonna open today! We've gotta go through!"

He stopped and blinked. "Only—it'll be different this time. The War of the Wizards never happened. They'll be thousands of wizards. And wizard schools. Gotta find Avani and Goban!" He frowned. "Probably won't remember me. Hafta convince em."

"What are you talking about?" She shook her head. "We're not going to the lab, it's your birthday!"

"Yes, we are!" Tom stared at his dog. "Max! You're the one. Help me?" Max glanced from one to the other.

"Ahhhh!" Tom froze. "We hafta go to the lab because—uhhh—you left your tablet there, right?"

"How did you know—" Tom bolted past her and down the hallway. "Besides!" he called over his shoulder. "It's my birthday. And you let me go, last time!

"Come on, Max! We're going to Elfhaven!"

## *** The End ***

## Awards & Reviews

### Thomas Holland and the Prophecy of Elfhaven

IPNE:
Finalist Award for the best new children's' book of the year

### Thomas Holland in the Realm of the Ogres

Writer's Digest:
1st Place winner in the middle-grade/young adult category

### Thomas Holland and Pandora's Portal

Mom's Choice Awards:
Gold Award Recipient

"This author has an excellent writing voice and even uses deep point of view which is a master skill. His characters are likable and make you want to turn the page instead of doing your chores. This author has great description skills, and he doesn't overuse them by telling the reader everything about the setting in the first paragraph-another master skill."

~Judge, 25th Annual Writer's Digest Self-Published Book Awards

"'Thomas Holland in the Realm of the Ogres' is a deftly crafted, impressively original, consistently entertaining, highly recommended addition to school and community library collections."

~Midwest Book Reviews

# More fun stuff!

Sign up for the author's newsletter and receive a free gift. In the newsletter you can find out where the author will be signing and dedicating books. Plus, the newsletter is packed with extra content like cut scenes and bloopers, more info on the characters, contests and prizes, the 'which character am I' quiz and lots more. Here's the link to sign up:

https://thomashollandbooks.com/newslettersignup/#newsletter

https://ThomasHollandBooks.com
https://facebook.com/kmdoherty.author
https://twitter.com/authorKMDoherty

# Thomas Holland

Enjoy author K. M. Doherty's
Award Winning Magical
Adventure Trilogy!

Thomas Holland and the Prophecy of Elfhaven

Thomas Holland in the Realm of the Ogres

Thomas Holland and Pandora's Portal

**** About the authors ****

Bellchar (the rock troll) is a critically acclaimed author in Elfhaven. Bellchar enjoys hiking, long walks by the swamp, candlelight dinners with that special she troll, as well as wrestling zhanderbeasts, and whacking ogres upside the head.

Award-winning author K. M. Doherty is a computer hardware and software engineer. During his life he raced sailboats, skied, flew hang gliders, studied martial arts, rode motorcycles, performed as a professional musician, acted in theater.

KM: Well Bellchar? Now that we've finished the trilogy—
Bellchar: We finished? I wrote da books.
KM: Now that *we've* finished, what are you going to with your share of

the royalties?

Bellchar: Build dream hut in Deathly Bog.

KM: The Bog? Isn't that a bit morbid, even for you?

Bellchar: What mean? Even fer me?

KM: I just meant—

Bellchar: You tink you better'n me!

KM: No. It's just that—

Bellchar: I wrote da books! I should get all da royalties!

KM: Now Bellchar, we've been through all that and you agreed—

Bellchar: It my story! Ya just put quill to parchment!

KM: Typed it on my laptop, to be accurate. Plus, I did all the editing, the formatting—

Bellchar: Der ya go again! Ya tink you smart, 'n me dumb!

KM: No. I know you're smart, smart as me, it's just that your fingers are too big for the keyboard. Remember that time you tried? You didn't just destroy my laptop, you snapped my whole desk in half!

Bellchar: Ya sayin' Bellchar clumsy, too?

KM: No! I was merely pointing out that… Bellchar? Put down that club! Can't we just have a civilized human to troll discussion for once without—

*Thwack!*

Narrator: Bellchar tossed KM's unconscious body from the chair, leaned over the keyboard, and using his little pinky (well quite large pinky, in fact), carefully typed:


*** The End ***


Bellchar grinned.